TALES FROM
SHAKSPEARE

TALES FROM
SHAKSPEARE

by
Charles
& Mary
Lamb

Illustrated by
FRANK C. PAPÉ

FREDERICK WARNE & Co., Ltd.
LONDON AND NEW YORK

PRINTED IN GREAT BRITAIN

PREFACE

THE following Tales are meant to be submitted to the young reader as an introduction to the study of Shakspeare, for which purpose his words are used whenever it seemed possible to bring them in; and in whatever has been added to give them the regular form of a connected story, diligent care has been taken to select such words as might least interrupt the effect of the beautiful English tongue in which he wrote; therefore, words introduced into our language since his time have been as far as possible avoided.

In those Tales which have been taken from the Tragedies, as my young readers will perceive when they come to see the source from which these stories are derived, Shakspeare's own words, with little alteration, recur very frequently in the narrative as well as in the dialogue; but in those made from the Comedies I found myself scarcely ever able to turn his words into the narrative form; therefore I fear in them I have

made use of dialogue too frequently for young people
not used to the dramatic form of writing. But this
fault—if it be as I fear a fault—has been caused by my
earnest wish to give as much of Shakspeare's own words
as possible; and if the "*He said*" and "*She said*," the
question and the reply, should sometimes seem tedious
to their young ears, they must pardon it, because it
was the only way I knew of in which I could give them
a few hints and little foretastes of the great pleasure
which awaits them in their elder years, when they come
to the rich treasures from which these small and value-
less coins are extracted, pretending to no other merit
than as faint and imperfect stamps of Shakspeare's
matchless image. Faint and imperfect images they must
be called, because the beauty of his language is too frequently destroyed by the necessity of changing many of
his excellent words into words far less expressive of his
true sense, to make it read something like prose; and
even in some few places where his blank verse is given
unaltered, as hoping from its simple plainness to cheat
the young readers into the belief that they are reading
prose, yet still, his language being transplanted from its
own natural soil and wild poetic garden, it must want
much of its native beauty.

I have wished to make these Tales easy reading for
very young children. To the utmost of my ability I
have constantly kept this in my mind; but the subjects
of most of them made this a very difficult task. It was
no easy matter to give the histories of men and women
in terms familiar to the apprehension of a very young
mind. For young ladies, too, it has been my intention

chiefly to write, because boys are generally permitted the use of their fathers' libraries at a much earlier age than girls are. They frequently having the best scenes of Shakspeare by heart before their sisters are permitted to look into this manly book; and therefore, instead of recommending these Tales to the perusal of young gentlemen who can read them so much better in the originals, I must rather beg their kind assistance in explaining to their sisters such parts as are hardest for them to understand; and when they have helped them to get over the difficulties, then perhaps they will read to them—carefully selecting what is proper for a young sister's ear—some passage which has pleased them in one of these stories, in the very words of the scene from which it is taken. And I trust they will find that the beautiful extracts, the select passages, they may choose to give their sisters in this way will be much better relished and understood from their having some notion of the general story from one of these imperfect abridgments, which, if they be fortunately so done as to prove delightful to any of you, my young readers, I hope will have no worse effect upon you than to make you wish yourselves a little older, that you may be allowed to read the Plays at full length: such a wish will be neither peevish nor irrational. When time and leave of judicious friends shall put them into your hands, you will discover in such of them as are here abridged—not to mention almost as many more which are left untouched —many surprising events and turns of fortune, which for their infinite variety could not be contained in this little book, besides a world of sprightly and cheerful

characters, both men and women, the humour of which
I was fearful of losing if I attempted to reduce the
length of them.

What these Tales have been to you in childhood,
that and much more it is my wish that the true Plays of
Shakspeare may prove to you in older years—enrichers
of the fancy, strengtheners of virtue, a withdrawing from
all selfish and mercenary thoughts, a lesson of all sweet
and honourable thoughts and actions, to teach you
courtesy, benignity, generosity, humanity; for of examples
teaching these virtues, his pages are full.

CONTENTS

TALES FROM SHAKSPEARE

THE TEMPEST

THERE was a certain island in the sea, the only inhabitants of which were an old man, whose name was Prospero, and his daughter Miranda, a very beautiful young lady. She came to this island so young, that she had no memory of having seen any other human face than her father's.

They lived in a cave or cell, made out of a rock: it was divided into several apartments, one of which Prospero called his study. There he kept his books, which chiefly treated of magic, a study at that time much affected by all learned men, and the knowledge of this art he found very useful to him; for, being thrown by a strange chance upon this island, which had been enchanted by a witch called Sycorax, who died there a short time before his arrival, Prospero, by virtue of his art, released many good spirits that Sycorax had imprisoned in the bodies of large trees, because they had refused to execute her wicked commands. These gentle spirits were ever after obedient to the will of Prospero. Of these Ariel was the chief.

The lively little sprite Ariel had nothing mischievous in his nature, except that he took rather too much pleasure in tormenting an ugly monster called Caliban, for he owed

him a grudge because he was the son of his old enemy
Sycorax. This Caliban Prospero found in the woods, a
strange mis-shapen thing, far less human in form than an
ape : he took him home to his cell, and taught him to
speak ; and Prospero would have been very kind to him,
but the bad nature which Caliban inherited from his mother
Sycorax would not let him learn anything good or useful,
therefore he was employed like a slave, to fetch wood and
do the most laborious offices ; and Ariel had the charge
of compelling him to these services.

When Caliban was lazy and neglected his work, Ariel
(who was invisible to all eyes but Prospero's) would come
slyly and pinch him, and sometimes tumble him down in
the mire ; and then Ariel, in the likeness of an ape, would
make mouths at him. Then swiftly changing his shape,
in the likeness of a hedgehog he would lie tumbling in
Caliban's way, who feared the hedgehog's sharp quills would
prick his bare feet. With a variety of such-like vexatious
tricks Ariel would often torment him, whenever Caliban
neglected the work which Prospero commanded him to do.

Having these powerful spirits obedient to his will,
Prospero could by their means command the winds and
the waves of the sea. By his orders they raised a violent
storm, in the midst of which, and struggling with the wild
sea-waves that every moment threatened to swallow it up,
he showed his daughter a fine large ship, which he told
her was full of living beings like themselves. " O my dear
father," said she, " if by your art you have raised this
dreadful storm, have pity on their sad distress. See !
the vessel will be dashed to pieces. Poor souls ! they
will all perish. If I had power, I would sink the sea
beneath the earth, rather than the good ship should be
destroyed, with all the precious souls within her."

" Be not so amazed, daughter Miranda," said Prospero ;
" there is no harm done. I have so ordered it that no
person in the ship shall receive any hurt. What I have

done has been in care of you, my dear child. You are
ignorant who you are, or where you came from, and you
know no more of me but that I am your father, and live in
this poor cave. Can you remember a time before you came
to this cell ? I think you cannot, for you were not then three
years of age."

" Certainly I can, sir," replied Miranda.

" By what ? " asked Prospero ; " by any other house
or person ? Tell me what you can remember, my child."

Miranda said, " It seems to me like the recollection
of a dream. But had I not once four or five women who
attended upon me ? "

Prospero answered, " You had, and more. How is it
that this still lives in your mind ? Do you remember how
you came here ? "

" No, sir," said Miranda, " I remember nothing more."

" Twelve years ago, Miranda," continued Prospero,
" I was Duke of Milan, and you were a princess and my
only heir. I had a younger brother, whose name was
Antonio, to whom I trusted everything ; and as I was fond
of retirement and deep study, I commonly left the management of my state affairs to your uncle, my false brother
(for so indeed he proved). I, neglecting all worldly ends,
buried among my books, did dedicate my whole time to
the bettering of my mind. My brother Antonio, being
thus in possession of my power, began to think himself
the duke indeed. The opportunity I gave him of making
himself popular among my subjects awakened in his bad
nature a proud ambition to deprive me of my dukedom :
this he soon effected with the aid of the King of Naples, a
powerful prince, who was my enemy."

" Wherefore," said Miranda, " did they not at that
hour destroy us ? "

" My child," answered her father, " they durst not,
so dear was the love that my people bore me. Antonio
carried us on board a ship, and when we were some leagues

out at sea, he forced us into a small boat, without either
tackle, sail, or mast : there he left us, as he thought, to
perish. But a kind lord of my court, one Gonzalo, who
loved me, had privately placed in the boat water, provisions, apparel, and some books which I prize above my
dukedom."

"O my father," said Miranda, "what a trouble must
I have been to you then ! "

"No, my love," said Prospero, "you were a little
cherub that did perserve me. Your innocent smiles made
me to bear up against my misfortunes. Our food lasted
till we landed on this desert island, since when my chief
delight has been in teaching you, Miranda, and well have
you profited by my instructions."

"Heaven thank you, my dear father," said Miranda.
"Now pray tell me, sir, your reason for raising this sea-
storm ? "

"Know, then," said her father, "that by means of
this storm my enemies, the King of Naples and my cruel
brother, are cast ashore upon this island."

Having so said, Prospero gently touched his daughter
with his magic wand, and she fell fast asleep ; for the spirit
Ariel just then presented himself before his master, to
give an account of the tempest, and how he had disposed
of the ship's company ; and, though the spirits were
always invisible to Miranda, Prospero did not choose she
should hear him holding converse (as would seem to her)
with the empty air.

"Well, my brave spirit," said Prospero to Ariel, "how
have you performed your task ? "

Ariel gave a lively description of the storm, and of the
terrors of the mariners; and how the King's son, Ferdinand,
was the first who leaped into the sea ; and his father thought
he saw his dear son swallowed up by the waves and lost.

"But he is safe," said Ariel, "in a corner of the isle,
sitting with his arms folded sadly, lamenting the loss of

the King his father, whom he concludes drowned. Not a hair of his head is injured, and his princely garments, though drenched in the sea-waves, look fresher than before."

" That's my delicate Ariel," said Prospero. " Bring him hither : my daughter must see this young prince. Where is the king and my brother ? "

" I left them," answered Ariel, " searching for Ferdinand, whom they have little hopes of finding, thinking they saw him perish. Of the ship's crew not one is missing, though each one thinks himself the only one saved ; and the ship, though invisible to them, is safe in the harbour."

" Ariel," said Prospero, " thy charge is faithfully performed ; but there is more work yet."

" Is there more work ? " said Ariel. " Let me remind you, master, you have promised me my liberty. I pray remember I have done you worthy service, told you no lies, made no mistakes, served you without grudge or grumbling."

" How now ! " said Prospero. " You do not recollect what a torment I freed you from. Have you forgot the wicked witch Sycorax, who with age and envy was almost bent double ? Where was she born ? Speak : tell me."

" Sir, in Algiers," said Ariel.

" O, was she so ? " said Prospero. " I must recount what you have been, which I find you do not remember. This bad witch Sycorax, for her witchcrafts, too terrible to enter human hearing, was banished from Algiers, and here left by the sailors ; and because you were a spirit too delicate to execute her wicked commands, she shut you up in a tree, where I found you howling. This torment, remember, I did free you from."

" Pardon me, dear master," said Ariel, ashamed to seem ungrateful ; " I will obey your commands."

" Do so," said Prospero, " and I will set you free." He then gave orders what further he would have him do,

B

and away went Ariel, first to where he had left Ferdinand,
and found him still sitting on the grass in the same melancholy posture.

"O my young gentleman," said Ariel, when he saw
him, "I will soon move you. You must be brought, I
find, for the Lady Miranda to have a sight of your pretty
person. Come, sir, follow me." He then began singing,

> "Full fathom five thy father lies:
>   Of his bones are coral made;
> Those are pearls that were his eyes:
>   Nothing of him that doth fade,
> But doth suffer a sea-change,
> Into something rich and strange.
> Sea-nymphs hourly ring his knell:
> Hark, now I hear them, ding-dong-bell."

This strange news of his lost father soon roused the
prince from the stupid fit into which he had fallen. He
followed in amazement the sound of Ariel's voice, till it
led him to Prospero and Miranda, who were sitting under
the shade of a large tree. Now, Miranda had never seen
a man before, except her own father.

"Miranda," said Prospero, "tell me what you are looking at yonder."

"O father," said Miranda, in a strange surprise,
"surely that is a spirit. Lord! how it looks about!
Believe me, sir, it is a beautiful creature. Is it not a
spirit?"

"No, girl," answered her father; "it eats, and sleeps,
and has senses such as we have. This young man you
see was in the ship. He is somewhat altered by grief,
or you might call him a handsome person. He has lost his
companions, and is wandering about to find them."

Miranda, who thought all men had grave faces and grey
beards like her father, was delighted with the appearance
of this beautiful young prince; and Ferdinand, seeing
such a lovely lady in this desert place, and from the strange
sounds he had heard expecting nothing but wonders,

thought he was upon an enchanted island, and that Miranda was the goddess of the place, and as such he began to address her.

She timidly answered, she was no goddess, but a simple maid, and was going to give an account of herself when Prospero interrupted her. He was well pleased to find they admired each other, for he plainly perceived they had (as we say) fallen in love at first sight; but to try Ferdinand's constancy, he resolved to throw some difficulties in their way: therefore advancing forward, he addressed the prince with a stern air, telling n. the came to the island as a spy, to take it from him who was the lord of it. "Follow me," said he. "I will tie your neck and feet together. You shall drink sea-water; shell-fish, withered roots, and husks of acorns shall be your food."

"No," said Ferdinand, "I will resist such entertain-ment, till I see a more powerful enemy," and drew his sword; but Prospero, waving his magic wand, fixed him to the spot where he stood, so that he had no power to move.

Miranda hung upon her father, saying, "Why are you so ungentle? Have pity, sir; I will be his surety. This is the second man I ever saw, and to me he seems a true one."

"Silence!" said her father; "one word more will make me chide you, girl. What, an advocate for an im-postor? You think there are no more such fine men, having seen only him and Caliban. I tell you, foolish girl, most men as far excel this as he does Caliban." This, he said to prove his daughter's constancy; and she replied, "My affections are most humble. I have no wish to see a goodlier man."

"Come on, young man," said Prospero to the prince; "you have no power to disobey me."

"I have not, indeed," answered Ferdinand; and not

knowing that it was by magic he was deprived of all power of resistance, he was astonished to find himself so strangely compelled to follow Prospero.   Looking back on Miranda as long as he could see her, he said, as he went after Prospero into the cave, " My spirits are all bound up, as if I were in a dream ; but this man's threats, and the weakness which I feel, would seem light to me if from my prison I might once a day behold this fair maid."

Prospero kept Ferdinand not long confined within the cell ; he soon brought out his prisoner, and set him a severe task to perform, taking care to let his daughter know the hard labour he had imposed on him, and then pretending to go into his study, he secretly watched them both.

Prospero had commanded Ferdinand to pile up some heavy logs of wood. Kings' sons not being much used to laborious work, Miranda soon after found her lover almost dying with fatigue.

" Alas ! " said she, " do not work so hard ; my father is at his studies, he is safe for these three hours : pray rest yourself."

" O my dear lady," said Ferdinand, " I dare not. I must finish my task before I take my rest."

" If you will sit down," said Miranda, " I will carry your logs the while."   But this Ferdinand would by no means agree to. Instead of a help Miranda became a hindrance, for they began a long conversation, so that the business of log-carrying went on very slowly.

Prospero, who had enjoined Ferdinand this task merely as a trial of his love, was not at his books as his daughter supposed, but was standing by them, invisible, to over-hear what they said.

Ferdinand inquired her name, which she told him, saying it was against her father's express command she did so.

Prospero only smiled at this first instance of his

daughter's disobedience, for having by his magic art caused his daughter to fall in love so suddenly, he was not angry that she showed her love by forgetting to obey his commands. And he listened well pleased to a long speech of Ferdinand's, in which he professed to love her above all the ladies he ever saw.

In answer to his praises of her beauty, which he said exceeded all the women in the world, she replied, " I do not remember the face of any woman, nor have I seen any more men than you, my good friend, and my dear father. How features are abroad, I know not ; but believe me, sir, I would not wish any companion in the world but you, nor can my imagination form any shape but yours that I could like. But, sir, I fear I talk to you too freely, and my father's precepts I forget."

At this Prospero smiled, and nodded his head, as much as to say, " This goes on exactly as I could wish ; my girl will be Queen of Naples."

And then Ferdinand, in another fine long speech (for young princes speak in courtly phrases), told the innocent Miranda he was heir to the crown of Naples, and that she should be his queen.

" Ah, sir ! " said she, " I am a fool to weep at what I am glad of. I will answer you in plain and holy innocence. I am your wife, if you will marry me."

Prospero prevented Ferdinand's thanks by appearing visible before them.

" Fear nothing, my child," said he ; " I have overheard, and approve of all you have said. And, Ferdinand, if I have too severely used you, I will make you rich amends, by giving you my daughter. All your vexations were but my trials of your love, and you have nobly stood the test. Then as my gift, which your true love has worthily purchased, take my daughter, and do not smile that I boast she is above all praise." He then, telling them that he had business which required his presence, desired they would sit down and talk together till he returned ; and this command Miranda seemed not at all disposed to disobey.

When Prospero left them, he called his spirit Ariel, who quickly appeared before him, eager to relate what he had done with Prospero's brother and the King of Naples. Ariel said he had left them almost out of their senses with fear at the strange things he had caused them to see and hear. When fatigued with wandering about, and famished for w. t of food, he had suddenly set before them a deliciou. banquet, and then, just as they were going to eat, he appeared visible before them in the shape of a harpy, a voracious monster with wings, and the feast vanished away. Then, to their utter amazement, this seeming harpy spoke to them, reminding them of their cruelty in driving Prospero from his dukedom, and leaving him and his infant daughter to perish in the sea, saying that for this cause these terrors were suffered to afflict them.

The King of Naples and Antonio, the false brother, repented the injustice they had done to Prospero ; and Ariel told his master he was certain their penitence was sincere, and that he, though a spirit, could not but pity them.

" Then bring them hither, Ariel," said Prospero : " if you, who are but a spirit, feel for their distress, shall not I, who am a human being like themselves, have compassion on them ? Bring them quickly, my dainty Ariel."

Ariel soon returned with the king, Antonio, and old Gonzalo in their train, who had followed him, wondering at the wild music he played in the air to draw them on to his master's presence. This Gonzalo was the same who had so kindly provided Prospero formerly with books and provisions, when his wicked brother left him, as he thought, to perish in an open boat in the sea.

Grief and terror had so stupefied their senses that they did not know Prospero. He first discovered himself to

the good old Gonzalo, calling him the preserver of his life ;
and then his brother and the king knew he was the injured
Prospero.

Antonio, with tears and sad words of sorrow and true
repentance, implored his brother's forgiveness ; and the
king expressed his sincere remorse for having assisted
Antonio to depose his brother : and Prospero forgave
them ; and upon their engaging to restore his dukedom,
he said to the King of Naples, " I have a gift in store for
you too " ; and opening a door, showed him his son
Ferdinand playing at chess with Miranda.

Nothing could exceed the joy of the father and the son
at this unexpected meeting, for they each thought the
other drowned in the storm.

" O wonder ! " said Miranda, " what noble creatures
these are ! It must surely be a brave world that has such
people in it."

The King of Naples was almost as much astonished
at the beauty and excellent graces of the young Miranda
as his son had been.

" Who is this maid ? " said he ; " she seems the goddess that has parted us, and brought us thus together."

" No, sir," answered Ferdinand, smiling to find his
father had fallen into the same mistake that he had done
when he first saw Miranda ; " she is a mortal, but by
immortal Providence she is mine : I chose her when I
could not ask you, my father, for your consent, not thinking you were alive. She is the daughter to this Prospero,
who is the famous Duke of Milan, of whose renown I have
heard so much, but never saw him till now : of him I
have received a new life ; he has made himself to me a
second father, giving me this dear lady."

" Then I must be her father," said the king ; " but,
on ! how oddly will it sound that I must ask my child
forgiveness ! "

" No more of that," said Prospero ; " let us not

remember our troubles past, since they so happily have ended." And then Prospero embraced his brother, and again assured him of his forgiveness, and said that a wise, overruling Providence had permitted that he should be driven from his poor dukedom of Milan that his daughter might inherit the crown of Naples, for that by their meeting in this desert island it had happened that the king's son had loved Miranda.

These kind words which Prospero spoke, meaning to comfort his brother, so filled Antonio with shame and remorse, that he wept and was unable to speak, and the kind old Gonzalo wept to see this joyful reconciliation, and prayed for blessings on the young couple.

Prospero now told them that their ship was safe in the harbour, and the sailors all on board her, and that he and his daughter would accompany them home the next morning. " In the meantime," said he, " partake of such refreshments as my poor cave affords, and for your evening's entertainment I will relate the history of my life from my first landing in this desert island." He then called for Caliban to prepare some food and set the cave in order, and the company were astonished at the uncouth form and savage appearance of this ugly monster, who (Prospero said) was the only attendant he had to wait upon him.

Before Prospero left the island he dismissed Ariel from his service, to the great joy of that lively little spirit, who, though he had been a faithful servant to his master, was always longing to enjoy his free liberty, to wander uncontrolled in the air, like a wild bird, under green trees, among pleasant fruits and sweet-smelling flowers.

" My quaint Ariel," said Prospero to the little sprite when he made him free, " I shall miss you ; yet you shall have your freedom."

" Thank you, my dear master," said Ariel ; " but give me leave to attend your ship home with prosperous gales, before you bid farewell to the assistance of your faithful spirit; and then, master, when I am free, how merrily I shall live!"

Here Ariel sang this pretty song:

> " Where the bee sucks, there suck I ;
> In a cowslip's bell I lie :
> There I couch when owls do cry,
> On the bat's back I do fly
> After summer merrily.
> Merrily, merrily, shall I live now
> Under the blossom that hangs on the bough."

Prospero then buried deep in the earth his magical books and wand, for he was resolved never more to make use of the magic art. And having thus overcome his enemies, and being reconciled to his brother and the King of Naples, nothing now remained to complete his happiness but to revisit his native land, to take possession of his dukedom, and to witness the happy nuptials of his daughter Miranda and Prince Ferdinand, which the king said should be instantly celebrated with great splendour on their return to Naples. At which place, under the safe convoy of the spirit Ariel, they, after a pleasant voyage, soon arrived.

A MIDSUMMER NIGHT'S DREAM

THERE was a law in the city of Athens which gave to its citizens the power of compelling their daughters to marry whomsoever they pleased; for upon a daughter's refusing to marry the man her father had chosen to be her husband, the father was empowered by this law to cause her to be put to death; but as fathers do not often desire the death of their own daughters, even though they do happen to prove a little refractory, this law was seldom or never put in execution, though perhaps the young ladies of that city were not unfrequently threatened by their parents with the terrors of it.

There was one instance, however, of an old man, whose name was Egeus, who actually did come before Theseus (at that time the reigning Duke of Athens) to complain that his daughter Hermia, whom he had commanded to marry Demetrius, a young man of a noble Athenian family, refused to obey him, because she loved another young Athenian, named Lysander. Egeus demanded justice of Theseus, and desired that this cruel law might be put in force against his daughter.

Hermia pleaded in excuse for her disobedience, that

Demetrius had formerly professed love for her dear friend Helena, and that Helena loved Demetrius to distraction ; but this honourable reason which Hermia gave for not obeying her father's command moved not the stern Egeus.

Theseus, though a great and merciful prince, had no power to alter the laws of his country ; therefore he could only give Hermia four days to consider of it ; and at the end of that time, if she still refused to marry Demetrius, she was to be put to death.

When Hermia was dismissed from the presence of the duke, she went to her lover, Lysander, and told him the peril she was in, and that she must either give him up and marry Demetrius, or lose her life in four days.

Lysander was in great affliction at hearing these evil tidings ; but recollecting that he had an aunt who lived at some distance from Athens, and that at the place where she lived the cruel law could not be put in force against Hermia (this law not extending beyond the boundaries of the city), he proposed to Hermia that she should steal out of her father's house that night, and go with him to his aunt's house, where he would marry her. " I will meet you," said Lysander, " in the wood a few miles without the city—in that delightful wood where we have so often walked with Helena in the pleasant month of May."

To this proposal Hermia joyfully agreed ; and she told no one of her intended flight but her friend Helena. Helena (as maidens will do foolish things for love) very ungenerously resolved to go and tell this to Demetrius, though she could hope no benefit from betraying her friend's secret, but the poor pleasure of following her faithless lover to the wood ; for she well knew that Demetrius would go thither in pursuit of Hermia.

The wood, in which Lysander and Hermia proposed to meet, was the favourite haunt of those little beings known by the name of *Fairies*.

Oberon the king, and Titania the queen, of the fairies, with all their tiny train of followers, in this wood held their midnight revels.

Between this little king and queen of sprites there happened, at this time, a sad disagreement : they never met by moonlight in the shady walks of this pleasant wood, but they were quarrelling, till all their fairy elves would creep into acorn-cups and hide themselves for fear.

The cause of this unhappy disagreement was Titania's refusing to give Oberon a little changeling boy, whose mother had been Titania's friend ; and upon her death the fairy queen stole the child from its nurse, and brought him up in the woods.

The night on which the lovers were to meet in this wood, as Titania was walking with some of her maids of honour, she met Oberon attended by his train of fairy courtiers.

" Ill met by moonlight, proud Titania," said the fairy king. The queen replied, " What, jealous Oberon, is it you ? Fairies, skip hence ; I have forsworn his company ! " " Tarry, rash fairy ! " said Oberon : " am not I thy lord ? Why does Titania cross her Oberon ? Give me your little changeling boy to be my page."

" Set your heart at rest," answered the queen ; " your whole fairy kingdom buys not the boy of me." She then left her lord in great anger. " Well, go your way," said Oberon : " before the morning dawns I will torment you for this injury."

Oberon then sent for Puck, his chief favourite and privy councillor.

Puck (or, as he was sometimes called, Robin Goodfellow) was a shrewd and knavish sprite, that used to play comical pranks in the neighbouring villages—sometimes getting into the dairies and skimming the milk, sometimes plunging his light and airy form into the butter-churn, and while he was dancing his fantastic shape in the churn, in vain the dairymaid would labour to change her cream into butter ; nor had the village swains any better success : whenever Puck chose to play his freaks in the brewing copper, the ale was sure to be spoiled. When a few good neighbours were met to drink some comfortable ale together, Puck would jump into the bowl of ale in the likeness of a roasted crab, and when some old goody was going to drink he would bob against her lips, and spill the ale over her withered chin ; and presently after, when the same old dame was gravely seating herself to tell her neighbours a sad and melancholy story, Puck would slip her three-legged stool from under her, and down toppled the poor old woman, and then the old gossips would hold their sides and laugh at her, and swear they never wasted a merrier hour.

" Come hither, Puck," said Oberon to this little merry wanderer of the night. " Fetch me the flower which maids call ' Love in Idleness ' ; the juice of that little purple flower laid on the eyelids of those who sleep will make them, when they awake, dote on the first thing they see. Some of the juice of that flower I will drop on the eyelids of my Titania when she is asleep, and the first thing she looks upon when she opens her eyes she will fall in love with, even though it be a lion, or a bear, a meddling monkey, or a busy ape ; and before I will take this charm from off her sight, which I can do with another charm I know of, I will make her give me that boy to be my page."

Puck, who loved mischief to his heart, was highly diverted with this intended frolic of his master, and ran to seek the flower ; and while Oberon was waiting the return of Puck, he observed Demetrius and Helena enter the wood : he overheard Demetrius reproaching Helena for following him, and after many unkind words on his part, and gentle expostulations from Helena, reminding him of his former love and professions of true faith to her, he left her (as he said) to the mercy of the wild beasts, and she ran after him as swiftly as she could.

The fairy king, who was always friendly to true lovers, felt great compassion for Helena, and perhaps, as Lysander said they used to walk by moonlight in this pleasant wood, Oberon might have seen Helena in those happy times when she was beloved by Demetrius. However that might be, when Puck returned with the little purple flower, Oberon said to his favourite, " Take a part of this flower : there has been a sweet Athenian lady here who is in love with a disdainful youth ; if you find him sleeping, drop some of the love-juice in his eyes, but contrive to do it when she is near him, that the first thing he sees when he awakes may be this despised lady. You will know the man by the Athenian garments which he wears." Puck promised to manage this matter very dexterously, and then Oberon went, unperceived by Titania, to her bower, where she was preparing to go to rest. Her fairy bower was a bank, where grew wild thyme, cowslips, and sweet violets, under a canopy of woodbine, musk-roses, and eglantine. There Titania always slept some part of the night ; her coverlet, the enamelled skin of a snake, which, though a small mantle, was wide enough to wrap a fairy in.

He found Titania giving orders to her fairies how they were to employ themselves while she slept. " Some of you," said her majesty, " must kill cankers in the musk-rose buds, and some wage war with the bats for their leathern wings to make my small elves coats, and some of you keep watch that the clamorous owl, that nightly hoots, come not near me ; but first sing me to sleep." Then they began to sing this song :—

'You spotted snakes with double tongue
Thorny hedgehogs, be not seen ;
Newts and blind-worms, do no wrong,
Come not near our fairy queen.
Philomel, with melody,

Sing in your sweet lullaby,
Lulla, lulla, lullaby ; lulla, lulla, lullaby :
Never harm, nor spell, nor charm,
Come our lovely lady nigh ;
So good night with lullaby."

When the fairies had sung their queen asleep with this pretty lullaby, they left her, to perform the important services she had enjoined them. Oberon then softly drew near his Titania, and dropped some of the love-juice on her eyelids, saying,

" What thou seest when thou dost wake
Do it for thy true-love take."

But to return to Hermia, who made her escape out of her father's house that night to avoid the death she was doomed to for refusing to marry Demetrius. When she entered the wood she found her dear Lysander waiting for her, to conduct her to his aunt's house, but before they had passed half through the wood Hermia was so much fatigued that Lysander, who was very careful of this dear lady, who had proved her affection for him even by hazarding her life for his sake, persuaded her to rest till morning on a bank of soft moss, and lying down himself on the ground at some little distance, they soon fell fast asleep. Here they were found by Puck, who, seeing a handsome young man asleep, and perceiving that his clothes were made in the Athenian fashion, and that a pretty lady was sleeping near him, concluded that this must be the Athenian maid, and her disdainful lover whom Oberon had sent him to seek, and he naturally enough conjectured that, as they were alone together, she must be the first thing he would see when he awoke, so without more ado he proceeded to pour some of the juice of the little purple flower into his eyes. But it so fell out that Helena came that way, and, instead of Hermia, was the first object Lysander beheld when he opened his eyes ; and, strange to relate, so

powerful was the love-charm, that all his love for
Hermia vanished away, and Lysander fell in love with
Helena.

Had he first seen Hermia when he awoke, the blunder
Puck committed would have been of no consequence,
for he could not love that faithful lady too well ; but for
poor Lysander to be forced by a fairy love-charm to forget his own true Hermia, and to run after another lady
and leave Hermia asleep quite alone in a wood at midnight, was a sad chance indeed.

Thus this misfortune happened. Helena, as has
been before related, endeavoured to keep pace with
Demetrius when he ran away so rudely from her, but she
could not continue this unequal race long, men being
always better runners in a long race than ladies. Helena
soon lost sight of Demetrius, and as she was wandering
about, dejected and forlorn, she arrived at the place where
Lysander was sleeping. " Ah ! " said she, " this is
Lysander lying on the ground : is he dead or asleep ? "
Then gently touching him, she said, " Good sir, if you
are alive, awake." Upon this Lysander opened his eyes,
and (the love-charm beginning to work) immediately
addressed her in terms of extravagant love and admiration,
telling her she as much excelled Hermia in beauty as
a dove does a raven, and that he would run through fire
for her sweet sake, and many more such lover-like
speeches. Helena knowing Lysander was her friend
Hermia's lover, and that he was solemnly engaged to
marry her, was in the utmost rage when she heard herself addressed in this manner, for she thought (as well she
might) that Lysander was making a jest of her. " Oh ! "
said she, " why was I born to be mocked and scorned by
every one ? Is it not enough, is it not enough, young
man, that I can never get a sweet look or a kind word
from Demetrius, but you, sir, must pretend in this disdainful manner to court me ? I thought, Lysander, you

were a lord of more true gentleness." Saying these words
in great anger, she ran away, and Lysander followed her,
quite forgetful of his own Hermia, who was still asleep.

When Hermia awoke, she was in a sad fright at finding herself alone. She wandered about the wood, not
knowing what was become of Lysander, or which way
to go to seek for him. In the meantime Demetrius, not
being able to find Hermia and his rival Lysander, and
fatigued with his fruitless search, was observed by Oberon
fast asleep. Oberon had learnt by some questions he had
asked of Puck that he had applied the love-charm to the
wrong person's eyes, and now, having found the person
first intended, he touched the eyelids of the sleeping
Demetrius with the love juice, and he instantly awoke,
and the first thing he saw being Helena, he, as Lysander
had done before, began to address love speeches to her,
and just at that movement Lysander, followed by Hermia
(for through Puck's unlucky mistake it was now become
Hermia's turn to run after her lover), made his appearance, and then Lysander and Demetrius, both speaking
together, made love to Helena, they being each one under
the influence of the same potent charm.

The astonished Helena thought that Demetrius,
Lysander, and her once dear friend Hermia were all in a
plot together to make a jest of her.

Hermia was as much surprised as Helena : she knew
not why Lysander and Demetrius, who both before loved
her, were now become the lovers of Helena, and to Hermia
the matter seemed to be no jest.

The ladies, who before had always been the dearest
of friends, now fell to high words together.

" Unkind Hermia," said Helena, " it is you have set
Lysander on to vex me with mock praises ; and your
other lover Demetrius, who used almost to spurn me
with his foot, have you not bid him call me goddess,
nymph, rare, precious, and celestial ? He would not

c

speak thus to me, whom he hates, if you did not set him on to make a jest of me. Unkind Hermia to join with men in scorning your poor friend. Have you forgot our school-day friendship? How often, Hermia, have we two, sitting on one cushion, both singing one song, with our needles working the same flower, both on the same sampler wrought, growing up together in fashion of a double cherry, scarcely seeming parted? Hermia, it is not friendly in you, it is not maidenly, to join with men in scorning your poor friend."

"I am amazed at your passionate words," said Hermia: "I scorn you not; it seems you scorn me." "Ay, do!" returned Helena, "persevere, counterfeit serious looks, and make mouths at me when I turn my back; then wink at each other, and hold the sweet jest up. If you had any pity, grace, or manners, you would not use me thus."

While Helena and Hermia were speaking these angry words to each other, Demetrius and Lysander left them, to fight together in the wood for the love of Helena.

When they found the gentlemen had left them, they departed, and once more wandered weary in the wood in search of their lovers.

As soon as they were gone, the fairy king, who with little Puck had been listening to their quarrels, said to him, "This is your negligence, Puck; or did you do this wilfully?" "Believe me, king of shadows," answered Puck, "it was a mistake: did not you tell me I should know the man by his Athenian garments? However, I am not sorry this has happened, for I think their jangling makes excellent sport." "You heard," said Oberon, "that Demetrius and Lysander are gone to seek a convenient place to fight in. I command you to overhang the night with a thick fog, and lead these quarrelsome lovers so astray in the dark that they shall not be able to find each other. Counterfeit each of their voices to the

other, and with bitter taunts provoke them to follow you,
while they think it is their rival's tongue they hear. See
you do this till they are so weary they can go no farther,
and when you find they are asleep, drop the juice of this
other flower into Lysander's eyes, and when he awakes
he will forget his new love for Helena, and return to his
old passion for Hermia ; and then the two fair ladies may
each one be happy with the man she loves, and they will
think all that has passed a vexatious dream. About this
quickly, Puck, and I will go and see what sweet love my
Titania has found."

Titania was still sleeping, and Oberon, seeing a clown
near her who had lost his way in the wood, and was likewise asleep :—" This fellow," said he, " shall be my
Titania's true-love ; " and clapping an ass's head over
the clown's it seemed to fit him as well as if it had grown
upon his own shoulders. Although Oberon fixed the
ass's head on very gently, it awakened him, and rising
up, unconscious of what Oberon had done to him, he went
towards the bower where the fairy queen slept.

" Ah ! what angel is that I see ? " said Titania, opening her eyes, and the juice of the little purple flower
beginning to take effect. " Are you as wise as you are
beautiful ? "

" Why, mistress," said the foolish clown, " if I have
wit enough to find the way out of this wood, I have enough
to serve my turn."

" Out of the wood do not desire to go," said the en-
amoured queen. " I am a spirit of no common rate. I
love you. Go with me, and I will give you fairies to
attend upon you." She then called four of her fairies :
their names were Peas-blossom, Cobweb, Moth, and
Mustard-seed.

" Attend," said the queen, " upon this sweet gentleman ; hop in his walks, and gambol in his sight ; feed him
with grapes and apricots, and steal for him the honey-bags

from the bees. Come, sit with me," said she to the clown,
" and let me play with your amiable hairy cheeks, my
beautiful ass ! and kiss your fair large ears, my gentle
joy ! "

" Where is Peas-blossom ? " said the ass-headed
clown, not much regarding the fairy queen's courtship,
but very proud of his new attendants.

" Here, sir," said little Peas-blossom.

" Scratch my head," said the clown. " Where is
Cobweb ? "

" Here, sir," said Cobweb.

" Good Mr. Cobweb," said the foolish clown, " kill
me the red humble-bee on the top of that thistle yonder ;
and, good Mr. Cobweb, bring me the honey-bag. Do not
fret yourself too much in the action, Mr. Cobweb, and
take care the honey-bag break not ; I should be sorry to
have you overflown with a honey-bag. Where is Mustard-
seed ? "

" Here, sir," said Mustard-seed. " What is your
will ? "

" Nothing," said the clown, " good Mr. Mustard-
seed, but to help Mr. Peas-blossom to scratch. I must
go to a barber's, Mr. Mustard-seed, for methinks I am
marvellous hairy about the face."

" My sweet love," said the queen, " what will you have
to eat ? I have a venturous fairy that shall seek the
squirrel's hoard, and fetch you some new nuts."

" I had rather have a handful of dried peas," said
the clown, who with his ass's head had got an ass's
appetite ; " but, I pray, let none of your people disturb
me, for I have a mind to sleep."

" Sleep, then," said the queen, " and I will wind you
in my arms. O how I love you ! How I dote upon
you ! "

When the fairy king saw the clown sleeping in the
arms of his queen, he advanced within her sight, and

O how I love you !
    how I dote upon you !"

reproached her with having lavished her favours upon an ass.

This she could not deny, as the clown was then sleeping within her arms, with his ass's head crowned by her with flowers.

When Oberon had teased her for some time, he again demanded the changeling boy, which she, ashamed of being discovered by her lord with her new favourite, did not dare to refuse him.

Oberon, having thus obtained the little boy he had so long wished for to be his page, took pity on the disgraceful situation into which, by his merry contrivance, he had brought his Titania, and threw some of the juice of the other flower into her eyes; and the fairy queen immediately recovered her senses, and wondered at her late dotage, saying how she now loathed the sight of the strange monster.

Oberon likewise took the ass's head from off the clown, and left him to finish his nap with his own fool's head upon his shoulders.

Oberon and his Titania being now perfectly reconciled, he related to her the history of the lovers, and their midnight quarrels; and she agreed to go with him, and see the end of their adventures.

The fairy king and queen found the lovers and their fair ladies, at no great distance from each other, sleeping on a grass-plot; for Puck, to make amends for his former mistake, had contrived with the utmost diligence to bring them all to the same spot, unknown to each other; and he had carefully removed the charm from off the eyes of Lysander with the antidote the fairy king gave to him.

Hermia first awoke, and finding her lost Lysander asleep so near her, was looking at him and wondering at his strange inconstancy. Lysander presently opening his eyes, and seeing his dear Hermia, recovered his reason which the fairy charm had before clouded, and with his reason his love for Hermia ; and they began to talk over the adventures of the night, doubting if these things had really happened, or if they had both been dreaming the same bewildering dream.

Helena and Demetrius were by this time awake, and a sweet sleep having quieted Helena's disturbed and angry spirits, she listened with delight to the professions of love which Demetrius still made to her, and which, to her surprise as well as pleasure, she began to perceive were sincere.

These fair night-wandering ladies, now no longer rivals, became once more true friends ; all the unkind words which had passed were forgiven, and they calmly consulted together what was best to be done in their present situation. It was soon agreed that, as Demetrius had given up his pretensions to Hermia, he should endeavour to prevail upon her father to revoke the cruel sentence of death which had been passed against her. Demetrius was preparing to return to Athens for this friendly purpose, when they were surprised with the sight of Egeus, Hermia's father, who came to the wood in pursuit of his runaway daughter.

When Egeus understood that Demetrius would not now marry his daughter, he no longer opposed her marriage with Lysander, but gave his consent that they should be wedded on the fourth day from that time, being the same day on which Hermia had been condemned to lose her life ; and on that same day Helena joyfully agreed to marry her beloved and now faithful Demetrius.

The fairy king and queen, who were invisible spectators of this reconciliation, and now saw the happy ending of the lovers' history brought about through the good offices of Oberon, received so much pleasure, that these kind spirits resolved to celebrate the approaching nuptials with sports and revels throughout their fairy kingdom.

And now, if any are offended with this story of fairies and their pranks, as judging it incredible and strange, they have only to think that they have been asleep and dreaming, and that all these adventures were visions which they saw in their sleep : and I hope none of my readers will be so unreasonable as to be offended with a pretty, harmless Midsummer Night's Dream.

THE WINTER'S TALE

LEONTES, King of Sicily, and his queen, the beautiful and virtuous Hermione, once lived in the greatest harmony together. So happy was Leontes in the love of this excellent lady, that he had no wish ungratified, except that he sometimes desired to see again, and to present to his queen, his old companion and school-fellow, Polixenes, King of Bohemia. Leontes and Polixenes were brought up together from their infancy; but being, by the death of their fathers, called to reign over their respective kingdoms, they had not met for many years, though they frequently interchanged gifts, letters, and loving embassies.

At length, after repeated invitations, Polixenes came from Bohemia to the Sicilian court, to make his friend Leontes a visit.

At first this visit gave nothing but pleasure to Leontes. He recommended the friend of his youth to the queen's particular attention, and seemed in the presence of his dear friend and old companion to have his felicity quite completed. They talked over old times; their school days and their youthful pranks were remembered, and

28

recounted to Hermione, who always took a cheerful part in these conversations.

When, after a long stay, Polixenes was preparing to depart, Hermione, at the desire of her husband, joined her entreaties to his that Polixenes would prolong his visit.

And now began this good queen's sorrow; for Polixenes refusing to stay at the request of Leontes, was won over by Hermione's gentle and persuasive words to put off his departure for some weeks longer. Upon this, although Leontes had so long known the integrity and honourable principles of his friend Polixenes, as well as the excellent disposition of his virtuous queen, he was seized with an ungovernable jealousy. Every attention Hermione showed to Polixenes, though by her husband's particular desire, and merely to please him, increased the unfortunate king's jealousy; and from being a loving and a true friend, and the best and fondest of husbands, Leontes became suddenly a savage and inhuman monster. Sending for Camillo, one of the lords of his court, and telling him of the suspicion he entertained, he commanded him to poison Polixenes.

Camillo was a good man; and he, well knowing that the jealousy of Leontes had not the slightest foundation in truth, instead of poisoning Polixenes, acquainted him with the king his master's orders, and agreed to escape with him out of the Sicilian dominions; and Polixenes, with the assistance of Camillo, arrived safe in his own kingdom of Bohemia, where Camillo lived from that time in the king's court, and became the chief friend and favourite of Polixenes.

The flight of Polixenes enraged the jealous Leontes still more; he went to the queen's apartment, where the good lady was sitting with her little son Mamillus, who was just beginning to tell one of his best stories to amuse his mother, when the king entered, and taking the child away, sent Hermione to prison.

Mamillus, though but a very young child, loved his mother tenderly ; and when he saw her so dishonoured, and found she was taken from him to be put into a prison, he took it deeply to heart, and drooped and pined away by slow degrees, losing his appetite and his sleep, till it was thought his grief would kill him.

The king, when he had sent his queen to prison, commanded Cleomenes, and Dion, two Sicilian lords, to go to Delphos, there to inquire of the oracle at the temple of Apollo if his queen had been unfaithful to him.

When Hermione had been a short time in prison, she had a little daughter ; and the poor lady received much comfort from the sight of her pretty baby, and she said to it, " My poor little prisoner, I am as innocent as you are."

Hermione had a kind friend in the noble-spirited Paulina, who was the wife of Antigonus, a Sicilian lord ; and when the lady Paulina heard her royal mistress had a new baby, she went to the prison where Hermione was confined, and she said to Emilia, a lady who attended upon Hermione, " I pray you, Emilia, tell the good queen, if her majesty dare trust me with her little babe, I will carry it to the king its father : we do not know how he may soften at the sight of his innocent child." " Most worthy madam," replied Emilia, " I will acquaint the queen with your noble offer : she was wishing to-day that she had any friend who would venture to present the child to the king." " And tell her," said Paulina, ' that I will speak boldly to Leontes in her defence." " May you be for ever blessed," said Emilia, " for your kindness to our gracious queen ! " Emilia then went to Hermione, who joyfully gave up her baby to the care of Paulina, for she had feared that no one would dare venture to present the child to its father.

Paulina took the new-born infant, and forcing herself into the king's presence, notwithstanding her husband, fearing the king's anger, endeavoured to prevent her, she laid the babe at its father's feet, and Paulina made a noble speech to the king in defence of Hermione, and she reproached him severely for his inhumanity, and implored him to have mercy on his innocent wife and child. But Paulina's spirited remonstrances only aggravated Leontes' displeasure, and he ordered her husband Antigonus to take her from his presence.

When Paulina went away, she left the little baby at its father's feet, thinking, when he was alone with it, he would look upon it, and have pity on its helpless innocence.

The good Paulina was mistaken; for no sooner was she gone than the merciless father ordered Antigonus, Paulina's husband, to take the child, and carry it out to sea, and leave it upon some desert shore to perish.

Antigonus, unlike the good Camillo, too well obeyed the orders of Leontes, for he immediately carried the child on shipboard, and put out to sea, intending to leave it on the first desert coast he could find.

So firmly was the king persuaded of the guilt of Hermione, that he would not wait for the return of Cleomenes and Dion, whom he had sent to consult the oracle of Apollo at Delphos; but before the queen was recovered from her grief for the loss of her precious baby, he had her brought to a public trial before all the lords and nobles of his court. And when all the great lords, the judges, and all the nobility of the land were assembled together to try Hermione, and that unhappy queen was standing as a prisoner before her subjects to receive their judgment, Cleomenes and Dion entered the assembly, and presented to the king the answer of the oracle sealed up; and Leontes commanded the seal to be broken, and the words of the oracle to be read aloud, and these were the words :—" *Hermione is innocent, Polixenes blameless, Camillo a true subject, Leontes a jealous tyrant, and the king*

shall live without an heir if that which is lost be not found."
The king would give no credit to the words of the oracle :
he said it was a falsehood invented by the queen's friends,
and he desired the judge to proceed in the trial of the
queen ; but while Leontes was speaking, a man entered
and told him that the Prince Mamillus, hearing his mother
was to be tried for her life, struck with grief and shame,
had suddenly died.

Hermione, upon hearing of the death of this dear
affectionate child, who had lost his life in sorrowing for
her misfortune, fainted ; and Leontes, pierced to the
heart by the news, began to feel pity for his unhappy
queen, and he ordered Paulina, and the ladies who were
her attendants, to take her away, and use means for her
recovery. Paulina soon returned and told the king that
Hermione was dead.

When Leontes heard that the queen was dead, he
repented of his cruelty to her ; and now that he thought
his ill usage had broken Hermione's heart, he believed her
innocent ; and he now thought the words of the oracle
were true, as he knew " if that which was lost was not
found," which he concluded was his young daughter, he
should be without an heir, the young prince Mamillus
being dead ; and he would give his kingdom now to recover his lost daughter : and Leontes gave himself up to
remorse, and passed many years in mournful thoughts
and repentant grief.

The ship in which Antigonus carried the infant
princess out to sea was driven by a storm upon the coast
of Bohemia, the very kingdom of the good King Polixenes.
Here Antigonus landed, and here he left the little baby.

Antigonus never returned to Sicily to tell Leontes
where he had left his daughter, for as he was going back
to the ship, a bear came out of the woods, and tore him
to pieces ; a just punishment on him for obeying the
wicked order of King Leontes.

He saw the old man's supposed daughter

The child was dressed in rich clothes and jewels; for Hermione had made it very fine when she sent it to Leontes, and Antigonus had pinned a paper to its mantle, with the name of *Perdita* written thereon, and words obscurely intimating its high birth and untoward fate.

This poor deserted baby was found by a shepherd. He was a humane man, and so he carried the little Perdita home to his wife, who nursed it tenderly; but poverty tempted the shepherd to conceal the rich prize he had found; therefore he left that part of the country, that no one might know where he got his riches, and with part of Perdita's jewels he bought herds of sheep, and became a wealthy shepherd. He brought up Perdita as his own child, and she knew not she was any other than a shepherd's daughter.

The little Perdita grew up a lovely maiden; and though she had no better education than that of a shepherd's daughter, yet so did the natural graces she inherited from her royal mother shine forth in her un-tutored mind, that no one from her behaviour would have known she had not been brought up in her father's court.

Polixenes, the King of Bohemia, had an only son, whose name was Florizel. As this young prince was hunting near the shepherd's dwelling, he saw the old man's sup-posed daughter; and the beauty, modesty, and queen-like deportment of Perdita caused him instantly to fall in love with her. He soon, under the name of Doricles, and in the disguise of a private gentleman, became a constant visitor to the old shepherd's house.

Florizel's frequent absences from court alarmed Polixenes; and setting people to watch his son, he dis-covered his love for the shepherd's fair daughter.

Polixenes then called for Camillo, the faithful Camillo, who had preserved his life from the fury of Leontes, and desired that he would accompany him to the house of the shepherd, the supposed father of Perdita.

Polixenes and Camillo, both in disguise, arrived at the old shepherd's dwelling while they were celebrating the feast of sheep-shearing; and though they were strangers, yet at the sheep-shearing every guest being made welcome, they were invited to walk in, and join in the general festivity.

Nothing but mirth and jollity was going forward. Tables were spread, and great preparations were making for the rustic feast. Some lads and lasses were dancing on the green before the house, while others of the young men were buying ribands, gloves, and such toys, of a pedlar at the door.

While this busy scene was going forward, Florizel and Perdita sat quietly in a retired corner, seemingly more pleased with the conversation of each other than desirous of engaging in the sports and silly amusements of those around them.

The king was so disguised that it was impossible his son could know him; he therefore advanced near enough to hear the conversation. The simple yet elegant manner in which Perdita conversed with his son did not a little surprise Polixenes; he said to Camillo, "This is the prettiest low-born lass I ever saw; nothing she does or says but looks like something greater than herself, too noble for this place."

Camillo replied, "Indeed, she is the very queen of curds and cream."

"Pray, my good friend," said the king to the old shepherd, "what fair swain is that talking with your daughter?" "They call him Doricles," replied the shepherd. "He says he loves my daughter; and to speak the truth, there is not a kiss to choose which loves the other best. If young Doricles can get her, she shall bring him that he little dreams of": meaning the remainder of

Perdita's jewels; which, after he had bought herds of sheep with part of them, he had carefully hoarded up for her marriage portion.

Polixenes then addressed his son. " How now, young man ! " said he : " your heart seems full of something that takes off your mind from feasting. When I was young, I used to load my love with presents ; but you have let the pedlar go, and have bought your lass no toy."

The young prince, who little thought he was talking to the king his father, replied, " Old sir, she prizes not such trifles ; the gifts which Perdita expects from me are locked up in my heart." Then turning to Perdita, he said to her, " O hear me, Perdita, before this ancient gentleman, who it seems was once himself a lover ; he shall hear what I profess." Florizel then called upon the old stranger to be a witness to a solemn promise of marriage which he made to Perdita, saying to Polixenes, " I pray you, mark our contract."

" Mark your divorce, young sir," said the king, discovering himself. Polixenes then reproached his son for daring to contract himself to this low-born maiden, calling Perdita " shepherd's-brat, sheep-hook," and other disrespectful names ; and threatening, if ever she suffered his son to see her again, he would put her, and the old shepherd her father, to a cruel death.

The king then left them in great wrath, and ordered Camillo to follow him with Prince Florizel.

When the king had departed, Perdita, whose royal nature was roused by Polixenes' reproaches, said, " Though we are all undone, I was not much afraid ; and once or twice I was about to speak, and tell him plainly that the self-same sun which shines upon his palace, hides not his face from our cottage, but looks on both alike." Then sorrowfully she said, " But now I am awakened from this dream, I will queen it no further. Leave me, sir ; I will go milk my ewes, and weep."

The kind-hearted Camillo was charmed with the spirit and propriety of Perdita's behaviour ; and perceiving that the young prince was too deeply in love to give up his mistress at the command of his royal father, he thought of a way to befriend the lovers, and at the same time to execute a favourite scheme he had in his mind.

Camillo had long known that Leontes, the King of Sicily, was become a true penitent ; and though Camillo was now the favoured friend of King Polixenes, he could not help wishing once more to see his late royal master and his native home. He therefore proposed to Florizel and Perdita, that they should accompany him to the Sicilian court, where he would engage Leontes should protect them, till through his mediation they could obtain pardon from Polixenes, and his consent to their marriage.

To this proposal they joyfully agreed ; and Camillo, who conducted everything relative to their flight, allowed the old shepherd to go along with them.

The shepherd took with him the remainder of Perdita's jewels, her baby clothes, and the paper which he had found pinned to her mantle.

After a prosperous voyage, Florizel and Perdita, Camillo and the old shepherd, arrived in safety at the court of Leontes. Leontes, who still mourned his dead Hermione and his lost child, received Camillo with great kindness, and gave a cordial welcome to Prince Florizel. But Perdita, whom Florizel introduced as his princess, seemed to engross all Leontes' attention : perceiving a resemblance between her and his dead Queen Hermione, his grief broke out afresh, and he said, such a lovely creature might his own daughter have been, if he had not so cruelly destroyed her. " And then, too," said he to Florizel, " I lost the society and friendship of your brave father, whom I now desire more than my life once again to look upon."

When the old shepherd heard how much notice the king had taken of Perdita, and that he had lost a daughter, who was exposed in infancy, he fell to comparing the time when he found the little Perdita with the manner of her exposure, the jewels and other tokens of her high birth; from all which it was impossible for him not to conclude that Perdita and the king's lost daughter were the same.

Florizel and Perdita, Camillo, and the faithful Paulina, were present when the old shepherd related to the king the manner in which he had found the child, and also the circumstance of Antigonus' death, he having seen the bear seize upon him. He showed the rich mantle in which Paulina remembered Hermione had wrapped the child; and he produced a jewel which she remembered Hermione had tied about Perdita's neck; and he gave up the paper which Paulina knew to be the writing of her husband: it could not be doubted that Perdita was Leontes' own daughter; but oh! the noble struggles of Paulina, between sorrow for her husband's death, and joy that the oracle was fulfilled, in the king's heir, his long-lost daughter, being found. When Leontes heard that Perdita was his daughter, the great sorrow that he felt that Hermione was not living to behold her child, made him that he could say nothing for a long time but " O thy mother! thy mother! "

Paulina interrupted this joyful yet distressful scene with saying to Leontes that she had a statue, newly finished by that rare Italian master Julio Romano, which was such a perfect resemblance of the queen, that would his majesty be pleased to go to her house and look upon it, he would almost be ready to think it was Hermione herself. Thither then they all went, the king anxious to see the semblance of his Hermione, and Perdita longing to behold what the mother she never saw did look like.

When Paulina drew back the curtain which concealed this famous statue, so perfectly did it resemble Hermione

D

that all the king's sorrow was renewed at the sight : for a
long time he had no power to speak or move.

"I like your silence, my liege," said Paulina ; "it the
more shows your wonder. Is not this statue very like
your queen ? "

At length the king said, "Oh, thus she stood, even
with such majesty, when I first wooed her. But yet, Paulina,
Hermione was not so aged as this statue looks." Paulina
replied, "So much the more the carver's excellence, who
has made the statue as Hermione would have looked had
she been living now. But let me draw the curtain, sire,
lest presently you think it moves."

The king then said, "Do not draw the curtain!
Would I were dead ! See, Camillo, would you not think it
breathed ? Her eye seems to have motion in it." "I
must draw the curtain, liege," said Paulina ; "you are
so transported, you will persuade yourself the statue lives."
"O sweet Paulina," said Leontes, "make me think so
twenty years together. Still methinks there is an air
comes from her. What fine chisel could ever yet cut
breath ? Let no man mock me, for I will kiss her."
"Good my lord, forbear ! " said Paulina. "The ruddi-
ness upon her lip is wet ; you will stain your own with
oily painting. Shall I draw the curtain ? " "No, not
these twenty years," said Leontes.

Perdita, who all this time had been kneeling and beholding in silent admiration the statue of her matchless
mother, said now, "And so long could I stay here looking
upon my dear mother."

"Either forbear this transport," said Paulina to
Leontes, "and let me draw the curtain, or prepare yourself for more amazement. I can make the statue move
indeed—ay, and descend from off the pedestal and take
you by the hand. But then you will think, which I protest I am not, that I am assisted by some wicked
powers."

"What you can make her do," said the astonished king, "I am content to look upon. What you can make her speak I am content to hear, for it is as easy to make her speak as move."

Paulina then ordered some slow and solemn music, which she had prepared for the purpose, to strike up, and to the amazement of all the beholders, the statue came down from off the pedestal and threw its arms around Leontes' neck. The statue then began to speak, praying for blessings on her husband, and on her child, the newly-found Perdita.

No wonder that the statue hung upon Leontes' neck and blessed her husband and her child. No wonder, for the statue was indeed Hermione herself, the real, the living queen!

Paulina had falsely reported to the king the death of Hermione, thinking that the only means to preserve her royal mistress's life, and with the good Paulina Hermione had lived ever since, never choosing Leontes should know she was living till she heard Perdita was found: for though she had long forgiven the injuries which Leontes had done to herself, she could not pardon his cruelty to his infant daughter.

His dead queen thus restored to life, his lost daughter found, the long-sorrowing Leontes could scarcely support the excess of his own happiness.

Nothing but congratulations and affectionate speeches where heard on all sides. Now the delighted parents thanked Prince Florizel for loving their lowly-seeming daughter, and now they blessed the good old shepherd for preserving their child. Greatly did Camillo and Paulina rejoice that they had lived to see so good an end of all their faithful services.

And as if nothing should be wanting to complete this strange and unlooked-for joy, King Polixenes himself now entered the palace.

When Polixenes first missed his son and Camillo, knowing that Camillo had long wished to return to Sicily, he conjectured he should find the fugitives here; and, following them with all speed, he happened to arrive just at this, the happiest moment of Leontes' life.

Polixenes took a part in the general joy; he forgave his friend Leontes the unjust jealousy he had conceived against him; and they once more loved each other with all the warmth of their first boyish friendship. And there was no fear that Polixenes would now oppose his son's marriage with Perdita. She was no " sheep-hook " now, but the heiress of the crown of Sicily.

Thus have we seen the patient virtues of the long-suffering Hermione rewarded. That excellent lady lived many years with her Leontes and her Perdita, the happiest of mothers and of queens.

MUCH ADO ABOUT NOTHING

THERE lived in the palace at Messina two ladies, whose names were Hero and Beatrice. Hero was the daughter, and Beatrice the niece, of Leonato, the Governor of Messina.

Beatrice was of a lively temper, and loved to divert her cousin Hero, who was of a more serious disposition, with her sprightly sallies. Whatever was going forward was sure to make matter of mirth for the light-hearted Beatrice.

At the time the history of these ladies commences some young men of high rank in the army, as they were passing through Messina on their return from a war then just ended, in which they had distinguished themselves by their great bravery, came to visit Leonato Among these were Don Pedro, the Prince of Arragon, and his friend Claudio, who was a lord of Florence, and with them came the wild and witty Benedick, and he was a lord of Padua.

These strangers had been at Messina before, and the hospitable governor introduced them to his daughter and his niece as their old friends and acquaintances.

Benedick, the moment he entered the room, began a lively conversation with Leonato and the prince. Beatrice, who liked not to be left out of any discourse, interrupted Benedick with saying, " I wonder that you will still be talking, Signior Benedick ; nobody marks you." Benedick was just such another rattle-brain as Beatrice, yet he was not pleased at this free salutation ; he thought it did not become a well-bred lady to be so flippant with her tongue, and he remembered when he was last at Messina that Beatrice used to select him to make her merry jests upon. And as there is no one who so little likes to be made a jest of as those who are apt to take the same liberty themselves, so it was with Benedick and Beatrice : these two sharp wits never met in former times but a perfect war of raillery was kept up between them, and they always parted mutually displeased with each other. Therefore when Beatrice stopped him in the middle of his discourse with telling him nobody marked what he was saying, Benedick, affecting not to have observed before that she was present, said, " What, my dear Lady Disdain, are you yet living ? " And now war broke out afresh between them, and a long jangling argument ensued, during which Beatrice, although she knew he had so well approved his valour in the late war, said that she would eat all he had killed there, and observing the prince take delight in Benedick's conversation, she called him " the prince's jester." This sarcasm sank deeper into the mind of Benedick than all Beatrice had said before. The hint she gave him that he was a coward, by saying she would eat all he had killed, he did not regard, knowing himself to be a brave man ; but there is nothing that great wits so much dread as the imputation of buffoonery, because the charge comes sometimes a little too near the truth, therefore Benedick perfectly hated Beatrice when she called him " the prince's jester."

The modest Lady Hero was silent before the noble guests ; and while Claudio was attentively observing the improvement which time had made in her beauty, and was contemplating the exquisite graces of her fine figure

MUCH ADO ABOUT NOTHING   43

(for she was an admirable young lady), the prince was highly amused with listening to the humorous dialogue between Benedick and Beatrice, and he said in a whisper to Leonato, " This is a pleasant-spirited young lady. She were an excellent wife for Benedick." Leonato replied to this suggestion, " O my lord, my lord, if they were but a week married they would talk themselves mad." But though Leonato thought they would make a discordant pair, the prince did not give up the idea of matching these two keen wits together.

When the prince returned with Claudio from the palace, he found that the marriage he had devised between Benedick and Beatrice was not the only one projected in that good company, for Claudio spoke in such terms of Hero, as made the prince guess at what was passing in his heart ; and he liked it well, and he said to Claudio, " Do you affect Hero ? " To this question Claudio replied, " O my lord, when I was last at Messina, I looked upon her with a soldier's eye, that liked, but had no leisure for loving ; but now, in this happy time of peace, thoughts of war have left their places vacant in my mind, and in their room come thronging soft and delicate thoughts, all prompting me how fair young Hero is, reminding me that I liked her before I went to the wars." Claudio's confession of his love for Hero so wrought upon the prince that he lost no time in soliciting the consent of Leonato to accept of Claudio for a son-in-law. Leonato agreed to this proposal, and the prince found no great difficulty in persuading the gentle Hero herself to listen to the suit of the noble Claudio, who was a lord of rare endowments and highly accomplished ; and Claudio, assisted by his kind prince, soon prevailed upon Leonato to fix an early day for the celebration of his marriage with Hero.

Claudio was to wait but a few days before he was to be married to his fair lady, yet he complained of the interval being tedious, as, indeed, most young men are impatient when they are waiting for the accomplishment of any event they have set their hearts upon : the prince, therefore, to make the time seem short to him, proposed, as a kind of merry pastime, that they should invent some artful scheme to make Benedick and Beatrice fall in love with each other. Claudio entered with great satisfaction into this whim of the prince, and Leonato promised them his assistance ; and even Hero said she would do any modest office to help her cousin to a good husband.

The device the prince invented was, that the gentlemen should make Benedick believe that Beatrice was in love with him, and that Hero should make Beatrice believe that Benedick was in love with her.

The prince, Leonato, and Claudio began their operations first, and, watching an opportunity when Benedick was quietly seated reading in an arbour, the prince and his assistants took their station among the trees behind the arbour, so near that Benedick could not choose but hear all they said ; and after some careless talk the prince said, " Come hither, Leonato. What was it you told me the other day—that your niece Beatrice was in love with Signior Benedick ? I did never think that lady would have loved any man." " No, nor I neither, my lord," answered Leonato. " It is most wonderful that she should so dote on Benedick, whom she in all outward behaviour seemed ever to dislike." Claudio confirmed all this, with saying that Hero had told him Beatrice was so in love with Benedick, that she would certainly die of grief if he could not be brought to love her ; which Leonato and Claudio seemed to agree was impossible, he having always been such a railer against all fair ladies, and in particular against Beatrice.

The prince affected to hearken to all this with great compassion for Beatrice, and he said, " It were good that Benedick were told of this." " To what end ? " said Claudio : " he would but make sport of it, and torment the poor lady worse." "And if he should," said the prince, " it were a good deed to hang him ; for Beatrice is an excellent sweet lady, and exceeding wise in everything but in loving Benedick." Then the prince motioned to his companions that they should walk on, and leave Benedick to meditate upon what he had overheard.

Benedick had been listening with great eagerness to this conversation, and he said to himself when he heard Beatrice loved him, " Is it possible ? Sits the wind in that corner ? " And when they were gone he began to reason in this manner with himself :—" This can be no trick ! they were very serious, and they have the truth from Hero, and seem to pity the lady. Love me ! Why, it must be requited ! I did never think to marry. But when I said I should die a bachelor, I did not think I should live to be married. They say the lady is virtuous and fair. She is so ; and wise in everything but in loving me. Why, that is no great argument of her folly. But here comes Beatrice. By this day, she is a fair lady ! I do spy some marks of love in her." Beatrice now approached him, and said, with her usual tartness, " Against my will I am sent to bid you to come in to dinner." Benedick, who never felt himself disposed to speak so politely to her before, replied, " Fair Beatrice, I thank you for your pains." And when Beatrice, after two or three more rude speeches, left him, Benedick thought he observed a concealed meaning of kindness under the uncivil words she uttered, and he said aloud, " If I do not take pity on her, I am a villain. If I do not love her, I am a Jew. I will go get her picture."

The gentleman being thus caught in the net they had spread for him, it was now Hero's turn to play her part with Beatrice ; and for this purpose she sent for Ursula and Margaret, two gentlewomen who attended upon her ; and she said to Margaret, " Good Margaret, run to the parlour ; there you will find my cousin Beatrice talking

with the prince and Claudio. Whisper in her ear that I
and Ursula are walking in the orchard, and that our discourse is all of her. Bid her steal into that pleasant arbour
where honeysuckles, ripened by the sun, like ungrateful
minions forbid the sun to enter." This arbour, into
which Hero desired Margaret to entice Beatrice, was the
very same pleasant arbour where Benedick had so lately
been an attentive listener. " I will make her come, I
warrant, presently," said Margaret.

Hero, then, taking Ursula with her into the orchard,
said to her, " Now, Ursula, when Beatrice comes we will
walk up and down this alley, and our talk must be only
of Benedick, and when I name him, let it be your part
to praise him more than ever man did merit. My talk
to you must be how Benedick is in love with Beatrice.
Now begin ; for look where Beatrice like a lapwing runs
close by the ground, to hear our conference." They
then began ; Hero saying, as if in answer to something
which Ursula had said, " No, truly, Ursula. She is too
disdainful ; her spirits are as coy as wild birds of the
rock." " But are you sure," said Ursula, " that Benedick
loves Beatrice so entirely ? " Hero replied, " So says
the prince and my lord Claudio, and they entreated me
to acquaint her with it ; but I persuaded them, if they
loved Benedick, never to let Beatrice know of it." " Certainly," replied Ursula ; " it were not good she knew his
love, lest she made sport of it." " Why, to say the truth,"
said Hero, " I never yet saw a man, how wise soever, or
noble, young, or rarely featured, but she would dispraise
him." " Sure, sure, such carping is not commendable,"
said Ursula. " No," replied Hero ; " but who dare tell
her so ? If I should speak, she would mock me into air."
" Oh, you wrong your cousin," said Ursula ; " she cannot be so much without true judgment as to refuse so rare
a gentleman as Signior Benedick." He hath an excellent good name." said Hero : " indeed, he is the first

man in Italy, always excepting my dear Claudio." And now, Hero giving her attendant a hint that it was time to change the discourse, Ursula said, " And when are you to be married, madam ? " Hero then told her that she was to be married to Claudio the next day, and desired she would go in with her and look at some new attire, as she wished to consult with her on what she would wear on the morrow. Beatrice, who had been listening with breathless eagerness to this dialogue, when they went away exclaimed, " What fire is in my ears ? Can this be true ? Farewell, contempt and scorn, and maiden pride, adieu ! Benedick, love on ! I will requite you, taming my wild heart to your loving hand."

It must have been a pleasant sight to see these old enemies converted into new and loving friends, and to behold their first meeting after being cheated into mutual liking by the merry artifice of the good-humoured prince. But a sad reverse in the fortunes of Hero must now be thought of. The morrow, which was to have been her wedding day, brought sorrow on the heart of Hero and her good father Leonato.

The prince had a half-brother, who came from the wars along with him to Messina. This brother (his name was Don John) was a melancholy, discontented man, whose spirits seemed to labour in the contriving of villanies. He hated the prince his brother, and he hated Claudio, because he was the prince's friend, and he determined to prevent Claudio's marriage with Hero, only for the malicious pleasure of making Claudio and the prince unhappy ; for he knew the prince had set his heart upon this marriage, almost as much as Claudio himself ; and to effect this wicked purpose, he employed one Borachio, a man as bad as himself, whom he encouraged with the offer of a great reward. This Borachio paid his court to Margaret, Hero's attendant ; and Don John, knowing this, prevailed upon him to make Margaret promise to talk with him from her lady's chamber window that night, after Hero was asleep, and also to dress herself in Hero's clothes, the better to deceive Claudio into the belief that it was Hero ; for that was the end he meant to compass by this wicked plot.

Don John then went to the prince and Claudio, and told them that Hero was an imprudent lady, and that she talked with men from her chamber window at midnight. Now this was the evening before the wedding, and he offered to take them that night where they should themselves hear Hero discoursing with a man from her window ; and they consented to go along with him, and Claudio said, " If I see anything to-night why I should not marry her, to-morrow in the congregation, where I intended to wed her, there will I shame her." The prince also said, " And as I assisted you to obtain her, I will join with you to disgrace her."

When Don John brought them near Hero's chamber that night, they saw Borachio standing under the window, and they saw Margaret looking out of Hero's window, and heard her talking with Borachio ; and Margaret being dressed in the same clothes they had seen Hero wear, the prince and Claudio believed it was the Lady Hero herself.

Nothing could equal the anger of Claudio, when he had made (as he thought) this discovery. All his love for the innocent Hero was at once converted into hatred, and he resolved to expose her in the church, as he had said he would, the next day ; and the prince agreed to this, thinking no punishment could be too severe for the naughty lady who talked with a man from her window the very night before she was going to be married to the noble Claudio.

The next day when they were all met to celebrate the marriage, and Claudio and Hero were standing before the priest, and the priest, or friar, as he was called, was proceeding to pronounce the marriage ceremony, Claudio, in the most passionate language, proclaimed the guilt of the blameless Hero, who, amazed at the strange words he uttered, said meekly, " Is my lord well, that he does speak so wide ? "

Leonato, in the utmost horror, said to the prince, " My lord, why speak not you ? " " What should I speak ? " said the prince ; " I stand dishonoured, that I have gone about to link my dear friend to an unworthy woman. Leonato, upon my honour, myself, my brother, and this grieved Claudio, did see and hear her last night at midnight talk with a man at her chamber window."

Benedick, in astonishment at what he heard, said, " This looks not like a nuptial."

" True, O God ! " replied the heart-struck Hero ; and then this hapless lady sank down in a fainting-fit, to all appearance dead.   The prince and Claudio left the church without staying to see if Hero would recover, or at all regarding the distress into which they had thrown Leonato. So hard-hearted had their anger made them.

Benedick remained, and assisted Beatrice to recover Hero from her swoon, saying, " How does the lady ? " " Dead, I think," replied Beatrice in great agony, for she loved her cousin ; and knowing her virtuous principles, she believed nothing of what she had heard spoken against her.   Not so the poor old father ; he believed the story of his child's shame, and it was piteous to hear him lamenting over her, as she lay like one dead before him, wishing she might never more open her eyes.

But the ancient friar was a wise man, and full of observation on human nature, and he had attentively marked the lady's countenance when she heard herself accused, and noted a thousand blushing shames to start into her face, and then he saw an angel-like whiteness bear away those blushes, and in her eye he saw a fire that did belie the error that the prince did speak against her maiden truth, and he said to the sorrowing father, " Call me a fool, trust not my reading nor my observation, trust not my age, my reverence, nor my calling, if this sweet lady lie not guiltless here under some biting error."

When Hero recovered from the swoon into which she had fallen, the friar said to her, " Lady, what man is he you are accused of ? " Hero replied, " They know that do accuse me ; I know of none " ; then turning to Leonato, she said, " O my father, if you can prove that any man has ever conversed with me at hours unmeet, or that I yesternight changed words with any creature, refuse me, hate me, torture me to death."

" There is," said the friar, " some strange misunderstanding in the prince and Claudio " ; and then he counselled Leonato, that he should report that Hero was dead ; and he said that the death-like swoon in which they had left Hero would make this easy of belief ; and he also advised him that he should put on mourning and erect a monument for her, and do all rites that appertain to a burial. " What shall become of this ? " said Leonato ; " what will this do ? " The friar replied, " This report of her death shall change slander into pity ; that is some good, but that is not all the good I hope for. When Claudio shall hear that she died upon hearing his words, the idea of her life shall sweetly creep into his imagination. Then shall he mourn if ever love had interest in his heart, and wish he had not so accused her ; yea, though he thought his accusation true."

Benedick now said, " Leonato, let the friar advise you ; and though you know how well I love the prince and Claudio, yet, on my honour, I will not reveal this secret to them."

Leonato, thus persuaded, yielded ; and he said sorrowfully, " I am so grieved that the smallest twine may lead me." The kind friar then led Leonato and Hero away to comfort and console them, and Beatrice and Benedick remained alone ; and this was the meeting from which

their friends, who contrived the merry plot against them,
expected so much diversion—those friends who were now
overwhelmed with affliction, and from whose minds all
thoughts of merriment seemed for ever banished.

Benedick was the first who spoke, and he said, " Lady
Beatrice, have you wept all this while ? " " Yea, and I
will weep a while longer," said Beatrice. " Surely," said
Benedick, " I do believe your fair cousin is wronged."
" Ah ! " said Beatrice, " how much might that man
deserve of me who would right her ! " Benedick then
said, " Is there any way to show such friendship ? I do
love nothing in the world so much as you ; is not that
strange ? " " It were as possible," said Beatrice, " for
me to say I loved nothing in the world so well as you ; but
believe me not, and yet I lie not. I confess nothing, nor
I deny nothing. I am sorry for my cousin." " By my
sword," said Benedick, " you love me, and I protest I love
you. Come, bid me do anything for you." " Kill
Claudio," said Beatrice. " Ha ! not for the wide world,"
said Benedick ; for he loved his friend Claudio, and he
believed he had been imposed upon. " Is not Claudio
a villain, that has slandered, scorned, and dishonoured
my cousin ? " said Beatrice : " O that I were a man ! "
" Hear me, Beatrice ! " said Benedick. But Beatrice would
hear nothing in Claudio's defence ; and she continued to
urge on Benedick to revenge her cousin's wrongs ; and she
said, " Talk with a man out of the window ; a proper
saying ! Sweet Hero ! she is wronged ; she is slandered ;
she is undone. O that I were a man for Claudio's sake !
or that I had any friend who would be a man for my sake !
but valour is melted into courtesies and compliments. I
cannot be a man with wishing, therefore I will die a
woman with grieving." " Tarry, good Beatrice," said
Benedick : " by this hand I love you." " Use it for my
love some other way than swearing by it," said Beatrice.
" Think you on your soul that Claudio has wronged

Hero ? " asked Benedick. " Yea," answered Beatrice ;
" as sure as I have a thought, or a soul." " Enough,"
said Benedick ; " I am engaged ; I will challenge him.
I will kiss your hand, and so leave you. By this hand,
Claudio shall render me a dear account ! As you hear
from me, so think of me. Go, comfort your cousin."

While Beatrice was thus powerfully pleading with Benedick, and working his gallant temper by the spirit of her
angry words to engage in the cause of Hero, and fight
even with his dear friend Claudio, Leonato was challenging
the prince and Claudio to answer with their swords the
injury they had done his child, who, he affirmed, had died
for grief. But they respected his age and his sorrow, and
they said, " Nay, do not quarrel with us, good old man."
And now came Benedick, and he also challenged Claudio
to answer with his sword the injury he had done to Hero ;
and Claudio and the prince said to each other, " Beatrice
has set him on to do this." Claudio nevertheless must
have accepted this challenge of Benedick, had not the
justice of Heaven at the moment brought to pass a better
proof of the innocence of Hero than the uncertain fortune
of a duel.

While the prince and Claudio were yet talking of the
challenge of Benedick, a magistrate brought Borachio as
a prisoner before the prince. Borachio had been overheard talking with one of his companions of the mischief
he had been employed by Don John to do.

Borachio made a full confession to the prince in
Claudio's hearing, that it was Margaret dressed in her
lady's clothes that he had talked with from the window,
whom they had mistaken for the Lady Hero herself ; and
no doubt continued on the minds of Claudio and the
prince of the innocence of Hero. If a suspicion had remained, it must have been removed by the flight of Don
John, who, finding his villanies were detected, fled from
Messina to avoid the just anger of his brother.

The heart of Claudio was sorely grieved when he found
he had falsely accused Hero, who, he thought, died upon
hearing his cruel words ; and the memory of his beloved
Hero's image came over him in the rare semblance that
he loved it first ; and the prince asking him if what he
heard did not run like iron through his soul, he answered,
that he felt as if he had taken poison while Borachio was
speaking.

And the repentant Claudio implored forgiveness of the
old man Leonato for the injury he had done his child ;
and promised, that whatever penance Leonato would lay
upon him for his fault in believing the false accusation
against his betrothed wife, for her dear sake he would
endure it.

The penance Leonato enjoined him was, to marry the
next morning a cousin of Hero's, who, he said, was now
his heir, and in person very like Hero.   Claudio, regarding the solemn promise he made to Leonato, said he would
marry this unknown lady, even though she were an Ethiop ;
but his heart was very sorrowful, and he passed that night
in tears, and in remorseful grief, at the tomb which
Leonato had erected for Hero.

When the morning came, the prince accompanied
Claudio to the church, where the good friar, and Leonato
and his niece, were already assembled, to celebrate a second
nuptial ; and Leonato presented to Claudio his promised
bride ; and she wore a mask, that Claudio might not discover her face.   And Claudio said to the lady in the
mask, " Give me your hand, before this holy friar ; I am
your husband if you will marry me."   " And when I
lived I was your other wife," said this unknown lady ;
and, taking off her mask, she proved to be no niece (as
was pretended), but Leonato's very daughter, the Lady
Hero herself.   We may be sure that this proved a most
agreeable surprise to Claudio, who thought her dead,
so that he could scarcely for joy believe his eyes ; and the

E

prince, who was equally amazed at what he saw, exclaimed, "Is not this Hero, Hero that was dead?" Leonato replied, "She died, my lord, but while her slander lived." The friar promised them an explanation of this seeming miracle, after the ceremony was ended; and was proceeding to marry them when he was interrupted by Benedick, who desired to be married at the same time to Beatrice. Beatrice making some demur to this match, and Benedick challenging her with her love for him, which he had learned from Hero, a pleasant explanation took place; and they found they had both been tricked into a belief of love, which had never existed, and had become lovers in truth by the power of a false jest; but the affection, which a merry invention had cheated them into, was grown too powerful to be shaken by a serious explanation; and since Benedick proposed to marry, he was resolved to think nothing to the purpose that the world could say against it; and he merrily kept up the jest, and swore to Beatrice, that he took her but for pity, and because he heard she was dying of love for him; and Beatrice protested, that she yielded upon great persuasion, and partly to save his life, for she heard he was in a consumption. So these two mad wits were reconciled, and made a match of it, after Claudio and Hero were married; and to complete the history, Don John, the contriver of the villany, was taken in his flight, and brought back to Messina; and a brave punishment it was to this gloomy discontented man, to see the joy and feastings which, by the disappointment of his plots, took place at the palace in Messina.

AS YOU LIKE IT

DURING the time that France was divided into provinces (or dukedoms, as they were called) there reigned in one of these provinces an usurper, who had deposed and banished his elder brother, the lawful duke.

The duke, who was thus driven from his dominions, retired with a few faithful followers to the forest of Arden ; and here the good duke lived with his loving friends, who had put themselves into a voluntary exile for his sake, while their land and revenues enriched the false usurper ; and custom soon made the life of careless ease they led here more sweet to them than the pomp and uneasy splendour of a courtier's life. Here they all lived like the old Robin Hood of England, and to this forest many noble youths daily resorted from the court, and did fleet the time carelessly, as they did who lived in the golden age. In the summer they lay along under the fine shade of the large forest trees, marking the playful sports of the wild deer ; and so fond were they of these poor dappled fools, who seemed to be the native inhabitants of the forest, that it grieved them to be forced to kill them to supply themselves with venison for food. When the cold winds of

55

winter made the duke feel the change of his adverse fortune, he would endure it patiently, and say, " These chilling winds which blow upon my body are true councillors : they do not flatter, but represent truly to me my condition ; and though they bite sharply, their tooth is nothing like so keen as that of unkindness and ingratitude. I find that, howsoever men speak against adversity, yet some sweet uses are to be extracted from it ; like the jewel, precious for medicine, which is taken from the head of the venomous and despised toad." In this manner did the patient duke draw a useful moral from everything that he saw ; and by the help of this moralizing turn, in that life of his, remote from public haunts, he could find tongues in trees, books in the running brooks, sermons in stones, and good in everything.

The banished duke had an only daughter, named Rosalind, whom the usurper, Duke Frederick, when he banished her father, still retained in his court as a companion for his own daughter Celia. A strict friendship subsisted between these ladies, which the disagreement between their fathers did not in the least interrupt, Celia striving by every means in her power to make amends to Rosalind for the injustice of her own father in deposing the father of Rosalind ; and whenever the thoughts of her father's banishment, and her own dependence on the false usurper, made Rosalind melancholy, Celia's whole care was to comfort and console her.

One day, when Celia was talking in her usual kind manner to Rosalind, saying, " I pray you, Rosalind, my sweet cousin, be merry," a messenger entered from the duke, to tell them that if they wished to see a wrestling match, which was just going to begin, they must come instantly to the court before the palace ; and Celia, thinking it would amuse Rosalind, agreed to go and see it.

In those times wrestling, which is only practised now by country clowns. was a favourite sport even in the courts of princes, and before fair ladies and princesses. To this wrestling match, therefore, Celia and Rosalind went. They found that it was likely to prove a very tragical sight, for a large and powerful man, who had long been practised in the art of wrestling, and had slain many men in contests of this kind, was just going to wrestle with a very young man, who, from his extreme youth and inexperience in the art, the beholders all thought would certainly be killed.

When the duke saw Celia and Rosalind, he said, " How now, daughter and niece, are you crept hither to see the wrestling ? You will take little delight in it, there is such odds in the men : in pity to this young man, I wish to persuade him from wrestling. Speak to him, ladies, and see if you can move him."

The ladies were well pleased to perform this humane office, and first Celia, entreated the young stranger that he would desist from the attempt ; and then Rosalind spoke so kindly to him, and with such feeling consideration for the danger he was about to undergo, that instead of being persuaded by her gentle words to forgo his purpose, all his thoughts were bent to distinguish himself by his courage in this lovely lady's eyes. He refused the request of Celia and Rosalind in such graceful and modest words, that they felt still more concern for him : he concluded his refusal with saying, " I am sorry to deny such fair and excellent ladies anything. But let your fair eyes and gentle wishes go with me to my trial, wherein if I be conquered, there is one shamed that was never gracious ; if I am killed, there is one dead that is willing to die : I shall do my friends no wrong, for I have none to lament me ; the world no injury, for in it I have nothing ; for I only fill up a place in the world which may be better supplied when I have made it empty."

And now the wrestling match began. Celia wished the young stranger might not be hurt, but Rosalind felt most for him. The friendless state which he said he was

in, and that he wished to die, made Rosalind think that
he was, like herself, unfortunate ; and she pitied him so
much, and so deep an interest she took in his danger while
he was wrestling, that she might almost be said at that
moment to have fallen in love with him.

The kindness shown this unknown youth by these fair
and noble ladies gave him courage and strength, so that
he performed wonders, and in the end completely conquered
his antagonist, who was so much hurt that for a while he
was unable to speak or move.

The Duke Frederick was much pleased with the
courage and skill shown by this young stranger, and
desired to know his name and parentage, meaning to take
him under his protection.

The stranger said his name was Orlando, and that he
was the youngest son of Sir Rowland de Boys.

Sir Rowland de Boys, the father of Orlando, had been
dead some years ; but when he was living he had been a
true subject and dear friend of the banished duke ; therefore when Frederick heard Orlando was the son of his
banished brother's friend, all his liking for this brave young
man was changed into displeasure, and he left the place
in very ill humour. Hating to hear the very name of any
of his brother's friends, and yet still admiring the valour
of the youth, he said, as he went out, " that he wished
Orlando had been the son of any other man."

Rosalind was delighted to hear that her new favourite
was the son of her father's old friend, and she said to Celia,
" My father loved Sir Rowland de Boys, and if I had
known this young man was his son, I would have added
tears to my entreaties before he should have ventured."

The ladies then went up to him, and seeing him
abashed by the sudden displeasure shown by the duke,
they spoke kind and encouraging words to him ; and
Rosalind, when they were going away, turned back to speak
some more civil things to the brave young son of her

father's old friend ; and taking a chain from off her neck, she said, " Gentleman, wear this for me. I am out of suits with fortune, or I would give you a more valuable present."

When the ladies were alone, Rosalind's talk being still of Orlando, Celia began to perceive her cousin had fallen in love with the handsome young wrestler, and she said to Rosalind, " Is it possible you should fall in love so suddenly ? " Rosalind replied, " The duke, my father, loved his father dearly." " But," said Celia, " does it therefore follow that you should love his son dearly ? for then I ought to hate him, for my father hated his father ; yet I do not hate Orlando."

Frederick being enraged at the sight of Sir Rowland de Boys' son, which reminded him of the many friends the banished duke had among the nobility, and having been for some time displeased with his niece, because the people praised her for her virtues and pitied her for her good father's sake, his malice suddenly broke out against her ; and while Celia and Rosalind were talking of Orlando, Frederick entered the room, and with looks full of anger ordered Rosalind instantly to leave the palace, and follow her father into banishment, telling Celia, who in vain pleaded for her, that " he had only suffered Rosalind to stay upon her account." " I did not then," said Celia, " entreat you to let her stay, for I was too young at that time to value her ; but now that I know her worth, and that we so long have slept together, rose at the same instant, learned, played, and eat together, I cannot live out of her company." Frederick replied, " She is too subtle for you : her smoothness, her very silence, and her patience, speak to the people, and they pity her. You are a fool to plead for her, for you will seem more bright and virtuous when she is gone ; therefore open not your lips in her favour, for the doom which I have passed upon her is irrevocable."

When Celia found she could not prevail upon her

father to let Rosalind remain with her, she generously resolved to accompany her ; and, leaving her father's palace that night, she went along with her friend to seek Rosalind's father, the banished duke, in the forest of Arden.

Before they set out, Celia considered that it would be unsafe for two young ladies to travel in the rich clothes they then wore : she therefore proposed that they should disguise their rank by dressing themselves like country maids. Rosalind said it would be a still greater protection if one of them was to be dressed like a man ; and so it was quickly agreed on between them that, as Rosalind was the tallest, she should wear the dress of a young countryman, and Celia should be habited like a country lass, and that they should say they were brother and sister, and Rosalind said she would be called Ganymede, and Celia chose the name Aliena.

In this disguise, and taking their money and jewels to defray their expenses, these fair princesses set out on their long travel ; for the forest of Arden was a long way off, beyond the boundaries of the duke's dominions.

The Lady Rosalind (or Ganymede as she must now be called) with her manly garb seemed to have put on a manly courage. The faithful friendship Celia had shown in accompanying Rosalind so many weary miles, made the new brother, in recompense for this true love, exert a cheerful spirit, as if he were indeed Ganymede, the rustic and stout-hearted brother of the gentle maiden, Aliena.

When at last they came to the forest of Arden, they no longer found the convenient inns and good accommodations they had met with on the road ; and being in want of food and rest, Ganymede, who had so merrily cheered his sister with pleasant speeches and happy remarks all the way, now owned to Aliena that he was so weary he could find in his heart to disgrace his man's apparel and cry like a woman ; and Aliena declared she could go no farther ; and then Ganymede tried to recollect that it was a man's duty to comfort and console a woman, as the weaker vessel ; and to seem courageous to his new sister, he said, " Come, have a good heart, my sister Aliena ; we are now at the end of our travel, in the forest of Arden." But feigned manliness and forced courage would no longer support them ; for though they were in the forest of Arden, they knew not where to find the duke ; and here the travel of these weary ladies might have come to a sad conclusion, for they might have lost themselves, and have perished for want of food ; but providentially, as they were sitting on the grass almost dying with fatigue and hopeless of any relief, a countryman chanced to pass that way, and Ganymede once more tried to speak with a manly boldness, saying, " Shepherd, if love or gold can in this desert place procure us entertainment, I pray you bring us where we may rest ourselves, for this young maid, my sister, is much fatigued with travelling, and faints for want of food."

The man replied that he was only a servant to a shepherd, and that his master's house was just going to be sold, and therefore they would find but poor entertainment, but that if they would go with him they would be welcome to what there was. They followed the man, the near prospect of relief giving them fresh strength, and bought the house and sheep of the shepherd, and took the man who conducted them to the shepherd's house to wait on them ; and being by this means so fortunately provided with a neat cottage, and well supplied with provisions, agreed to stay here till they could learn in what part of the forest the duke dwelt.

When they were rested after the fatigue of their journey, they began to like their new way of life, and almost fancied themselves the shepherd and shepherdess they feigned to be ; yet sometimes Ganymede remembered he had once been the same Lady Rosalind who had so dearly loved the brave Orlando, because he was the son of old Sir Rowland, her father's friend ; and though Ganymede thought that Orlando was many miles distant, even so many weary miles as they had travelled, yet it soon appeared that Orlando was also in the forest of Arden ; and in this manner this strange event came to pass :

Orlando was the youngest son of Sir Rowland de Boys, who, when he died, left him (Orlando being then very young) to the care of his eldest brother Oliver, charging Oliver on his blessing to give his brother a good education, and provide for him as became the dignity of their ancient house.   Oliver proved an unworthy brother ; and disregarding the commands of his dying father, he never put his brother to school, but kept him at home untaught and entirely neglected.   But in his nature and in the noble qualities of his mind Orlando so much resembled his excellent father, that without any advantages of education he seemed like a youth who had been bred with the utmost care ;   and Oliver so envied the fine person and dignified manners of his untutored brother, that at last he wished to destroy him ;   and to effect this he set on people to persuade him to wrestle with the famous wrestler, who, as has been before related, had killed so many men.   Now it was this cruel brother's neglect of him which made Orlando say he wished to die, being so friendless.

When, contrary to the wicked hopes he had formed, his brother proved victorious, his envy and malice knew no bounds, and he swore he would burn the chamber where Orlando slept.   He was overheard making this vow by one that had been an old and faithful servant to their father, and that loved Orlando because he resembled Sir Rowland. This old man went out to meet him when he returned from the duke's palace, and when he saw Orlando, the peril his dear young master was in made him break out into these passionate exclamations : " O my gentle master, my sweet master !   O you memory of old Sir Rowland !   why are you virtuous ?   why are you gentle, strong, and valiant ? and why would you be so fond to overcome the famous wrestler ? Your praise is come too swiftly home before you." Orlando, wondering what all this meant, asked him what was the matter. And then the old man told him how his wicked brother, envying the love all people bore him, and now hearing the fame he had gained by his victory in the duke's palace, intended to destroy him by setting fire to his chamber that night ; and in conclusion, advised him to escape the danger he was in by instant flight ; and knowing Orlando had no money, Adam (for that was the good old man's name) had brought out with him his own little hoard, and he said, " I have five hundred crowns, the thrifty hire I saved under your father, and laid by to be provision for me when my old limbs should become unfit for service ; take that, and He that doth the ravens feed be comfort to my age ! Here is the gold : all this I give to you ; let me be your servant : though I look old, I will do the service of a younger man in all your business and necessities." " O good old man ! " said Orlando, " how well appears in you the constant service of the old world ! You are not for the fashion of these times. We will go along together, and before your youthful wages are spent I shall light upon some means for both our maintenance."

Together then this faithful servant and his loved master set out, and Orlando and Adam travelled on, uncertain what course to pursue, till they came to the forest of Arden, and there they found themselves in the same distress for want of food that Ganymede and Aliena had been. They wandered on, seeking some human habitation, till they were almost spent with hunger and fatigue. Adam at last said, " O my dear master, I die for want of food, I can go no farther ! " He then laid himself down, thinking to make that place his grave, and bade his dear master farewell. Orlando, seeing him in this weak state, took his old servant up in his arms, and carried him under the shelter of some pleasant trees, and he said to him,

" Cheerly, old Adam, rest your weary limbs here awhile, and do not talk of dying ! "

Orlando then searched about to find some food, and he happened to arrive at that part of the forest where the duke was, and he and his friends were just going to eat their dinner, this royal duke being seated on the grass under no other canopy than the shady covert of some large trees.

Orlando, whom hunger had made desperate, drew his sword, intending to take their meat by force, and said, " Forbear, and eat no more ; I must have your food ! " The duke asked him if distress had made him so bold, or if he were a rude despiser of good manners ? On this Orlando said he was dying with hunger ; and then the duke told him he was welcome to sit down and eat with them. Orlando, hearing him speak so gently, put up his sword, and blushed with shame at the rude manner in which he had demanded their food. " Pardon me, I pray you," said he : " I thought that all things had been savage here, and therefore I put on the countenance of stern command ; but whatever men you are, that in this desert, under the shade of melancholy boughs, lose and neglect the creeping hours of time : if ever you have looked on better days ; if ever you have been where bells have knolled to church ; if you have ever sat at any good man's feast ; if ever from your eyelids you have wiped a tear, and know what it is to pity or be pitied, may gentle speeches now move you to do me human courtesy ! " The duke replied, " True it is that we are men (as you say) who have seen better days, and though we have now our habitation in this wild forest, we have lived in towns and cities, and have with holy bell been knolled to church, have sat at good men's feasts, and from our eyes have wiped the drops which sacred pity has engendered : therefore sit you down, and take of our refreshment as much as will minister to your wants." " There is an old poor man," answered Orlando, " who has limped after me many a weary step in pure love, oppressed at once with two sad infirmities, age and hunger : till he be satisfied, I must not touch a bit." " Go, find him out and bring him hither," said the duke ; " we will forbear to eat till you return." Then Orlando went like a doe to find its fawn and give it food ; and presently returned, bringing Adam in his arms ; and the duke said, " Set down your venerable burthen ; you are both welcome." And they fed the old man, and cheered his heart, and he revived, and recovered his health and strength again.

The duke inquired who Orlando was ; and when he found that he was the son of his old friend, Sir Rowland de Boys, he took him under his protection, and Orlando and his old servant lived with the duke in the forest.

Orlando arrived in the forest not many days after Ganymede and Aliena came there and (as has been before related) bought the shepherd's cottage.

Ganymede and Aliena were strangely surprised to find the name of Rosalind carved on the trees, and love-sonnets fastened to them, all addressed to Rosalind ; and while they were wondering how this could be, they met Orlando, and they perceived the chain which Rosalind had given him about his neck.

Orlando little thought that Ganymede was the fair Princess Rosalind, who, by her noble condescension and favour, had so won his heart that he passed his whole time in carving her name upon the trees, and writing sonnets in praise of her beauty ; but being much pleased with the graceful air of this pretty shepherd youth, he entered into conversation with him, and he thought he saw a likeness in Ganymede to his beloved Rosalind, but that he had none of the dignified deportment of that noble lady ; for Ganymede assumed the forward manners often seen in youths when they are between boys and men, and with much archness and humour talked to Orlando of a certain

lover, "who," said he, "haunts our forest, and spoils
our young trees with carving ' Rosalind ' upon their barks ;
and he hangs odes upon hawthorns, and elegies on
brambles, all praising this same Rosalind. If I could
find this lover, I would give him some good counsel that
would soon cure him of his love."

Orlando confessed that he was the fond lover of whom
he spoke, and asked Ganymede to give him the good counsel
he talked of. The remedy Ganymede proposed, and the
counsel he gave him, was that Orlando should come every
day to the cottage where he and his sister Aliena dwelt :
" And then," said Ganymede, " I will feign myself to be
Rosalind, and you shall feign to court me in the same
manner as you would do if I was Rosalind, and then
I will imitate the fantastic ways of ladies to their lovers,
till I make you ashamed of your love ; and this is the way
I propose to cure you." Orlando had no great faith in
the remedy, yet he agreed to come every day to Ganymede's
cottage, and feign a playful courtship ; and every day
Orlando visited Ganymede and Aliena, and Orlando called
the shepherd Ganymede his Rosalind, and every day talked
over all the fine words and flattering compliments which
young men delight to use when they court their mistresses.
It does not appear, however, that Ganymede made any
progress in curing Orlando of his love for Rosalind.

Though Orlando thought all this was but a sportive
play (not dreaming that Ganymede was his very Rosalind),
yet the opportunity it gave him of saying all the fond
things he had in his heart, pleased his fancy almost as well
as it did Ganymede's who enjoyed the secret jest in knowing
these fine love speeches were all addressed to the right
person.

In this manner many days passed pleasantly on with
these young people ; and the good-natured Aliena, seeing
it made Ganymede happy, let him have his own way, and
was diverted at the mock courtship, and did not care to

remind Ganymede that the Lady Rosalind had not yet made herself known to the duke her father, whose place of resort in the forest they had learnt from Orlando. Ganymede met the duke one day, and had some talk with him, and the duke asked of what parentage he came. Ganymede answered that he came of as good parentage as he did ; which made the duke smile, for he did not suspect the pretty shepherd boy came of royal lineage. Then seeing the duke look well and happy, Ganymede was content to put off all further explanation for a few days longer.

One morning, as Orlando was going to visit Ganymede, he saw a man lying asleep on the ground, and a large green snake had twisted itself about his neck. The snake, seeing Orlando approach, glided away among the bushes. Orlando went nearer, and then he discovered a lioness lie couching, with her head on the ground, with a cat-like watch, waiting till the sleeping man awaked (for it is said that lions will prey on nothing that is dead or sleeping). It seemed as if Orlando was sent by Providence to free the man from the danger of the snake and lioness ; but when Orlando looked in the man's face, he perceived that the sleeper who was exposed to this double peril was his own brother Oliver, who had so cruelly used him, and had threatened to destroy him by fire ; and he was almost tempted to leave him a prey to the hungry lioness ; but brotherly affection and the gentleness of his nature soon overcame his first anger against his brother ; and he drew his sword, and attacked the lioness and slew her, and thus preserved his brother's life both from the venomous snake and the furious lioness ; but before Orlando could conquer the lioness, she had torn one of his arms with her sharp claws.

While Orlando was engaged with the lioness, Oliver awaked, and perceiving that his brother Orlando, whom he had so cruelly treated, was saving him from the fury of a wild beast at the risk of his own life, shame and

remorse at once seized him, and he repented of his unworthy conduct, and besought with many tears his
brother's pardon for the injuries he had done him. Orlando rejoiced to see him so penitent, and readily forgave
him : they embraced each other ; and from that hour
Oliver loved Orlando with a true brotherly affection,
though he had come to the forest bent on his destruction.

The wound in Orlando's arm having bled very much,
he found himself too weak to go to visit Ganymede, and
therefore he desired his brother to go and tell Ganymede,
" whom," said Orlando, " I in sport do call my Rosalind,"
the accident which had befallen him.

Thither then Oliver went, and told to Ganymede and
Aliena how Orlando had saved his life ; and when he had
finished the story of Orlando's bravery, and his own pro-
vidential escape, he owned to them that he was Orlando's
brother, who had so cruelly used him ; and then he told
them of their reconciliation.

The sincere sorrow that Oliver expressed for his
offences made such a lively impression on the kind heart
of Aliena, that she instantly fell in love with him ; and
Oliver observing how much she pitied the distress he told
her he felt for his fault, he as suddenly fell in love
with her. But while love was thus stealing into the hearts
of Aliena and Oliver, he was no less busy with Ganymede,
who hearing of the danger Orlando had been in, and that
he was wounded by the lioness, fainted ; and when he
recovered, he pretended that he had counterfeited the
swoon in the imaginary character of Rosalind, and
Ganymede said to Oliver, " Tell your brother Orlando how
well I counterfeited a swoon." But Oliver saw by the
paleness of his complexion that he did really faint, and
much wondering at the weakness of the young man, he
said, " Well, if you did counterfeit, take a good heart, and
counterfeit to be a man." " So I do," replied Ganymede,
truly, " but I should have been a woman by right."

Oliver made this visit a very long one, and when at last
he returned back to his brother, he had much news to
tell him ; for besides the account of Ganymede's fainting
at the hearing that Orlando was wounded, Oliver told him
how he had fallen in love with the fair shepherdess Aliena,
and that she had lent a favourable ear to his suit, even in
this their first interview ; and he talked to his brother,
as a thing almost settled, that he should marry Aliena,
saying, that he so well loved her, that he would live here
as a shepherd, and settle his estate and house at home
upon Orlando.

"You have my consent," said Orlando. "Let your
wedding be to-morrow, and I will invite the duke and his
friends. Go and persuade your shepherdess to agree to
this : she is now alone ; for look, here comes her brother."
Oliver went to Aliena ; and Ganymede, whom Orlando
had perceived approaching, came to inquire after the
health of his wounded friend.

When Orlando and Ganymede began to talk over the
sudden love which had taken place between Oliver and Aliena,
Orlando said he had advised his brother to persuade his
fair shepherdess to be married on the morrow, and then
he added how much he could wish to be married on the
same day to his Rosalind.

Ganymede, who well approved of this arrangement,
said that if Orlando really loved Rosalind as well as he
professed to do, he should have his wish ; for on the
morrow he would engage to make Rosalind appear in her
own person, and also that Rosalind should be willing to
marry Orlando.

This seemingly wonderful event, which, as Ganymede
was the Lady Rosalind, he could so easily perform, he
pretended he would bring to pass by the aid of magic,
which he said he had learnt of an uncle who was a famous
magician.

The fond lover Orlando, half believing and half

F

doubting what he heard, asked Ganymede if he spoke in sober meaning. " By my life I do," said Ganymede ; " therefore put on your best clothes, and bid the duke and your friends to your wedding ; for if you desire to be married to-morrow to Rosalind, she shall be here."

The next morning, Oliver having obtained the consent of Aliena, they came into the presence of the duke, and with them also came Orlando.

They being all assembled to celebrate this double marriage, and as yet only one of the brides appearing, there was much of wondering and conjecture, but they mostly thought that Ganymede was making a jest of Orlando.

The duke, hearing that it was his own daughter that was to be brought in this strange way, asked Orlando if he believed the shepherd boy could really do what he had promised ; and while Orlando was answering that he knew not what to think, Ganymede entered, and asked the duke, if he brought his daughter, whether he would consent to her marriage with Orlando. " That I would," said the duke, " if I had kingdoms to give with her." Ganymede then said to Orlando, " And you say you will marry her if I bring her here ? " " That I would," said Orlando, " If I were king of many kingdoms."

Ganymede and Aliena then went out together, and Ganymede throwing off his male attire, and being once more dressed in woman's apparel, quickly became Rosalind without the power of magic ; and Aliena, changing her country garb for her own rich clothes, was with as little trouble transformed into the Lady Celia.

While they were gone, the duke said to Orlando, that he thought the shepherd Ganymede looked very like his daughter Rosalind ; and Orlando said he also had observed the resemblance.

They had no time to wonder how all this would end, for Rosalind and Celia in their own clothes entered ; and no longer pretending that it was by the power of magic that she came there, Rosalind threw herself on her knees before her father, and begged his blessing. It seemed so wonderful to all present that she should so suddenly appear, that it might well have passed for magic ; but Rosalind would no longer trifle with her father, and told him the story of her banishment, and of her dwelling in the forest as a shepherd boy, her cousin Celia passing as her sister.

The duke ratified the consent he had already given to the marriage, and Orlando and Rosalind, Oliver and Celia, were married at the same time. And though their wedding could not be celebrated in this wild forest with any of the parade or splendour usual on such occasions, yet a happier wedding day was never passed ; and while they were eating their venison under the cool shade of the pleasant trees, as if nothing should be wanting to complete the felicity of this good duke and the true lovers, an unexpected messenger arrived to tell the duke the joyful news that his dukedom was restored to him.

The usurper, enraged at the flight of his daughter Celia, and hearing that every day men of great worth resorted to the forest of Arden to join the lawful duke in his exile, much envying that his brother should be so highly respected in his adversity, put himself at the head of a large force, and advanced towards the forest, intending to seize his brother, and put him, with all his faithful followers, to the sword ; but, by a wonderful interposition of Providence, this bad brother was converted from his evil intention ; for just as he entered the skirts of the wild forest, he was met by an old religious man, a hermit, with whom he had much talk, and who in the end completely turned his heart from his wicked design   Thenceforward he became a true penitent, and resolved, relinquishing his unjust dominion, to spend the remainder of his days in a religious house. The first act of his newly-conceived penitence was to send a messenger to his brother (as has been related), to offer to restore to him his dukedom, which he had usurped so long, and with it the lands and revenues of his friends, the faithful followers of his adversity.

This joyful news, as unexpected as it was welcome, came opportunely to heighten the festivity and rejoicings at the wedding of the princesses. Celia complimented her cousin on this good fortune which had happened to the duke, Rosalind's father, and wished her joy very sincerely, though she herself was no longer heir to the dukedom, but, by this restoration which her father had made, Rosalind was now the heir, so completely was the love of these two cousins unmixed with anything of jealousy or envy.

The duke had now an opportunity of rewarding those true friends who had stayed with him in his banishment, and these worthy followers, though they had patiently shared his adverse fortune, were very well pleased to return in peace and prosperity to the palace of their lawful duke.

THE TWO GENTLEMEN OF VERONA

THERE lived in the city of Verona two young gentlemen, whose names were Valentine and Proteus, between whom a firm and uninterrupted friendship had long subsisted. They pursued their studies together, and their hours of leisure were always passed in each other's company, except when Proteus visited a lady he was in love with; and these visits to his mistress, and this passion of Proteus for the fair Julia, were the only topics on which these two friends disagreed; for Valentine, not being himself a lover, was sometimes a little weary of hearing his friend for ever talking of his Julia, and then he would laugh at Proteus, and in pleasant terms ridicule the passion of love, and declare that no such idle fancies should ever enter his head, greatly preferring (as he said) the free and happy life he led, to the anxious hopes and fears of the lover Proteus.

One morning Valentine came to Proteus to tell him that they must for a time be separated, for that he was going to Milan. Proteus, unwilling to part with his friend, used many arguments to prevail upon Valentine not to leave him; but Valentine said, " Cease to persuade me, my loving Proteus. I will not, like a sluggard, wear out my youth in idleness at home. Home-keeping youths have ever homely wits. If your affection were not chained to the sweet glances of your honoured Julia, I would entreat you to accompany me, to see the wonders of the world abroad; but since you are a lover, love on still, and may your love be prosperous!"

They parted with mutual expressions of unalterable friendship. "Sweet Valentine, adieu!" said Proteus; "think on me when you see some rare object worthy of notice in your travels, and wish me partaker of your happiness."

Valentine began his journey that same day towards Milan, and when his friend had left him, Proteus sat down to write a letter to Julia, which he gave to her maid Lucetta to deliver to her mistress.

Julia loved Proteus as well as he did her, but she was a lady of a noble spirit, and she thought it did not become her maiden dignity too easily to be won; therefore she affected to be insensible of his passion, and gave him much uneasiness in the prosecution of his suit.

And when Lucetta offered the letter to Julia, she would not receive it, and chid her maid for taking letters from Proteus, and ordered her to leave the room. But she so much wished to see what was written in the letter, that she soon called in her maid again; and when Lucetta returned, she said, "What o'clock is it?" Lucetta, who knew her mistress more desired to see the letter than to know the time of day, without answering her question again offered the rejected letter. Julia, angry that her maid should thus take the liberty of seeming to know what she really wanted, tore the letter in pieces and threw it on the floor, ordering her maid once more out of the room. As Lucetta was retiring, she stooped to pick up the fragments of the torn letter; but Julia, who meant not so to

part with them, said in pretended anger, " Go, get you
gone, and let the papers lie ; you would be fingering them
to anger me."

Julia then began to piece together as well as she could
the torn fragments. She first made out these words,
" Love-wounded Proteus " ; and lamenting over these
and suchlike loving words which she made out, though
they were all torn asunder, or, she said, *wounded* (the expression " love-wounded Proteus " giving her that idea),
she talked to these kind words, telling them she would
lodge them in her bosom as in a bed, till their wounds
were healed, and that she would kiss each several piece,
to make amends.

In this manner she went on talking with a pretty lady-
like childishness, till finding herself unable to make out
the whole, and vexed at her own ingratitude in destroying
such sweet and loving words, as she called them, she wrote
a much kinder letter to Proteus than she had ever done
before.

Proteus was greatly delighted at receiving this favourable answer to his letter, and while he was reading it he
exclaimed, " Sweet love, sweet lines, sweet life ! " In
the midst of his raptures he was interrupted by his father.
" How now ! " said the old gentleman : " what letter are
you reading there ? "

" My lord," replied Proteus, " it is a letter from my
friend Valentine, at Milan."

" Lend me the letter," said his father : " let me see
what news."

" There are no news, my lord," said Proteus, greatly
alarmed, " but that he writes how well beloved he is of
the Duke of Milan, who daily graces him with favours ;
and how he wishes me with him, the partner of his
fortune."

" And how stand you affected to his wish ? " asked the
father.

" As one relying on your lordship's will, and not depending on his friendly wish," said Proteus.

Now it had happened that Proteus' father had just been talking with a friend on this very subject : his friend had said he wondered his lordship suffered his son to spend his youth at home, while most men were sending their sons to seek preferment abroad ; " some," said he, " to the wars, to try their fortunes there, and some to discover islands far away, and some to study in foreign universities ; and there is his companion Valentine, he is gone to the Duke of Milan's court. Your son is fit for any of these things, and it will be a great disadvantage to him in his riper age, not to have travelled in his youth."

Proteus' father thought the advice of his friend was very good, and upon Proteus telling him that Valentine " wished him with him, the partner of his fortune," he at once determined to send his son to Milan ; and without giving Proteus any reason for this sudden resolution, it being the usual habit of this positive old gentleman to command his son, not reason with him, he said, " My will is the same as Valentine's wish " ; and seeing his son look astonished, he added, " Look not amazed, that I so suddenly resolve you shall spend some time in the Duke of Milan's court, for what I will I will, and there is an end. To-morrow be in readiness to go. Make no excuses, for I am peremptory."

Proteus knew it was of no use to make objections to his father, who never suffered him to dispute his will ; and he blamed himself for telling his father an untruth about Julia's letter, which had brought upon him the sad necessity of leaving her.

Now that Julia found she was going to lose Proteus for so long a time, she no longer pretended indifference ; and they bade each other a mournful farewell, with many vows of love and constancy. Proteus and Julia exchanged rings, which they both promised to keep for ever in remembrance of each other ; and thus, taking a sorrowful leave, Proteus set out on his journey to Milan, the abode of his friend Valentine.

Valentine was in reality what Proteus had feigned to his father, in high favour with the Duke of Milan ; and another event had happened to him, of which Proteus did not even dream, for Valentine had given up the freedom of which he used so much to boast, and was become as passionate a lover as Proteus.

She who had wrought this wondrous change in Valentine was the Lady Silvia, daughter of the Duke of Milan, and she also loved him ; but they concealed their love from the duke, because although he showed much kindness for Valentine, and invited him every day to his palace, yet he designed to marry his daughter to a young courtier whose name was Thurio. Silvia despised this Thurio, for he had none of the fine sense and excellent qualities of Valentine.

These two rivals, Thurio and Valentine, were one day on a visit to Silvia, and Valentine was entertaining Silvia with turning everything Thurio said into ridicule, when the duke himself entered the room, and told Valentine the welcome news of his friend Proteus' arrival. Valentine said, " If I had wished a thing, it would have been to have seen him here ! " and then he highly praised Proteus to the duke, saying, " My lord, though I have been a truant of my time, yet hath my friend made use and fair advantage of his days, and is complete in person and in mind, and in all good grace to grace a gentleman."

" Welcome him, then, according to his worth," said the duke : " Silvia, I speak to you, and you, Sir Thurio ; for Valentine, I need not bid him do so." They were here interrupted by the entrance of Proteus, and Valentine introduced him to Silvia, saying, " Sweet lady, entertain him to be my fellow-servant to your ladyship."

When Valentine and Proteus had ended their visit, and were alone together, Valentine said, " Now tell me how all does from whence you came ? How does your lady, and how thrives your love ? " Proteus replied, " My tales of love used to weary you. I know you joy not in a love discourse."

" Ay, Proteus," returned Valentine, " but that life is altered now. I have done penance for contemning love ; for in revenge of my contempt of love, Love has chased sleep from my enthralled eyes. O gentle Proteus, Love is a mighty lord, and hath so humbled me, that I confess there is no woe like his correction, nor no such joy on earth as in his service. I now like no discourse except it be of love. Now I can break my fast, dine, sup, and sleep upon the very name of love."

This acknowledgment of the change which love had made in the disposition of Valentine, was a great triumph to his friend Proteus. But " friend " Proteus must be called no longer, for the same all-powerful deity Love, of whom they were speaking (yea, even while they were talking of the change he had made in Valentine), was working in the heart of Proteus, and he, who had till this time been a pattern of true love and perfect friendship, was now, in one short interview with Silvia, become a false friend and a faithless lover ; for at the first sight of Silvia, all his love for Julia vanished away like a dream, nor did his long friendship for Valentine deter him from endeavouring to supplant him in her affections ; and although, as it will always be when people of dispositions naturally good become unjust, he had many scruples before he determined to forsake Julia, and become the rival of Valentine, yet he at length overcame his sense of duty, and yielded himself up, almost without remorse, to his new unhappy passion.

Valentine imparted to him in confidence the whole history of his love, and how carefully they had concealed

it from the duke her father, and told him that, despair-
ing of ever being able to obtain his consent, he had prevailed upon Silvia to leave her father's palace that night,
and go with him to Mantua : then he showed Proteus a
ladder of ropes, by help of which he meant to assist Silvia
to get out of one of the windows of the palace, after it was
dark.

Upon hearing this faithful recital of his friend's dearest
secrets, it is hardly possible to be believed, but so it was
that Proteus resolved to go to the duke and disclose the
whole to him.

This false friend began his tale with many artful
speeches to the duke, such as that by the laws of
friendship he ought to conceal what he was going to reveal,
but that the gracious favour the duke had shown him, and
the duty he owed his grace, urged him to tell that which
else no worldly good should draw from him. He then told
all he had heard from Valentine, not omitting the ladder of
ropes, and the manner in which Valentine meant to conceal
them under a long cloak.

The duke thought Proteus quite a miracle of integrity,
in that he preferred telling his friend's intention rather
than he would conceal an unjust action, highly commended
him, and promised him not to let Valentine know from
whom he had learnt this intelligence, but by some artifice
to make Valentine betray the secret himself. For this
purpose the duke awaited the coming of Valentine in the
evening, whom he soon saw hurrying towards the palace,
and he perceived somewhat was wrapped within his cloak,
which he concluded was the rope ladder.

The duke upon this stopped him, saying, " Whither
away so fast, Valentine ? " " May it please your grace,"
said Valentine, " there is a messenger, that stays to bear
my letters to my friends, and I am going to deliver them."
Now this falsehood of Valentine's had no better success
in the event than the untruth Proteus told his father.

" Be they of much import ? " said the duke.

" No more, my lord," said Valentine, " than to tell my father I am well and happy at your grace's court."

" Nay, then," said the duke, " no matter : stay with me a while. I wish your counsel about some affairs that concern me nearly." He then told Valentine an artful story, as a prelude to draw his secret from him, saying that Valentine knew he wished to match his daughter with Thurio, but that she was stubborn and disobedient to his commands, " neither regarding," said he, " that she is my child, nor fearing me as if I were her father. And I may say to thee, this pride of hers has drawn my love from her. I had thought my age should have been cherished by her childlike duty. I now am resolved to take a wife, and turn her out to whosoever will take her in. Let her beauty be her wedding dower, for me and my possessions she esteems not."

Valentine, wondering where all this would end, made answer, " And what would your grace have me do in all this ? "

" Why," said the duke, " the lady I would wish to marry is nice and coy, and does not much esteem my aged eloquence. Besides, the fashion of courtship is much changed since I was young : now I would willingly have you to be my tutor to instruct me how I am to woo."

Valentine gave him a general idea of the modes of courtship then practised by young men, when they wished to win a fair lady's love, such as presents, frequent visits, and the like.

The duke replied to this, that the lady did refuse a present which he sent her, and that she was so strictly kept by her father, that no man might have access to her by day.

" Why, then," said Valentine, ' you must visit her by night."

"But at night," said the artful duke, who was now coming to the drift of his discourse, "her doors are fast locked."

Valentine then unfortunately proposed that the duke should get into the lady's chamber at night, by means of a ladder of ropes, saying he would procure him one fitting for that purpose ; and in conclusion advised him to conceal this ladder of ropes under such a cloak as that which he now wore. "Lend me your cloak," said the duke, who had feigned this long story on purpose to have a pretence to get off the cloak : so upon saying these words, he caught hold of Valentine's cloak, and throwing it back, he discovered not only the ladder of ropes, but also a letter of Silvia's, which he instantly opened and read ; and this letter contained a full account of their intended elopement. The duke, after upbraiding Valentine for his ingratitude in thus returning the favour he had shown him by endeavouring to steal away his daughter, banished him from the court and city of Milan for ever ; and Valentine was forced to depart that night, without even seeing Silvia.

While Proteus at Milan was thus injuring Valentine, Julia at Verona was regretting the absence of Proteus ; and her regard for him at last so far overcame her sense of propriety that she resolved to leave Verona, and seek her lover at Milan ; and to secure herself from danger on the road she dressed her maid Lucetta and herself in men's clothes, and they set out in this disguise, and arrived at Milan soon after Valentine was banished from that city through the treachery of Proteus.

Julia entered Milan about noon, and she took up her abode at an inn ; and her thoughts being all on her dear Proteus, she entered into conversation with the inn-keeper, or host, as he was called, thinking by that means to learn some news of Proteus.

The host was greatly pleased that this handsome

young gentleman (as he took her to be), who, from his appearance, he concluded was of high rank, spoke so familiarly to him ; and being a good-natured man, he was sorry to see him look so melancholy ; and to amuse his young guest he offered to take him to hear some fine music, with which, he said, a gentleman that evening was going to serenade his mistress.

The reason Julia looked so very melancholy was, that she did not well know what Proteus would think of the imprudent step she had taken, for she knew he had loved her for her noble maiden pride and dignity of character, and she feared she should lower herself in his esteem ; and this it was that made her wear a sad and thoughtful countenance.

She gladly accepted the offer of the host to go with him and hear the music, for she secretly hoped she might meet Proteus by the way.

But when she came to the palace whither the host conducted her, a very different effect was produced to what the kind host intended, for there, to her heart's sorrow, she beheld her lover, the inconstant Proteus, serenading the Lady Silvia with music, and addressing discourse of love and admiration to her. And Julia overheard Silvia from a window talk with Proteus, and reproach him for forsaking his own true lady, and for his ingratitude to his friend Valentine ; and then Silvia left the window, not choosing to listen to his music and his fine speeches, for she was a faithful lady to her banished Valentine, and abhorred the ungenerous conduct of his false friend Proteus.

Though Julia was in despair at what she had just witnessed, yet did she still love the truant Proteus ; and hearing that he had lately parted with a servant, she contrived, with the assistance of her host, the friendly innkeeper, to hire herself to Proteus as a page ; and Proteus knew not she was Julia, and he sent her with letters and

presents to her rival Silvia, and he even sent by her the
very ring she gave him as a parting gift at Verona.

When she went to that lady with the ring, she was
most glad to find that Silvia utterly rejected the suit of
Proteus ; and Julia, or the page Sebastian as she was
called, entered into conversation with Silvia about Proteus' first love, the forsaken Lady Julia.   She, putting
in (as one may say) a good word for herself, said she knew
Julia, as well she might, being herself the Julia of whom she
spoke ; telling how fondly Julia loved her master Proteus,
and how his unkind neglect would grieve her ; and then
she with a pretty equivocation went on : " Julia is about
my height and of my complexion, the colour of her eyes
and hair the same as mine " ; and indeed Julia looked a
most beautiful youth in her boy's attire.   Silvia was moved
to pity this lovely lady who was so sadly forsaken by the
man she loved ; and when Julia offered the ring which
Proteus had sent, refused it, saying, " The more shame
for him that he sends me that ring ; I will not take it, for
I have often heard him say his Julia gave it to him.   I
love thee, gentle youth, for pitying her, poor lady ! Here
is a purse ; I give it you for Julia's sake."   These comfortable words coming from her kind rival's tongue cheered
the drooping heart of the disguised lady.

But to return to the banished Valentine, who scarce
knew which way to bend his course, being unwilling to
return home to his father a disgraced and banished man.
As he was wandering over a lonely forest, not far distant
from Milan, where he had left his heart's dear treasure,
the Lady Silvia, he was set upon by robbers, who demanded his money.

Valentine told them that he was a man crossed by
adversity, that he was going into banishment, and that
he had no money, the clothes he had on being all his
riches.

The robbers, hearing that he was a distressed man,

and being struck with his noble air and manly behaviour, told him, if he would live with them, and be their chief or captain, they would put themselves under his command; but that if he refused to accept their offer they would kill him.

Valentine, who cared little what became of himself, said he would consent to live with them and be their captain, provided they did no outrage on women or poor passengers.

Thus the noble Valentine became, like Robin Hood, of whom we read in ballads, a captain of robbers and outlawed banditti; and in this situation he was found by Silvia, and in this manner it came to pass:

Silvia, to avoid a marriage with Thurio, whom her father insisted upon her no longer refusing, came at last to the resolution of following Valentine to Mantua, at which place she had heard her lover had taken refuge; but in this account she was misinformed, for he still lived in the forest among the robbers, bearing the name of their captain, but taking no part in their depredations, and using the authority which they had imposed upon him in no other way than to compel them to show compassion to the travellers they robbed.

Silvia contrived to effect her escape from her father's palace in company with a worthy old gentleman whose name was Eglamour, whom she took along with her for protection on the road. She had to pass through the forest where Valentine and the banditti dwelt; and one of these robbers seized on Silvia, and would also have taken Eglamour, but he escaped.

The robber who had taken Silvia, seeing the terror she was in, bid her not be alarmed, for that he was only going to carry her to a cave where his captain lived, and that she need not be afraid, for their captain had an honourable mind, and always showed humanity to women. Silvia found little comfort in hearing she was going to be

carried as a prisoner before the captain of a lawless banditti.   " O Valentine," she cried, " this I endure for
thee ! "

But as the robber was conveying her to the cave of his
captain, he was stopped by Proteus, who, still attended
by Julia in the disguise of a page, having heard of the
flight of Silvia, had traced her steps to this forest.
Proteus now rescued her from the hands of the robber ;
but scarce had she time to thank him for the service he
had done her, before he began to distress her afresh with
his love-suit ; and while he was rudely pressing her to
consent to marry him, and his page (the forlorn Julia)
was standing beside him in great anxiety of mind, fearing
lest the great service which Proteus had just done to
Silvia should win her to show him some favour, they were
all strangely surprised with the sudden appearance of
Valentine, who, having heard his robbers had taken a
lady prisoner, came to console and relieve her.

Proteus was courting Silvia, and he was so much
ashamed of being caught by his friend, that he was all
at once seized with penitence and remorse ; and he expressed such a lively sorrow for the injuries he had done
to Valentine, that Valentine, whose nature was noble and
generous, even to a romantic degree, not only forgave and
restored him to his former place in his friendship, but
in a sudden flight of heroism he said, " I freely do forgive
you ; and all the interest I have in Silvia, I give it up to
you." Julia, who was standing beside her master as a
page, hearing this strange offer, and fearing Proteus
would not be able with this new-found virtue to refuse
Silvia, fainted, and they were all employed in recovering
her : else would Silvia have been offended at being thus
made over to Proteus, though she could scarcely think
that Valentine would long persevere in this overstrained
and too generous act of friendship. When Julia recovered
from the fainting-fit, she said, " I had forgot : my master

G

ordered me to deliver this ring to Silvia." Proteus, looking upon the ring, saw that it was the one he gave to Julia, in return for that which he received from her, and which he had sent by the supposed page to Silvia. " How is this ? " said he, " this is Julia's ring : how came you by it, boy ? " Julia answered, " Julia herself did give it me, and Julia herself hath brought it hither."

Proteus, now looking earnestly upon her, plainly perceived that the page Sebastian was no other than the Lady Julia herself ; and the proof she had given of her constancy and true love so wrought in him, that his love for her returned into his heart, and he took again his own dear lady, and joyfully resigned all pretentions to the Lady Silvia to Valentine, who had so well deserved her.

Proteus and Valentine were expressing their happiness in their reconciliation, and in the love of their faithful ladies, when they were surprised with the sight of the Duke of Milan and Thurio, who came there in pursuit of Silvia.

Thurio first approached, and attempted to seize Silvia, saying, " Silvia is mine." Upon this Valentine said to him in a very spirited manner, " Thurio, keep back : if once again you say that Silvia is yours, you shall embrace your death. Here she stands, take but possession of her with a touch ! I dare you but to breathe upon my love." Hearing this threat, Thurio, who was a great coward, drew back, and said he cared not for her, and that none but a fool would fight for a girl who loved him not.

The duke, who was a very brave man himself, said now in great anger, " The more base and degenerate in you to take such means for her as you have done, and leave her on such slight conditions." Then turning to Valentine, he said, " I do applaud your spirit, Valentine, and think you worthy of an empress's love. You shall have Silvia, for you have well deserved her." Valentine then with great humility kissed the duke's hand, and accepted the noble present which he had made him of his daughter with becoming thankfulness; taking occasion of this joyful minute to entreat the good-humoured duke to pardon the thieves with whom he had associated in the forest, assuring him that, when reformed and restored to society, there would be found among them many good, and fit for great employment; for the most of them had been banished, like Valentine, for state offences, rather than for any black crimes they had been guilty of. To this the ready duke consented; and now nothing remained but that Proteus, the false friend, was ordained, by way of penance for his love-prompted faults, to be present at the recital of the whole story of his loves and falsehoods before the duke; and the shame of the recital to his awakened conscience was judged sufficient punishment; which being done, the lovers, all four, returned back to Milan, and their nuptials were solemnised in presence of the duke, with high triumphs and feasting.

THE MERCHANT OF VENICE

SHYLOCK the Jew lived at Venice; he was an usurer, who had amassed an immense fortune by lending money at great interest to Christian merchants. Shylock, being a hard-hearted man, exacted the payment of the money he lent with such severity, that he was much disliked by all good men, and particularly by Antonio, a young merchant of Venice; and Shylock as much hated Antonio, because he used to lend money to people in distress, and would never take any interest for the money he lent; therefore there was great enmity between this covetous Jew and the generous merchant Antonio. Whenever Antonio met Shylock on the Rialto (or Exchange), he used to reproach him with his usuries and hard dealings, which the Jew would bear with seeming patience, while he secretly meditated revenge.

Antonio was the kindest man that lived, the best conditioned, and had the most unwearied spirit in doing courtesies; indeed, he was one in whom the ancient Roman honour more appeared than in any that drew breath in Italy. He was greatly beloved by all his fellow-citizens, but the friend who was nearest and dearest to his heart was Bassanio, a noble Venetian, who, having but a small patrimony, had nearly exhausted his little fortune by living in too expensive a manner for his slender means, as young men of high rank with small fortunes are too apt to do. Whenever Bassanio wanted money, Antonio assisted him; and it seemed as if they had but one heart and one purse between them.

One day Bassanio came to Antonio, and told him that he wished to repair his fortune by a wealthy marriage with a lady whom he dearly loved, whose father, that was lately dead, had left her sole heiress to a large estate; and that in her father's lifetime he used to visit at her house, when he thought he had observed this lady had sometimes from her eyes sent speechless messages, that seemed to say he would be no unwelcome suitor; but not having money to furnish himself with an appearance befitting the lover of so rich an heiress, he besought Antonio to add to the many favours he had shown him, by lending him three thousand ducats.

Antonio had no money by him at that time to lend his friend, but expecting soon to have some ships come home laden with merchandise, he said he would go to Shylock, the rich money-lender, and borrow the money upon the credit of those ships.

Antonio and Bassanio went together to Shylock, and Antonio asked the Jew to lend him three thousand ducats upon an interest he should require, to be paid out of the merchandise contained in his ships at sea. On this Shylock thought within himself, " If I can once catch him on the hip, I will feed fat the ancient grudge I bear him : he hates our Jewish nation ; he lends out money gratis ; and among the merchants he rails at me and my well-earned bargains, which he calls interest. Cursed be my tribe if I forgive him ! " Antonio finding he was musing within himself and did not answer, and being impatient for the money, said, " Shylock, do you hear? will you

lend the money?" To this question the Jew replied,
"Signior Antonio, on the Rialto many a time and often
you have railed at me about my monies and my usuries,
and I have borne it with a patient shrug, for sufferance
is the badge of all our tribe; and then you have called
me unbeliever, cut-throat dog, and spit upon my Jewish
garments, and spurned at me with your foot, as if I were
a cur. Well, then, it now appears you need my help;
and you come to me and say, *Shylock, lend me monies.*
Has a dog money? Is it possible a cur should lend three
thousand ducats? Shall I bend low and say, Fair sir,
you spit upon me on Wednesday last, another time you
called me dog, and for these courtesies I am to lend you
monies?" Antonio replied, "I am as like to call you
so again, to spit on you again, and spurn you too. If you
will lend me this money, lend it not to me as to a friend,
but rather lend it to me as to an enemy, that, if I break,
you may with better face exact the penalty." "Why,
look you," said Shylock, "how you storm! I would be
friends with you, and have your love. I will forget the
shames you have put upon me. I will supply your wants,
and take no interest for my money." This seemingly
kind offer greatly surprised Antonio; and then Shylock,
still pretending kindness, and that all he did was to gain
Antonio's love, again said he would lend him the three
thousand ducats, and take no interest for his money,—
only Antonio should go with him to a lawyer, and there
sign in merry sport a bond, that if he did not repay the
money by a certain day, he would forfeit a pound of flesh, to
be cut off from any part of his body that Shylock pleased.

"Content," said Antonio. "I will sign to this bond,
and say there is much kindness in the Jew."

Bassanio said Antonio should not sign to such a bond
for him, but still Antonio insisted that he would sign it,
for that before the day of payment came his ships would
return, laden with many times the value of the money.

Shylock, hearing this debate, exclaimed, " O father Abraham, what suspicious people these Christians are! Their own hard dealings teach them to suspect the thoughts of others. I pray you tell me this, Bassanio : if he should break his day, what should I gain by the exaction of the forfeiture ? A pound of man's flesh, taken from a man, is not so estimable, nor profitable neither, as the flesh of mutton or of beef. I say, to buy his favour I offer this friendship : if he will take it, so ; if not, adieu."

At last, against the advice of Bassanio, who, notwithstanding all the Jew had said of his kind intentions, did not like his friend should run the hazard of this shocking penalty for his sake, Antonio signed the bond, thinking it really was (as the Jew said) merely in sport.

The rich heiress that Bassanio wished to marry lived near Venice, at a place called Belmont : her name was Portia, and in the graces of her person and her mind she was nothing inferior to that Portia, of whom we read, who was Cato's daughter, and the wife of Brutus.

Bassanio, being so kindly supplied with money by his friend Antonio at the hazard of his life, set out for Belmont with a splendid train, and attended by a gentleman of the name of Gratiano.

Bassanio proving successful in his suit, Portia in a short time consented to accept of him for a husband.

Bassanio confessed to Portia that he had no fortune, and that his high birth and noble ancestry were all that he could boast of ; she, who loved him for his worthy qualities, and had riches enough not to regard wealth in a husband, answered with a graceful modesty, that she would wish herself a thousand times more fair, and ten thousand times more rich, to be more worthy of him ; and then the accomplished Portia prettily dispraised herself, and said she was an unlessoned girl, unschooled, unpractised, yet not so old but that she could learn, and that she would commit her gentle spirit to be directed and governed by him in all things ; and she said, " Myself and what is mine, to you and yours is now converted. But yesterday, Bassanio, I was the lady of this fair mansion, queen of myself, and mistress over these servants ; and now this house, these servants, and myself, are yours, my lord ; I give them with this ring " : presenting a ring to Bassanio.

Bassanio was so overpowered with gratitude and wonder at the gracious manner in which the rich and noble Portia accepted of a man of his humble fortunes that he could not express his joy and reverence to the dear lady who so honoured him, by anything but broken words of love and thankfulness ; and taking the ring, he vowed never to part with it.

Gratiano, and Nerissa, Portia's waiting-maid, were in attendance upon their lord and lady, when Portia so gracefully promised to become the obedient wife of Bassanio ; and Gratiano, wishing Bassanio and the generous lady joy, desired permission to be married at the same time.

" With all my heart, Gratiano," said Bassanio, " if you can get a wife."

Gratiano then said that he loved the Lady Portia's fair waiting gentlewoman, Nerissa, and that she had promised to be his wife, if her lady married Bassanio. Portia asked Nerissa if this was true. Nerissa replied, " Madam, it is so, if you approve of it." Portia willingly consenting, Bassanio pleasantly said, " Then our wedding feast shall be much honoured by your marriage, Gratiano."

The happiness of these lovers was sadly crossed at this moment by the entrance of a messenger, who brought a letter from Antonio containing fearful tidings. When Bassanio read Antonio's letter, Portia feared it was to tell him of the death of some dear friend, he looked so pale ; and inquiring what was the news which had so distressed him, he said, " O sweet Portia, here are a few of the unpleasantest words that ever blotted paper: gentle lady, when I first imparted my love to you, I freely told you all the wealth I had ran in my veins; but I should have told you that I had less than nothing, being in debt." Bassanio then told Portia, what has been here related, of his borrowing the money of Antonio, and of Antonio's procuring it of Shylock the Jew, and of the bond by which Antonio had engaged to forfeit a pound of flesh, if it was not repaid by a certain day; and then Bassanio read Antonio's letter, the words of which were, "*Sweet Bassanio, my ships are all lost, my bond to the Jew is forfeited, and since in paying it is impossible I should live, I could wish to see you at my death; notwithstanding, use your pleasure: if your love for me do not persuade you to come, let not my letter.*" "O my dear love," said Portia, "dispatch all business and be gone: you shall have gold to pay the money twenty times over, before this kind friend shall lose a hair by my Bassanio's fault; and as you are so dearly bought, I will dearly love you." Portia then said she would be married to Bassanio before he set out, to give him a legal right to her money; and that same day they were married, and Gratiano was also married to Nerissa; and Bassanio and Gratiano, the instant they were married, set out in great haste for Venice, where Bassanio found Antonio in prison.

The day of payment being past, the cruel Jew would not accept of the money which Bassanio offered him, but insisted upon having a pound of Antonio's flesh. A day was appointed to try this shocking cause before the Duke of Venice, and Bassanio awaited in dreadful suspense the event of the trial.

When Portia parted with her husband, she spoke cheeringly to him, and bade him bring his dear friend along with him when he returned; yet she feared it would go hard with Antonio, and when she was left alone, she began to think and consider within herself if she could

94 TALES FROM SHAKSPEARE

by any means be instrumental in saving the life of her
dear Bassanio's friend; and notwithstanding, when she
wished to honour her Bassanio, she had said to him with
such a meek and wife-like grace, that she would submit
in all things to be governed by his superior wisdom, yet
being now called forth into action by the peril of her
honoured husband's friend, she did nothing doubt her
own powers, and, by the sole guidance of her own true
and perfect judgment, at once resolved to go herself to
Venice, and speak in Antonio's defence.

Portia had a relation who was a counsellor in the law:
to this gentleman, whose name was Bellario, she wrote,
and stating the case to him, desired his opinion, and that
with his advice he would also send her the dress worn
by a counsellor. When the messenger returned, he
brought letters from Bellario of advice how to proceed,
and also everything necessary for her equipment.

Portia dressed herself and her maid Nerissa in men's
apparel, and putting on the robes of a counsellor, she
took Nerissa along with her as her clerk; and setting out
immediately, they arrived at Venice on the very day of the
trial. The cause was just going to be heard before the
duke and senators of Venice in the senate house, when
Portia entered this high court of justice, and presented
a letter from Bellario, in which that learned counsellor
wrote to the duke, saying he would have come himself
to plead for Antonio, but that he was prevented by sickness, and he requested that the learned young Doctor
Balthasar (so he called Portia) might be permitted to plead
in his stead. This the duke granted, much wondering
at the youthful appearance of the stranger, who was
prettily disguised by her counsellor's robes and her large
wig.

And now began this important trial. Portia looked
around her, and she saw the merciless Jew; and she saw
Bassanio, but he knew her not in her disguise. He was

standing beside Antonio, in an agony of distress and fear for his friend.

The importance of the arduous task Portia had engaged in gave this tender lady courage, and she boldly proceeded in the duty she had undertaken to perform ; and first of all she addressed herself to Shylock, and allowing that he had a right by the Venetian law to have the forfeit expressed in the bond, she spoke so sweetly of the noble quality of *mercy*, as would have softened any heart but the unfeeling Shylock's, saying that it dropped as the gentle rain from heaven upon the place beneath, and how mercy was a double blessing—it blessed him that gave and him that received it ; and how it became monarchs better than their crowns, being an attribute of God Himself, and that earthly power came nearest to God's in proportion as mercy tempered justice ; and she bid Shylock remember that as we all pray for mercy, that same prayer should teach us to show mercy. Shylock only answered her by desiring to have the penalty forfeited in the bond. " Is he not able to pay the money ? " asked Portia. Bassanio then offered the Jew the payment of the three thousand ducats as many times over as he should desire ; which Shylock refusing, and still insisting upon having a pound of Antonio's flesh, Bassanio begged the learned young counsellor would endeavour to wrest the law a little, to save Antonio's life. But Portia gravely answered that laws once established must never be altered. Shylock hearing Portia say that the law might not be altered, it seemed to him that she was pleading in his favour, and he said, " A Daniel is come to judgment ! O wise young judge, how I do honour you ! How much elder are you than your looks ! "

Portia now desired Shylock to let her look at the bond, and when she had read it, she said, " This bond is forfeited, and by this the Jew may lawfully claim a pound of flesh, to be by him cut off nearest Antonio's heart."

Then she said to Shylock, " Be merciful : take the money, and bid me tear the bond." But no mercy would the cruel Shylock show ; and he said, " By my soul, I swear there is no power in the tongue of man to alter me." " Why, then, Antonio," said Portia, " you must prepare your bosom for the knife " ; and while Shylock was sharpening a long knife with great eagerness to cut off the pound of flesh, Portia said to Antonio, " Have you any-thing to say ? " Antonio, with a calm resignation, replied that he had but little to say, for that he had prepared his mind for death. Then he said to Bassanio, " Give me your hand, Bassanio. Fare you well. Grieve not that I am fallen into this misfortune for you. Commend me to your honourable wife, and tell her how I have loved you ! " Bassanio in the deepest affliction replied, " Antonio, I am married to a wife, who is as dear to me as life itself ; but life itself, my wife and all the world, are not esteemed with me above your life. I would lose all, I would sacrifice all to this devil here, to deliver you."

Portia hearing this, though the kind-hearted lady was not at all offended with her husband for expressing the love he owed to so true a friend as Antonio in these strong terms, yet could not help answering, " Your wife would give you little thanks, if she were present, to hear you make this offer." And then Gratiano, who loved to copy what his lord did, thought he must make a speech like Bassanio's, and he said, in Nerissa's hearing, who was writing in her clerk's dress by the side of Portia, " I have a wife, whom I protest I love ; I wish she were in heaven, if she could but entreat some power there to change the cruel temper of this currish Jew." " It is well you wish this behind her back, else you would have but an unquiet house," said Nerissa.

Shylock now cried out impatiently, " We trifle time ; I pray pronounce the sentence." And now all was awful expectation in the court, and every heart was full of grief for Antonio.

Portia asked if the scales were ready to weigh the flesh; and she said to the Jew, " Shylock, you must have some surgeon by, lest he bleed to death." Shylock, whose whole intent was that Antonio *should* bleed to death, said, " It is not so named in the bond." Portia replied, " It is not so named in the bond, but what of that? It were good you did so much for charity." To this all the answer Shylock would make was, " I cannot find it; it is not in the bond." " Then," said Portia, " a pound of Antonio's flesh is thine. The law allows it, and the court awards it. And you may cut this flesh from off his breast. The law allows it, and the court awards it." Again Shylock exclaimed, " O wise and upright judge! A Daniel is come to judgment! " And then he sharpened his long knife again, and looking eagerly on Antonio, he said, " Come, prepare! "

" Tarry a little, Jew," said Portia; " there is something else. This bond here gives you no drop of blood; the words expressly are, ' a pound of flesh.' If in the cutting off the pound of flesh you shed one drop of Christian blood, your land and goods are by the law to be confiscated to the state of Venice." Now, as it was utterly impossible for Shylock to cut off the pound of flesh without shedding some of Antonio's blood, this wise discovery of Portia's, that it was flesh and not blood that was named in the bond, saved the life of Antonio; and all admiring the wonderful sagacity of the young counsellor, who had so happily thought of this expedient, plaudits resounded from every part of the senate house, and Gratiano exclaimed, in the words which Shylock had used, " O wise and upright judge! mark, Jew, a Daniel is come to judgment! "

Shylock, finding himself defeated in his cruel intent, said, with a disappointed look, that he would take the

money ; and Bassanio, rejoiced beyond measure at Antonio's
unexpected deliverance, cried out, " Here is the money ! "
But Portia stopped him, saying, " Softly ; there is no
haste : the Jew shall have nothing but the penalty ; therefore, prepare, Shylock, to cut off the flesh ; but mind
you shed no blood ; nor do not cut off more nor less than
just a pound ; be it more nor less than by one poor
scruple, nay, if the scale turn but by the weight of a single
hair, you are condemned by the laws of Venice to die, and
all your wealth is forfeited to the senate." " Give me
my money, and let me go," said Shylock. " I have it
ready," said Bassanio ; " here it is."

Shylock was going to take the money, when Portia
again stopped him, saying, " Tarry, Jew ; I have yet
another hold upon you. By the laws of Venice, your
wealth is forfeited to the state for having conspired against
the life of one of its citizens, and your life lies at the mercy
of the duke ; therefore, down on your knees, and ask him
to pardon you."

The duke then said to Shylock, " That you may see
the difference of our Christian spirit, I pardon you your
life before you ask it ; half your wealth belongs to Antonio,
the other half comes to the state."

The generous Antonio then said that he would give
up his share of Shylock's wealth, if Shylock would sign
a deed to make it over at his death to his daughter and her
husband ; for Antonio knew that the Jew had an only
daughter, who had lately been married against his consent
to a young Christian, named Lorenzo, a friend of Antonio's,
which had so offended Shylock, that he had disinherited
her.

The Jew agreed to this ; and being thus disappointed
in his revenge, and despoiled of his riches, he said, " I am
ill. Let me go home : send the deed after me, and I
will sign over half my riches to my daughter." " Get
thee gone, then," said the duke, " and sign it ; and if

you repent your cruelty and turn Christian, the stɛte will forgive you the fine of the other half of your riches."

The duke now released Antonio, and dismissed the court. He then highly praised the wisdom and ingenuity of the young counsellor, and invited him home to dinner. Portia, who meant to return to Belmont before her husband, replied, " I humbly thank your grace, but I must away directly." The duke said he was sorry he had not leisure to stay and dine with him ; and, turning to Antonio, he added, " Reward this gentleman ; for, in my mind, you are much indebted to him."

The duke and his senators left the court ; and then Bassanio said to Portia, " Most worthy gentleman, I and my friend Antonio have by your wisdom been this day acquitted of grievous penalties, and beg you will accept of the three thousand ducats due unto the Jew." " And we shall stand indebted to you over and above," said Antonio, " in love and service evermore."

Portia could not be prevailed upon to accept the money ; but upon Bassanio still pressing her to accept of some reward, she said, " Give me your gloves ; I will wear them for your sake " ; and then, Bassanio taking off his gloves, she espied the ring which she had given him upon his finger. Now it was the ring the wily lady wanted to get from him to make a merry jest when she saw her Bassanio again, that made her ask him for his gloves ; and she said, when she saw the ring, " And for your love I will take this ring from you." Bassanio was sadly distressed that the counsellor should ask him for the only thing he could not part with, and he replied in great confusion, that he could not give him that ring, because it was his wife's gift, and he had vowed never to part with it ; but that he would give him the most valuable ring in Venice, and find it out by proclamation. On this Portia affected to be affronted, and left the court, saying, " You teach me, sir, how a beggar should be answered."

" Dear Bassanio," said Antonio, " let him have the ring ; let my love and the great service he has done for me be valued against your wife's displeasure." Bassanio, ashamed to appear so ungrateful, yielded, and sent Gratiano after Portia with the ring ; and then the *clerk* Nerissa, who had also given Gratiano a ring, she begged his ring, and Gratiano (not choosing to be outdone in generosity by his lord) gave it to her. And there was laughing among these ladies, to think, when they got home how they could tax their husbands with giving away their rings, and swear that they had given them as a present to some woman.

Portia, when she returned, was in that happy temper of mind which never fails to attend the consciousness of having performed a good action ; her cheerful spirits enjoyed everything she saw. The moon never seemed to shine so bright before ; and when that pleasant moon was hid behind a cloud, then a light which she saw from her house at Belmont as well pleased her charmed fancy, and she said to Nerissa, " That light we see is burning in my hall. How far that little candle throws its beams ! So shines a good deed in a naughty world." And hearing the sound of music from her house, she said, " Methinks that music sounds much sweeter than by day."

And now Portia and Nerissa entered the house, and, dressing themselves in their own apparel, they awaited the arrival of their husbands, who soon followed them with Antonio ; and Bassanio presenting his dear friend to the Lady Portia, the congratulations and welcomings of that lady were hardly over, when they perceived Nerissa and her husband quarrelling in a corner of the room. " A quarrel already ? " said Portia. " What is the matter ? " Gratiano replied, " Lady, it is about a paltry gilt ring that Nerissa gave me, with words upon it like the poetry on a cutler's knife : ' *Love me, and leave me not.*' "

" What does the poetry or the value of the ring

signify ? " said Nerissa. " You swore to me, when I gave
it to you, that you would keep it until the hour of death ;
and now you say you gave it to the lawyer's clerk.   I
know you gave it to a woman." " By this hand," replied
Gratiano, " I gave it to a youth, a kind of boy, a little
scrubbed boy no higher than yourself ; he was clerk to
the young counsellor that by his wise pleading saved
Antonio's life. This prating boy begged it for a fee,
and I could not for my life deny him." Portia said,
" You were to blame, Gratiano, to part with your wife's
first gift. I gave my Lord Bassanio a ring, and I am
sure he would not part with it for all the world."
Gratiano, in excuse for his fault, now said, " My Lord
Bassanio gave his ring away to the counsellor, and then
the boy, his clerk, that took some pains in writing, he
begged my ring."

Portia, hearing this, seemed very angry, and reproached Bassanio for giving away her ring ; and she said
Nerissa had taught her what to believe, and that she knew
some woman had the ring. Bassanio was very unhappy
to have so offended his dear lady, and he said, with great
earnestness, " No, by my honour, no woman had it, but
a civil doctor, who refused three thousand ducats of me,
and begged the ring, which, when I denied him, he went
displeased away. What could I do, sweet Portia ? I
was so beset with shame for my seeming ingratitude that
I was forced to send the ring after him. Pardon me, good
lady : had you been there, I think you would have begged
the ring of me to give the worthy doctor."

" Ah ! " said Antonio, " I am the unhappy cause of
these quarrels."

Portia bid Antonio not to grieve at that, for that he
was welcome notwithstanding ; and then Antonio said,
" I once did lend my body for Bassanio's sake ; and but
for him to whom your husband gave the ring, I should
have now been dead. I dare be bound again, my soul

H

upon the forfeit, your lord will never more break his faith with you." " Then you shall be his surety," said Portia ; " give him this ring, and bid him keep it better than the other."

When Bassanio looked at this ring, he was strangely surprised to find it was the same he gave away ; and then Portia told him, how she was the young counsellor, and Nerissa was her clerk ; and Bassanio found, to his unspeakable wonder and delight, that it was by the noble courage and wisdom of his wife that Antonio's life was saved.

And then Portia again welcomed Antonio, and gave him letters which by some chance had fallen into her hands, which contained an account of Antonio's ships, that were supposed lost, being safely arrived in the harbour. So these tragical beginnings of this rich merchant's story were all forgotten in the unexpected good fortune which ensued ; and there was leisure to laugh at the comical adventure of the rings, and the husbands that did not know their own wives ; Gratiano merrily swearing, in a sort of rhyming speech, that

> " —— while he lived, he'd fear no other thing
>   So sore, as keeping safe Nerissa's ring."

CYMBELINE

DURING the time of Augustus Cæsar, Emperor of Rome, there reigned in England (which was then called Britain) a king whose name was Cymbeline.

Cymbeline's first wife died when his three children (two sons and a daughter) were very young. Imogen, the eldest of these children, was brought up in her father's court; but by a strange chance the two sons of Cymbeline were stolen out of their nursery, when the eldest was but three years of age, and the youngest quite an infant; and Cymbeline could never discover what was become of them, or by whom they were conveyed away.

Cymbeline was twice married: his second wife was a wicked, plotting woman, and a cruel stepmother to Imogen, Cymbeline's daughter by his first wife.

The queen, though she hated Imogen, yet wished her to marry a son of her own by a former husband (she also having been twice married); for by this means she hoped upon the death of Cymbeline to place the crown of Britain upon the head of her son Cloten; for she knew that, if the king's sons were not found, the Princess Imogen must be the king's heir;

but this design was prevented by Imogen herself, who married without the consent or even knowledge of her father or the queen.

Posthumus (for that was the name of Imogen's husband) was the best scholar and most accomplished gentleman of that age. His father died fighting in the wars for Cymbeline, and soon after his birth his mother died also for grief at the loss of her husband.

Cymbeline, pitying the helpless state of this orphan, took Posthumus (Cymbeline having given him that name, because he was born after his father's death), and educated him in his own court.

Imogen and Posthumus were both taught by the same masters, and were playfellows from their infancy: they loved each other tenderly when they were children, and their affection continuing to increase with their years, when they grew up they privately married.

The disappointed queen soon learnt this secret, for she kept spies constantly in watch upon the actions of her step-daughter, and she immediately told the king of the marriage of Imogen with Posthumus.

Nothing could exceed the wrath of Cymbeline, when he heard that his daughter had been so forgetful of her high dignity as to marry a subject. He commanded Posthumus to leave Britain, and banished him from his native country for ever.

The queen, who pretended to pity Imogen for the grief she suffered at losing her husband, offered to procure them a private meeting before Posthumus set out on his journey to Rome, which place he had chosen for his residence in his banishment: this seeming kindness she showed, the better to succeed in her future designs in regard to her son Cloten; for she meant to persuade Imogen, when her husband was gone, that her marriage was not lawful, being contracted without the consent of the king.

Imogen and Posthumus took a most affectionate leave

of each other. Imogen gave her husband a diamond
ring which had been her mother's, and Posthumus promised never to part with the ring ; and he fastened a
bracelet on the arm of his wife, which he begged she would
preserve with great care, as a token of his love : they then
bid each other farewell, with many vows of everlasting
love and fidelity.

Imogen remained a solitary and dejected lady in her
father's court, and Posthumus arrived at Rome, the place
he had chosen for his banishment.

Posthumus fell into company at Rome with some gay
young men of different nations, who were talking freely
of ladies : each one praising the ladies of his country, and
his own mistress. Posthumus, who had ever his own dear
lady in his mind, affirmed that his wife, the fair Imogen,
was the most virtuous, wise, and constant lady in the
world.

One of these gentlemen, whose name was Iachimo,
being offended that a lady of Britain should be so praised
above the Roman ladies, his countrywomen, provoked
Posthumus by seeming to doubt the constancy of his so
highly-praised wife ; and at length, after much alterca-
tion, consented to a proposal of Iachimo's, that he
(Iachimo) should go to Britain, and endeavour to gain the
love of the married Imogen. They then laid a wager,
that if Iachimo did not succeed in this wicked design, he
was to forfeit a large sum of money ; but if he could win
Imogen's favour, and prevail upon her to give him the
bracelet which Posthumus had so earnestly desired she
would keep as a token of his love, then the wager was to
terminate with Posthumus giving to Iachimo the ring,
which was Imogen's love-present when she parted with
her husband. Such firm faith had Posthumus in the
fidelity of Imogen, that he thought he ran no hazard in
this trial of her honour.

Iachimo, on his arrival in Britain, gained admittance,

and a courteous welcome from Imogen, as a friend of her husband ; but when he began to make professions of love to her, she repulsed him with disdain, and he soon found that he could have no hope in succeeding in his dishonourable design.

The desire Iachimo had to win the wager made him now have recourse to a stratagem to impose upon Posthumus, and for this purpose he bribed some of Imogen's attendants, and was by them conveyed into her bedchamber, concealed in a large trunk, where he remained shut up till Imogen was retired to rest and had fallen asleep ; and then getting out of the trunk, he examined the chamber with great attention, and wrote down everything he saw there, and particularly noticed a mole which he observed upon Imogen's neck, and then softly unloosing the bracelet from her arm, which Posthumus had given to her, he retired into the chest again ; and the next day set off for Rome with great expedition, and boasted to Posthumus that Imogen had given him the bracelet, and likewise permitted him to pass a night in her chamber ; and in this manner Iachimo told his false tale : " Her bedchamber," said he, " was hung with tapestry of silk and silver, the story was *the proud Cleopatra when she met her Antony*, a piece of work most bravely wrought."

" This is true," said Posthumus ; " but this you might have heard spoken of without seeing."

" Then the chimney," said Iachimo, " is south of the chamber, and the chimney-piece is *Diana bathing* ; never saw I figures more life-like."

" This is a thing you might have likewise heard," said Posthumus, " for it is much talked of."

Iachimo as accurately described the roof of the chamber, and added, " I had almost forgot her andirons, they were *two winking Cupids* made of silver, each on one foot standing." He then took out the bracelet, and said,

" Know you this jewel, sir ? She gave me this. She took it from her arm. I see her yet ; her pretty action did outsell her gift, and yet enriched it too. She gave it me, and said, *she prized it once*." He last of all de- scribed the mole he had observed upon her neck.

Posthumus, who had heard the whole of this artful recital in an agony of doubt, now broke out into the most passionate exclamations against Imogen. He delivered up the diamond ring to Iachimo which he had agreed to forfeit to him if he obtained the bracelet from Imogen.

Posthumus then in a jealous rage wrote to Pisanio, a gentleman of Britain, who was one of Imogen's attendants, and had long been a faithful friend to Posthumus ; and after telling him what proof he had of his wife's dis- loyalty, he desired Pisanio would take Imogen to Milford Haven, a seaport of Wales, and there kill her. And at the same time he wrote a deceitful letter to Imogen, desir- ing her to go with Pisanio, for that finding he could live no longer without seeing her, though he was forbidden upon pain of death to return to Britain, he would come to Milford Haven, at which place he begged she would meet him. She, good unsuspecting lady, who loved her husband above all things, and desired more than her life to see him, hastened her departure with Pisanio, and the same night she received the letter she set out.

When their journey was nearly at an end, Pisanio, who, though faithful to Posthumus, was not faithful to serve him in an evil deed, disclosed to Imogen the cruel order he had received.

Imogen, who, instead of meeting a loving and beloved husband, found herself doomed by that husband to suffer death, was afflicted beyond measure.

Pisanio persuaded her to take comfort, and wait with patient fortitude for the time when Posthumus should see and repent his injustice : in the meantime, as she refused

in her distress to return to her father's court, he advised
her to dress herself in boy's clothes for more security in
travelling; to which advice she agreed, and thought in
that disguise she would go over to Rome and see her
husband, whom, though he had used her so barbarously,
she could not forget to love.

When Pisanio had provided her with her new apparel,
he left her to her uncertain fortune, being obliged to return
to court; but before he departed he gave her a phial of
cordial, which he said the queen had given him as a sovereign remedy in all disorders.

The queen, who hated Pisanio because he was a friend
to Imogen and Posthumus, gave him this phial, which
she supposed contained poison, she having ordered her
physician to give her some poison, to try its effects (as
she said) upon animals; but the physician, knowing her
malicious disposition, would not trust her with real poison,
but gave her a drug which would do no other mischief
than causing a person to sleep with every appearance of
death for a few hours. This mixture, which Pisanio
thought a choice cordial, he gave to Imogen, desiring her,
if she found herself ill upon the road, to take it; and so,
with blessings and prayers for her safety and happy deliverance from her undeserved troubles, he left her.

Providence strangely directed Imogen's steps to the
dwelling of her two brothers who had been stolen away
in their infancy. Bellarius, who stole them away, was
lord in the court of Cymbeline, and having been falsely
accused to the king of treason, and banished from the
court, in revenge he stole away the two sons of Cymbeline,
and brought them up in a forest, where he lived concealed
in a cave. He stole them through revenge, but he soon
loved them as tenderly as if they had been his own
children, educated them carefully, and they grew up fine
youths, their princely spirits leading them to bold and
daring actions; and as they subsisted by hunting, they were

active and hardy, and were always pressing their supposed
father to let them seek their fortune in the wars.

At the cave where these youths dwelt it was Imogen's
fortune to arrive. She had lost her way in a large forest
through which her road lay to Milford Haven, from
whence she meant to embark for Rome; and being unable to find any place where she could purchase food,
she was with weariness and hunger almost dying, for it is
not merely putting on a man's apparel that will enable a
young lady, tenderly brought up, to bear the fatigue of
wandering about lonely forests like a man. Seeing this
cave, she entered, hoping to find some one within of whom
she could procure food. She found the cave empty, but
looking about she discovered some cold meat, and her
hunger was so pressing that she could not wait for an invitation, but sat down and began to eat. " Ah ! " said she,
talking to herself, " I see a man's life is a tedious one :
how tired am I ! for two nights together I have made the
ground my bed ; my resolution helps me, or I should be
sick. When Pisanio showed me Milford Haven from the
mountain-top, how near it seemed ! " Then the thoughts
of her husband and his cruel mandate came across her,
and she said, " My dear Posthumus, thou art a false one ! "

The two brothers of Imogen, who had been hunting
with their reputed father Bellarius, were by this time
returned home. Bellarius had given them the names of
Polidore and Cadwal, and they knew no better, but supposed that Bellarius was their father ; but the real names
of these princes were Guiderius and Arviragus.

Bellarius entered the cave first, and seeing Imogen,
stopped them, saying, " Come not in yet ! it eats our
victuals, or I should think that it was a fairy."

" What is the matter, sir ? " said the young men. " By
Jupiter ! " said Bellarius again, " there is an angel in the
cave, or if not, an earthly paragon." So beautiful did
Imogen look in her boy's apparel.

She, hearing the sound of voices, came forth from the cave and addressed them in these words : " Good masters, do not harm me : before I entered your cave I had thought to have begged or bought what I have eaten. Indeed, I have stolen nothing, nor would I though I had found gold strewed on the floor. Here is money for my meat, which I would have left on the board when I had made my meal, and parted with prayers for the provider." They refused her money with great earnestness. " I see you are angry with me," said the timid Imogen ; " but, sirs, if you kill me for my fault, know that I should have died if I had not made it."

" Whither are you bound ? " asked Bellarius, " and what is your name ? "

" Fidele is my name," answered Imogen. " I have a kinsman who is bound for Italy ; he embarked at Milford Haven, to whom being going, almost spent with hunger, I am fallen into this offence."

" Prithee, fair youth," said old Bellarius, " do not think us churls, nor measure our good minds by this rude place we live in. You are well encountered ; it is almost night. You shall have better cheer before you depart, and thanks to stay and eat it. Boys, bid him welcome."

The gentle youths, her brothers, then welcomed Imogen to their cave with many kind expressions, saying they would love her (or, as they said, *him*) as a brother ; and they entered the cave, where (they having killed venison when they were hunting) Imogen delighted them with her neat housewifery, assisting them in preparing their supper ; for though it is not the custom now for young women of high birth to understand cookery, it was then, and Imogen excelled in this useful art, and, as her brothers prettily expressed it, Fidele cut their roots in characters, and sauced their broth as if Juno had been sick and Fidele were her dieter. " And then," said Polidore to his brother, " how angel-like he sings ! "

They also remarked to each other that though Fidele
smiled so sweetly, yet so sad a melancholy did overcloud
his lovely face, as if grief and patience had together taken
possession of him.

For these her gentle qualities (or perhaps it was their
near relationship, though they knew it not) Imogen (or,
as the boys called her, Fidele) became the doting-piece
of her brothers, and she scarcely less loved them, thinking
that, but for the memory of her dear Posthumus, she could
live and die in the cave with these wild forest youths, and
she gladly consented to stay with them till she was enough
rested from the fatigue of travelling to pursue her way to
Milford Haven.

When the venison they had taken was all eaten, and
they were going out to hunt for more, Fidele could not
accompany them because she was unwell. Sorrow, no
doubt, for her husband's cruel usage, as well as the fatigue
of wandering in the forest, was the cause of her illness.

They then bid her farewell and went to their hunt,
praising all the way the noble parts and graceful demean-
our of the youth Fidele.

Imogen was no sooner left alone than she recollected
the cordial Pisanio had given her, and drank if off, and
presently fell into a sound and deathlike sleep.

When Bellarius and her brother returned from hunting, Polidore went first into the cave, and supposing her
asleep, pulled off his heavy shoes that he might tread
softly and not awake her—so did true gentleness spring
up in the minds of these princely foresters ; but he soon
discovered that she could not be awakened by any noise,
and concluded her to be dead, and Polidore lamented
over her with dear and brotherly regret, as if they had
never from their infancy been parted.

Bellarius also proposed to carry her out into the forest
and there celebrate her funeral with songs and solemn
dirges, as was then the custom.

Imogen's two brothers then carried her to a shady covert, and there laying her gently on the grass, they sang repose to her departed spirit, and covering her over with leaves and flowers, Polidore said, " While summer lasts and I live here, Fidele, I will daily strew thy sad grave. The pale primrose, that flower most like thy face ; the bluebell, like thy clear veins ; and the leaf of eglantine, which is not sweeter than was thy breath ; all these I will strew over thee. Yea, and the furred moss in winter, when there are no flowers to cover thy sweet corse."

When they had finished her funeral obsequies, they departed very sorrowful.

Imogen had not been long left alone when, the effect of the sleepy drug going off, she awakened, and easily shaking off the slight covering of leaves and flowers they had thrown over her, she arose, and imagining she had been dreaming, she said, " I thought I was a cave-keeper and cook to honest creatures. How came I here covered with flowers ? " Not being able to find her way back to the cave, and seeing nothing of her new companions, she concluded it was certainly all a dream, and once more Imogen set out on her weary pilgrimage, hoping at last she should find her way to Milford Haven, and thence get a passage in some ship bound for Italy ; for all her thoughts were still with her husband Posthumus, whom she intended to seek in the disguise of a page.

But great events were happening at this time, of which Imogen knew nothing ; for a war had suddenly broken out between the Roman Emperor Augustus Cæsar, and Cymbeline the King of Britain ; and a Roman army had landed to invade Britain, and was advanced into the very forest over which Imogen was journeying. With this army came Posthumus.

Though Posthumus came over to Britain with the Roman army, he did not mean to fight on their side against his own countrymen, but intended to join the army of

How came I here covered with flowers?

Britain and fight in the cause of his king who had banished him.

He still believed Imogen false to him, yet the death of her he had so fondly loved, and by his own orders too (Pisanio having written him a letter to say he had obeyed his command, and that Imogen was dead), sat heavy on his heart, and therefore he returned to Britain, desiring either to be slain in battle or to be put to death by Cymbeline for returning home from banishment.

Imogen, before she reached Milford Haven, fell into the hands of the Roman army, and her presence and deportment recommending her, she was made a page to Lucius, the Roman general.

Cymbeline's army now advanced to meet the enemy, and when they entered this forest Polidore and Cadwal joined the king's army. The young men were eager to engage in acts of valour, though they little thought they were going to fight for their own royal father, and old Bellarius went with them to the battle. He had long since repented of the injury he had done to Cymbeline in carrying away his sons, and having been a warrior in his youth, he gladly joined the army to fight for the king he had so injured.

And now a great battle commenced between the two armies, and the Britons would have been defeated and Cymbeline himself killed but for the extraordinary valour of Posthumus, and Bellarius, and the two sons of Cymbeline. They rescued the king and saved his life, and so entirely turned the fortune of the day that the Britons gained the victory. When the battle was over, Posthumus, who had not found the death he sought for, surrendered himself up to one of the officers of Cymbeline, willing to suffer the death which was to be his punishment if he returned from banishment.

Imogen and the master she served were taken prisoners, and brought before Cymbeline, as was also her old enemy

Iachimo, who was an officer in the Roman army; and when these prisoners were before the king, Posthumus was brought in to receive his sentence of death; and at this strange juncture of time, Bellarius, with Polidore and Cadwal, were also brought before Cymbeline to receive the rewards due to the great services they had by their valour done for the king. Pisanio, being one of the king's attendants, was likewise present.

Therefore there were now standing in the king's presence (but with very different hopes and fears) Posthumus and Imogen, with her new master the Roman general; the faithful servant Pisanio and the false friend Iachimo; and likewise the two lost sons of Cymbeline, with Bellarius, who had stolen them away.

The Roman general was the first who spoke; the rest stood silent before the king, though there was many a beating heart among them.

Imogen saw Posthumus and knew him, though he was in the disguise of a peasant, but he did not know her in her male attire, and she knew Iachimo, and she saw a ring on his finger which she perceived to be her own, but she did not know him as yet to have been the author of all her troubles; and she stood before her own father a prisoner of war.

Pisanio knew Imogen, for it was he who had dressed her in the garb of a boy. " It is my mistress," thought he : " since she is living, let the time run on to good or bad." Bellarius knew her too, and softly said to Cadwal, " Is not this boy revived from death ? " " One sand," replied Cadwal, " does not more resemble another than that sweet rosy lad is like the dead Fidele." " The same dead thing alive," said Polidore. " Peace, peace ! " said Bellarius ; " if it were he, I am sure he would have spoken to us." " But we saw him dead," again whispered Polidore " Be silent," replied Bellarius.

Posthumus waited in silence to hear the welcome

sentence of his own death ; and he resolved not to disclose to the king that he had saved his life in the battle,
lest that should move Cymbeline to pardon him.

Lucius, the Roman general who had taken Imogen
under his protection as his page, was the first (as has been
before said) who spoke to the king. He was a man of high
courage and noble dignity, and this was his speech to the
king :

" I hear you take no ransom for your prisoners, but
doom them all to death. I am a Roman, and with a
Roman heart will suffer death. But there is one thing
for which I would entreat." Then bringing Imogen
before the king, he said, " This boy is a Briton born. Let
him be ransomed. He is my page. Never master had
a page so kind, so duteous, so diligent on all occasions,
so true, so nurse-like. He hath done no Briton wrong,
though he hath served a Roman. Save him, if you spare
no one beside."

Cymbeline looked earnestly on his daughter Imogen.
He knew her not in that disguise ; but it seemed that all-
powerful nature spake in his heart, for he said, " I have
surely seen him, his face appears familiar to me. I know
not why or wherefore I say, Live, boy ; but I give you
your life, and ask of me what boon you will, and I will
grant it you. Yea, even though it be the life of the noblest
prisoner I have."

" I humbly thank your highness," said Imogen.

What was then called granting a boon was the same
as a promise to give any one thing, whatever it might be,
that the person on whom that favour was conferred might
ask for. They all were attentive to hear what thing the
page would ask for ; and Lucius, her master, said to her,
" I do not beg my life, good lad, but I know that is what
you will ask for." " No, no, alas ! " said Imogen, " I
have other work in hand, good master ; your life I cannot
ask for."

This seeming want of gratitude in the boy astonished the Roman general.

Imogen then, fixing her eye on Iachimo, demanded no other boon than this ; that Iachimo should be made to confess whence he had the ring he wore on his finger.

Cymbeline granted her this boon, and threatened Iachimo with the torture if he did not confess how he came by the diamond ring on his finger.

Iachimo then made a full acknowledgment of all his villany, telling, as he had before related, the whole story of his wager with Posthumus, and how he had succeeded in imposing upon his credulity.

What Posthumus felt at hearing this proof of the innocence of his lady cannot be expressed. He instantly came forward, and confessed to Cymbeline the cruel sentence which he had enjoined Pisanio to execute upon the princess, exclaiming wildly, " O Imogen, my queen, my life, my wife ! O Imogen, Imogen, Imogen ! "

Imogen could not see her beloved husband in this distress without discovering herself, to the unutterable joy of Posthumus, who was thus relieved from a weight of guilt and woe, and restored to the good graces of the dear lady he had so cruelly treated.

Cymbeline, almost as much overwhelmed as he with joy at finding his lost daughter so strangely recovered, received her to her former place in his fatherly affection, and not only gave her husband Posthumus his life, but consented to acknowledge him for his son-in-law.

Bellarius chose this time of joy and reconciliation to make his confession. He presented Polidore and Cadwal to the king, telling him they were his two lost sons Guiderius and Arviragus.

Cymbeline forgave old Bellarius ; for who could think of punishments at a season of such universal happiness ? To find his daughter living, and his lost sons in the persons of his young deliverers, that he had seen so bravely fight in his defence, was unlooked-for joy indeed !

Imogen was now at leisure to perform good services for her late master, the Roman general Lucius, whose life the king her father readily granted at her request ; and by the mediation of the same Lucius a peace was concluded between the Romans and the Britons, which was kept inviolate many years.

How Cymbeline's wicked queen, through despair of bringing her projects to pass, and touched with remorse of conscience, sickened and died, having first lived to see her foolish son Cloten slain in a quarrel which he had provoked, are events too tragical to interrupt this happy conclusion by more than merely touching upon. It is sufficient that all were made happy who were deserving ; and even the treacherous Iachimo, in consideration of his villany having missed its final aim, was dismissed without punishment.

King Lear

LEAR, King of Britain, had three daughters—Goneril, wife to the Duke of Albany, Regan, wife to the Duke of Cornwall, and Cordelia, a young maid, for whose love the King of France and Duke of Burgundy were joint suitors, and were at this time making stay for that purpose in the court of Lear.

The old king, worn out with age and the fatigues of government, he being more than fourscore years old, determined to take no further part in state affairs, but to leave the management to younger strengths, that he might have time to prepare for death, which must at no long period ensue. With this intent, he called his three daughters to him, to know from their own lips which of them loved him best, that he might part his kingdom among them in such proportions as their affection for him seemed to deserve.

Goneril, the eldest, declared that she loved her father more than words could give out, that he was dearer to her than the light of her own eyes, dearer than life and liberty, with a deal of such professing stuff, which is easy to counterfeit where there is no real love, only a few fine words delivered with confidence being wanted in that case.

The king, delighted to hear from her own mouth this assurance of her love, and thinking truly that her heart went with it, in a fit of fatherly fondness bestowed upon her and her husband one-third of his ample kingdom.

Then calling to him his second daughter, he demanded what she had to say. Regan, who was made of the same hollow metal as her sister, was not a whit behind in her professions, but rather declared that what her sister had spoken came short of the love which she professed to bear for his highness ; insomuch that she found all other joys dead, in comparison with the pleasure which she took in the love of her dear king and father.

Lear blessed himself in having such loving children, as he thought, and could do no less, after the handsome assurances which Regan had made, than bestow a third of his kingdom upon her and her husband, equal in size to that which he had already given away to Goneril.

Then turning to his youngest daughter Cordelia, whom he called his joy, he asked what she had to say ; thinking, no doubt, that she would glad his ears with the same loving speeches which her sisters had uttered, or rather that her expressions would be so much stronger than theirs, as she had always been his darling, and favoured by him above either of them. But Cordelia, disgusted with the flattery of her sisters, whose hearts she knew were far from their lips, and seeing that all their coaxing speeches were only intended to wheedle the old king out of his dominions, that they and their husbands might reign in his lifetime, made no other reply but this, that she loved his majesty according to her duty, neither more nor less.

The king, shocked with this appearance of ingratitude in his favourite child, desired her to consider her words, and to mend her speech, lest it should mar her fortunes.

Cordelia then told her father that he was her father, that he had given her breeding, and loved her, that she returned those duties back as was most fit, and did obey him, love him, and most honour him. But that she could not frame her mouth to such large speeches as her sisters had done, or promise to love nothing else in the world. Why had her sisters husbands if (as they said) they had no love for anything but their father? If she should ever wed, she was sure the lord to whom she gave her hand would want half her love, half of her care and duty; she would never marry like her sisters, to love her father all.

Cordelia, who in earnest loved her old father even almost as extravagantly as her sisters pretended to do, would have plainly told him so at any other time, in more daughter-like and loving terms, and without these qualifications, which did indeed sound a little ungracious; but after the crafty flattering speeches of her sisters, which she had seen draw such extravagant rewards, she thought the handsomest thing she could do was to love and be silent. This put her affection out of suspicion of mercenary ends, and showed that she loved, but not for gain; and that her professions, the less ostentatious they were, had so much the more of truth and sincerity than her sisters'.

The plainness of speech, which Lear called pride, so enraged the old monarch—who in his best of times always showed much of spleen and rashness, and in whom the dotage incident to old age had so clouded over his reason, that he could not discern truth from flattery, nor a gay painted speech from words that came from the heart—that in a fury of resentment he retracted the third part of his kingdom which yet remained, and which he had reserved for Cordelia, and gave it away from her, sharing it equally between her two sisters and their husbands, the Dukes of Albany and Cornwall; whom he now called to him, and in presence of all his courtiers, bestowing a coronet between them, invested them jointly with all the power, revenue, and execution of government, only retaining to

himself the name of king. All the rest of royalty he resigned ; with this reservation, that himself, with a hundred
knights for his attendants, was to be maintained by
monthly course in each of his daughter's palaces in turn.

So preposterous a disposal of his kingdom, so little
guided by reason, and so much by passion, filled all his
courtiers with astonishment and sorrow ; but none of
them had the courage to interpose between this incensed
king and his wrath, except the Earl of Kent, who was beginning to speak a good word for Cordelia, when the
passionate Lear on pain of death commanded him to desist ;
but the good Kent was not so to be repelled. He had been
ever loyal to Lear, whom he had honoured as a king, loved
as a father, followed as a master, and had never esteemed
his life further than as a pawn to wage against his royal
master's enemies, nor feared to lose it when Lear's safety
was the motive ; nor now that Lear was most his own
enemy, did this faithful servant of the king forget his old
principles, but manfully opposed Lear to do Lear good,
and was unmannerly only because Lear was mad. He
had been a most faithful counsellor in times past to the
king, and he besought him now, that he would see with
his eyes (as he had done in many weighty matters) and go
by his advice still, and in his best consideration recall this
hideous rashness ; for he would answer with his life, his
judgment that Lear's youngest daughter did not love him
least, nor were those empty-hearted whose low sound
gave no token of hollowness. When power bowed to
flattery, honour was bound to plainness. For Lear's
threats, what could he do to him whose life was already
at his service? That should not hinder duty from
speaking.

The honest freedom of this good Earl of Kent only
stirred up the king's wrath the more, and like a frantic
patient who kills his physician and loves his mortal disease,
he banished this true servant, and allotted him but five

days to make his preparations for departure ; but if on the sixth his hated person was found within the realm of Britain, that moment was to be his death. And Kent bade farewell to the king, and said that since he chose to show himself in such fashion, it was but banishment to stay there ; and before he went, he recommended Cordelia to the protection of the gods, the maid who had so rightly thought and so discreetly spoken, and only wished that her sisters' large speeches might be answered with deeds of love ; and then he went, as he said, to shape his old course to a new country.

The King of France and Duke of Burgundy were now called in to hear the determination of Lear about his youngest daughter, and to know whether they would persist in their courtship to Cordelia, now that she was under her father's displeasure, and had no fortune but her own person to recommend her ; and the Duke of Burgundy declined the match, and would not take her to wife upon such conditions ; but the King of France, understanding what the nature of the fault had been which had lost her the love of her father, that it was only a tardiness of speech, and the not being able to frame her tongue to flattery like her sisters, took this young maid by the hand, and saying that her virtues were a dowry above a kingdom, bade Cordelia to take farewell of her sisters, and of her father, though he had been unkind, and she should go with him, and be queen of him and of fair France, and reign over fairer possessions than her sisters ; and he called the Duke of Burgundy in contempt a waterish duke, because his love for this young maid had in a moment run all away like water.

Then Cordelia, with weeping eyes, took leave of her sisters, and besought them to love their father well, and make good their professions ; and they sullenly told her not to prescribe to them, for they knew their duty, but to strive to content her husband, who had taken her (as they tauntingly expressed it) as Fortune's alms. And Cordelia with a heavy heart departed, for she knew the cunning of her sisters, and she wished her father in better hands than she was about to leave him in.

Cordelia was no sooner gone, than the devilish dispositions of her sisters began to show themselves in their true colours. Even before the expiration of the first month, which Lear was to spend by agreement with his eldest daughter Goneril, the old king began to find out the difference between promises and performances. This wretch having got from her father all that he had to bestow, even to the giving away of the crown from off his head, began to grudge even those small remnants of royalty which the old man had reserved to himself, to please his fancy with the idea of being still a king. She could not bear to see him and his hundred knights. Every time she met her father she put on a frowning countenance ; and when the old man wanted to speak with her, she would feign sickness, or anything, to be rid of the sight of him ; for it was plain that she esteemed his old age a useless burden, and his attendants an unnecessary expense : not only she herself slackened in her expressions of duty to the king, but by her example, and (it is to be feared) not without her private instructions, her very servants affected to treat him with neglect, and would either refuse to obey his orders, or still more contemptuously pretend not to hear them. Lear could not but perceive this alteration in the behaviour of his daughter, but he shut his eyes against it as long as he could, as people commonly are unwilling to believe the unpleasant consequences which their own mistakes and obstinacy have brought upon them.

True love and fidelity are no more to be estranged by *ill*, than falsehood and hollow-heartedness can be conciliated by *good usage*. This eminently appears in the instance of the good Earl of Kent, who, though banished

by Lear, and his life made forfeit if he were found in
Britain, chose to stay and abide all consequences, as long
as there was a chance of his being useful to the king
his master. See to what mean shifts and disguises poor
loyalty is forced to submit sometimes ; yet it counts nothing base or unworthy, so as it can but do service where
it owes an obligation ! In the disguise of a serving-man,
all his greatness and pomp laid aside, this good earl
proffered his services to the king, who, not knowing him
to be Kent in that disguise, but pleased with a certain
plainness, or rather bluntness in his answers which the
earl put on (so different from that smooth, oily flattery
which he had so much reason to be sick of, having found
the effects not answerable in his daughter), a bargain was
quickly struck, and Lear took Kent into his service by the
name of Caius, as he called himself, never suspecting him
to be his once great favourite, the high and mighty Earl
of Kent.

This Caius quickly found means to show his fidelity
and love to his royal master ; for Goneril's steward that
same day behaving in a disrespectful manner to Lear,
and giving him saucy looks and language, as no doubt
he was secretly encouraged to do by his mistress, Caius,
not enduring to hear so open an affront put upon majesty,
made no more ado but presently tripped up his heels, and
laid the unmannerly slave in the kennel ; for which friendly
service Lear became more and more attached to him.

Nor was Kent the only friend Lear had. In his degree, and as far as so insignificant a personage could show
his love, the poor fool or jester, that had been of his
palace while Lear had a palace, as it was the custom of
kings and great personages at that time to keep a fool (as
he was called) to make them sport after serious business.
This poor fool clung to Lear after he had given away his
crown, and by his witty sayings would keep up his good
humour, though he could not refrain sometimes from

jeering at his master for his imprudence in uncrowning himself and giving all away to his daughters ; at which time, as he rhymingly expressed it, these daughters

> " For sudden joy did weep,
>   And he for sorrow sung
>   That such a king should play bo-peep,
>   And go the fools among."

And in such wild sayings, and scraps of songs, of which he had plenty, this pleasant, honest fool poured out his heart even in the presence of Goneril herself, in many a bitter taunt and jest which cut to the quick : such as comparing the king to the hedge-sparrow, who feeds the young of the cuckoo till they grow old enough, and then has its head bit off for its pains ; and saying that an ass may know when the cart draws the horse (meaning that Lear's daughters, that ought to go behind, now ranked before their father) ; and that Lear was no longer Lear, but the shadow of Lear : for which free speeches he was once or twice threatened to be whipped.

The coolness and falling off of respect which Lear had begun to perceive, were not all which this foolish, fond father was to suffer from his unworthy daughter. She now plainly told him that his staying in her palace was inconvenient so long as he insisted upon keeping up an establishment of a hundred knights ; that this establishment was useless and expensive, and only served to fill her court with riot and feasting ; and she prayed him that he would lessen their number, and keep none but old men about him, such as himself, and fitting his age.

Lear at first could not believe his eyes or ears, nor that it was his daughter who spoke so unkindly. He could not believe that she who had received a crown from him could seek to cut off his train, and grudge him the respect due to his old age. But she persisting in her undutiful demand, the old man's rage was so excited, that he called her a detested kite, and said that she spoke an untruth ;

and so indeed she did, for the hundred knights were all men
of choice behaviour and sobriety of manners, skilled in all
particulars of duty, and not given to rioting and feasting,
as she said. And he bid his horses to be prepared, for
he would go to his other daughter, Regan, he and his
hundred knights ; and he spoke of ingratitude, and said
it was a marble-hearted devil, and showed more hideous
in a child than the sea-monster. And he cursed his eldest
daughter Goneril so as was terrible to hear ; praying that
she might never have a child, or, if she had, that it might
live to return that scorn and contempt upon her which
she had shown to him ; that she might feel how sharper
than a serpent's tooth it was to have a thankless child.
And Goneril's husband, the Duke of Albany, beginning
to excuse himself for any share which Lear might suppose he had in the unkindness, Lear would not hear him
out, but in a rage ordered his horses to be saddled, and
set out with his followers for the abode of Regan, his other
daughter. And Lear thought to himself how small the
fault of Cordelia (if it was a fault) now appeared, in comparison with her sister's, and he wept ; and then he was
ashamed that such a creature as Goneril should have so
much power over his manhood as to make him weep.

Regan and her husband were keeping their court in
great pomp and state at their palace ; and Lear dispatched
his servant Caius with letters to his daughter, that she
might be prepared for his reception, while he and his train
followed after. But it seems that Goneril had been before-
hand with him, sending letters also to Regan, accusing
her father of waywardness and ill humours, and advising
her not to receive so great a train as he was bringing with
him. This messenger arrived at the same time with
Caius, and Caius and he met ; and who should it be but
Caius's old enemy the steward, whom he had formerly
tripped up by the heels for his saucy behaviour to Lear.
Caius not liking the fellow's look, and suspecting what

he came for, began to revile him, and challenged him to fight, which the fellow refusing, Caius, in a fit of honest passion, beat him soundly, as such a mischief-maker and carrier of wicked messages deserved; which coming to the ears of Regan and her husband, they ordered Caius to be put in the stocks, though he was a messenger from the king her father, and in that character demanded the highest respect: so that the first thing the king saw, when he entered the castle, was his faithful servant Caius sitting in that disgraceful situation.

This was but a bad omen of the reception which he was to expect; but a worse followed, when, upon inquiry for his daughter and her husband, he was told they were weary with travelling all night, and could not see him; and when, lastly, upon insisting in a positive and angry manner to see him, they came to greet him, whom should be seen in their company but the hated Goneril, who had come to tell her own story, and set her sister against the king her father!

This sight much moved the old man, and still more to see Regan take her by the hand; and he asked Goneril if she was not ashamed to look upon his old white beard. And Regan advised him to go home again with Goneril, and live with her peaceably, dismissing half of his attendants, and to ask her forgiveness; for he was old and wanted discretion, and must be ruled and led by persons that had more discretion than himself. And Lear showed how preposterous that would sound, if he were to down on his knees and beg of his own daughter for food and raiment, and he argued against such an unnatural dependence, declaring his resolution never to return with her, but to stay where he was with Regan, he and his hundred knights; for he said that she had not forgot the half of the kingdom which he had endowed her with, and that her eyes were not fierce, like Goneril's, but mild and kind. And he said that rather than return to Goneril, with half his train cut off, he would go over to France, and beg a wretched pension of the king there, who had married his youngest daughter without a portion.

But he was mistaken in expecting kinder treatment of Regan than he had experienced from her sister Goneril. As if willing to outdo her sister in unfilial behaviour, she declared that she thought fifty knights too many to wait upon him; that five-and-twenty were enough. Then Lear, nigh broken-hearted, turned to Goneril, and said that he would go back with her, for her fifty doubled five-and-twenty, and so her love was twice as much as Regan's. But Goneril excused herself, and said, " What need of so many as five-and-twenty ? or even ten ? or five ? when he might be waited upon by her servants, or her sister's servants." So these two wicked daughters, as if they strove to exceed each other in cruelty to their old father who had been so good to them, by little and little would have abated him of all his train, all respect (little enough for him that once commanded a kingdom), which was left him to show that he had once been a king ! Not that a splendid train is essential to happiness ; but from a king to a beggar is a hard change, from commanding millions to be without one attendant ; and it was the ingratitude in his daughters' denying it, more than what he would suffer by the want of it, which pierced this poor king to the heart ; insomuch that, with this double ill-usage, and vexation for having so foolishly given away a kingdom, his wits began to be unsettled, and while he said he knew not what, he vowed vengeance against those unnatural hags, and to make examples of them that should be a terror to the earth !

While he was thus idly threatening what his weak arm could never execute, night came on, and a loud storm of thunder and lightning, with rain ; and his daughters still persisting in their resolution not to admit his followers, he called for his horses, and chose rather to encounter the

utmost fury of the storm abroad, than stay under the same
roof with these ungrateful daughters ; and they, saying
that the injuries which wilful men procure to themselves
are their just punishment, suffered him to go in that condition, and shut their doors upon him.

The winds were high, and the rain and storm increased,
when the old man sallied forth to combat with the elements, less sharp than his daughters' unkindness. For
many miles about there was scarcely a bush, and there upon
a heath, exposed to the fury of the storm in a dark night,
did King Lear wander out, and defy the winds and the
thunder ; and he bid the winds to blow the earth into the
sea, or swell the waves of the sea till they drowned the
earth, that no token might remain of any such ungrateful
animal as man. The old king was now left with no other
companion than the poor fool, who still abided with him,
with his merry conceits striving to outjest misfortune,
saying, it was but a naughty night to swim in, and truly
the king had better go in and ask his daughters' blessing :

> But he that has a little tiny wit,
> With heigh ho, the wind and the rain !
> Must make content with his fortunes fit,
> Though the rain it raineth every day ;

and swearing it was a brave night to cool a lady's
pride.

Thus poorly accompanied, this once great monarch
was found by his ever-faithful servant the good Earl of
Kent, now transformed to Caius, who ever followed close
at his side, though the king did not know him to be the
earl ; and he said, " Alas ! sir, are you here ? creatures
that love night, love not such nights as these. This dreadful storm has driven the beasts to their hiding-places.
Man's nature cannot endure the affliction or the fear."
And Lear rebuked him and said, these lesser evils were
not felt where a greater malady was fixed. When the mind
is at ease, the body has leisure to be delicate ; but the

tempest in his mind did take all feeling else from his senses, but of that which beat at his heart. And he spoke of filial ingratitude, and said it was all one as if the mouth should tear the hand for lifting food to it ; for parents were hands and food and everything to children.

But the good Caius, still persisting in his entreaties that the king would not stay out in the open air, at last persuaded him to enter a little wretched hovel which stood upon the heath, where the fool first entering, suddenly ran back terrified saying that he had seen a spirit. But upon examination this spirit proved to be nothing more than a poor Bedlam beggar, who had crept into this deserted hovel for shelter, and with his talk about devils frighted the fool, one of those poor lunatics who are either mad, or feign to be so, the better to extort charity from the compassionate country people, who go about the country, calling themselves Poor Tom and Poor Turlygood, saying, " Who gives anything to Poor Tom ? " sticking pins and nails and sprigs of rosemary into their arms to make them bleed ; and with such horrible actions, partly by prayers, and partly with lunatic curses, they move or terrify the ignorant country folks into giving them alms. This poor fellow was such a one, and the king seeing him in so wretched a plight, with nothing but a blanket about his loins to cover his nakedness, could not be persuaded but that the fellow was some father who had given all away to his daughters, and brought himself to that pass ; for nothing he thought could bring a man to such wretchedness but the having unkind daughters.

And from this and many such wild speeches which he uttered, the good Caius plainly perceived that he was not in his perfect mind, but that his daughters' ill usage had really made him go mad. And now the loyalty of this worthy Earl of Kent showed itself in more essential services than he had hitherto found opportunity to perform ; for with the assistance of some of the king's attendants who remained loyal, he had the person of his royal master removed at daybreak to the castle of Dover, where his own friends and influence, as Earl of Kent, chiefly lay ; and himself embarking for France, hastened to the court of Cordelia, and did there in such moving terms represent the pitiful condition of her royal father, and set out in such lively colours the inhumanity of her sisters, that this good and loving child with many tears besought the king her husband that he would give her leave to embark for England with a sufficient power to subdue these cruel daughters and their husbands, and restore the old king her father to his throne ; which being granted, she set forth, and with a royal army landed at Dover.

Lear having by some chance escaped from the guardians which the good Earl of Kent had put over him to take care of him in his lunacy, was found by some of Cordelia's train wandering about the fields near Dover, in a pitiable condition, stark mad, and singing aloud to himself, with a crown upon his head which he had made of straw and nettles and other wild weeds that he had picked up in the corn-fields. By the advice of the physicians, Cordelia, though earnestly desirous of seeing her father, was prevailed upon to put off the meeting till, by sleep and the operation of herbs which they gave him, he should be restored to greater composure. By the aid of these skilful physicians, to whom Cordelia promised all her gold and jewels for the recovery of the old king, Lear was soon in a condition to see his daughter.

A tender sight it was to see the meeting between this father and daughter—to see the struggles between the joy of this poor old king at beholding again his once darling child, and the shame at receiving such filial kindnesses from her whom he had cast off for so small a fault in his displeasure ; both these passions struggling with the remains of his malady, which in his half-crazed brain sometimes made him that he scarce remembered where he was, or who it was that so kindly kissed him and spoke to him ; and then he would beg the standers-by not to laugh at him if he were mistaken in thinking this lady to be his daughter Cordelia. And then to see him fall on his knees to beg pardon of his child ; and she, good lady, kneeling all the while to ask a blessing of him, and telling him that it did not become him to kneel, but it was her duty, for she was his child, his true and very child Cordelia ! And she kissed him (as she said) to kiss away all her sisters' unkindness, and said that they might be ashamed of themselves, to turn their old kind father with his white beard out into the cold air, when her enemy's dog, though it had bit her (as she prettily expressed it), should have stayed by her fire such a night as that, and warmed himself. And she told her father how she had come from France with purpose to bring him assistance ; and he said that she must forget and forgive, for he was old and foolish, and did not know what he did ; but that to be sure she had great cause not to love him, but her sisters had none. And Cordelia said that she had no cause, no more than they had.

So we will leave this old king in the protection of this dutiful and loving child, where, by the help of sleep and medicine, she and her physicians at length succeeded in winding up the untuned and jarring senses which the cruelty of his other daughters had so violently shaken. Let us return to say a word or two about those cruel daughters.

These monsters of ingratitude, who had been so false to their old father, could not be expected to prove more faithful to their own husbands. They soon grew tired of paying even the appearance of duty and affection, and in an open way showed they had fixed their loves upon another. It happened that the object of their guilty loves was the same. It was Edmund, a natural son of the late Earl of Gloucester, who by his treacheries had succeeded in dis-inheriting his brother Edgar, the lawful heir, from his earldom, and by his wicked practices was now earl himself : a wicked man, and a fit object for the love of such wicked creatures as Goneril and Regan. It falling out about this time that the Duke of Cornwall, Regan's husband, died, Regan immediately declared her intention of wedding this Earl of Gloucester, which rousing the jealousy of her sister, to whom as well as to Regan this wicked earl had at sundry times professed love, Goneril found means to make away with her sister by poison ; but being detected in her practices, and imprisoned by her husband the Duke of Albany for this deed, and for her guilty passion for the earl, which had come to his ears, she in a fit of disappointed love and rage shortly put an end to her own life. Thus the justice of Heaven at last overtook these wicked daughters.

While the eyes of all men were upon this event, admiring the justice displayed in their deserved deaths, the same eyes were suddenly taken off from this sight to admire at the mysterious ways of the same Power in the melancholy fate of the young and virtuous daughter, the Lady Cordelia, whose good deeds did seem to deserve a more fortunate conclusion ; but it is an awful truth, that innocence and piety are not always successful in this world. The forces which Goneril and Regan had sent out under the command of the bad Earl of Gloucester were victorious, and Cordelia, by the practices of this wicked earl, who did not like that any should stand between him and the throne, ended her life in prison. Thus Heaven took this innocent lady to itself in her young years, after showing her to the world an illustrious example of filial duty. Lear did not long survive her.

Before he died, the good Earl of Kent, who had still attended his old master's steps from the first of his daughters' ill usage to this sad period of his decay, tried to make him understand that it was he who had followed him under the name of Caius ; but Lear's care-crazed

K

brain at that time could not comprehend how that could be, or how Kent and Caius could be the same person; so Kent thought it needless to trouble him with explanations at such a time, and Lear soon after expiring, this faithful servant to the king, between age and grief for his old master's vexations, soon followed him to the grave.

How the judgment of Heaven overtook the bad Earl of Gloucester, whose treasons were discovered, and himself slain in single combat with his brother, the lawful earl; and how Goneril's husband, the Duke of Albany, who was innocent of the death of Cordelia, and had never encouraged his lady in her wicked proceedings against her father, ascended the throne of Britain after the death of Lear, is needless here to narrate; Lear and his three daughters being dead, whose adventures alone concern our story.

MACBETH

WHEN Duncan the Meek reigned King of Scotland, there lived a great thane, or lord, called Macbeth. This Macbeth was a near kinsman to the king, and in great esteem at court for his valour and conduct in the wars; an example of which he had lately given, in defeating a rebel army assisted by the troops of Norway in terrible numbers.

The two Scottish generals, Macbeth and Banquo, returning victorious from this great battle, their way lay over a blasted heath, where they were stopped by the strange appearance of three figures like women, except that they had beards, and their withered skins and wild attire made them look not like any earthly creatures. Macbeth first addressed them, when they, seemingly offended, laid each one her choppy finger upon her skinny lips, in token of silence; and the first of them saluted Macbeth with the title of Thane of Glamis. The general was not a little startled to find himself known by such creatures; but how much more, when the second of them followed up that salute by giving him the title of Thane of Cawdor, to which honour he had no pretensions; and again the third bid him " All hail! king that shalt be hereafter ! " Such a prophetic greeting might well amaze him, who knew that while the king's sons lived he could not hope to succeed to the throne. Then turning to Banquo, they pronounced him, in a sort of riddling terms, to be *lesser than Macbeth and greater ! not so happy, but much happier !* and prophesied that though he should never reign, yet his sons after him should be kings in Scotland. They then turned into air, and vanished ; by which the generals knew them to be weird sisters, or witches.

While they stood pondering on the strangeness of this adventure, there arrived certain messengers from the king, who were empowered by him to confer upon Macbeth the dignity of Thane of Cawdor. An event so miraculously corresponding with the prediction of the witches astonished Macbeth, and he stood wrapped in amazement, unable to make any reply to the messengers ; and in that point of time swelling hopes arose in his mind that the prediction of the third witch might in like manner have its accomplishment, and that he should one day reign king in Scotland.

Turning to Banquo, he said, " Do you not hope that your children shall be kings, when what the witches promised to me has so wonderfully come to pass ? " " That hope," answered the general, " might enkindle you to aim at the throne ; but oftentimes these ministers of darkness tell us truths in little things to betray us into deeds of greatest consequence."

But the wicked suggestions of the witches had sunk too deep into the mind of Macbeth to allow him to attend to the warnings of the good Banquo. From that time he bent all his thoughts how to compass the throne of Scotland.

Macbeth had a wife, to whom he communicated the strange prediction of the weird sisters and its partial accomplishment. She was a bad, ambitious woman, and, so as her husband and herself could arrive at greatness, she cared not much by what means. She spurred on the reluctant purpose of Macbeth, who felt compunction at the thoughts of blood, and did not cease to represent the murder of the king as a step absolutely necessary to the fulfilment of the flattering prophecy.

It happened at this time that the king, who out of his royal condescension would oftentimes visit his principal nobility upon gracious terms, came to Macbeth's house, attended by his two sons, Malcolm and Donalbain, and a numerous train of thanes and attendants, the more to honour Macbeth for the triumphal success of his wars.

The castle of Macbeth was pleasantly situated, and the air about it was sweet and wholesome, which appeared by the nests which the martlet, or swallow, had built under all the jutting friezes and buttresses of the building, wherever it found a place of advantage ; for where those birds most breed and haunt the air is observed to be delicate. The king entered well pleased with the place, and not less so with the attentions and respect of his honoured hostess, Lady Macbeth, who had the art of covering treacherous purposes with smiles, and could look like the innocent flower, while she was indeed the serpent under it.

The king, being tired with his journey, went early to bed, and in his state-room two grooms of his chamber (as was the custom) slept beside him. He had been un-usually pleased with his reception, and had made presents before he retired to his principal officers, and among the rest had sent a rich diamond to Lady Macbeth, greeting her by the name of his most kind hostess.

Now was the middle of night, when over half the world nature seems dead, and wicked dreams abuse men's minds asleep, and none but the wolf and the murderer is abroad. This was the time when Lady Macbeth waked to plot the murder of the king. She would not have undertaken a deed so abhorrent to her sex, but that she

feared her husband's nature, that it was too full of the
milk of human kindness to do a contrived murder. She
knew him to be ambitious, but withal to be scrupulous,
and not yet prepared for that height of crime which
commonly in the end accompanies inordinate ambition.
She had won him to consent to the murder, but she
doubted his resolution ; and she feared that the natural
tenderness of his disposition (more humane than her own)
would come between and defeat the purpose. So with
her own hands armed with a dagger she approached the
king's bed, having taken care to supply the grooms of his
chamber so with wine that they slept intoxicated and careless of their charge. There lay Duncan in a sound sleep
after the fatigues of his journey, and as she viewed him
earnestly, there was something in his face as he slept which
resembled her own father, and she had not the courage
to proceed.

She returned to confer with her husband. His resolution had begun to stagger. He considered that there
were strong reasons against the deed. In the first place,
he was not only a subject, but a near kinsman to the king ;
and he had been his host and entertainer that day, whose
duty, by the laws of hospitality, it was to shut the door
against his murderers, not bear the knife himself. Then
he considered how just and merciful a king this Duncan
had been, how clear of offence to his subjects, how loving
to his nobility, and in particular to him ; that such kings
are the peculiar care of Heaven, and their subjects doubly
bound to revenge their deaths. Besides, by the favours
of the king, Macbeth stood high in the opinion of all sorts
of men, and how would those honours be stained by the
reputation of so foul a murder !

In these conflicts of the mind Lady Macbeth found
her husband, inclining to the better part, and resolving
to proceed no further. But she being a woman not easily
shaken in her evil purpose, began to pour in at his ears

words which infused a portion of her own spirit into his
mind, assigning reason upon reason why he should not
shrink from what he had undertaken ; how easy the
deed was ; how soon it would be over ; and how the
action of one short night would give to all their nights and
days to come sovereign sway and royalty !   Then she
threw contempt on his change of purpose, and accused
him of fickleness and cowardice ; and declared that she
had given suck, and knew how tender it was to love the
babe that milked her ; but she would, while it was smiling
in her face, have plucked it from her breast and dashed its
brains out, if she had so sworn to do it as he had sworn
to perform that murder.   Then she added how practic-
able it was to lay the guilt of the deed upon the drunken
sleepy grooms.   And with the valour of her tongue she so
chastised his sluggish resolutions, that he once more
summoned up courage to the bloody business.

So, taking the dagger in his hand, he softly stole in
the dark to the room where Duncan lay ; and as he went,
he thought he saw another dagger in the air, with the
handle towards him, and on the blade and at the point
of it drops of blood ; but when he tried to grasp at it, it
was nothing but air,—a mere phantasm proceeding from
his own hot and oppressed brain and the business he had
in hand.

Getting rid of this fear, he entered the king's room,
whom he dispatched with one stroke of his dagger. Just
as he had done the murder, one of the grooms, who slept
in the chamber, laughed in his sleep, and the other cried
" Murder ! " which woke them both ; but they said a
short prayer ; one of them said, " God bless us ! " and
the other answered " Amen ! " and addressed themselves
to sleep again.   Macbeth, who stood listening to them,
tried to say " Amen," when the fellow said " God bless
us ! " but, though he had most need of a blessing, the
word stuck in his throat, and he could not pronounce it.

Again he thought he heard a voice which cried " Sleep no more! Macbeth doth murder sleep, the innocent sleep, that nourishes life." Still it cried " Sleep no more ! " to all the house : " Glamis hath murdered sleep, and therefore Cawdor shall sleep no more, Macbeth shall sleep no more."

With such horrible imaginations Macbeth returned to his listening wife, who began to think he had failed of his purpose, and that the deed was somehow frustrated. He came in so distracted a state, that she reproached him with his want of firmness, and sent him to wash his hands of the blood which stained them, while she took his dagger, with purpose to stain the cheeks of the grooms with blood, to make it seem their guilt.

Morning came, and with it the discovery of the murder, which could not be concealed ; and though Macbeth and his lady made a great show of grief, and the proofs against the grooms (the dagger being produced against them and their faces smeared with blood) were sufficiently strong, yet the entire suspicion fell upon Macbeth, whose inducements to such a deed were so much more forcible than such poor silly grooms could be supposed to have ; and Duncan's two sons fled. Malcolm, the eldest, sought for refuge in the English court ; the younger, Donalbain, made his escape to Ireland.

The king's sons, who should have succeeded him, having thus vacated the throne, Macbeth as next heir was crowned king, and thus the prediction of the weird sisters was literally accomplished.

Though placed so high, Macbeth and his queen could not forget the prophecy of the weird sisters, that, though Macbeth should be king, yet not his children, but the children of Banquo, should be kings after him. The thought of this, and that they had defiled their hands with blood, and done so great crimes, only to place the posterity of Banquo upon the throne, so rankled within them, that

him with false confidence, and he remembered the saying
of the spirits, that none of woman born was to hurt
him, and that he was never to be vanquished till Birnam
Wood should come to Dunsinane, which he thought could
never be. So he shut himself up in his castle, whose
impregnable strength was such as defied a siege : here he
sullenly waited the approach of Malcolm. When, upon
a day, there came a messenger to him, pale and shaking
with fear, almost unable to report that which he had seen ;
for he averred that as he stood upon his watch on the hill
he looked towards Birnam, and to his thinking the wood
began to move. " Liar and slave ! " cried Macbeth :
" if thou speakest false thou shalt hang alive upon the
next tree till famine end thee. If thy tale be true, I care
not if thou dost as much by me " ; for Macbeth now began
to faint in resolution, and to doubt the equivocal speeches
of the spirits. He was not to fear till Birnam Wood should
come to Dunsinane, and now a wood did move. " However," said he, " if this which he avouches be true, let us
arm and out. There is no flying hence, nor staying here.
I begin to be weary of the sun, and wish my life at an
end." With these desperate speeches he sallied forth
upon the besiegers, who had now come up to the castle.

The strange appearance which had given the messenger
an idea of a wood moving is easily solved. When the
besieging army marched through the Wood of Birnam,
Malcolm, like a skilful general, instructed his soldiers to
hew down every one a bough, and bear it before him by
way of concealing the true numbers of his host. This
marching of the soldiers with boughs had, at a distance,
the appearance which had frightened the messenger. Thus
were the words of the spirit brought to pass, in a sense
different from that in which Macbeth had understood
them, and one great hold of his confidence was gone.

And now a severe skirmishing took place, in which
Macbeth, though feebly supported by those who called

themselves his friends, but in reality hated the tyrant and inclined to the party of Malcolm and Macduff, yet fought with the extreme of rage and valour, cutting to pieces all who were opposed to him, till he came to where Macduff was fighting. Seeing Macduff, and remembering the caution of the spirit who had counselled him to avoid Macduff above all men, he would have turned, but Macduff, who had been seeking him through the whole fight, opposed his turning, and a fierce contest ensued, Macduff giving him many foul reproaches for the murder of his wife and children. Macbeth, whose soul was charged enough with blood of that family already, would still have declined the combat, but Macduff still urged him to it, calling him tyrant, murderer, hell-hound, and villain.

Then Macbeth remembered the words of the spirit, how none of woman born should hurt him, and smiling confidently, he said to Macduff, " Thou losest thy labour, Macduff. As easily thou mayest impress the air with thy sword as make me vulnerable. I bear a charmed life, which must not yield to one of woman born."

" Despair thy charm," said Macduff, " and let that lying spirit whom thou hast served tell thee that Macduff was never born of woman, never as the ordinary manner of men is to be born, but was untimely taken from his mother."

" Accursed be the tongue which tells me so ! " said the trembling Macbeth, who felt his last hold of confidence give way ; " and let never man in future believe the lying equivocation of witches and juggling spirits, who deceive us in words which have double senses, and while they keep their promise literally, disappoint our hopes with a different meaning. I will not fight with thee."

" Then live ! " said the scornful Macduff ; " we will have a show of thee, as men show monsters, and a painted board, on which shall be written, ' Here men may see the tyrant ! ' "

"Never!" said Macbeth, whose courage returned
with despair; "I will not live to kiss the ground before
young Malcolm's feet, and to be baited with the curses
of the rabble. Though Birnam Wood be come to Dunsinane, and thou opposed to me, who was never born of
woman, yet will I try the last." With these frantic words
he threw himself upon Macduff, who, after a severe
struggle, in the end overcame him, and cutting off his
head, made a present of it to the young and lawful King
Malcolm, who took upon him the government which,
by the machinations of the usurper, he had so long been
deprived of, and ascended the throne of Duncan the Meek
amid the acclamations of the nobles and the people.

ALL'S WELL
THAT ENDS WELL

BERTRAM, Count of Rousillon, had newly come
to his title and estate,
by the death of his father. The
King of France loved the father
of Bertram, and when he heard
of his death, he sent for his son
to come immediately to his royal
court in Paris, intending, for the
friendship he bore the late count,
to grace young Bertram with his
especial favour and protection.

Bertram was living with his mother, the widowed
countess, when Lafeu, an old lord of the French court,
came to conduct Bertram to the king. The King of France
was an absolute monarch, and the invitation to court was
in the form of a royal mandate, or positive command, which
no subject, of what high dignity soever, might disobey;
therefore though the countess, in parting with this dear
son, seemed a second time to bury her husband, whose
loss she had so lately mourned, yet she dared not to keep
him a single day, but gave instant orders for his departure.
Lafeu, who came to fetch him, tried to comfort the
countess for the loss of her late lord, and her son's sudden
absence; and he said, in a courtier's flattering manner,
that the king was so kind a prince, she would find in his
majesty a husband, and that he would be a father to her

son ; meaning only that the good king would befriend the fortunes of Bertram. Lafeu told the countess that the king had fallen into a sad malady, which was pronounced by his physicians to be incurable. The lady expressed great sorrow on hearing this account of the king's ill health, and said she wished the father of Helena (a young gentlewoman who was present in attendance upon her) were living, for that she doubted not he could have cured his Majesty of his disease. And she told Lafeu something of the history of Helena, saying she was the only daughter of the famous physician Gerard de Narbon, and that he had recommended his daughter to her care when he was dying, so that since his death she had taken Helena under her protection ; then the countess praised the virtuous disposition and excellent qualities of Helena, saying she inherited these virtues from her worthy father. While she was speaking, Helena wept in sad and mournful silence, which made the countess gently reprove her for too much grieving for her father's death.

Bertram now bade his mother farewell. The countess parted with her dear son with tears and many blessings, and commended him to the care of Lafeu, saying, " Good my lord, advise him, for he is an unseasoned courtier."

Bertram's last words were spoken to Helena, but they were words of mere civility, wishing her happiness ; and he concluded his short farewell to her with saying, " Be comfortable to my mother, your mistress, and make much of her."

Helena had long loved Bertram, and when she wept in sad and mournful silence, the tears she shed were not for Gerard de Narbon. Helena loved her father, but in the present feeling of a deeper love, the object of which she was about to lose, she had forgotten the very form and features of her dead father, her imagination presenting no image to her mind but Bertram's.

L

Helena had long loved Bertram, yet she always remembered that he was the Count of Roussillon, descended from the most ancient family in France. She of humble birth ; her parents of no note at all, his ancestors all noble. And therefore she looked up to the high-born Bertram as to her master and to her dear lord, and dared not form any wish but to live his servant, and so living to die his vassal. So great the distance seemed to her between his height of dignity and her lowly fortunes, that she would say, " It were all one that I should love a bright particular star, and think to wed it ; Bertram is so far above me."

Bertram's absence filled her eyes with tears and her heart with sorrow ; for though she loved without hope, yet it was a pretty comfort to her to see him every hour ; and Helena would sit and look upon his dark eye, his arched brow, and the curls of his fine hair, till she seemed to draw his portrait on the tablet of her heart, that heart too capable of retaining the memory of every line in the features of that loved face.

Gerard de Narbon, when he died, left her no other portion than some prescriptions of rare and well-proved virtue, which by deep study and long experience in medicine he had collected as sovereign and almost infallible remedies. Among the rest, there was one set down as an approved medicine for the disease under which Lafeu said the king at that time languished ; and when Helena heard of the king's complaint, she, who till now had been so humble and so hopeless, formed an ambitious project in her mind to go herself to Paris, and undertake the cure of the king. But though Helena was the possessor of this choice prescription, it was unlikely, as the king as well as his physicians were of opinion that his disease was incurable, that they would give credit to a poor unlearned virgin, if she should offer to perform a cure. The firm hopes that Helena had of succeeding, if she might be permitted to make the trial, seemed more than even her

father's skill warranted, though he was the most famous
physician of his time ; for she felt a strong faith that this
good medicine was sanctified by all the luckiest stars in
heaven to be the legacy that should advance her fortune,
even to the high dignity of being Count Roussillon's
wife.

Bertram had not been long gone, when the countess
was informed by her steward that he had overheard Helena
talking to herself, and that he understood from some words
she uttered that she was in love with Bertram, and had
thought of following him to Paris. The countess dismissed the steward with thanks, and desired him to tell
Helena she wished to speak with her. What she had
just heard of Helena brought the remembrance of days
long past into the mind of the countess—those days, probably, when her love for Bertram's father first began ; and
she said to herself, " Even so it was with me when I was
young. Love is a thorn that belongs to the rose of youth ;
for in the season of youth, if ever we are Nature's
children, these faults are ours, though then we think not
they are faults." While the countess was thus meditating
on the loving errors of her own youth, Helena entered,
and she said to her, " Helena, you know I am a mother
to you." Helena replied, " You are my honourable mistress." " You are my daughter," said the countess again :
" I say I am your mother. Why do you start and look
pale at my words ? " With looks of alarm and confused
thoughts, fearing the countess suspected her love, Helena
still replied, " Pardon me, madam, you are not my mother ;
the Count Roussillon cannot be my brother, nor I your
daughter." " Yet, Helena," said the countess, " you
might be my daughter-in-law ; and I am afraid that is
what you mean to be, the words *mother* and *daughter* so
disturb you. Helena, do you love my son ? " " Good
madam, pardon me," said the affrighted Helena. Again
the countess repeated her question, " Do you love my

son ? " " Do not you love him, madam ? " said Helena.
The countess replied, " Give me not this evasive answer,
Helena. Come, come, disclose the state of your affections,
for your love has to the full appeared." Helena on her
knees now owned her love, and with shame and terror
implored the pardon of her noble mistress ; and with
words expressive of the sense she had of the inequality
between their fortunes, she protested Bertram did not
know she loved him, comparing her humble unaspiring
love to a poor Indian, who adores the sun, that looks upon
his worshipper, but knows of him no more. The countess
asked Helena if she had not lately an intent to go to Paris.
Helena owned the design she had formed in her mind,
when she heard Lafeu speak of the king's illness. " This
was your motive for wishing to go to Paris," said the
countess, " was it ? Speak truly." Helena honestly
answered, " My lord your son made me to think of this ;
else Paris, and the medicine, and the king, had from the
conversation of my thoughts been absent then." The
countess heard the whole of this confession without saying a word either of approval or blame, but she strictly
questioned Helena as to the probability of the medicine
being useful to the king. She found that it was the most
prized by Gerard de Narbon of all he possessed, and that
he had given it to his daughter on his death-bed ; and,
remembering the solemn promise she had made at that
awful hour in regard to this young maid, whose destiny,
and the life of the king himself, seemed to depend
on the execution of a project (which though conceived
by the fond suggestions of a loving maiden's thoughts,
the countess knew not but it might be the unseen workings of Providence to bring to pass the recovery of the
king, and to lay the foundation of the future fortunes of
Gerard de Narbon's daughter), free leave she gave to
Helena to pursue her own way, and generously furnished
her with ample means and suitable attendants ; and

Helena set out for Paris with the blessings of the countess, and her kindest wishes for her success.

Helena arrived at Paris, and by the assistance of her friend the old Lord Lafeu, she obtained an audience of the king. She had still many difficulties to encounter, for the king was not easily prevailed on to try the medicine offered him by this fair young doctor. But she told him she was Gerard de Narbon's daughter (with whose fame the king was well acquainted), and she offered the precious medicine as the darling treasure which contained the essence of all her father's long experience and skill, and she boldly engaged to forfeit her life if it failed to restore his majesty to perfect health in the space of two days. The king at length consented to try it, and in two days' time Helena was to lose her life if the king did not recover, but if she succeeded he promised to give her the choice of any man throughout all France (the princes only excepted) whom she could like for a husband, the choice of a husband being the fee Helena demanded if she cured the king of his disease.

Helena did not deceive herself in the hope she conceived of the efficacy of her father's medicine. Before two days were at an end the king was restored to perfect health, and he assembled all the young noblemen of his court together, in order to confer the promised reward of a husband upon his fair physician, and he desired Helena to look round on this youthful parcel of noble bachelors, and choose her husband. Helena was not slow to make her choice, for among these young lords she saw the Count Roussillon, and turning to Bertram she said, " This is the man. I dare not say, my lord, I take you, but I give me and my service ever whilst I live into your guiding power." " Why, then," said the king, " young Bertram, take her ; she is your wife." Bertram did not hesitate to declare his dislike to this present of the king's of the self-offered Helena, who, he said, was a poor physician's daughter, bred at his father's charge, and now living a dependent on his mother's bounty. Helena heard him speak these words of rejection and of scorn, and she said to the king, " That you are well, my lord, I am glad. Let the rest go." But the king would not suffer his royal command to be so slighted, for the power of bestowing their nobles in marriage was one of the many privileges of the kings of France, and that same day Bertram was married to Helena, a forced and uneasy marriage to Bertram, and of no promising hope to the poor lady, who, though she gained the noble husband she had hazarded her life to obtain, seemed to have won but a splendid blank, her husband's love not being a gift in the power of the King of France to bestow.

Helena was no sooner married than she was desired by Bertram to apply to the king for him for leave of absence from court ; and when she brought him the king's permission for his departure, Bertram told her that as he was not prepared for this sudden marriage, it had much unsettled him, and therefore she must not wonder at the course he should pursue. If Helena wondered not, she grieved when she found it was his intention to leave her. He ordered her to go home to his mother. When Helena heard this unkind command, she replied, " Sir, I can nothing say to this but that I am your most obedient servant, and shall ever with true observance seek to eke out that desert, wherein my homely stars have failed to equal my great fortunes." But this humble speech of Helena's did not at all move the haughty Bertram to pity his gentle wife, and he parted from her without even the common civility of a kind farewell.

Back to the countess then Helena returned. She had accomplished the purport of her journey, she had pre-served the life of the king, and she had wedded her heart's dear lord, the Count Roussillon ; but she returned back a dejected lady to her noble mother-in-law, and as soon as she entered the house she received a letter from Bertram which almost broke her heart.

The good countess received her with a cordial welcome, as if she had been her son's own choice and a lady of high degree, and she spoke kind words to comfort her for the unkind neglect of Bertram in sending his wife home on her bridal day alone. But this gracious reception failed to cheer the sad mind of Helena, and she said, " Madam, my lord is gone, for ever gone ! " She then read these words out of Bertram's letter : *When you can get the ring from my finger, which never shall come off, then call me husband, but in such a Then I write a Never.* " This is a dreadful sentence ! " said Helena. The countess begged her to have patience, and said now Bertram was gone she should be her child, and that she deserved a lord that twenty such rude boys as Bertram might tend upon and hourly call her mistress. But in vain, by respectful condescension and kind flattery, this matchless mother tried to soothe the sorrows of her daughter-in-law. Helena still kept her eyes fixed upon the letter, and cried out in an agony of grief, " *Till I have no wife, I have nothing in France.*" The countess asked her if she found those words in the letter ? " Yes, madam," was all poor Helena could answer.

The next morning Helena was missing. She left a letter to be delivered to the countess after she was gone, to acquaint her with the reason of her sudden absence : in this letter she informed her that she was so much grieved at having driven Bertram from his native country and his home, that to atone for her offence she had undertaken a pilgrimage to the shrine of St. Jaques le Grand, and concluded with requesting the countess to inform her son that the wife he so hated had left his house for ever.

Bertram, when he left Paris, went to Florence, and there became an officer in the Duke of Florence's army, and after a successful war, in which he distinguished himself by many brave actions, Bertram received letters from his mother, containing the acceptable tidings that Helena would no more disturb him, and he was preparing to return home when Helena herself, clad in her pilgrim's weeds, arrived at the city of Florence.

Florence was a city through which the pilgrims used to pass on their way to St. Jaques le Grand, and when Helena arrived at that city she heard that a hospitable widow dwelt there, who used to receive into her house the female pilgrims that were going to visit the shrine of that saint, giving them lodging and kind entertainment. To this good lady, therefore, Helena went, and the widow gave her a courteous welcome, and invited her to see whatever was curious in that famous city, and told her that if she would like to see the duke's army, she would take her where she might have a full view of it. " And you will see a countryman of yours," said the widow ; " his name is Count Roussillon, who has done worthy service in the duke's wars." Helena wanted no second invitation when she found Bertram was to make a part of the show. She accompanied her hostess, and a sad and mournful pleasure it was to her to look once more upon her dear husband's face. " Is he not a handsome man ? " said the widow. " I like him well," replied Helena with great truth. All the way they walked the talkative widow's discourse was all of Bertram : she told Helena the story of Bertram's marriage, and how he had deserted the poor lady his wife, and entered into the duke's army to avoid living with her. To this account of her own misfortunes Helena patiently listened, and when it was ended, the history of Bertram was not yet done, for then the widow began another tale, every word of which sank deep into the mind of Helena ; for the story she now told was of Bertram's love for her daughter.

Though Bertram did not like the marriage forced on

him by the king, it seems he was not insensible to love, for since he had been stationed with the army at Florence he had fallen in love with Diana, a fair young gentle-woman, the daughter of this widow who was Helena's hostess, and every night, with music of all sorts, and songs composed in praise of Diana's beauty, he would come under her window and solicit her love, and all his suit to her was that she would permit him to visit her by stealth after the family were retired to rest ; but Diana would by no means be persuaded to grant this improper request, nor give any encouragement to his suit, knowing him to be a married man ; for Diana had been brought up under the counsels of a prudent mother, who, though she was now in reduced circumstances, was well born, and descended from the noble family of the Capulets.

All this the good lady related to Helena, highly prais-ing the virtuous principles of her discreet daughter, which she said were entirely owing to the excellent education and good advice she had given her ; and she further said that Bertram had been particularly importunate with Diana to admit him to the visit he so much desired that night, because he was going to leave Florence early the next morning.

Though it grieved Helena to hear of Bertram's love for the widow's daughter, yet from this story the ardent mind of Helena conceived a project (nothing discouraged at the ill success of her former one) to recover her truant lord. She disclosed to the widow that she was Helena, the deserted wife of Bertram, and requested that her kind hostess and her daughter would suffer this visit from Bertram to take place, and allow her to pass herself upon Bertram for Diana ; telling them her chief motive for desiring to have this secret meeting with her husband was to get a ring from him, which he had said if ever she was in possession of he would acknowledge her as his wife.

The widow and her daughter promised to assist her

in this affair, partly moved by pity for this unhappy for-saken wife, and partly won over to her interest by the promises of reward which Helena made them, giving them a purse of money in earnest of her future favour. In the course of that day Helena caused information to be sent to Bertram that she was dead, hoping that when he thought himself free to make a second choice by the news of her death, he would offer marriage to her in her feigned character of Diana. And if she could obtain the ring and this promise too, she doubted not she should make some future good come of it.

In the evening, after it was dark, Bertram was ad-mitted into Diana's chamber, and Helena was there ready to receive him. The flattering compliments and love dis-course he addressed to Helena were precious sounds to her, though she knew they were meant for Diana; and Bertram was so well pleased with her that he made her a solemn promise to be her husband and to love her for ever, which she hoped would be prophetic of a real affection when he should know it was his own wife, the despised Helena, whose conversation had so delighted him.

Bertram never knew how sensible a lady Helena was, else perhaps he would not have been so regardless of her; and seeing her every day, he had entirely overlooked her beauty, a face we are accustomed to see constantly losing the effect which is caused by the first sight either of beauty or of plainness; and of her understanding it was impos-sible he should judge, because she felt such reverence, mixed with her love for him, that she was always silent in his presence; but now that her future fate and the happy ending of all her love projects seemed to depend upon her leaving a favourable impression on the mind of Bertram from this night's interview, she exerted all her wit to please him; and the simple graces of her lively conversation and the endearing sweetness of her manners so charmed Bertram that he vowed she should be his wife.

Helena begged the ring from off his finger as a token of his regard, and he gave it to her ; and in return for this ring, which it was of such importance for her to possess, she gave him another ring, which was one the king had made her a present of. Before it was light in the morning she sent Bertram away, and he immediately set out on his journey towards his mother's house.

Helena prevailed on the widow and Diana to accompany her to Paris, their further assistance being necessary to the full accomplishment of the plan she had formed. When they arrived there they found the king had gone upon a visit to the Countess of Roussillon, and Helena followed the king with all the speed she could make.

The king was still in perfect health, and his gratitude to her who had been the means of his recovery was so lively in his mind, that the moment he saw the Countess of Roussillon he began to talk of Helena, calling her a precious jewel that was lost by the folly of her son ; but seeing the subject distressed the countess, who sincerely lamented the death of Helena, he said, " My good lady, I have forgiven and forgotten all." But the good-natured old Lafeu, who was present, and could not bear that the memory of his favourite Helena should be so lightly passed over, said, " This I must say, the young lord did great offence to his Majesty, his mother, and his lady, but to himself he did the greatest wrong of all, for he has lost a wife whose beauty astonished all eyes, whose words took all ears captive, whose deep perfection made all hearts wish to serve her." The king said, " Praising what is lost makes the remembrance dear. Well, call him hither," meaning Bertram, who now presented himself before the king, and, on his expressing deep sorrow for the injuries he had done to Helena, the king, for his dead father's and his admirable mother's sake, pardoned him and restored him once more to his favour. But the gracious countenance of the king was soon changed towards him, for he perceived that Bertram wore the very ring upon his finger which he had given to Helena ; and he well remembered that Helena had called all the saints in heaven to witness she would never part with that ring unless she sent it to the king himself upon some great disaster befalling her ; and Bertram, on the king's questioning him how he came by the ring, told an improbable story of a lady throwing it to him out of a window, and denied ever having seen Helena since the day of their marriage. The king, knowing Bertram's dislike to his wife, feared he had destroyed her, and he ordered his guards to seize Bertram, saying, " I am wrapped in dismal thinking, for I fear the life of Helena was foully snatched." At this moment Diana and her mother entered and presented a petition to the king, wherein they begged his Majesty to exert his royal power to compel Bertram to marry Diana, he having made her a solemn promise of marriage. Bertram, fearing the king's anger, denied he had made any such promise ; and then Diana produced the ring (which Helena had put into her hands) to confirm the truth of her words, and she said that she had given Bertram the ring he then wore in exchange for that, at the time he vowed to marry her. On hearing this the king ordered the guards to seize her also, and her account of the ring differing from Bertram's, the king's suspicions were confirmed, and he said if they did not confess how they came by this ring of Helena's they should be both put to death. Diana requested her mother might be permitted to fetch the jeweller of whom she bought the ring, which being granted, the widow went out, and presently returned leading in Helena herself.

The good countess, who in silent grief had beheld her son's danger, and had even dreaded that the suspicion of his having destroyed his wife might possibly be true, finding her dear Helena, whom she loved with even a maternal affection, was still living, felt a delight she was hardly able to support ; and the king, scarce believing for joy that it was Helena, said, " Is this indeed the wife of Bertram that I see ? " Helena, feeling herself yet an unacknowledged wife, replied, " No, my good lord, it is but the shadow of a wife you see, the name and not the thing."

Bertram cried out, " Both, both ! O pardon ! "

" O my lord," said Helena, " when I personated this fair maid I found you wondrous kind ; and look, here is your letter ! " reading to him in a joyful tone those words which she had once repeated so sorrowfully : *When from my finger you can get this ring.* " This is done,—it was to me you gave the ring. Will you be mine, now that you are doubly won ? "

Bertram replied, " If you can make it plain that you were the lady I talked with that night, I will love you dearly, ever, ever dearly."

This was no difficult task, for the widow and Diana came with Helena purposely to prove this fact ; and the king was so well pleased with Diana for the friendly assistance she had rendered the dear lady he so truly valued for the service she had done him, that he promised her also a noble husband ; Helena's history giving him a hint that it was a suitable reward for kings to bestow upon fair ladies when they perform notable services.

Thus Helena at last found that her father's legacy was indeed sanctified by the luckiest stars in heaven ; for she was now the beloved wife of her dear Bertram, the daughter-in-law of her noble mistress, and herself the Countess of Rousillon.

THE TAMING
OF THE
SHREW

KATHARINE the Shrew was the eldest daughter of Baptista, a rich gentleman of Padua. She was a lady of such an ungovernable spirit and fiery temper, such a loud-tongued scold, that she was known in Padua by no other name than Katharine the Shrew. It seemed very unlikely, indeed impossible, that any gentleman would ever be found who would venture to marry this lady, and therefore Baptista was much blamed for deferring his consent to many excellent offers that were made to her gentle sister Bianca, putting off all Bianca's suitors with this excuse, that when the eldest sister was fairly off his hands, they should have free leave to address young Bianca.

It happened, however, that a gentleman named Petruchio came to Padua, purposely to look out for a wife, who, nothing discouraged by these reports of Katharine's temper, and hearing she was rich and handsome, resolved upon marrying this famous termagant, and taming her into a meek and manageable wife. And truly none was so fit to set about this herculean labour as Petruchio, whose spirit was as high as Katharine's, and he was a witty and most happy-tempered humorist, and withal so wise, and

of such a true judgment, that he well knew how to feign
a passionate and furious deportment, when his spirits were
so calm that himself could have laughed merrily at his
own angry feigning, for his natural temper was careless
and easy ; the boisterous airs he assumed when he became the husband of Katharine being but in sport, or
more properly speaking affected by his excellent discern-
ment, as the only means to overcome in her own way the
passionate ways of the furious Katharine.

A-courting then Petruchio went to Katharine the
Shrew, and first of all he applied to Baptista, her father,
for leave to woo his *gentle daughter* Katharine, as
Petruchio called her, saying archly, that having heard of
her bashful modesty and mild behaviour, he had come
from Verona to solicit her love. Her father, though he
wished her married, was forced to confess Katharine
would ill answer this character, it being soon apparent of
what manner of gentleness she was composed, for her
music-master rushed into the room to complain that the
gentle Katharine, his pupil, had broken his head with her
lute for presuming to find fault with her performance ;
which, when Petruchio heard, he said, " It is a brave
wench ; I love her more than ever, and long to have some
chat with her " ; and hurrying the old gentleman for a
positive answer, he said, " My business is in haste, Signior
Baptista, I cannot come every day to woo. You knew
my father. He is dead, and has left me heir to all his
lands and goods. Then tell me, if I get your daughter's
love, what dowry you will give with her." Baptista
thought his manner was somewhat blunt for a lover ; but
being glad to get Katharine married, he answered that he
would give her twenty thousand crowns for her dowry,
and half his estate at his death. So this odd match was
quickly agreed on, and Baptista went to apprise his shrewish
daughter of her lover's addresses, and sent her in to
Petruchio to listen to his suit.

In the meantime Petruchio was settling with himself the mode of courtship he should pursue ; and he said, " I will woo her with some spirit when she comes. If she rails at me, why, then I will tell her she sings as sweetly as a nightingale ; and if she frowns, I will say she looks as clear as roses newly washed with dew. If she will not speak a word, I will praise the eloquence of her language ; and if she bids me leave her, I will give her thanks as if she bid me stay with her a week." Now the stately Katharine entered, and Petruchio first addressed her with " Good morrow, Kate, for that is your name, I hear." Katharine, not liking this plain salutation, said disdainfully, " They call me Katharine who do speak to me." " You lie," replied the lover ; " for you are called plain Kate, and bonny Kate, and sometimes Kate the Shrew ; but, Kate, you are the prettiest Kate in Christendom, and therefore, Kate, hearing your mildness praised in every town, I am come to woo you for my wife."

A strange courtship they made of it. She in loud and angry terms showing him how justly she had gained the name of Shrew, while he still praised her sweet and courteous words, till at length, hearing her father coming, he said (intending to make as quick a wooing as possible), "Sweet Katharine, let us set this idle chat aside, for your father has consented that you shall be my wife, your dowry is agreed on, and whether you will or no, I will marry you."

And now Baptista entering, Petruchio told him his daughter had received him kindly, and that she had promised to be married the next Sunday. This Katharine denied, saying she would rather see him hanged on Sunday, and reproached her father for wishing to wed her to such a madcap ruffian as Petruchio. Petruchio desired her father not to regard her angry words, for they had agreed she should seem reluctant before him, but that when they were alone he had found her very fond and loving ; and he said to her, " Give me your hand, Kate,

I will go to Venice to buy you fine apparel against our wedding-day. Provide the feast, father, and bid the wedding guests. I will be sure to bring rings, fine array, and rich clothes, that my Katharine may be fine ; and kiss me, Kate, for we will be married on Sunday."

On the Sunday all the wedding guests were assembled, but they waited long before Petruchio came, and Katharine wept for vexation to think that Petruchio had only been making a jest of her. At last, however, he appeared, but he brought none of the bridal finery he had promised Katharine, nor was he dressed himself like a bridegroom, but in strange disordered attire, as if he meant to make a sport of the serious business he came about ; and his servant and the very horses on which they rode were in like manner in mean and fantastic fashion habited.

Petruchio could not be persuaded to change his dress : he said, Katharine was to be married to *him*, and not to his clothes ; and finding it was in vain to argue with him, to the church they went, he still behaving in the same mad way, for when the priest asked Petruchio if Katharine should be his wife, he swore so loud that she should, that all amazed the priest let fall his book, and as he stooped to take it up, this mad-brained bridegroom gave him such a cuff, that down fell the priest and his book together. And all the while they were being married he stamped and swore so, that the high-spirited Katharine trembled and shook with fear. After the ceremony was over, while they were yet in the church, he called for wine, and drank a loud health to the company, and threw a sop which was at the bottom of the glass full in the sexton's face, giving no other reason for this strange act, than that the sexton's beard grew thin and hungerly, and seemed to ask the sop as he was drinking. Never sure was there such a mad marriage ; but Petruchio did but put this wildness on, the better to succeed in the plot he had formed to tame his shrewish wife.

M

Baptista had provided a sumptuous marriage feast, but when they returned from church, Petruchio, taking hold of Katharine, declared his intention of carrying his wife home instantly ; and no remonstrance of his father-in-law, or angry words of the enraged Katharine, could make him change his purpose : he claimed a husband's right to dispose of his wife as he pleased, and away he hurried Katharine off ; he seeming so daring and resolute that no one dared attempt to stop him.

Petruchio mounted his wife upon a miserable horse, lean and lank, which he had picked out for the purpose, and himself and his servant no better mounted ; they journeyed on through rough and miry ways, and ever when this horse of Katharine's stumbled, he would storm and swear at the poor jaded beast, who could scarce crawl under his burthen, as if he had been the most passionate man alive.

At length, after a weary journey, during which Katharine had heard nothing but the wild ravings of Petruchio at the servant and the horses, they arrived at his house. Petruchio welcomed her kindly to her home, but he resolved she should have neither rest nor food that night. The tables were spread, and supper soon served ; but Petruchio, pretending to find fault with every dish, threw the meat about the floor, and ordered the servants to remove it away ; and all this he did, as he said, in love for his Katharine, that she might not eat meat that was not well dressed. And when Katharine, weary and supper-less, retired to rest, he found the same fault with the bed, throwing the pillows and bed-clothes about the room, so that she was forced to sit down in a chair, where if she chanced to drop asleep, she was presently awakened by the loud voice of her husband, storming at the servants for the ill making of his wife's bridal bed.

The next day Petruchio pursued the same course, still speaking kind words to Katharine ; but when she attempted

"How fares my sweet KATE?"

to eat, finding fault with everything that was set before
her, throwing the breakfast on the floor as he had done
the supper ; and Katharine, the haughty Katharine, was
fain to beg the servants would bring her secretly a morsel
of food ; but they being instructed by Petruchio, replied,
they dared not give her anything unknown to their master.
" Ah ! " said she, " did he marry me to famish me ?
Beggars that come to my father's door have food given them.
But I, who never knew what it was to entreat for anything, am starved for want of food, giddy for want of sleep,
with oaths kept waking, and with brawling fed ; and that
which vexes me more than all, he does it under the name
of perfect love, pretending that if I sleep or eat, it were
present death to me." Here her soliloquy was interrupted
by the entrance of Petruchio : he, not meaning she should
be quite starved, had brought her a small portion of meat,
and he said to her, " How fares my sweet Kate ? Here,
love, you see how diligent I am : I have dressed your meat
myself. I am sure this kindness merits thanks. What,
not a word ? Nay, then you love not the meat, and all
the pains I have taken is to no purpose." He then ordered
the servant to take the dish away. Extreme hunger, which
had abated the pride of Katharine, made her say, though
angered to the heart, " I pray you let it stand." But this
was not all Petruchio intended to bring her to, and he
replied : " The poorest service is repaid with thanks, and
so shall mine before you touch the meat." On this
Katharine brought out a reluctant " I thank you, sir."
And now he suffered her to make a slender meal, saying,
" Much good may it do your gentle heart, Kate ; eat apace.
And now, my honey love, we will return to your father's
house, and revel it as bravely as the best, with silken coats
and caps and golden rings ; with ruffs and scarfs and fans,
and double change of finery " ; and to make her believe
he really intended to give her these gay things, he called
in a tailor and a haberdasher, who brought some new

clothes he had ordered for her, and then giving her plate to the servant to take away before she had half satisfied her hunger, he said, " What, have you dined ? " The haberdasher presented a cap, saying, " Here is the cap your worship bespoke " ; on which Petruchio began to storm afresh, saying the cap was moulded in a porringer, and that it was no bigger than a cockle or walnut-shell ; desiring the haberdasher to take it away and make a bigger. Katharine said, " I will have this : all gentlewomen wear such caps as these." " When you are gentle," replied Petruchio, " you shall have one too, and not till then." The meat Katharine had eaten had a little revived her fallen spirits, and she said, " Why, sir, I trust I may have leave to speak, and speak I will. I am no child, no babe ; your betters have endured to hear me say my mind ; and if you cannot, you had better stop your ears." Petruchio would not hear these angry words, for he had happily discovered a better way of managing his wife than keeping up a jangling argument with her ; therefore his answer was, " Why, you say true, it is a paltry cap, and I love you for not liking it." " Love me, or love me not," said Katharine, " I like the cap, and I will have this cap or none." " You say you wish to see the gown ? " said Petruchio, still affecting to misunderstand her. The tailor then came forward, and showed her a fine gown he had made for her. Petruchio, whose intent was that she should have neither cap nor gown, found much fault with that. " O mercy, Heaven ! " said he, " what masking stuff is here ? What, do you call this a sleeve ? it is like a demi-cannon, carved up and down like an apple tart." The tailor said, " You bid me make it according to the fashion of the times " ; and Katharine said she never saw a better fashioned gown. This was enough for Petruchio, and privately desiring these people might be paid for their goods, and excuses made to them for the seemingly strange treatment he bestowed upon them, he with fierce words and furious gestures drove the tailor and the haberdasher out of the room ; and then, turning to Katharine, he said, " Well, come, my Kate, we will go to your father's even in these mean garments we now wear."

And then he ordered his horses, affirming they should reach Baptista's house by dinner-time, for that it was but seven o'clock. Now, it was not early morning, but the very middle of the day, when he spoke this ; therefore Katharine ventured to say, though modestly—being almost overcome by the vehemence of his manner—" I dare assure you, sir, it is two o'clock, and will be supper-time before we get there." But Petruchio meant that she should be so completely subdued that she should assent to everything he said before he carried her to her father ; and therefore, as if he were lord even of the sun, and could command the hours, he said it should be what time he pleased to have it, before he set forward ; " For," said he, " whatever I say or do, you still are crossing it. I will not go to-day, and when I go it shall be what o'clock I say it is." Another day Katharine was forced to practise her newly-found obedience ; and not till he had brought her proud spirit to such a perfect subjection that she dared not remember there was such a word as contradiction, would Petruchio allow her to go to her father's house ; and even while they were upon their journey thither, she was in danger of being turned back again, only because she happened to hint it was the sun, when he affirmed the moon shone brightly at noonday.

" Now, by my mother's son," said he, " and that is myself, it shall be the moon, or stars, or what I list, before I journey to your father's house." He then made as if he were going back again ; but Katharine, no longer Katharine the Shrew, but the obedient wife, said, " Let us go forward, I pray, now we have come so far, and it shall be the sun, or moon, or what you please, and if you please to call it a rush candle henceforth, I vow it shall be so for me."

This he was resolved to prove, therefore he said again, " I say it is the moon." " I know it is the moon," replied Katharine. " You lie, it is the blessed sun," said Petruchio. " Then it is the blessed sun," replied Katharine ; " but sun it is not, when you say it is not. What you will have it named, even so it is, and so it ever shall be for Katharine." Now, then, he suffered her to proceed on her journey ; but further to try if this yielding humour would last, he addressed an old gentleman they met on the road as if he had been a young woman, saying to him, " Good morrow, gentle mistress " ; and asked Katharine if she had ever beheld a fairer gentlewoman, praising the red and white of the old man's cheeks, and comparing his eyes to two bright stars ; and again he addressed him, saying, " Fair lovely maid, once more good day to you ! " and said to his wife, " Sweet Kate, embrace her for her beauty's sake." The now completely vanquished Katharine quickly adopted her husband's opinion, and made her speech in like sort to the old gentleman, saying to him, " Young budding virgin, you are fair, and fresh, and sweet : whither are you going, and where is your dwelling ? Happy are the parents of so fair a child." " Why, how now, Kate ! " said Petruchio ; " I hope you are not mad. This is a man, old and wrinkled, faded and withered, and not a maiden, as you say he is." On this Katharine said, " Pardon me, old gentleman : the sun has so dazzled my eyes, that everything I look on seemeth green. Now I perceive you are a reverend father : I hope you will pardon me for my sad mistake." " Do, good old grandsire," said Petruchio, " and tell us which way you are travelling. We shall be glad of your company, if you are going our way." The old gentleman replied, " Fair sir, and you my merry mistress, your strange encounter has much amazed me. My name is Vincentio, and I am going to visit a son of mine who lives at Padua." Then Petruchio knew the old gentleman to be the father of Lucentio, a young gentleman who was to be married to Baptista's younger daughter, Bianca, and he made Vincentio very happy by telling him the rich marriage his son was about to make ; and they all journeyed on pleasantly together till they came to Baptista's house, where there was a large company assembled to celebrate the wedding of Bianca and Lucentio, Baptista having willingly consented to the marriage of Bianca when he had got Katharine off his hands.

When they entered, Baptista welcomed them to the marriage feast, and there was present also another newly married pair.

Lucentio, Bianca's husband, and Hortensio, the other new-married man, could not forbear sly jests, which seemed to hint at the shrewish disposition of Petruchio's wife, and these fond bridegrooms seemed highly pleased with the mild tempers of the ladies they had chosen, laughing at Petruchio at his less fortunate choice. Petruchio took little notice of their jokes till the ladies were retired after dinner, and then he perceived Baptista joined in the laugh against him ; for when Petruchio affirmed that his wife would prove more obedient than theirs, the father of Katharine said, " Now, in good sadness, son Petruchio, I fear you have got the veriest shrew of all." " Well," said Petruchio, " I say no, and therefore for assurance that I speak the truth, let us each send for his wife, and he whose wife is most obedient to come at first when she is sent for, shall win a wager which we will propose." To this the other two husbands willingly consented, for they were quite confident that their gentle wives would prove more obedient than the headstrong Katharine ; and they proposed a wager of twenty crowns ; but Petruchio merrily said, he would lay as much as that upon his hawk or hound, but twenty times as much upon his wife. Lucentio and Hortensio raised the wager to a hundred crowns, and Lucentio first sent his servant to desire Bianca would come to him. But the servant returned, and said, " Sir, my mistress sends you word she is busy and cannot come." " How ! " said Petruchio, " does she say she is busy and cannot come ? Is that an answer for a wife ? " Then they laughed at him, and said it would be well if Katharine did not send a worse answer. And now it was Hortensio's turn to send for his wife ; and he said to his servant, " Go, and entreat my wife to come to me." " Oho ! entreat her ! " said Petruchio ; " nay, then she needs must come." " I am afraid, sir," said Hortensio, " your wife will not be entreated." But presently this civil husband looked a little blank, when the servant returned without his mistress ; and he said to him, " How now ! where is my wife ? " " Sir," said the servant, " my mistress says, you have some goodly jest in hand, and therefore she will not come. She bids you come to her." " Worse and worse ! " said Petruchio ; and then he sent his servant, saying, " Sirrah, go to your mistress, and tell her I command her to come to me." The company had scarcely time to think she would not obey this summons, when Baptista all in amaze exclaimed, " Now, by my holidame, here comes Katharine ! " and she entered, saying meekly to Petruchio, " What is your will, sir, that you send for me ? " " Where is your sister and Hortensio's wife ? " said he. Katharine replied, " They sit conferring by the parlour fire." " Go, fetch them hither ! " said Petruchio. Away went Katharine without reply to perform her husband's command. " Here is a wonder," said Lucentio, " if you talk of a wonder." " And so it is," said Hortensio ; " I marvel what it bodes." " Marry, peace it bodes," said Petruchio, " and love, and quiet life, and right supremacy ; and, to be short, everything that is sweet and happy." Katharine's father, overjoyed to see this reformation in his daughter, said, " Now fair befall thee, son Petruchio ! you have won the wager, and I will add another twenty thousand crowns to her dowry, as if she were another daughter, for she is changed as if she had never been." " Nay," said Petruchio, " I

will win the wager better yet, and show more signs of
her new-built virtue and obedience." Katharine now
entering with the two ladies, he continued, " See where
she comes, and brings your froward wives as prisoners to
her womanly persuasion. Katharine, that cap of yours
does not become you ; off with that bauble, and throw it
underfoot." Katharine instantly took off her cap and
threw it down. " Lord ! " said Hortensio's wife, " may
I never have a cause to sigh till I am brought to such a
silly pass ! " And Bianca, she too said, " Fie, what foolish
duty call you this ? " On this Bianca's husband said to
her, " I wish your duty were as foolish too. The wisdom
of your duty, fair Bianca, has cost me a hundred crowns
since dinner-time." " The more fool you," said Bianca,
" for laying on my duty." " Katharine," said Petruchio,
" I charge you tell these headstrong women what duty
they owe their lords and husbands." And to the 'wonder
of all present, the reformed shrewish lady spoke as elo-
quently in praise of the wife-like duty of obedience, as
she had practised it implicitly in a ready submission to
Petruchio's will. And Katharine once more became
famous in Padua, not as heretofore, as Katharine the
Shrew, but as Katharine the most obedient and duteous
wife in Padua.

THE COMEDY OF ERRORS

THE states of Syracuse and Ephesus being at variance, there was a cruel law made at Ephesus, ordaining that if any merchant of Syracuse was seen in the city of Ephesus, he was to be put to death, unless he could pay a thousand marks for the ransom of his life.

Ægeon, an old merchant of Syracuse, was discovered in the streets of Ephesus, and brought before the duke, either to pay this heavy fine or to receive sentence of death.

Ægeon had no money to pay the fine, and the duke, before he pronounced the sentence of death upon him, desired him to relate the history of his life, and to tell for what cause he had ventured to come to the city of Ephesus, which it was death for any Syracusan merchant to enter.

Ægeon said that he did not fear to die, for sorrow had made him weary of his life, but that a heavier task could not have been imposed upon him than to relate the events of his unfortunate life. He then began his own history, in the following words :

" I was born at Syracuse, and brought up to the profession of a merchant. I married a lady with whom I

174

lived very happily ; but being obliged to go to Epidamnum, I was detained there by my business six months, and then, finding I should be obliged to stay some time longer, I sent for my wife, who, as soon as she arrived, was brought to bed of two sons, and what was very strange, they were both so exactly alike that it was impossible to distinguish the one from the other. At the same time that my wife was brought to bed of these twin boys, a poor woman in the inn where my wife lodged was brought to bed of two sons, and these twins were as much like each other as my two sons were. The parents of these children being exceedingly poor, I bought the two boys, and brought them up to attend upon my sons.

" My sons were very fine children, and my wife was not a little proud of two such boys ; and she daily wishing to return home, I unwillingly agreed, and in an evil hour we got on shipboard ; for we had not sailed above a league from Epidamnum before a dreadful storm arose, which continued with such violence, that the sailors, seeing no chance of saving the ship, crowded into the boat to save their own lives, leaving us alone in the ship, which we every moment expected would be destroyed by the fury of the storm.

" The incessant weeping of my wife, and the piteous complaints of the pretty babes, who, not knowing what to fear, wept for fashion, because they saw their mother weep, filled me with terror for them, though I did not myself fear death ; and all my thoughts were bent to contrive means for their safety. I tied my youngest son to the end of a small spare mast, such as seafaring men provide against storms ; at the other end I bound the youngest of the twin slaves, and at the same time I directed my wife how to fasten the other children in like manner to another mast. She thus having the care of the two eldest children, and I of the two younger, we bound ourselves separately to these masts with the children ;

and but for this contrivance we had all been lost, for the ship split on a mighty rock, and was dashed in pieces, and we clinging to these slender masts were supported above the water, where I, having the care of two children, was unable to assist my wife, who with the other children was soon separated from me; but while they were yet in my sight, they were taken up by a boat of fishermen, from Corinth (as I supposed), and seeing them in safety, I had no care but to struggle with the wild sea-waves, to preserve my dear son and the youngest slave. At length we in our turn were taken up by a ship, and the sailors knowing me, gave us kind welcome and assistance, and landed us in safety at Syracuse; but from that sad hour I have never known what became of my wife and eldest child.

" My youngest son, and now my only care, when he was eighteen years of age, began to be inquisitive after his mother and his brother, and often importuned me that he might take his attendant, the young slave, who had also lost his brother, and go in search of them; at length I unwillingly gave consent, for though I anxiously desired to hear tidings of my wife and eldest son, yet in sending my younger one to find them, I hazarded the loss of him also. It is now seven years since my son left me; five years have I passed in travelling through the world in search of him. I have been in farthest Greece, and through the bounds of Asia; and coasting homewards, I landed here in Ephesus, being unwilling to leave any place unsought that harbours men; but this day must end the story of my life, and happy should I think myself in my death, if I were assured my wife and sons were living."

Here the hapless Ægeon ended the account of his misfortunes; and the duke, pitying this unfortunate father, who had brought upon himself this great peril by his love for his lost son, said, if it were not against the laws, which his oath and dignity did not permit him to alter, he would freely pardon him ; yet, instead of dooming him to instant death, as the strict letter of the law required, he would give him that day, to try if he could beg or borrow the money to pay the fine.

This day of grace did seem no great favour to Ægeon ; for not knowing any man in Ephesus, there seemed to him but little chance that any stranger would lend or give him a thousand marks to pay the fine ; and helpless and hopeless of any relief, he retired from the presence of the duke in the custody of a jailer.

Ægeon supposed he knew no person in Ephesus ; but at the very time he was in danger of losing his life through the careful search he was making after his youngest son, that son and his eldest son also were both in the city of Ephesus.

Ægeon's sons, besides being exactly alike in face and person, were both named alike, being both called Antipholus, and the two twin slaves were also both named Dromio. Ægeon's youngest son, Antipholus of Syracuse, he whom the old man had come to Ephesus to seek, happened to arrive at Ephesus with his slave Dromio that very same day that Ægeon did ; and he being also a merchant of Syracuse, he would have been in the same danger that his father was, but by good fortune he met a friend, who told him the peril an old merchant of Syracuse was in, and advised him to pass for a merchant of Epidamnum ; this Antipholus agreed to do, and he was sorry to hear one of his countrymen was in this danger ; but he little thought this old merchant was his own father.

The eldest son of Ægeon (who must be called Antipholus of Ephesus, to distinguish him from his brother, Antipholus of Syracuse) had lived at Ephesus twenty years, and, being a rich man, was well able to have paid the money for the ransom of his father's life ; but Antipholus knew nothing of his father, being so young when he was taken out of the sea with his mother by the fishermen, that he only remembered he had been so preserved, but he had no recollection of either his father or his mother ; the fishermen who took up this Antipholus and his mother and the young slave Dromio, having carried the two children away from her (to the great grief of that unhappy lady), intending to sell them.

Antipholus and Dromio were sold by them to Duke Menaphon, a famous warrior, who was uncle to the Duke of Ephesus, and he carried the boys to Ephesus, when he went to visit the duke his nephew.

The Duke of Ephesus taking a liking to young Antipholus when he grew up made him an officer in his army, in which he distinguished himself by his great bravery in the wars, where he saved the life of his patron the duke, who rewarded his merit by marrying him to Adriana, a rich lady of Ephesus, with whom he was living, his slave Dromio still attending him, at the time his father came there.

Antipholus of Syracuse, when he parted with his friend, who advised him to say he came from Epidamnum, gave his slave Dromio some money to carry to the inn where he intended to dine, and in the meantime he said he would walk about and view the city, and observe the manners of the people.

Dromio was a pleasant fellow ; and when Antipholus was dull and melancholy, he used to divert himself with the odd humours and merry jests of his slave, so that the freedoms of speech he allowed in Dromio were greater than is usual between masters and their servants.

When Antipholus of Syracuse had sent Dromio away, he stood awhile thinking over his solitary wanderings in search of his mother and his brother, of whom in no place where he landed could he hear the least tidings ; and he said sorrowfully to himself, " I am like a drop of water in the ocean, which seeking to find its fellow-drop, loses itself in the wide sea. So I, unhappily, to find a mother and a brother, do lose myself."

While he was thus meditating on his weary travels, which had hitherto been so useless, Dromio (as he thought) returned. Antipholus, wondering that he came back so soon, asked him where he had left the money. Now, it was not his own Dromio, but the twin-brother that lived with Antipholus of Ephesus, that he spoke to. The two Dromios and the two Antipholuses were still as much alike as Ægeon had said they were in their infancy; therefore no wonder Antipholus thought it was his own slave returned, and asked him why he came back so soon. Dromio replied, " My mistress sent me to bid you come to dinner. The capon burns, and the pig falls from the spit, and the meat will be all cold if you do not come home." " These jests are out of season," said Antipholus : " where did you leave the money ? " Dromio still answering that his mistress had sent him to fetch Antipholus to dinner : " What mistress ? " said Antipholus. " Why, your worship's wife, sir," replied Dromio. Antipholus having no wife, he was very angry with Dromio, and said, " Because I familiarly sometimes chat with you, you presume to jest with me in this free manner. I am not in a sportive humour now : where is the money ? We being strangers here, how dare you trust so great a charge from your own custody ? " Dromio hearing his master, as he thought him, talk of their being strangers, supposing Antipholus was jesting, replied merrily, " I pray you, sir, jest as you sit at dinner : I had no charge but to fetch you home, to dine with my mistress and her sister." Now Antipholus lost all patience, and beat Dromio, who ran home and told his mistress that his master had refused to come to dinner, and said that he had no wife.

Adriana, the wife of Antipholus of Ephesus, was very angry when she heard that her husband said he had no wife, for she was of a jealous temper, and she said her husband meant that he loved another lady better than herself; and she began to fret, and say unkind words of jealousy and reproach of her husband; and her sister Luciana, who lived with her, tried in vain to persuade her out of her groundless suspicions.

Antipholus of Syracuse went to the inn, and found Dromio with the money in safety there, and seeing his own Dromio, he was going again to chide him for his free jests, when Adriana came up to him, and not doubting but it was her husband she saw, she began to reproach him for looking strange upon her (as well he might, never having seen this angry lady before); and then she told him how well he loved her before they were married, and that now he loved some other lady instead of her. " How comes it now, my husband," said she, " oh! how comes it that I have lost your love ? " " Plead you to me, fair dame ? " said the astonished Antipholus. It was in vain he told her he was not her husband, and that he had been in Ephesus but two hours : she insisted on his going home with her ; and Antipholus at last, being unable to get away, went with her to his brother's house, and dined with Adriana and her sister, the one calling him husband, and the other brother, he, all amazed, thinking he must have been married to her in his sleep, or that he was sleeping now. And Dromio, who followed them, was no less surprised, for the cook-maid, who was his brother's wife, also claimed him for her husband.

While Antipholus of Syracuse was dining with his brother's wife, his brother, the real husband, returned home to dinner with his slave Dromio ; but the servants would not open the door, because their mistress had ordered them not to admit any company ; and when they repeatedly knocked, and said they were Antipholus and Dromio, the maids laughed at them, and said that Antipholus was at dinner with their mistress, and Dromio was in the kitchen ; and though they almost knocked the door down, they could not gain admittance, and at last Antipholus went away very angry, and strangely surprised at hearing a gentleman was dining with his wife.

When Antipholus of Syracuse had finished his dinner, he was so perplexed at the lady's still persisting in calling him husband, and at hearing that Dromio had also been claimed by the cook-maid, that he left the house as soon as he could find any pretence to get away ; for though he was very much pleased with Luciana the sister, yet the jealous-tempered Adriana he disliked very much, nor was Dromio at all better satisfied with his fair wife in the kitchen ; therefore both master and man were glad to get away from their new wives as fast as they could.

The moment Antipholus of Syracuse had left the house, he was met by a goldsmith, who, mistaking him as Adriana had done for Antipholus of Ephesus, gave him a gold chain, calling him by his name ; and when Antipholus would have refused the chain, saying it did not belong to him, the goldsmith replied he made it by his own orders, and went away, leaving the chain in the hands of Antipholus, who ordered his man Dromio to get his things on board a ship, not choosing to stay in a place any longer where he met with such strange adventures that he surely thought himself bewitched.

The goldsmith, who had given the chain to the wrong Antipholus, was arrested immediately after for a sum of money he owed ; and Antipholus, the married brother, to whom the goldsmith thought he had given the chain, happened to come to the place where the officer was arresting the goldsmith, who, when he saw Antipholus, asked him to pay for the gold chain he had just delivered to him, the price amounting to nearly the same sum as that for which he had been arrested. Antipholus denying the having received the chain, and the goldsmith persisting to declare that he had but a few minutes before given it to him, they disputed this matter a long time, both thinking they were

N

right, for Antipholus knew the goldsmith never gave him the chain, and, so like were the two brothers, the goldsmith was as certain he had delivered the chain into his hands, till at last the officer took the goldsmith away to prison for the debt he owed, and at the same time the goldsmith made the officer arrest Antipholus for the price of the chain ; so that at the conclusion of their dispute, Antipholus and the merchant were both taken away to prison together.

As Antipholus was going to prison, he met Dromio of Syracuse, his brother's slave, and mistaking him for his own, he ordered him to go to Adriana his wife, and tell her to send the money for which he was arrested. Dromio, wondering that his master should send him back to the strange house where he dined, and from which he had just before been in such haste to depart, did not dare to reply, though he came to tell his master the ship was ready to sail ; for he saw Antipholus was in no humour to be jested with. Therefore he went away, grumbling within himself that he must return to Adriana's house, " where," said he, " Dowsabel claims me for a husband ; but I must go, for servants must obey their masters' commands."

Adriana gave him the money, and as Dromio was returning he met Antipholus of Syracuse, who was still in amaze at the surprising adventures he met with, for his brother being well known in Ephesus, there was hardly a man he met in the streets but saluted him as an old acquaintance : some offered him money which they said was owing to him, some invited him to come and see them, and some gave him thanks for kindnesses they said he had done them, all mistaking him for his brother. A tailor showed him some silks he had bought for him, and insisted upon taking measure of him for some clothes.

Antipholus began to think he was among a nation of sorcerers and witches, and Dromio did not at all relieve his master from his bewildered thoughts, by asking how he got free from the officer who was carrying him to prison, and giving him the purse of gold which Adriana had sent to pay the debt with. This talk of Dromio's of the arrest and of a prison, and of the money he had brought from Adriana, perfectly confounded Antipholus, and he said, " This fellow Dromio is certainly distracted, and we wander here in illusions ; " and quite terrified at his own confused thoughts, he cried out, " Some blessed power deliver us from this strange place ! "

And now another stranger came up to him, and she was a lady, and she too called him Antipholus, and told him he had dined with her that day, and asked him for a gold chain which she said he had promised to give her. Antipholus now lost all patience, and calling her a sorceress he denied that he had ever promised her a chain, or dined with her, or had even seen her face before that moment. The lady persisted in affirming he had dined with her, and had promised her a chain, which Antipholus still denying, she further said that she had given him a valuable ring, and if he would not give her the gold chain, she insisted upon having her own ring again. On this Antipholus became quite frantic, and again calling her sorceress and witch, and denying all knowledge of her or her ring, ran away from her, leaving her astonished at his words and his wild looks, for nothing to her appeared more certain than that he had dined with her, and that she had given him a ring, in consequence of his promising to make her a present of a gold chain. But this lady had fallen into the same mistake the others had done, for she had taken him for his brother : the married Antipholus had done all the things she taxed this Antipholus with.

When the married Antipholus was denied entrance into his own house (those within supposing him to be already there), he had gone away very angry, believing it to be one of his wife's jealous freaks, to which she was very subject, and remembering that she had often falsely accused him of visiting other ladies, he, to be revenged on her for shutting him out of his own house, determined to go and dine with this lady, and she receiving him with great civility, and his wife having so highly offended him, Antipholus promised to give her a gold chain which he had intended as a present for his wife : it was the same chain which the goldsmith by mistake had given to his brother. The lady liked so well the thoughts of having a fine gold chain that she gave the married Antipholus a ring, which when, as she supposed (taking his brother for him), he denied, and said he did not know her, and left her in such a wild passion, she began to think he was certainly out of his senses, and presently she resolved to go and tell Adriana that her husband was mad. And while she was telling it to Adriana he came, attended by the jailer (who allowed him to come home to get the money to pay the debt), for the purse of money which Adriana had sent by Dromio, and he had delivered to the other Antipholus.

Adriana believed the story the lady told her of her husband's madness must be true, when he reproached her for shutting him out of his own house, and remembering how he had protested all dinner-time that he was not her husband, and had never been in Ephesus till that day, she had no doubt that he was mad ; she therefore paid the jailer the money, and, having discharged him, she ordered her servants to bind her husband with ropes and had him conveyed into a dark room, and sent for a doctor to come and cure him of his madness, Antipholus all the while hotly exclaiming against this false accusation, which the exact likeness he bore to his brother had brought upon him But his rage only the more confirmed them in the belief that he was mad, and Dromio persisting in the same story, they bound him also, and took him away along with his master.

Soon after Adriana had put her husband into confinement, a servant came to tell her that Antipholus and Dromio must have broken loose from their keepers, for that they were both walking at liberty in the next street.   On hearing this, Adriana ran out to fetch him home, taking some people with her to secure her husband again, and her sister went along with her.   When they came to the gates of a convent in their neighbourhood, there they saw Antipholus and Dromio, as they thought, being again deceived by the likeness of the twin brothers.

Antipholus of Syracuse was still beset with the per-plexities this likeness had brought upon him.   The chain which the goldsmith had given him was about his neck, and the goldsmith was reproaching him for denying that he had it and refusing to pay for it, and Antipholus was protesting that the goldsmith freely gave him the chain in the morning, and that from that hour he had never seen the goldsmith again.

And now Adriana came up to him, and claimed him as her lunatic husband who had escaped from his keepers, and the men she brought with her were going to lay violent hands on Antipholus and Dromio, but they ran into the convent, and Antipholus begged the abbess to give him shelter in her house.

And now came out the lady abbess herself to inquire into the cause of this disturbance.   She was a grave and venerable lady, and wise to judge of what she saw, and she would not too hastily give up the man who had sought protection in her house ; so she strictly questioned the wife about the story she told of her husband's madness, and she said, " What is the cause of this sudden distemper of your husband's ?   Has he lost his wealth at sea ?   Or is it the death of some dear friend that has disturbed his mind ? "   Adriana replied that no such things as these had been the cause.   " Perhaps," said the abbess, " he has fixed his affections on some other lady than you his wife, and that has driven him to this state."   Adriana said she had long thought the love of some other lady was the

cause of his frequent absences from home. Now it was
not his love for another, but the teasing jealousy of his
wife's temper that often obliged Antipholus to leave his
home, and (the abbess suspecting this from the vehemence
of Adriana's manner) to learn the truth she said, " You
should have reprehended him for this." " Why, so I did,"
replied Adriana. " Ay," said the abbess, " but perhaps
not enough." Adriana, willing to convince the abbess
that she had said enough to Antipholus on this subject,
replied, " It was the constant subject of our conversation :
in bed I would not let him sleep for speaking of it ; at
table I would not let him eat for speaking of it ; when
I was alone with him I talked of nothing else ; and in
company I gave him frequent hints of it. Still all my
talk was how vile and bad it was in him to love any lady
better than me."

The lady abbess, having drawn this full confession from
the jealous Adriana, now said, " And therefore comes it
that your husband is mad. The venomous clamour of a
jealous woman is a more deadly poison than a mad dog's
tooth. It seems his sleep was hindered by your railing,
no wonder that his head is light ; and his meat was sauced
with your upbraidings : unquiet meals make ill digestions,
and that has thrown him into this fever. You say his
sports were disturbed by your brawls : being debarred
from the enjoyment of society and recreation, what could
ensue but dull melancholy and comfortless despair ? The
consequence is, then, that your jealous fits have made your
husband mad."

Luciana would have excused her sister, saying she
always reprehended her husband mildly, and she said
to her sister, " Why do you hear these rebukes without
answering them ? " But the abbess had made her so
plainly perceive her fault that she could only answer, " She
has betrayed me to my own reproof."

Adriana, though ashamed of her own conduct, still

insisted on having her husband delivered up to her, but
the abbess would suffer no person to enter her house, nor
would she deliver up this unhappy man to the care of the
jealous wife, determining herself to use gentle means for
his recovery ; and she retired into her house again, and
ordered her gates to be shut against them.

During the course of this eventful day, in which so
many errors had happened from the likeness the twin
brothers bore to each other, old Ægeon's day of grace was
passing away, it being now near sunset, and at sunset he
was doomed to die if he could not pay the money.

The place of his execution was near this convent, and
here he arrived just as the abbess retired into the convent ;
the duke attending in person, that if any offered to pay
the money, he might be present to pardon him.

Adriana stopped this melancholy procession and cried
out to the duke for justice, telling him that the abbess had
refused to deliver up her lunatic husband to her care.
While she was speaking, her real husband and his servant
Dromio, who had got loose, came before the duke to
demand justice, complaining that his wife had confined
him on a false charge of lunacy, and telling in what manner
he had broken his bands and eluded the vigilance of his
keepers. Adriana was strangely surprised to see her
husband, when she thought he had been within the
convent.

Ægeon, seeing his son, concluded this was the son who
had left him to go in search of his mother and his brother,
and he felt secure that this dear son would readily pay
the money demanded for his ransom. He therefore spoke
to Antipholus in words of fatherly affection, with joyful
hope that he should now be released. But to the utter
astonishment of Ægeon, his son denied all knowledge of
him, as well he might, for this Antipholus had never seen
his father since they were separated in the storm in his
infancy ; but while the poor Ægeon was in vain endeavouring

to make his son acknowledge him, thinking surely that either his griefs and the anxieties he had suffered had so strangely altered him that his son did not know him, or else that he was ashamed to acknowledge his father in his misery ; in the midst of this perplexity the lady abbess and the other Antipholus and Dromio came out, and the wondering Adriana saw two husbands and two Dromios standing before her !

And now these riddling errors, which had so perplexed them all, were clearly made out. When the duke saw the two Antipholuses and the two Dromios both so exactly alike, he at once conjectured aright of these seeming mysteries, for he remembered the story Ægeon had told him in the morning, and he said these men must be the two sons of Ægeon and their twin slaves.

But now an unlooked-for joy indeed completed the history of Ægeon, and the tale he had in the morning told in sorrow and under sentence of death, before the setting sun went down was brought to a happy conclusion, for the venerable lady abbess made herself known to be the long lost wife of Ægeon, and the fond mother of the two Antipholuses.

When the fishermen took the eldest Antipholus and Dromio away from her, she entered a nunnery, and by her wise and virtuous conduct she was at length made lady abbess of this convent, and in discharging the rites of hospitality to an unhappy stranger, she had unknowingly protected her own son.

Joyful congratulations and affectionate greetings between these long-separated parents and their children made them for a while forget that Ægeon was yet under sentence of death ; but when they were become a little calm, Antipholus of Ephesus offered the duke the ransom money for his father's life ; but the duke freely pardoned Ægeon, and would not take the money. And the duke went with the abbess and her newly-found husband and children into the convent, to hear this happy family discourse at leisure of the blessed ending of their adverse fortunes. And the two Dromios' humble joy must not be forgotten : they had their congratulations and greetings too, and each Dromio pleasantly complimented his brother on his good looks, being well pleased to see his own person (as in a glass) show so handsome in his brother.

Adriana had so well profited by the good counsel of her mother-in-law, that she never after cherished unjust suspicions, or was jealous of her husband.

Antipholus of Syracuse married the fair Luciana, the sister of his brother's wife ; and the good old Ægeon, with his wife and sons, lived at Ephesus many years. Nor did the unravelling of these perplexities so entirely remove every ground of mistake for the future, but that sometimes, to remind them of adventures past, comical blunders would happen, and the one Antipholus, and the one Dromio, be mistaken for the other, making altogether a pleasant and diverting Comedy of Errors.

MEASURE FOR MEASURE

IN the city of Vienna there
once reigned a duke of
such a mild and gentle
temper, that he suffered his subjects to neglect the laws with
impunity; and there was in
particular one law, the existence
of which was almost forgotten,
the duke never having put it in
force during his whole reign.
This was a law dooming any
man to the punishment of death,
who should live with a woman that was not his wife;
and this law through the lenity of the duke being utterly
disregarded, the holy institution of marriage became neglected, and complaints were every day made to the duke
by the parents of the young ladies in Vienna, that their
daughters had been seduced from their protection, and
were living as the companions of single men.

The good duke perceived with sorrow this growing
evil among his subjects, but he thought that a sudden
change in himself from the indulgence he had hitherto
shown, to the strict severity requisite to check this abuse,
would make his people (who had hitherto loved him) consider him as a tyrant; therefore he determined to absent
himself awhile from his dukedom, and depute another
to the full exercise of his power, that the law against

these dishonourable lovers might be put in effect, without giving offence by an unusual severity in his own person.

Angelo, a man who bore the reputation of a saint in Vienna for his strict and rigid life, was chosen by the duke as a fit person to undertake this important charge ; and when the duke imparted his design to Lord Escalus, his chief counsellor, Escalus said, " If any man in Vienna be of worth to undergo such ample grace and honour, it is Lord Angelo." And now the duke departed from Vienna under pretence of making a journey into Poland, leaving Angelo to act as the lord-deputy in his absence ; but the duke's absence was only a feigned one, for he privately returned to Vienna, habited like a friar, with the intent to watch unseen the conduct of the saintly-seeming Angelo.

It happened just about the time that Angelo was in vested with this new dignity, that a gentleman, whose name was Claudio, had seduced a young lady from her parents, and for this offence, by command of the new lord deputy, Claudio was taken up and committed to prison, and by virtue of the old law which had been so long neglected, Angelo sentenced Claudio to be beheaded. Great interest was made for the pardon of young Claudio, and the good Lord Escalus himself interceded for him. " Alas ! " said he, " this gentleman whom I would save had an honourable father, for whose sake I pray you pardon the young man's transgression." But Angelo replied, " We must not make a scarecrow of the law, set-ting it up to frighten birds of prey, till custom, finding it harmless, makes it their perch, and not their terror. Sir, he must die."

Lucio, the friend of Claudio, visited him in the prison, and Claudio said to him, " I pray you, Lucio, do me this kind service. Go to my sister Isabel, who this day pro-poses to enter the convent of Saint Clare, acquaint her with the danger of my state, implore her that she may make friends with the strict deputy ; bid her go herself to Angelo. I have great hopes in that, for she can discourse with prosperous art, and well she can persuade ; besides, there is a speechless dialect in youthful sorrow, such as moves men."

Isabel, the sister of Claudio, had, as he said, that day entered upon her noviciate in the convent, and it was her intent, after passing through her probation as a novice, to take the veil ; and she was inquiring of a nun concerning the rules of the convent, when they heard the voice of Lucio, who, as he entered that religious house, said, "Peace be in this place!" "Who is it that speaks?" said Isabel. "It is a man's voice," replied the nun. "Gentle Isabel, go to him, and learn his business : you may, I may not. When you have taken the veil, you must not speak with men but in the presence of the prioress ; then if you speak, you must not show your face, or if you show your face you must not speak." "And have you nuns no further privileges?" said Isabel. "Are not these large enough?" replied the nun. "Yes, truly," said Isabel : "I speak not as desiring more, but rather wishing a more strict restraint upon the sisterhood, the votarists of St. Clare." Again they heard the voice of Lucio, and the nun said, "He calls again. I pray you answer him." Isabel then went out to Lucio, and in answer to his salutation said, "Peace and prosperity! Who is it that calls?" Then Lucio, approaching her with reverence, said, "Hail, virgin, if such you be, as the roses in your cheeks proclaim you are no less. Can you bring me to the sight of Isabel, a novice of this place, and the fair sister to her unhappy brother Claudio?" "Why her unhappy brother?" said Isabel, "let me ask; for I am that Isabel, and his sister." "Fair and gentle lady," he replied, "your brother kindly greets you by me : he is in prison." "Woe is me! for what?" said Isabel. Lucio then told her Claudio was imprisoned for seducing a young maiden. "Ah," said she, "I fear it is my cousin Juliet." Juliet and Isabel were not related, but they called each other cousin in remembrance of their schoolday friendship; and as Isabel knew that Juliet loved Claudio, she feared she had been led by her affection for him into this transgression. "She it is," replied Lucio. "Why, then, let my brother marry Juliet," said Isabel. Lucio replied that Claudio would gladly marry Juliet, but that the lord deputy had sentenced him to die for his offence, "unless," said he, "you have the grace by your fair prayer to soften Angelo; and that is my business between you and your poor brother." "Alas!" said Isabel, "what poor ability is there in me to do him good? I doubt I have no power to move Angelo." "Our doubts are traitors," said Lucio, "and make us lose the good we might often win, by fearing to attempt it. Go to Lord Angelo! When maidens sue, and kneel, and weep, men give like gods." "I will see what I can do," said Isabel: "I will but stay to give the prioress notice of the affair, and then I will go to Angelo. Commend me to my brother; soon at night I will send him word of my success."

Isabel hastened to the palace and threw herself on her knees before Angelo, saying, "I am a woeful suitor to your honour, if it will please your honour to hear me." "Well, what is your suit?" said Angelo. She then made her petition in the most moving terms for her brother's life. But Angelo said, "Maiden, there is no remedy: your brother is sentenced, and he must die." "Oh, just but severe law!" said Isabel; "I *had* a brother, then— Heaven keep your honour!" and she was about to depart.

But Lucio, who had accompanied her, said, "Give it not over so; return to him again—entreat him, kneel down before him, hang upon his gown. You are too cold: if you should need a pin you could not with a more tame tongue desire it." Then again Isabel on her knees implored for mercy. "He is sentenced," said Angelo; "it is too late." "Too late!" said Isabel; "why, no:

I that do speak a word may call it back again. Believe this, my lord, no ceremony that to great ones belongs—not the king's crown, nor the deputed sword, the marshal's truncheon, nor the judge's robe—becomes them with one half so good a grace as mercy does." "Pray you begone," said Angelo. But still Isabel entreated ; and she said, " If my brother had been as you and you as he, you might have slipped like him, but he like you would not have been so stern. I would to Heaven I had your power, and you were Isabel. Should it then be thus ? No, I would tell you what it were to be a judge and what a prisoner." " Be content, fair maid," said Angelo ; " it is the law, not I, condemns your brother. Were he my kinsman, my brother, or my son, it should be thus with him. He must die to-morrow." " To-morrow ? " said Isabel ; " oh, that is sudden ! Spare him, spare him ! he is not prepared for death. Even for our kitchens we kill the fowl in season. Shall we serve Heaven with less respect than we minister to our gross selves ? Good, good my lord, bethink you, none have died for my brother's offence, though many have committed it. So you would be the first that gives this sentence, and he the first that suffers it. Go to your own bosom, my lord ; knock there and ask your heart what it does know that is like my brother's fault ; if it confess a natural guiltiness such as his is, let it not sound a thought against my brother's life." Her last words more moved Angelo than all she had before said, for the beauty of Isabel had raised a guilty passion in his heart, and he began to form thoughts of dishonourable love such as Claudio's crime had been ; and the conflict in his mind made him to turn away from Isabel, but she called him back, saying, " Gentle my lord, turn back ; hark how I will bribe you. Good my lord, turn back." " How, bribe me ! " said Angelo, astonished that she should think of offering him a bribe " Ay," said Isabel, " with such gifts that Heaven itself shall share with you ; not with golden treasures, or those glittering stones whose price is either rich or poor as fancy values them, but with true prayers that shall be up to heaven before sunrise—prayers from preserved souls, from fasting maids whose minds are dedicated to nothing temporal." " Well, come to me to-morrow," said Angelo. And for this short respite of her brother's life, and for this permission that she might be heard again, she left him with the joyful hope that she should at last prevail over his stern nature ; and as she went away she said, " Heaven keep your honour safe ! Heaven save your honour ! " Which when Angelo heard, he said within his heart, " Amen ! I would be saved from thee and from thy virtues " ; and then, affrighted at his own evil thoughts, he said, " What is this ? what is this ? Do I love her, that I desire to hear her speak again and feast upon her eyes ? What is it I dream on ? The cunning enemy of mankind to catch a saint with saints does bait the hook. Never could an immodest woman once stir my temper, but this virtuous woman subdues me quite. Ever till now, when men were fond I smiled and wondered at them."

In the guilty conflict in his mind Angelo suffered more that night than the prisoner he had so severely sentenced ; for in the prison Claudio was visited by the good duke, who in his friar's habit taught the young man the way to heaven, preaching to him the words of penitence and peace. But Angelo felt all the pangs of irresolute guilt : now wishing to seduce Isabel from the paths of innocence and honour, and now suffering remorse and horror for a crime as yet but intentional. But in the end his evil thoughts prevailed, and he who had so lately started at the offer of a bribe resolved to tempt this maiden with so high a bribe as she might not be able to resist—even with the precious gift of her dear brother's life.

When Isabel came in the morning, Angelo desired

she might be admitted alone to his presence ; and being there, he said to her, if she would yield to him her virgin honour, and transgress even as Juliet had done with Claudio, he would give her her brother's life ; " For," said he, " I love you, Isabel." " My brother," said Isabel, " did so love Juliet, and yet you tell me he shall die for it." " But," said Angelo, " Claudio shall not die if you will consent to visit me by stealth at night, even as Juliet left her father's house at night to come to Claudio." Isabel, in amazement at his words, that he should tempt her to the same fault for which he passed sentence of death upon her brother, said, " I would do as much for my poor brother as for myself ; that is, were I under sentence of death, the impression of keen whips I would wear as rubies, and go to my death as to a bed that longing I had been sick for, ere I would yield myself up to this shame." And then she told him she hoped he only spoke these words to try her virtue. But he said, " Believe me, on my honour my words express my purpose." Isabel, angered to the heart to hear him use the word honour to express such dishonourable purposes, said, " Ha ! little honour to be much believed, and most pernicious purpose ! I will proclaim thee, Angelo ; look for it ! Sign me a present pardon for my brother, or I will tell the world aloud what man thou art ! " " Who will believe you, Isabel ? " said Angelo : " my unsoiled name, the austereness of my life, my word vouched against yours, will outweigh your accusation. Redeem your brother by yielding to my will, or he shall die to-morrow. As for you, say what you can, my false will overweigh your true story. Answer me to-morrow."

" To whom should I complain ? Did I tell this, who would believe me ? " said Isabel, as she went towards the dreary prison where her brother was confined. When she arrived there, her brother was in pious conversation with the duke, who in his friar's habit had also visited

Juliet, and brought both these guilty lovers to a proper
sense of their fault; and unhappy Juliet, with tears and
a true remorse, confessed that she was more to blame
than Claudio, in that she willingly consented to his dishonourable solicitations.

As Isabel entered the room where Claudio was confined, she said, "Peace be here, grace and good company." "Who is there?" said the disguised duke;
"come in: the wish deserves a welcome." "My business is a word or two with Claudio," said Isabel. Then
the duke left them together, and desired the provost who
had the charge of the prisoners to place him where he
might overhear their conversation.

"Now, sister, what is the comfort?" said Claudio.
Isabel told him he must prepare for death on the morrow.
"Is there no remedy?" said Claudio. "Yes, brother,"
replied Isabel, "there is; but such a one as, if you consented to it, would strip your honour from you and leave
you naked." "Let me know the point," said Claudio.
"Oh, I do fear you, Claudio," replied his sister; "and
I quake lest you should wish to live, and more respect the
trifling term of six or seven winters added to your life
than your perpetual honour. Do you dare to die? The
sense of death is most in apprehension, and the poor beetle
that we tread upon feels a pang as great as when a giant
dies." "Why do you give me this shame?" said
Claudio. "Think you I can fetch a resolution from
flowery tenderness? If I must die, I will encounter darkness as a bride and hug it in my arms." "There spoke
my brother," said Isabel; "there my father's grave did
utter forth a voice. Yes, you must die; yet—would you
think it, Claudio?—this outward sainted deputy, if I
would yield to him my virgin honour, would grant your
life. Oh, were it but my life, I would lay it down for
your deliverance as frankly as a pin!" "Thanks, dear
Isabel," said Claudio. "Be ready to die to-morrow,"

O

said Isabel. " Death is a fearful thing," said Claudio.
" And shamed life a hateful," replied his sister. But the
thoughts of death now overcame the constancy of
Claudio's temper, and terrors, such as the guilty only at
their deaths do know, assailing him, he cried out, " Sweet
sister, let me live ! The sin you do to save a brother's
life, nature dispenses with the deed so far that it becomes
a virtue." " Oh, faithless coward ! oh, dishonest
wretch ! " said Isabel ; " would you preserve your life
by your sister's shame ? Oh ! fie, fie, fie ! I thought, my
brother, you had in you such a mind of honour, that had
you twenty heads to render up on twenty blocks, you
would have yielded them up all before your sister should
stoop to such dishonour." " Nay, hear me, Isabel ! "
said the agonised Claudio.

But what he would have said in defence of his weakness in desiring to live by the dishonour of his virtuous
sister, was interrupted by the entrance of the duke, who
said, " Claudio, I have overheard what has passed
between you and your sister. Angelo had never the purpose to corrupt her ; what he said has only been to make
trial of her virtue. She having the truth of honour in
her, has given to him that gracious denial which he is
most glad to receive. There is no hope that he will
pardon you, therefore pass your hours in prayer, and
make ready for death." Then Claudio repented of his
weakness, and said, " Let me ask my sister's pardon. I
am so out of love with life that I will sue to be rid of it."
And Claudio retired, overwhelmed with shame and sorrow
for his fault.

The duke being now alone with Isabel, commended
her virtuous resolution, saying, " The hand that made
you fair has made you good." " Oh," said Isabel, " how
much is the good duke deceived in Angelo ! if ever he
return, and I can speak to him, I will discover his government." Isabel knew not that she was even now making

the discovery she threatened. The duke replied, ' That shall not be much amiss ; yet as the matter now stands, Angelo will repel your accusation ; therefore lend an attentive ear to my advisings. I believe that you may most righteously do a poor wronged lady a merited benefit, redeem your brother from the angry law, do no stain to your own most gracious person, and much please the absent duke, if peradventure he shall ever return to have notice of this business." Isabel said she had a spirit to do anything he desired, provided it was nothing wrong. " Virtue is bold, and never fearful," said the duke ; and then he asked her if she had ever heard of Mariana, the sister of Frederick, the great soldier who was drowned at sea. " I have heard of the lady," said Isabel, " and good words went with her name." " This lady," said the duke, " is the wife of Angelo ; but her marriage dowry was on board the vessel in which her brother perished, and mark how heavily this befell to the poor gentlewoman ! for, beside the loss of a most noble and renowned brother, who in his love towards her was ever most kind and natural, in the wreck of her fortune she lost the affections of her husband, the well-seeming Angelo, who, pretending to discover some dishonour in this honourable lady (though the true cause was the loss of her dowry), left her in her tears, and dried not one of them with his comfort. His unjust unkindness, that in all reason should have quenched her love, has, like an impediment in the current, made it more unruly, and Mariana loves her cruel husband with the full continuance of her first affection. The duke then more plainly unfolded his plan. It was that Isabel should go to Lord Angelo, and seemingly consent to come to him as he desired, at midnight ; that by this means she would obtain the promised pardon ; and that Mariana should go in her stead to the appointment, and pass herself upon Angelo in the dark for Isabel   " Nor, gentle daughter,"

said the feigned friar, " fear you to do this thing : Angelo
is her husband, and to bring them thus together is no
sin." Isabel, being pleased with this project, departed to
do as he directed her ; and he went to apprise Mariana
of their intention. He had before this time visited this
unhappy lady in his assumed character, giving her
religious instruction and friendly consolation, at which
times he had learned her sad story from her own lips ;
and now she, looking upon him as a holy man, readily
consented to be directed by him in this undertaking.

When Isabel returned from her interview with Angelo
to the house of Mariana, where the duke had appointed
her to meet him, he said, " Well met, and in good time !
what is the news from this good deputy ? " Isabel
related the manner in which she had settled the affair.
" Angelo," said she, " has a garden surrounded with a
brick wall, on the western side of which is a vineyard,
and to that vineyard is a gate." And then she showed
to the duke and Mariana two keys that Angelo had given
her, and she said, " This bigger key opens the vineyard
gate, this other a little door which leads from the vineyard
to the garden. There I have made my promise at the
dead of night to call upon him, and have got from him
his word of assurance for my brother's life. I have taken
a due and wary note of the place, and with whispering
and most guilty diligence he showed me the way twice
over." " Are there no other tokens agreed upon
between you that Mariana must observe ? " said the duke.
" No, none," said Isabel, " only to go when it is dark.
I have told him my time can be but short, for I have
made him think a servant comes along with me, and that
this servant is persuaded I come about my brother."
The duke commended her discreet management, and
she, turning to Mariana, said, " Little have you to say to
Angelo when you depart from him, but soft and low,
Remember now my brother ! "

Mariana was that night conducted to the appointed place by Isabel, who rejoiced that she had, as she supposed, by this device preserved both her brother's life and her own honour. But that her brother's life was safe the duke was not well satisfied, and therefore at midnight he again repaired to the prison, and it was well for Claudio that he did so, else would Claudio have that night been beheaded, for soon after the duke entered the prison an order came from the cruel deputy commanding that Claudio should be beheaded, and his head sent to him by five o'clock in the morning. But the duke persuaded the provost to put off the execution of Claudio, and to deceive Angelo by sending him the head of a man who died that morning in the prison. And to prevail upon the provost to agree to this, the duke, whom still the provost suspected not to be anything more or greater than he seemed, showed the provost a letter written with the duke's hand, and sealed with his seal, which, when the provost saw, he concluded this friar must have some secret order from the absent duke, and therefore he consented to spare Claudio, and he cut off the dead man's head and carried it to Angelo.

Then the duke, in his own name, wrote to Angelo a letter, saying that certain accidents had put a stop to his journey, and that he should be in Vienna by the following morning, requiring Angelo to meet him at the entrance of the city, there to deliver up his authority; and the duke also commanded it to be proclaimed that if any of his subjects craved redress for injustice, they should exhibit their petitions in the street on his first entrance into the city.

Early in the morning Isabel came to the prison, and the duke, who there awaited her coming, for secret reasons thought it good to tell her that Claudio was beheaded; therefore when Isabel inquired if Angelo had sent the pardon for her brother, he said, " Angelo has released Claudio from this world. His head is off, and sent to the deputy." The much-grieved sister cried out, " O unhappy Claudio, wretched Isabel, injurious world, most wicked Angelo ! " The seeming friar bid her take comfort, and when she was become a little calm, he acquainted her with the near prospect of the duke's return, and told her in what manner she should proceed in preferring her complaint against Angelo ; and he bade her not to fear if the cause should seem to go against her for a while. Leaving Isabel sufficiently instructed, he next went to Mariana, and gave her counsel in what manner she also should act.

Then the duke laid aside his friar's habit, and in his own royal robes, amidst a joyful crowd of his faithful subjects assembled to greet his arrival, he entered the city of Vienna, where he was met by Angelo, who delivered up his authority in the proper form. And there came Isabel in the manner of a petitioner for redress, and said, " Justice, most royal duke ! I am the sister of one Claudio, who for the seducing a young maid was condemned to lose his head. I made my suit to Lord Angelo for my brother's pardon. It were needless to tell your Grace how I prayed and kneeled, how he repelled me, and how I replied, for this was of much length. The vile conclusion I now begin with grief and shame to utter. Angelo would not but by my yielding to his dishonourable love release my brother ; and after much debate within myself, my sisterly remorse overcame my virtue, and I did yield to him. But the next morning betimes Angelo, forfeiting his promise, sent a warrant for my poor brother's head ! " The duke affected to disbelieve her story, and Angelo said that grief for her brother's death, who had suffered by the due course of the law, had disordered her senses. And now another suitor approached, which was Mariana, and Mariana said, " Noble prince, as there comes light from heaven and truth from breath, as there is sense in truth and truth in virtue, I am this man's wife, and, my good lord, the words of Isabel are false, for the night she says she was with Angelo, I passed that night with him in the garden-house. As this is true, let me in safety rise, or else for ever be fixed here a marble monument." Then did Isabel appeal for the truth of what she had said to Friar Lodowick, that being the name the duke had assumed in his disguise. Isabel and Mariana had both obeyed his instructions in what they said, the duke intending that the innocence of Isabel should be plainly proved in that public manner before the whole city of Vienna ; but Angelo little thought that it was from such a cause that they thus differed in their story, and he hoped from their contradictory evidence to be able to clear himself from the accusation of Isabel, and he said, assuming the look of offended innocence, " I did but smile till now ; but, good my lord, my patience here is touched, and I perceive these poor distracted women are but the instruments of some greater one who sets them on. Let me have way, my lord, to find this practice out." " Ay, with all my heart," said the duke, " and punish them to the height of your pleasure. You, Lord Escalus, sit with Lord Angelo, lend him your pains to discover this abuse : the friar is sent for that set them on, and when he comes do with your injuries as may seem best in any chastisement. I for a while will leave you, but stir not you, Lord Angelo, till you have well determined upon this slander."

The duke then went away, leaving Angelo well pleased to be deputed judge and umpire in his own cause. But the duke was absent only while he threw off his royal robes and put on his friar's habit ; and in that disguise again he presented himself before Angelo and Escalus ; and the good old Escalus, who thought Angelo had been falsely accused, said to the supposed friar, " Come, sir, did you set these women on to slander Lord Angelo ? "

He replied, " Where is the duke? It is he should hear me speak." Escalus said, " The duke is in us, and we will hear you. Speak justly." " Boldly at least," retorted the friar ; and then he blamed the duke for leaving the cause of Isabel in the hands of him she had accused, and spoke so freely of many corrupt practices he had observed, while, as he said, he had been a looker-on in Vienna, that Escalus threatened him with torture for speaking against the state, and for censuring the conduct of the duke, and ordered him to be taken away to prison. Then, to the amazement of all present, and to the utter confusion of Angelo, the supposed friar threw off his disguise, and they saw it was the duke himself.

The duke first addressed Isabel. He said to her, " Come hither, Isabel. Your friar is now your prince ; but with my habit I have not changed my heart. I am still devoted to your service." " Oh, give me pardon," said Isabel, " that I, your vassal, have employed and troubled your unknown sovereignty." He answered that he had most need of forgiveness from her, for not having prevented the death of her brother, for not yet would he tell her that Claudio was living, meaning first to make a further trial of her goodness. Angelo now knew the duke had been a secret witness of his bad deeds, and he said, " O my dread lord, I should be guiltier than my guiltiness, to think I can be undiscernible, when I perceive your grace, like power divine, has looked upon my actions. Then, good prince, no longer prolong my shame, but let my trial be my own confession. Immediate sentence and death is all the grace I beg." The duke replied, " Angelo thy faults are manifest. We do condemn thee to the very block where Claudio stooped to death ; and with like haste away with him ; and for his possessions, Mariana, we do instate and widow you withal to buy you a better husband." " O my dear lord," said Mariana, " I crave no other, nor no better man " ; and

then on her knees, even as Isabel had begged the life of
Claudio, did this kind wife of an ungrateful husband beg
the life of Angelo ; and she said, " Gentle my liege,
O good my lord ! Sweet Isabel, take my part ! Lend
me your knees, and all my life to come I will lend you all
my life to do you service ! " The duke said, " Against all
sense you importune her. Should Isabel kneel down to
beg for mercy, her brother's ghost would break his paved
bed, and take her hence in horror." Still Mariana said,
" Isabel, sweet Isabel, do but kneel by me, hold up your
hand ! say nothing—I will speak all. They say, best men
are moulded out of faults, and for the most part become
much the better for being a little bad. So may my husband. O Isabel, will you not lend a knee ? " The duke
then said, " He dies for Claudio." But much pleased
was the good duke, when his own Isabel, from whom he
expected all gracious and honourable acts, kneeled down
before him, and said, " Most bounteous sir, look, if it
please you, on this man condemned, as if my brother
lived. I partly think a due sincerity governed his deeds,
till he did look on me. Since it is so, let him not die !
My brother had but justice, in that he did the thing for
which he died."

The duke, as the best reply he could make to this
noble petitioner for her enemy's life, sending for Claudio
from his prison-house, where he lay doubtful of his
destiny, presented to her this lamented brother living ;
and he said to Isabel, " Give me your hand, Isabel ; for
your lovely sake I pardon Claudio. Say you will be mine,
and he shall be my brother too." By this time Lord
Angelo perceived he was safe ; and the duke observing
his eye to brighten up a little, said, " Well, Angelo, look
that you love your wife ; her worth has obtained your
pardon. Joy to you, Mariana ! Love her, Angelo ! I
have confessed her, and know her virtue." Angelo
remembered, when dressed in a little brief authority,

how hard his heart had been, and felt how sweet is mercy.

The duke commanded Claudio to marry Juliet, and offered himself again to the acceptance of Isabel, whose virtuous and noble conduct had won her prince's heart. Isabel, not having taken the veil, was free to marry ; and the friendly offices, while hid under the disguise of a humble friar, which the noble duke had done for her, made her with grateful joy accept the honour he offered her ; and when she became Duchess of Vienna, the excellent example of the virtuous Isabel worked such a complete reformation among the young ladies of that city, that from that time none ever fell into the transgression of Juliet, the repentant wife of the reformed Claudio. And the mercy-loving duke long reigned with his beloved Isabel, the happiest of husbands and of princes.

TWELFTH NIGHT,
OR, WHAT YOU WILL

S EBASTIAN and his sister Viola, a young gentleman and lady of Messaline, were twins, and (which was accounted a great wonder) from their birth they so much resembled each other that, but for the difference in their dress, they could not be known apart. They were both born in one hour, and in one hour they were both in danger of perishing, for they were shipwrecked on the coast of Illyria as they were making a sea voyage together. The ship on board of which they were split on a rock in a violent storm, and a very small number of the ship's company escaped with their lives. The captain of the vessel, with a few of the sailors that were saved, got to land in a small boat, and with them they brought Viola safe on shore, where she, poor lady, instead of rejoicing at her own deliverance, began to lament her brother's loss; but the captain comforted her with the assurance that he had seen her brother, when the ship split, fasten himself to a strong mast, on which, as long as he could see anything of him for the distance, he perceived him borne up above the waves. Viola was much consoled by the hope this account gave her, and now considered how she was to dispose of herself in a strange country so far from home, and she asked the captain if he knew anything of Illyria. " Ay, very well, madam," replied the captain, " for I was born not three hours' travel from this place." " Who governs here ? " said Viola. The captain told her Illyria was governed by Orsino, a duke noble in nature as well as dignity. Viola said she had heard her father speak of this Orsino, and that he was unmarried then. " And he is so now," replied the captain ; " or was so very lately, for but a month ago I went from here, and then it was the general talk (as you know what great ones do the people will prattle of) that Orsino sought the love of fair Olivia, a virtuous maid, the daughter of a count who died twelve months ago, leaving Olivia to the protection of her brother, who shortly after died also ; and for the love of this dear brother, they say, she has abjured the sight and company of men." Viola, who was herself in such a sad affliction for her brother's loss, wished she could live with this lady who so tenderly mourned a brother's death. She asked the captain if he could introduce her to Olivia, saying she would willingly serve this lady. But he replied this would be a hard thing to accomplish, because the Lady Olivia would admit no person into her house since her brother's death, not even the duke himself. Then Viola formed another project in her mind, which was, in a man's habit, to serve the Duke Orsino as a page. It was a strange fancy in a young lady to put on male attire and pass for a boy, but the forlorn and unprotected state of Viola, who was young and of uncommon beauty, alone, and in a foreign land, must plead her excuse.

She having observed a fair behaviour in the captain, and that he showed a friendly concern for her welfare, entrusted him with her design, and he readily engaged to assist her. Viola gave him money and directed him to furnish her with suitable apparel, ordering her clothes to be made of the same colour and in the same fashion her brother Sebastian used to wear, and when she was dressed in her manly garb she looked so exactly like her brother, that some strange errors happened by means of their being mistaken for each other, for, as will afterwards appear, Sebastian was also saved.

Viola's good friend, the captain, when he had transformed this pretty lady into a gentleman, having some interest at court, got her presented to Orsino under the feigned name of Cesario. The duke was wonderfully pleased with the address and graceful deportment of this handsome youth, and made Cesario one of his pages, that being the office Viola wished to obtain, and she so well fulfilled the duties of her new station, and showed such a ready observance and faithful attachment to her lord, that she soon became his most favoured attendant. To Cesario Orsino confided the whole history of his love for the Lady Olivia. To Cesario he told the long and unsuccessful suit he had made to one who, rejecting his long services and despising his person, refused to admit him to her presence ; and for the love of this lady, who had so unkindly treated him, the noble Orsino, forsaking the sports of the field and all manly exercises in which he used to delight, passed his hours in ignoble sloth, listening to the effeminate sounds of soft music, gentle airs, and passionate love songs, and, neglecting the company of the wise and learned lords with whom he used to associate, he was now all day long conversing with young Cesario. Unmeet companion no doubt his grave courtiers thought Cesario was for their once noble master, the great Duke Orsino.

It is a dangerous matter for young maidens to be the confidants of handsome young dukes, which Viola too soon found to her sorrow, for all that Orsino told her he endured for Olivia she presently perceived she suffered for the love of him, and much it moved her wonder that Olivia could be so regardless of this her peerless lord and master, whom she thought no one should behold without the deepest admiration, and she ventured gently to hint to Orsino that it was a pity he should affect a lady who was so blind to his worthy qualities, and she said, " If a lady were to love you, my lord, as you love Olivia (and perhaps there may be one who does), if you could not love her in return, would you not tell her that you could not love, and must not she be content with this answer ? " But Orsino would not admit of this reasoning, for he denied that it was possible for any woman to love as he did. He said no woman's heart was big enough to hold so much love, and therefore it was unfair to compare the love of any lady for him to his love for Olivia. Now, though Viola had the utmost deference for the duke's opinions, she could not help thinking this was not quite true, for she thought her heart had full as much love in it as Orsino's had, and she said, " Ah ! but I know, my lord—— " " What do you know, Cesario ? " said Orsino. " Too well I know," replied Viola, " what love women may owe to men. They are as true of heart as we are. My father had a daughter who loved a man as I, perhaps, were I a woman, should love your lordship." " And what is her history ? " said Orsino. " A blank, my lord," replied Viola : " she never told her love, but let concealment, like a worm in the bud, prey on her damask cheek. She pined in thought, and, with a green and yellow melancholy, she sat like Patience on a monument, smiling at grief." The duke inquired if this lady died of her love ; but to this question Viola returned an evasive answer, as probably she had feigned the story, to speak words expressive of the secret love and silent grief she suffered for Orsino.

While they were talking, a gentleman entered whom the duke had sent to Olivia, and he said, " So please you, my lord, I might not be admitted to the lady, but by her handmaid she returned you this answer : ' Until seven

years hence, the element itself shall not behold her face ;
but, like a cloisteress, she will walk veiled, watering her
chamber with her tears for the sad remembrance of her
dead brother.'" On hearing this, the duke exclaimed,
" Oh ! she that has a heart of this fine frame, to pay this
debt of love to a dead brother, how will she love, when
the rich golden shaft has touched her heart ! " And then
he said to Viola, " You know, Cesario, I have told you
all the secrets of my heart ; therefore, good youth, go to
Olivia's house. Be not denied access ; stand at her
doors, and tell her there your fixed foot shall grow
till you have audience." " And if I do speak to her, my
lord, what then ? " said Viola. " Oh, then," replied
Orsino, " unfold to her the passion of my love. Make a
long discourse to her of my dear faith. It will well become you to act my woes, for she will attend more to you
than to one of graver aspect."

Away then went Viola ; but not willingly did she
undertake this courtship, for she was to woo a lady to
become a wife to him she wished to marry ; but having
undertaken the affair, she performed it with fidelity, and
Olivia soon heard that a youth was at her door who insisted upon being admitted to her presence. " I told
him," said the servant, " that you were sick : he said
he knew you were, and therefore he came to speak with
you. I told him that you were asleep : he seemed to
have a foreknowledge of that too, and said that therefore
he must speak with you. What is to be said to him,
lady ? for he seems fortified against all denial, and will
speak with you, whether you will or no." Olivia, curious
to see who this peremptory messenger might be, desired
he might be admitted ; and throwing her veil over her face,
she said she would once more hear Orsino's embassy, not
doubting but that he came from the duke, by his importunity Viola entering, put on the most manly air she
could assume, and affecting the fine courtier's language of

great men's pages, she said to the veiled lady, " Most
radiant, exquisite, and matchless beauty, I pray you tell
me if you are the lady of the house, for I should be sorry
to cast away my speech upon another ; for besides that it
is excellently well penned, I have taken great pains to
learn it." " Whence come you, sir ? " said Olivia. " I
can say little more than I have studied," replied Viola ;
" and that question is out of my part." " Are you
a comedian ? " said Olivia. " No," replied Viola ; " and
yet I am not that which I play " ; meaning that she,
being a woman, feigned herself to be a man. And again
she asked Olivia if she were the lady of the house. Olivia
said she was ; and then Viola, having more curiosity to
see her rival's features than haste to deliver her master's
message, said, " Good madam, let me see your face."
With this bold request Olivia was not averse to comply ;
for this haughty beauty, whom the Duke Orsino had
loved so long in vain, at first sight conceived a passion for
the supposed page, the humble Cesario.

When Viola asked to see her face, Olivia said, " Have
you any commission from your lord and master to nego-
tiate with my face ? " And then, forgetting her determination to go veiled for seven long years, she drew aside
her veil, saying, " But I will draw the curtain and show
the picture. Is it not well done ? " Viola replied, " It is
beauty truly mixed ; the red and white upon your cheeks
is by Nature's own cunning hand laid on. You are the
most cruel lady living, if you will lead these graces to the
grave, and leave the world no copy." " O sir," replied
Olivia, " I will not be so cruel. The world may have an
inventory of my beauty. As, *item*, two lips, indifferent
red ; *item*, two grey eyes, with lids to them ; one neck ;
one chin, and so forth. Were you sent here to praise
me ? " Viola replied, " I see what you are ; you are too
proud, but you are fair. My lord and master loves you.
Oh, such a love could but be recompensed, though you

were crowned the queen of beauty ; for Orsino loves you with adoration and with tears, with groans that thunder love, and sighs of fire." " Your lord," said Olivia, " knows well my mind. I cannot love him ; yet I doubt not he is virtuous : I know him to be noble and of high estate, of fresh and spotless youth. All voices proclaim him learned, courteous, and valiant ; yet I cannot love him, he might have taken his answer long ago." " If I did love you as my master does," said Viola, " I would make me a willow cabin at your gates, and call upon your name. I would write complaining sonnets on Olivia, and sing them in the dead of the night ; your name should sound among the hills, and I would make Echo, the babbling gossip of the air, cry out, *Olivia !* Oh, you should not rest between the elements of earth and air, but you should pity me." " You might do much," said Olivia : " what is your parentage ? " Viola replied, " Above my fortunes, yet my state is well. I am a gentleman." Olivia now reluctantly dismissed Viola, saying, " Go to your master, and tell him I cannot love him. Let him send no more, unless perchance you come again to tell me how he takes it." And Viola departed, bidding the lady farewell by the name of Fair Cruelty. When she was gone, Olivia repeated the words, *Above my fortunes, yet my state is well. I am a gentleman.* And she said aloud, " I will be sworn he is ; his tongue, his face, his limbs, action, and spirit, plainly show he is a gentleman." And then she wished Cesario was the duke ; and perceiving the fast hold he had taken on her affections, she blamed herself for her sudden love ; but the gentle blame which people lay upon their own faults has no deep root, and presently the noble Lady Olivia so far forgot the inequality between her fortunes and those of this seeming page, as well as the maidenly reserve which is the chief ornament of a lady's character, that she resolved to court the love of young Cesario, and sent a servant after him

P

with a diamond ring, under the pretence that he had left it with her as a present from Orsino. She hoped by thus artfully making Cesario a present of the ring, she should give him some intimation of her design ; and truly it did make Viola suspect, for knowing that Orsino had sent no ring by her, she began to recollect that Olivia's looks and manner were expressive of admiration, and she presently guessed her master's mistress had fallen in love with her. " Alas ! " said she, " the poor lady might as well love a dream. Disguise I see is wicked, for it has caused Olivia to breathe as fruitless sighs for me as I do for Orsino."

Viola returned to Orsino's palace, and related to her lord the ill success of the negotiation, repeating the command of Olivia, that the duke should trouble her no more. Yet still the duke persisted in hoping that the gentle Cesario would in time be able to persuade her to show some pity, and therefore he bade him he should go to her again the next day. In the meantime, to pass away the tedious interval, he commanded a song which he loved to be sung ; and he said, " My good Cesario, when I heard that song last night, methought it did relieve my passion much. Mark it, Cesario, it is old and plain. The spinsters and the knitters when they sit in the sun, and the young maids that weave their thread with bone, chant this song. It is silly, yet I love it, it tells of the innocence of love in the old times."

SONG.

Come away, come away, Death !
   And in sad cypress let me be laid ;
Fly away, fly away, breath !
   I am slain by a fair cruel maid.
My shroud of white stuck all with yew, O, prepare it,
My part of death no one so true did share it.

Not a flower, not a flower sweet,
   On my black coffin let there be strown :
Not a friend, not a friend greet
   My poor corpse, where my bones shall be thrown.
A thousand thousand sighs to save, lay me, O, where
Sad true lover never finds my grave, to weep there.

Viola did not fail to mark the words of the old song, which in such true simplicity described the pangs of unrequited love, and she bore testimony in her countenance of feeling what the song expressed. Her sad looks were observed by Orsino, who said to her, " My life upon it, Cesario, though you are so young, your eye has looked upon some face that it loves; has it not, boy?" "A little, with your leave," replied Viola. " And what kind of woman, and of what age is she?" said Orsino. " Of your age, and of your complexion, my lord," said Viola; which made the duke smile to hear this fair young boy loved a woman so much older than himself and of a man's dark complexion; but Viola secretly meant Orsino, and not a woman like him.

When Viola made her second visit to Olivia, she found no difficulty in gaining access to her. Servants soon discover when their ladies delight to converse with handsome young messengers; and the instant Viola arrived, the gates were thrown wide open, and the duke's page was shown into Olivia's apartment with great respect; and when Viola told Olivia that she was come once more to plead in her lord's behalf, this lady said, " I desired you never to speak of him again; but if you would undertake another suit, I had rather hear you solicit than music from the spheres." This was pretty plain speaking, but Olivia soon explained herself still more plainly, and openly confessed her love; and when she saw displeasure with perplexity expressed in Viola's face, she said, " Oh, what a deal of scorn looks beautiful in the contempt and anger of his lip! Cesario, by the roses of the spring, by maidhood honour, and by truth, I love you so, that, in spite of your pride, I have neither wit nor reason to conceal my passion." But in vain the lady wooed: Viola hastened from her presence, threatening never more to come to plead Orsino's love; and all the reply she made to Olivia's fond solicitations was a declaration of a resolution *Never to love any woman*.

No sooner had Viola left the lady than a claim was made upon her valour. A gentleman, a rejected suitor of Olivia, who had learned how that lady had favoured the duke's messenger, challenged him to fight a duel. What should poor Viola do, who, though she carried a manlike outside, had a true woman's heart, and feared to look on her own sword ?

When she saw her formidable rival advancing towards her with his sword drawn, she began to think of confessing that she was a woman ; but she was relieved at once from her terror, and the shame of such a discovery, by a stranger that was passing by, who made up to them, and as if he had been long known to her, and were her dearest friend, said to her opponent, " If this young gentleman has done offence, I will take the fault on me ; and if you offend him, I will for his sake defy you." Before Viola had time to thank him for his protection, or to inquire the reason of his kind interference, her new friend met with an enemy where his bravery was of no use to him ; for the officers of justice coming up at that instant, apprehended the stranger in the duke's name to answer for an offence he had committed some years before ; and he said to Viola, " This comes with seeking you ; " and then he asked her for a purse, saying, " Now my necessity makes me ask for my purse, and it grieves me much more for what I cannot do for you, than for what befalls myself. You stand amazed, but be of comfort." His words did indeed amaze Viola, and she protested she knew him not, nor had ever received a purse from him ; but for the kindness he had just shown her, she offered him a small sum of money, being nearly the whole she possessed. And now the stranger spoke severe things, charging her with ingratitude and unkindness. He said, " This youth whom you see here

I snatched from the jaws of death, and for his sake alone I came to Illyria, and have fallen into this danger." But the officers cared little for hearkening to the complaints of their prisoner, and they hurried him off, saying, " What is that to us ? " And as he was carried away he called Viola by the name of Sebastian, reproaching the supposed Sebastian for disowning his friend, as long as he was within hearing. When Viola heard herself called Sebastian, though the stranger was taken away too hastily for her to ask an explanation, she conjectured that this seeming mystery might arise from her being mistaken for her brother ; and she began to cherish hopes that it was her brother whose life this man said he had preserved. And so indeed it was. The stranger, whose name was Antonio, was a sea captain. He had taken Sebastian up into his ship when, almost exhausted with fatigue, he was floating on the mast to which he had fastened him self in the storm. Antonio conceived such a friendship for Sebastian that he resolved to accompany him whithersoever he went ; and when the youth expressed a curiosity to visit Orsino's court, Antonio, rather than part from him, came to Illyria, though he knew if his person should be known there his life would be in danger, because in a sea-fight he had once dangerously wounded the Duke Orsino's nephew. This was the offence for which he was now made prisoner.

Antonio and Sebastian had landed together but a few hours before Antonio met Viola. He had given his purse to Sebastian, desiring him to use it freely if he saw anything he wished to purchase, telling him he would wait at the inn while Sebastian went to view the town ; but, Sebastian not returning at the time appointed, Antonio had ventured out to look for him, and Viola being dressed the same, and in face so exactly resembling her brother, Antonio drew his sword (as he thought) in defence of the youth he had saved, and when Sebastian (as he supposed) disowned him, and denied him his own purse, no wonder he accused him of ingratitude.

Viola, when Antonio was gone, fearing a second invita-- tion to fight, slunk home as fast as she could. She had not been long gone, when her adversary thought he saw her return ; but it was her brother Sebastian, who happened to arrive at this place ; and he said, " Now, sir, have I met with you again ? there's for you " ; and struck Sebastian a blow. Sebastian was no coward ; he returned the blow with interest, and drew his sword.

A lady now put a stop to this duel, for Olivia came out of the house, and she too, mistaking Sebastian for Cesario, invited him to come into her house, expressing much sorrow at the rude attack he had met with. Though Sebastian was as much surprised at the courtesy of the lady as the rudeness of his unknown foe, yet he went very willingly into the house, and Olivia was delighted to find Cesario (as she thought him) become more sensible of her attentions ; for though their features were exactly the same, there was none of the contempt and anger to be seen in his face, which she had complained of when she told her love to Cesario.

Sebastian did not at all object to the fondness the lady lavished on him. He seemed to take it in very good part, yet he wondered how it had come to pass, and he was rather inclined to think Olivia was not in her right senses ; but perceiving that she was mistress of a fine house, and that she ordered her affairs and seemed to govern her family discreetly, and that in all but her so sudden love for him she appeared in the full possession of her reason, he well approved of the courtship ; and Olivia, finding Cesario in this good humour, and fearing he might change his mind, proposed that, as she had a priest in the house, they should be instantly married. Sebastian assented to this proposal, and when the marriage ceremony was over he left his lady for a short time,

intending to go and tell his friend Antonio the good
fortune that he had met with. In the meantime Orsino
came to visit Olivia, and at the moment he arrived before
Olivia's house the officers of justice brought their prisoner
Antonio before the duke. Viola was with Orsino, her
master; and when Antonio saw Viola, whom he still
imagined to be Sebastian, he told the duke in what manner
he had rescued this youth from the perils of the sea; and
after fully relating all the kindness he had really shown to
Sebastian, he ended his complaint with saying that for
three months, both day and night, this ungrateful youth
had been with him. But now, the Lady Olivia coming
forth from her house, the duke could no longer attend to
Antonio's story, and he said, " Here comes the countess :
now heaven walks on earth ! but for thee, fellow, thy
words are madness ; three months has this youth attended
on me ! " and then he ordered Antonio to be taken aside.
But Orsino's heavenly countess soon gave the duke cause
to accuse Cesario as much of ingratitude as Antonio had
done, for all the words he could hear Olivia speak were
words of kindness to Cesario ; and when he found his
page had obtained this high place in Olivia's favour, he
threatened him with all the terrors of his just revenge.
And as he was going to depart he called Viola to follow
him, saying, " Come, boy, with me ; my thoughts are
ripe for mischief." Though it seemed in his jealous rage
he was going to doom Viola to instant death, yet her love
made her no longer a coward, and she said she would
most joyfully suffer death to give her master ease. But
Olivia would not so lose her husband, and she cried,
" Where goes my Cesario ? " Viola replied, " After him
I love more than my life." Olivia, however, prevented
their departure by loudly proclaiming that Cesario was her
husband, and sent for the priest, who declared that not
two hours had passed since he had married the Lady
Olivia to this young man. In vain Viola protested she

was not married to Olivia ; the evidence of that lady and the priest made Orsino believe that his page had robbed him of the treasure he prized above his life. But thinking that it was past recall, he was bidding farewell to his faith-less mistress and the *young dissembler*, her husband, as he called Viola, warning her never to come in his sight again, when (as it seemed to them) a miracle appeared, for another Cesario entered and addressed Olivia as his wife. This new Cesario was Sebastian, the real husband of Olivia ; and when their wonder had a little ceased at seeing two persons with the same face, the same voice, and the same habit, the brother and sister began to ques-tion each other, for Viola could scarce be persuaded that her brother was living, and Sebastian knew not how to account for the sister he supposed drowned being found in the habit of a young man. But Viola presently ac-knowledged that she was indeed Viola and his sister under that disguise.

When all the errors were cleared up which the extreme likeness between this twin brother and sister had occasioned, they laughed at the Lady Olivia for the pleasant mistake she had made in falling in love with a woman ; and Olivia showed no dislike to her exchange when she found she had wedded the brother instead of the sister.

The hopes of Orsino were for ever at an end by this marriage of Olivia, and with his hopes all his fruitless love seemed to vanish away, and all his thoughts were fixed on the event of his favourite, young Cesario, being changed into a fair lady. He viewed Viola with great attention, and he remembered how very handsome he had always thought Cesario was, and he concluded she would look very beautiful in a woman's attire ; and then he remembered how often she had said *she loved him*, which at the time seemed only the dutiful expressions of a faith-ful page, but now he guessed that something more was meant, for many of her pretty sayings, which were like riddles to him, came now into his mind, and he no sooner remembered all these things than he resolved to make Viola his wife ; and he said to her (he still could not help calling her *Cesario* and *boy*), " Boy, you have said to me a thousand times that you should never love a woman like to me, and for the faithful service you have done for me so much beneath your soft and tender breeding, and since you have called me master so long, you shall now be your master's mistress and Orsino's true duchess."

Olivia, perceiving Orsino was making over that heart, which she had so ungraciously rejected, to Viola, invited them to enter her house, and offered the assistance of the good priest who had married her to Sebastian in the morning to perform the same ceremony in the remaining part of the day for Orsino and Viola. Thus the twin brother and sister were both wedded on the same day, the storm and shipwreck which had separated them being the means of bringing to pass their high and mighty fortunes. Viola was the wife of Orsino, the duke of Illyria, and Sebastian the husband of the rich and noble countess, the Lady Olivia.

TIMON
OF ATHENS

TIMON, a lord of Athens, in the enjoyment of a princely fortune, affected a humour of liberality which knew no limits. His almost infinite wealth could not flow in so fast, but he poured it out faster upon all sorts and degrees of people. Not the poor only tasted of his bounty, but great lords did not disdain to rank themselves among his dependants and followers. His table was resorted to by all the luxurious feasters, and his house was open to all comers and goers, at Athens. His large wealth combined with his free and prodigal nature to subdue all hearts to his love : men of all minds and dispositions tendered their services to Lord Timon, from the glass-faced flatterer, whose face reflects as in a mirror the present humour of his patron, to the rough and unbending cynic, who affecting a contempt of men's persons, and an indifference to worldly things, yet could not stand out against the gracious manners and munificent soul of Lord Timon, but would come (against his nature) to partake of his royal entertainments, and return most rich in his own estimation if he had received a nod or a salutation from Timon.

If a poet had composed a work which wanted **a**

recommendatory introduction to the world, he had no more
to do but to dedicate it to Lord Timon, and the poem was
sure of a sale, besides a present purse from the patron,
and daily access to his house and table. If a painter had
a picture to dispose of, he had only to take it to Lord
Timon, and pretend to consult his taste as to the merits
of it ; nothing more was wanting to persuade the liberal-
hearted lord to buy it. If a jeweller had a stone of price,
or a mercer rich costly stuffs, which for their costliness
lay upon his hands, Lord Timon's house was a ready
mart always open, where they might get off their wares or
their jewellery at any price, and the good-natured lord
would thank them into the bargain, as if they had done
him a piece of courtesy in letting him have the refusal of
such precious commodities. So that by these means his
house was thronged with superfluous purchases, of no
use but to swell uneasy and ostentatious pomp ; and his
person was still more inconveniently beset with a crowd
of these idle visitors, lying poets, painters, sharking trades-
men, lords, ladies, needy courtiers, and expectants, who
continually filled his lobbies, raining their fulsome flat-
teries in whispers in his ears, sacrificing to him with
adulation as to a god, making sacred the very stirrup by
which he mounted his horse, and seeming as though
they drank the free air but through his permission and
bounty.

Some of these daily dependants were young men of
birth, who (their means not answering to their extrava-
gance) had been put in prison by creditors, and redeemed
thence by Lord Timon ; these young prodigals thenceforward fastened upon his lordship, as if by common
sympathy he were necessarily endeared to all such spend-
thrifts and loose livers, who, not being able to follow him
in his wealth, found it easier to copy him in prodigality
and copious spending of what was not their own. One
of these flesh-flies was Ventidius, for whose debts,

unjustly contracted, Timon but lately had paid down the sum of five talents.

But among this confluence, this great flood of visitors, none were more conspicuous than the makers of presents and givers of gifts. It was fortunate for these men if Timon took a fancy to a dog or a horse, or any piece of cheap furniture which was theirs. The thing so praised, whatever it was, was sure to be sent the next morning with the compliments of the giver for Lord Timon's acceptance, and apologies for the unworthiness of the gift ; and this dog or horse, or whatever it might be, did not fail to produce from Timon's bounty, who would not be outdone in gifts, perhaps twenty dogs or horses, certainly presents of far richer worth, as these pretended donors knew well enough, and that their false presents were but the putting out of so much money at large and speedy interest. In this way Lord Lucius had lately sent to Timon a present of four milk-white horses trapped in silver, which this cunning lord had observed Timon upon some occasion to commend ; and another lord, Lucullus, had bestowed upon him in the same pretended way of free gift a brace of greyhounds, whose make and fleetness Timon had been heard to admire. These presents the easy-hearted lord accepted without suspicion of the dishonest views of the presenters ; and the givers of course were rewarded with some rich return—a diamond or some jewel of twenty times the value of their false and mercenary donation.

Sometimes these creatures would go to work in a more direct way, and with gross and palpable artifice, which yet the credulous Timon was too blind to see, would affect to admire and praise something that Timon possessed, a bargain that he had bought, or some late purchase, which was sure to draw from this yielding and soft-hearted lord a gift of the thing commended, for no service in the world done for it but the easy expense of a little cheap and obvious flattery. In this way Timon but the other day had given to one of these mean lords the bay courser which he himself rode upon, because his lordship had been pleased to say that it was a handsome beast and went well ; and Timon knew that no man ever justly praised what he did not wish to possess. For Lord Timon weighed his friends' affection with his own, and so fond was he of bestowing, that he could have dealt kingdoms to these supposed friends, and never have been weary.

Not that Timon's wealth all went to enrich these wicked flatterers : he could do noble and praiseworthy actions ; and when a servant of his once loved the daughter of a rich Athenian, but could not hope to obtain her by reason that in wealth and rank the maid was so far above him, Lord Timon freely bestowed upon his servant three Athenian talents, to make his fortune equal with the dowry which the father of the young maid demanded of him who should be her husband. But for the most part knaves and parasites had the command of his fortune, false friends whom he did not know to be such ; but, because they flocked around his person, he thought they must needs love him ; and because they smiled and flattered him, he thought surely that his conduct was approved by all the wise and good. And when he was feasting in the midst of all these flatterers and mock friends, when they were eating him up, and draining his fortunes dry with large draughts of richest wines drunk to his health and prosperity, he could not perceive the difference of a friend from a flatterer, but to his deluded eyes (made proud with the sight) it seemed a precious comfort to have so many, like brothers, commanding one another's fortunes (though it was his own fortune which paid all the costs), and with joy they would run over at the spectacle of such, as it appeared to him, truly festive and fraternal meeting.

But while he thus outwent the very heart of kindness, and poured out his bounty, as if Plutus, the god of gold, had been but his steward ; while thus he proceeded without care or stop, so senseless of expense that he would neither inquire how he could maintain it, nor cease his wild flow of riot ; his riches, which were not infinite, must needs melt away before a prodigality which knew no limits. But who should tell him so ? his flatterers ? they had an interest in shutting his eyes.

In vain did his honest steward Flavius try to represent to him his condition, laying his accounts before him, begging of him, praying of him, with an importunity that on any other occasion would have been unmannerly in a servant, beseeching him with tears to look into the state of his affairs. Timon would still put him off, and turn the discourse to something else ; for nothing is so deaf to remonstrance as riches turned to poverty, nothing is so unwilling to believe its situation, nothing so incredulous to its own true state, and hard to give credit to a reverse. Often had this good steward, this honest creature, when all the rooms of Timon's great house have been choked up with riotous feeders at his master's cost, when the floors have wept with drunken spilling of wine, and every apartment has blazed with lights and resounded with music and feasting, often had he retired by himself to some solitary spot, and wept faster than the wine ran from the wasteful casks within, to see the mad bounty of his lord, and to think, when the means were gone which bought him praises from all sorts of people, how quickly the breath would be gone of which the praise was made ; praises won in feasting would be lost in fasting, and at one cloud of winter showers these flies would disappear.

But now the time was come that Timon could shut his ears no longer to the representations of this faithful steward. Money must be had ; and when he ordered Flavius to sell some of his land for that purpose, Flavius informed him what he had in vain endeavoured at several times before to make him listen to, that most of his land was already sold or forfeited, and that all he possessed at present was not enough to pay the one-half of what he owed. Struck with wonder at this representation, Timon hastily replied, " My lands extended from Athens to Lacedæmon." " O my good lord," said Flavius, " the world is but a world, and has bounds : were it all yours to give it in a breath, how quickly were it gone ! "

Timon consoled himself that no villainous bounty had yet come from him, that if he had given his wealth away unwisely, it had not been bestowed to feed his vices but to cherish his friends ; and he bade the kind-hearted steward (who was weeping) to take comfort in the assurance that his master could never lack means while he had so many noble friends ; and this infatuated lord persuaded himself that he had nothing to do but to send and borrow—to use every man's fortune (that had ever tasted his bounty) in this extremity, as freely as his own. Then with a cheerful look, as if confident of the trial, he severally dispatched messengers to Lord Lucius, to Lords Lucullus and Sempronius, men upon whom he had lavished his gifts in past times without measure or moderation, and to Ventidius, whom he had lately released out of prison by paying his debts, and who by the death of his father was now come into possession of an ample fortune, and well enabled to requite Timon's courtesy ; to request of Ventidius the return of those five talents which he had paid for him, and of each of those noble lords the loan of fifty talents ; nothing doubting that their gratitude would supply his wants (if he needed it) to the amount of five hundred times fifty talents.

Lucullus was the first applied to. This mean lord had been dreaming overnight of a silver basin and cup, and when Timon's servant was announced, his sordid mind suggested to him that this was surely a making out

of his dream, and that Timon had sent him such a
present ; but when he understood the truth of the matter,
and that Timon wanted money, the quality of his faint
and watery friendship showed itself, for with many protestations he vowed to the servant that he had long fore-
seen the ruin of his master's affairs, and many a time had
he come to dinner, to tell him of it, and had come again
to supper, to try to persuade him to spend less, but he
would take no counsel nor warning by his coming ; and
true it was that he had been a constant attender (as he
said) at Timon's feasts, as he had in greater things tasted
his bounty ; but that he ever came with that intent, or
gave good counsel or reproof to Timon, was a base unworthy lie, which he suitably followed up with meanly
offering the servant a bribe, to go home to his master and
tell him that he had not found Lucullus at home.

As little success had the messenger who was sent to
Lord Lucius. This lying lord, who was full of Timon's
meat, and enriched almost to bursting with Timon's costly
presents, when he found the wind changed, and the fountain of so much bounty suddenly stopped, at first could
hardly believe it ; but on its being confirmed, he affected
great regret that he should not have it in his power to
serve Lord Timon, for unfortunately (which was a base
falsehood) he had made a great purchase the day before,
which had quite disfurnished him of the means at present
—the more beast he, he called himself, to put it out of
his power to serve so good a friend ; and he counted it
one of his greatest afflictions that his ability should fail
him to pleasure such an honourable gentleman.

Who can call any man friend that dips in the same
dish with him ? Just of this metal is every flatterer. In
the recollection of everybody Timon had been a father to
this Lucius, had kept up his credit with his purse.
Timon's money had gone to pay the wages of his servants,
to pay the hire of the labourers who had sweat to build

the fine houses which Lucius' pride had made necessary to him ; yet, oh ! the monster which man makes himself when he proves ungrateful ! This Lucius now denied to Timon a sum which, in respect of what Timon had bestowed on him, was less than charitable men afford to beggars.

Sempronius and every one of these mercenary lords to whom Timon applied in their turn returned the same evasive answer or direct denial ; even Ventidius, the redeemed and now rich Ventidius, refused to assist him with the loan of those five talents which Timon had not lent but generously given him in his distress.

Now was Timon as much avoided in his poverty as he had been courted and resorted to in his riches. Now the same tongues which had been loudest in his praises, extolling him as bountiful, liberal, and open-handed, were not ashamed to censure that very bounty as folly, that liberality as profuseness, though it had shown itself folly in nothing so truly as in the selection of such unworthy creatures as themselves for its objects. Now was Timon's princely mansion forsaken, and become a shunned and hated place, a place for men to pass by, not a place as formerly where every passenger must stop and taste of his wine and good cheer : now, instead of being thronged with feasting and tumultuous guests, it was beset with impatient and clamorous creditors, usurers, extortioners, fierce and intolerable in their demands, pleading bonds, interest, mortgages—iron-hearted men that would take no denial nor putting off, that Timon's house was now his jail, which he could not pass nor go in nor out for them, one demanding his due of fifty talents, another bringing in a bill of five thousand crowns, which if he would tell out his blood by drops, and pay them so, he had not enough in his body to discharge drop by drop.

In this desperate and irremediable state (as it seemed of his affairs, the eyes of all men were suddenly surprised

Q

at a new and incredible lustre which this setting sun put
forth. Once more Lord Timon proclaimed a feast, to
which he invited his accustomed guests—lords, ladies, all
that was great or fashionable in Athens. Lords Lucius
and Lucullus came, Ventidius, Sempronius, and the rest.
Who more sorry now than these fawning wretches when
they found (as they thought) that Lord Timon's poverty
was all pretence, and had been only put on to make trial
of their loves, to think that they should not have seen
through the artifice at the time, and have had the cheap
credit of obliging his lordship ? Yet who more glad to
find the fountain of that noble bounty, which they had
thought dried up, still fresh and running ? They came
dissembling, protesting, expressing deepest sorrow and
shame that when his lordship sent to them they should
have been so unfortunate as to want the present means to
oblige so honourable a friend. But Timon begged them
not to give such trifles a thought, for he had altogether
forgotten it. And these base fawning lords, though they
had denied him money in his adversity, yet could not
refuse their presence at this new blaze of his returning
prosperity. For the swallow follows not summer more
willingly than men of these dispositions follow the good
fortunes of the great, nor more willingly leaves winter
than these shrink from the first appearance of a reverse :
such summer birds are men. But now with music and
state the banquet of smoking dishes was served up, and
when the guests had a little done admiring whence the
bankrupt Timon could find means to furnish so costly a
feast, some doubting whether the scene which they saw
was real, as scarce trusting their own eyes ; at a signal
given the dishes were uncovered, and Timon's drift appeared : instead of those varieties and far-fetched dainties
which they expected, that Timon's epicurean table in past
times had so liberally presented, now appeared under the
covers of these dishes a preparation more suitable to

Timon's poverty, nothing but a little smoke and luke-warm water, fit feast for this knot of mouth-friends, whose professions were indeed smoke, and their hearts lukewarm and slippery as the water with which Timon welcomed his astonished guests, bidding them " Uncover, dogs, and lap ! " and, before they could recover their surprise, sprinkling it in their faces, that they might have enough, and throwing dishes and all after them, who now ran huddling out, lords and ladies, with their caps snatched up in haste, a splendid confusion ; Timon pursuing them, still calling them what they were, " Smooth smiling para-sites, destroyers under the mask of courtesy, affable wolves, meek bears, fools of fortune, feast-friends, time-flies ! " They, crowding out to avoid him, left the house more willingly than they had entered it, some losing their gowns and caps and some their jewels in the hurry, all glad to escape out of the presence of such a mad lord and the ridicule of his mock banquet.

This was the last feast which ever Timon made, and in it he took farewell of Athens and the society of men, for after that he betook himself to the woods, turning his back upon the hated city and upon all mankind ; wishing the walls of that detestable city might sink, and the houses fall upon their owners ; wishing all plagues which infest humanity, war, outrage, poverty, diseases, might fasten upon its inhabitants ; praying the just gods to confound all Athenians, both young and old, high and low ; so wishing, he went to the woods, where he said he should find the unkindest beast much kinder than mankind. He stripped himself naked, that he might retain no fashion of a man, and dug a cave to live in, and lived solitary in the manner of a beast, eating the wild roots and drinking water, flying from the face of his kind, and choosing rather to herd with wild beasts as more harmless and friendly than man.

What a change from Lord Timon the rich, Lord

Timon the delight of mankind, to Timon the naked, Timon the man-hater ! Where were his flatterers now ? Where were his attendants and retinue ? Would the bleak air, that boisterous servitor, be his chamberlain, to put his shirt on warm ? Would those stiff trees, that had outlived the eagle, turn young and airy pages to him, to skip on his errands when he bade them ? Would the cold brook, when it was iced with winter, administer to him his warm broths, and caudles when sick of an overnight's surfeit ? Or would the creatures that lived in those wild woods come and lick his hand and flatter him ?

Here on a day when he was digging for roots, his poor sustenance, his spade struck against something heavy, which proved to be gold, a great heap which some miser had probably buried in a time of alarm, thinking to have come again and taken it from its prison, but died before the opportunity had arrived, without making any man privy to the concealment ; so it lay, doing neither good nor harm, in the bowels of the earth, its mother, as if it had never come from thence, till the accidental striking of Timon's spade against it once more brought it to light.

Here was a mass of treasure which, if Timon had retained his old mind, was enough to have purchased him friends and flatterers again ; but Timon was sick of the false world, and the sight of gold was poisonous to his eyes, and he would have restored it to the earth, but that, thinking of the infinite calamities which by means of gold happen to mankind, how the lure of it causes robberies, oppression, injustice, briberies, violence, and murder among men, he had a pleasure in imagining (such a rooted hatred did he bear to his species) that out of this heap which in digging he had discovered might arise some mischief to plague mankind. And some soldiers passing through the woods near to his cave at that instant, which proved to be a part of the troops of the Athenian captain Alcibiades, who, upon some disgust taken against the

senators of Athens (the Athenians were ever noted to be
a thankless and ungrateful people, giving disgust to their
generals and best friends) was marching at the head of the
same triumphant army which he had formerly headed in
their defence, to war against them; Timon, who liked
their business well, bestowed upon their captain the gold
to pay his soldiers, requiring no other service from him
than that he should with his conquering army lay Athens
level with the ground, and burn, slay, kill all her inhabitants, not sparing the old men for their white beards, for
(he said) they were usurers, nor the young children for
their seeming innocent smiles, for those (he said) would
live, if they grew up, to be traitors; but to steel his eyes
and ears against any sights or sounds that might awaken
compassion, and not to let the cries of virgins, babes, or
mothers hinder him from making one universal massacre
of the city, but to confound them all in his conquest;
and when he had conquered, he prayed that the gods
would confound him also, the conqueror, so thoroughly
did Timon hate Athens, Athenians, and all mankind.

While he lived in this forlorn state, leading a life more
brutal than human, he was suddenly surprised one day
with the appearance of a man standing in an admiring
posture at the door of his cave.   It was Flavius, the
honest steward, whom love and zealous affection to his
master had led to seek him out at his wretched dwelling,
and to offer his services; and the first sight of his master,
the once noble Timon, in that abject condition, naked as
he was born, living in the manner of a beast among
beasts, looking like his own sad ruins and a monument
of decay, so affected this good servant, that he stood
speechless, wrapped up in horror, and confounded.   And
when he found utterance at last to his words, they were
so choked with tears, that Timon had much ado to know
him again, or to make out who it was that had come (so
contrary to the experience he had had of mankind) to

offer him service in extremity. And being in the form
and shape of a man, he suspected him for a traitor, and
his tears for false ; but the good servant by so many
tokens confirmed the truth of his fidelity, and made it
clear that nothing but love and zealous duty to his once
dear master had brought him there, that Timon was forced
to confess that the world contained one honest man ;
yet, being in the shape and form of a man, he could not
look upon his face without abhorrence, or hear words
uttered from his man's lips without loathing ; and this
singly honest man was forced to depart, because he was
a man, and because, with a heart more gentle and compassionate than is usual to man, he bore man's detested
form and outward feature.

But greater visitants than a poor steward were about
to interrupt the savage quiet of Timon's solitude. For
now the day was come when the ungrateful lords of
Athens sorely repented the injustice which they had done
to the noble Timon. For Alcibiades, like an incensed
wild boar, was raging at the walls of their city, and with
his hot siege threatened to lay fair Athens in the dust.
And now the memory of Lord Timon's former prowess
and military conduct came fresh into their forgetful minds,
for Timon had been their general in past times, and was
a valiant and expert soldier, who alone of all the
Athenians was deemed able to cope with a besieging army
such as then threatened them, or to drive back the furious
approaches of Alcibiades.

A deputation of the senators was chosen in this
emergency to wait upon Timon. To him they came in
their extremity, to whom, when he was in extremity, they
had shown but small regard ; as if they presumed upon
his gratitude whom they had disobliged, and had derived
a claim to his courtesy from their own most discourteous
and unpiteous treatment.

Now they earnestly beseech him, implore him with

tears, to return and save that city, from which their
ingratitude had so lately driven him ; now they offer him
riches, power, dignities, satisfaction for past injuries, and
public honours and the public love ; their persons, lives,
and fortunes, to be at his disposal, if he will but come back
and save them. But Timon the naked, Timon the man-
hater, was no longer Lord Timon, the lord of bounty, the
flower of valour, their defence in war, their ornament in
peace. If Alcibiades killed his countrymen, Timon cared
not. If he sacked fair Athens and slew her old men and
her infants, Timon would rejoice. So he told them ; and
that there was not a knife in the unruly camp which he
did not prize above the reverendest throat in Athens.

This was all the answer he vouchsafed to the weeping
disappointed senators ; only at parting he bade them commend him to his countrymen, and tell them, that to ease
them of their griefs and anxieties, and to prevent the consequences of fierce Alcibiades' wrath, there was yet a way
left, which he would teach them, for he had yet so much
affection left for his dear countrymen as to be willing to
do them a kindness before his death. These words a
little revived the senators, who hoped that his kindness
for their city was returning. Then Timon told them he
had a tree, which grew near his cave, which he should
shortly have occasion to cut down, and he invited all his
friends in Athens, high or low, of what degree soever, who
wished to shun affliction, to come and take a taste of his
tree before he cut it down ; meaning, that they might
come and hang themselves on it, and escape affliction
that way.

And this was the last courtesy of all his noble bounties
which Timon showed to mankind, and this the last sight
of him which his countrymen had ; for not many days
after, a poor soldier passing by the sea-beach, which was
at a little distance from the woods which Timon
frequented, found a tomb on the verge of the sea, with an

inscription upon it, purporting that it was the grave of Timon the man-hater, who, " While he lived, did hate all living men, and dying wished a plague might consume all caitiffs left ! "

Whether he finished his life by violence, or whether mere distaste of life and the loathing he had for mankind brought Timon to his conclusion, was not clear, yet all men admired the fitness of his epitaph, and the consistency of his end—dying, as he had lived, a hater of mankind. And some there were who fancied a conceit in the very choice which he made of the sea-beach for his place of burial, where the vast sea might weep for ever upon his grave as in contempt of the transient and shallow tears of hypocritical and deceitful mankind.

ROMEO AND JULIET

THE two chief families in Verona were the rich Capulets and the Montagues. There had been an old quarrel between these families, which was grown to such a height, and so deadly was the enmity between them, that it extended to the remotest kindred, to the followers and retainers of both sides, insomuch that a servant of the house of Montague could not meet a servant of the house of Capulet, nor a Capulet encounter with a Montague by chance, but fierce words and sometimes bloodshed ensued; and frequent were the brawls from such accidental meetings which disturbed the happy quiet of Verona's streets.

Old Lord Capulet made a great supper, to which many fair ladies and many noble guests were invited. All the admired beauties of Verona were present, and all comers were made welcome if they were not of the house of Montague. At this feast of the Capulets, Rosaline, beloved of Romeo, son to the old Lord Montague, was present; and though it was dangerous for a Montague to be seen in this assembly, yet Benvolio, a friend of Romeo, persuaded the young lord to go to this assembly in the disguise of

a mask, that he might see his Rosaline, and seeing her,
compare her with some choice beauties of Verona, who,
he said, would make him think his swan a crow. Romeo
had small faith in Benvolio's words ; nevertheless, for
the love of Rosaline, he was persuaded to go ; for Romeo
was a sincere and passionate lover, and one that lost his
sleep for love, and fled society to be alone thinking on
Rosaline, who disdained him and never requited his love
with the least show of courtesy or affection ; and Benvolio wished to cure his friend of this love by showing
him diversity of ladies and company. To this feast of
the Capulets, then, young Romeo, with Benvolio and their
friend Mercutio, went masked. Old Capulet bid them
welcome, and told them that ladies who had their toes
unplagued with corns would dance with them ; and the
old man was light-hearted and merry, and said that he
had worn a mask when he was young, and could have
told a whispering tale in a fair lady's ear. And they fell
to dancing, and Romeo was suddenly struck with the exceeding beauty of a lady who danced there, who seemed to
him to teach the torches to burn bright, and her beauty
to show by night like a rich jewel worn by a blackamoor
—beauty too rich for use, too dear for earth ; like a snowy
dove trooping with crows, he said, so richly did her
beauty and perfections shine above the ladies her companions. While he uttered these praises he was overheard by Tybalt, a nephew of Lord Capulet, who knew
him by his voice to be Romeo. And this Tybalt, being
of a fiery and passionate temper, could not endure that
a Montague should come under cover of a mask to fleer
and scorn, as he said, at their solemnities ; and he stormed
and raged exceedingly, and would have struck young
Romeo dead, but his uncle, the old Lord Capulet, would
not suffer him to do any injury at that time, both out of
respect to his guests and because Romeo had borne himself like a gentleman, and all tongues in Verona bragged

of him to be a virtuous and well-governed youth. Tybalt, thus forced to be patient against his will, restrained himself, but swore that this vile Montague should at another time dearly pay for his intrusion.

The dancing being done, Romeo watched the place where the lady stood, and under favour of his masking habit, which might seem to excuse in part the liberty, he presumed in the gentlest manner to take her by her hand, calling it a shrine, which if he profaned by touching it, he was a blushing pilgrim and would kiss it for atonement. " Good pilgrim," answered the lady, " your devotion shows by far too mannerly and too courtly ; saints have hands, which pilgrims may touch but kiss not." " Have not saints lips, and pilgrims too ? " said Romeo. " Ay," said the lady, " lips which they must use in prayer." " Oh, then, my dear saint," said Romeo, " hear my prayer, and grant it lest I despair ! " In suchlike allusions and loving conceits they were engaged when the lady was called away to her mother ; and Romeo, inquiring who her mother was, discovered that the lady whose peerless beauty he was so much struck with was young Juliet, daughter and heir to the Lord Capulet, the great enemy of the Montagues, and that he had unknowingly engaged his heart to his foe. This troubled him, but it could not dissuade him from loving. As little rest had Juliet when she found that the gentleman that she had been talking with was Romeo and a Montague, for she had been suddenly smit with the same hasty and inconsiderate passion for Romeo which he had conceived for her ; and a prodigious birth of love it seemed to her, that she must love her enemy, and that her affections should settle there where family considerations should induce her chiefly to hate.

It being midnight, Romeo with his companions departed ; but they soon missed him, for unable to stay away from the house where he had left his heart, he leaped the wall of an orchard which was at the back of Juliet's house : here he had not been long, ruminating on his new love, when Juliet appeared above at a window, through which her exceeding beauty seemed to break like the light of the sun in the east ; and the moon, which shone in the orchard with a faint light, appeared to Romeo as if sick and pale with grief at the superior lustre of this new sun. And she leaning her hand upon her cheek, he passionately wished himself a glove upon that hand, that he might touch her cheek. She all this while thinking herself alone, fetched a deep sigh, and exclaimed, " Ah me ! " Romeo, enraptured to hear her speak, said softly and unheard by her, " Oh, speak again, bright angel, for such you appear, being over my head like a winged messenger from heaven, whom mortals fall back to gaze upon ! " She, unconscious of being overheard, and full of the passion which that night's adventure had given birth to, called upon her lover by name, whom she supposed absent, " O Romeo, Romeo ! " said she, " wherefore art thou Romeo ? Deny thy father and refuse thy name for my sake ; or if thou wilt not, be but my sworn love, and I no longer will be a Capulet." Romeo, having this encouragement, would fain have spoken, but he was desirous of hearing more ; and the lady continued her passionate discourse with herself, as she thought, still chiding Romeo for being Romeo and a Montague, and wishing him some other name, or that he would put away that hated name, and for that name, which was no part of himself, he should take all herself. At this loving word Romeo could no longer refrain, but taking up the dialogue as if her words had been addressed to him personally, and not merely in fancy, he bade her call him Love or by whatever other name she pleased, for he was no longer Romeo if that name was displeasing to her. Juliet, alarmed to hear a man's voice in the garden, did not at first know who it was that, by favour of the night and darkness, had thus stumbled upon the discovery of her secret ; but when he spoke again, though her ears had

not yet drunk a hundred words of that tongue's uttering,
yet so nice is a lover's hearing that she immediately knew
him to be young Romeo, and she expostulated with him
on the danger to which he had exposed himself by climb-
ing the orchard walls, for if any of her kinsmen should
find him there, it would be death to him, being a Montague.
" Alack ! " said Romeo, " there is more peril in your eye
than in twenty of their swords. Do you but look kind
upon me, lady, and I am proof against their enmity. Better
my life should be ended by their hate, than that hated
life should be prolonged to live without your love." " How
came you into this place," said Juliet, " and by whose
direction ? " " Love directed me," answered Romeo.
" I am no pilot, yet wert thou as far apart from me as
that vast shore which is washed with the farthest sea, I
should adventure for such merchandise." A crimson blush
came over Juliet's face, yet unseen by Romeo by reason
of the night, when she reflected upon the discovery she
had made, yet not meaning to make it, of her love to
Romeo. She would fain have recalled her words, but that
was impossible. Fain would she have stood upon form and
have kept her lover at a distance, as the custom of discreet
ladies is, to frown and be perverse, and give their suitors
harsh denials at first ; to stand off, and affect a coyness
or indifference where they most love, that their lovers
may not think them too lightly or too easily won—for the
difficulty of attainment increases the value of the object.
But there was no room in her case for denials, or puttings
off, or any of the customary arts of delay and protracted
courtship. Romeo had heard from her own tongue, when
she did not dream that he was near her, a confession of
her love. So, with an honest frankness which the novelty
of her situation excused, she confirmed the truth of what
he had before heard, and addressing him by the name of
fair Montague (love can sweeten a sour name), she begged
him not to impute her easy yielding to levity, or an

unworthy mind, but that he must lay the fault of it, if it were a fault, upon the accident of the night, which had so strangely discovered her thoughts ; and she added, that though her behaviour to him might not be sufficiently prudent, measured by the custom of her sex, yet that she would prove more true than many whose prudence was dissembling, and their modesty artificial cunning.

Romeo was beginning to call the heavens to witness that nothing was farther from his thoughts than to impute a shadow of dishonour to such an honoured lady, when she stopped him, begging him not to swear, for although she joyed in him, yet she had no joy of that night's contract, it was too rash, too unadvised, too sudden. But he being urgent with her to exchange a vow of love with him that night, she said that she already had given him hers before he requested it, meaning when he overheard her confession, but she would retract what she then bestowed, for the pleasure of giving it again, for her bounty was as infinite as the sea, and her love as deep. From this loving conference she was called away by her nurse, who slept with her, and thought it time for her to be in bed, for it was near to daybreak, but hastily returning, she said three or four words more to Romeo, the purport of which was, that if his love was indeed honourable, and his purpose marriage, she would send a messenger to him to-morrow, to appoint a time for their marriage, when she would lay all her fortunes at his feet, and follow him as her lord through the world. While they were settling this point, Juliet was repeatedly called for by her nurse, and went in and returned, and went and returned again, for she seemed as jealous of Romeo going from her as a young girl of her bird, which she will let hop a little from her hand, and pluck it back with a silken thread ; and Romeo was as loth to part as she, for the sweetest music to lovers is the sound of each other's tongues at night   But

The day was breaking when they parted

at last they parted, wishing mutually sweet sleep and rest for that night.

The day was breaking when they parted, and Romeo, who was too full of thoughts of his mistress and that blessed meeting to allow him to sleep, instead of going home, bent his course to a monastery hard by, to find Friar Lawrence. The good friar was already up at his devotions, but seeing young Romeo abroad so early, he conjectured rightly that he had not been abed that night, but that some distemper of youthful affection had kept him waking. He was right in imputing the cause of Romeo's wakefulness to love, but he made a wrong guess at the object, for he thought that his love for Rosaline had kept him waking. But when Romeo revealed his new passion for Juliet, and requested the assistance of the friar to marry them that day, the holy man lifted up his eyes and hands in a sort of wonder at the sudden change in Romeo's affections, for he had been privy to all Romeo's love for Rosaline, and his many complaints of her disdain, and he said that young men's love lay not truly in their hearts, but in their eyes. But Romeo replying that he himself had often chidden him for doting on Rosaline, who could not love him again, whereas Juliet both loved and was beloved by him, the friar assented in some measure to his reasons, and thinking that a matrimonial alliance between young Juliet and Romeo might happily be the means of making up the long breach between the Capulets and the Montagues, which no one more lamented than this good friar, who was a friend to both the families, and had often interposed his mediation to make up the quarrel without effect, partly moved by policy, and partly by his fondness for young Romeo, to whom he could deny nothing, the old man consented to join their hands in marriage.

Now was Romeo blessed indeed, and Juliet, who knew his intent from a messenger which she had dispatched

according to promise, did not fail to be early at the cell
of Friar Lawrence, where their hands were joined in holy
marriage, the good friar praying the heavens to smile
upon that act, and in the union of this young Montague
and young Capulet to bury the old strife and long dissensions
of their families.

The ceremony being over, Juliet hastened home, where
she stayed impatient for the coming of night, at which
time Romeo promised to come and meet her in the
orchard where they had met the night before, and the
time between seemed as tedious to her as the night before
some great festival seems to an impatient child, that
has got new finery which it may not put on till the
morning.

That same day about noon, Romeo's friends, Benvolio
and Mercutio, walking through the streets of Verona,
were met by a party of the Capulets with the impetuous
Tybalt at their head. This was the same angry Tybalt
who would have fought with Romeo at old Lord Capulet's
feast. He, seeing Mercutio, accused him bluntly of asso-
ciating with Romeo, a Montague. Mercutio, who had as
much fire and youthful blood in him as Tybalt, replied to
this accusation with some sharpness ; and, in spite of all
Benvolio could say to moderate their wrath, a quarrel was
beginning, when Romeo himself passing that way, the
fierce Tybalt turned from Mercutio to Romeo, and gave
him the disgraceful appellation of " villain." Romeo
wished to avoid a quarrel with Tybalt above all men, because
he was the kinsman of Juliet, and much beloved by her ;
and besides, this young Montague had never thoroughly
entered into the family quarrel, being by nature wise and
gentle ; and the name of a Capulet, which was his dear
lady's name, was now rather a charm to allay resentment
than a watchword to excite fury. So he tried to reason
with Tybalt, whom he saluted mildly by the name of *good
Capulet*, as if he, though a Montague, had some secret

pleasure in uttering that name ; but Tybalt, who hated all
Montagues as he hated hell, would hear no reason, but
drew his weapon, and Mercutio, who knew not of Romeo's
secret motive for desiring peace with Tybalt, but looked
upon his present forbearance as a sort of calm dishonourable submission, with many disdainful words provoked
Tybalt to the prosecution of his first quarrel with him,
and Tybalt and Mercutio fought till Mercutio fell, receiving
his death's wound while Romeo and Benvolio were vainly
endeavouring to part the combatants. Mercutio being
dead, Romeo kept his temper no longer, but returned the
scornful appellation of " villain " which Tybalt had given
him, and they fought till Tybalt was slain by Romeo.
This deadly broil falling out in the midst of Verona at
noonday, the news of it quickly brought a crowd of citizens
to the spot, and among them the old Lords Capulet and
Montague, with their wives ; and soon after arrived the
prince himself, who being related to Mercutio, whom
Tybalt had slain, and having had the peace of his government often disturbed by these brawls of Montagues and
Capulets, came determined to put the law in strictest force
against those who should be found to be offenders. Benvolio, who had been eye-witness to the fray, was commanded by the prince to relate the origin of it, which he
did, keeping as near to the truth as he could without injury
to Romeo, softening and excusing the part which his friends
took in it. Lady Capulet, whose extreme grief for the loss
of her kinsman Tybalt made her keep no bounds in her
revenge, exhorted the prince to do strict justice upon his
murderer, and to pay no attention to Benvolio's representation, who, being Romeo's friend and a Montague,
spoke partially. Thus she pleaded against her new son-in-
law, but she knew not yet that he was her son-in-law and
Juliet's husband. On the other hand was to be seen Lady
Montague pleading for her child's life, and arguing with
some justice that Romeo had done nothing worthy of

R

punishment in taking the life of Tybalt, which was already forfeited to the law by his having slain Mercutio. The prince, unmoved by the passionate exclamations of these women, on a careful examination of the facts, pronounced his sentence, and by that sentence Romeo was banished from Verona.

Heavy news to young Juliet, who had been but a few hours a bride, and now by this decree seemed everlastingly divorced ! When the tidings reached her, she at first gave way to rage against Romeo, who had slain her dear cousin. She called him a beautiful tyrant, a fiend angelical, a ravenous dove, a lamb with a wolf's nature, a serpent heart hid with a flowering face, and other like contradictory names, which denoted the struggles in her mind between her love and her resentment. But, in the end, love got the mastery, and the tears which she shed for grief that Romeo had slain her cousin, turned to drops of joy that her husband lived whom Tybalt would have slain. Then came fresh tears, and they were altogether of grief for Romeo's banishment. That word was more terrible to her than the death of many Tybalts.

Romeo, after the fray, had taken refuge in Friar Law-rence's cell, where he was first made acquainted with the prince's sentence, which seemed to him far more terrible than death. To him it appeared there was no world out of Verona's walls, no living out of the sight of Juliet. Heaven was there where Juliet lived, and all beyond was purgatory, torture, hell. The good friar would have applied the consolation of philosophy to his griefs, but this frantic young man would hear of none, but like a madman he tore his hair, and threw himself all along upon the ground, as he said, to take the measure of his grave. From this unseemly state he was roused by a message from his dear lady, which a little revived him, and then the friar took the advantage to expostulate with him on the unmanly weakness which he had shown. He had

slain Tybalt, but would he also slay himself, slay his dear
lady who lived but in his life ? The noble form of man,
he said, was but a shape of wax, when it wanted the
courage which should keep it firm. The law had been
lenient to him, that, instead of death which he had
incurred, had pronounced by the prince's mouth only
banishment. He had slain Tybalt, but Tybalt would
have slain him, there was a sort of happiness in that.
Juliet was alive, and (beyond all hope) had become his dear
wife, therein he was most happy. All these blessings, as
the friar made them out to be, did Romeo put from him
like a sullen misbehaved wench. And the friar bade him
beware, for such as despaired (he said) died miserable.
Then when Romeo was a little calmed, he counselled
him that he should go that night and secretly take his
leave of Juliet, and thence proceed straightway to Mantua,
at which place he should sojourn, till the friar found a fit
occasion to publish his marriage, which might be a joyful
means of reconciling their families, and then he did not
doubt but the prince would be moved to pardon him,
and he would return with twenty times more joy than he
went forth with grief. Romeo was convinced by these
wise counsels of the friar, and took his leave to go and
seek his lady, purposing to stay with her that night, and
by daybreak pursue his journey alone to Mantua, to which
place the good friar promised to send him letters from
time to time, acquainting him with the state of affairs at
home.

That night Romeo passed with his dear wife, gaining
secret admission to her chamber from the orchard in
which he had heard her confession of love the night before.
That had been a night of unmixed joy and rapture ; but
the pleasures of this night, and the delight which these
lovers took in each other's society, were sadly allayed with
the prospect of parting, and the fatal adventures of the
past day. The unwelcome daybreak seemed to come too

soon, and when Juliet heard the morning song of the lark, she would fain have persuaded herself that it was the nightingale, which sings by night, but it was too truly the lark which sang, and a discordant and unpleasing note it seemed to her, and the streaks of day in the east too certainly pointed out that it was time for these lovers to part. Romeo took his leave of his dear wife with a heavy heart, promising to write to her from Mantua every hour in the day; and when he had descended from her chamber window, as he stood below her on the ground, in that sad foreboding state of mind in which she was, he appeared to her eyes as one dead in the bottom of a tomb. Romeo's mind misgave him in like manner, but now he was forced hastily to depart, for it was death for him to be found within the walls of Verona after daybreak.

This was but the beginning of the tragedy of this pair of star-crossed lovers. Romeo had not been gone many days before the old Lord Capulet proposed a match for Juliet. The husband he had chosen for her, not dreaming that she was married already, was Count Paris, a gallant, young, and noble gentleman, no unworthy suitor to the young Juliet, if she had never seen Romeo.

The terrified Juliet was in a sad perplexity at her father's offer. She pleaded her youth unsuitable to marriage, the recent death of Tybalt, which had left her spirits too weak to meet a husband with any face of joy, and how indecorous it would show for the family of the Capulets to be celebrating a nuptial feast, when his funeral solemnities were hardly over: she pleaded every reason against the match but the true one, namely, that she was married already. But Lord Capulet was deaf to all her excuses, and in a peremptory manner ordered her to get ready, for by the following Thursday she should be married to Paris; and having found her a husband rich, young, and noble, such as the proudest maid in Verona might joyfully accept, he could not bear that out of an affected coyness, as he construed her denial, she should oppose obstacles to her own good fortune. ·

In this extremity Juliet applied to the friendly friar, always her counsellor in distress, and he asking her if she had resolution to undertake a desperate remedy, and she answering that she would go into the grave alive rather than marry Paris, her own dear husband living ; he directed her to go home, and appear merry, and give her consent to marry Paris, according to her father's desire ; and on the next night, which was the night before the marriage, to drink off the contents of a phial which he then gave her, the effect of which would be, that for two-and-forty hours after drinking it she should appear cold and lifeless ; that when the bridegroom came to fetch her in the morning, he would find her to appearance dead ; that then she would be borne, as the manner in that country was, uncovered on a bier, to be buried in the family vault ; that if she could put off womanish fear, and consent to this terrible trial, in forty-two hours after swallowing the liquid (such was its certain operation) she would be sure to awake, as from a dream ; and before she would awake, he would let her husband know their drift, and he should come in the night, and bear her thence to Mantua. Love, and the dread of marrying Paris, gave young Juliet strength to undertake this horrible adventure ; and she took the phial of the friar, promising to observe his directions.

Going from the monastery, she met the young Count Paris, and, modestly dissembling, promised to become his bride. This was joyful news to the Lord Capulet and his wife : it seemed to put youth into the old man ; and Juliet, who had displeased him exceedingly by her refusal of the count, was his darling again, now she promised to be obedient. All things in the house were in a bustle against the approaching nuptials. No cost was spared to prepare such festival rejoicings as Verona had never before witnessed.

On the Wednesday night Juliet drank off the potion. She had many misgivings, lest the friar, to avoid the blame which might be imputed to him for marrying her to Romeo, had given her poison ; but then he was always known for a holy man ; then lest she should awake before the time that Romeo was to come for her ; whether the terror of the place, a vault full of dead Capulets' bones, and where Tybalt, all bloody, lay festering in his shroud, would not be enough to drive her distracted ; again she thought of all the stories she had heard of spirits haunting the place where their bodies were bestowed. But then her love for Romeo, and her aversion for Paris, returned, and she desperately swallowed the draught, and became insensible.

When young Paris came early in the morning with music, to awaken his bride, instead of a living Juliet, her chamber presented the dreary spectacle of a lifeless corse. What death to his hopes ! What confusion then reigned through the whole house ! Poor Paris lamenting his bride, whom most detestable death had beguiled him of, had divorced from him even before their hands were joined. But still more piteous it was to hear the mournings of the old Lord and Lady Capulet, who having but this one, one poor loving child, to rejoice and solace in, cruel death had snatched her from their sight, just as these careful parents were on the point of seeing her advanced (as they thought) by a promising and advantageous match. Now all things that were ordained for the festival were turned from their properties to do the office of a black funeral. The wedding cheer served for a sad burial feast, the bridal hymns were changed to sullen dirges, the sprightly instruments to melancholy bells, and the flowers that should have been strewed in the bride's path now served but to strew her corse. Now, instead of a priest

to marry her, a priest was needed to bury her ; and she
was borne to church indeed, not to augment the cheerful
hopes of the living, but to swell the dreary numbers of
the dead.

Bad news, which always travels faster than good, now
brought the dismal story of his Juliet's death to Romeo at
Mantua, before the messenger could arrive, who was sent
from Friar Lawrence to apprise him that these were mock
funerals only, and but the shadow and representation of
death ; and that his dear lady lay in the tomb but for a
short while, expecting when Romeo should come to release her from that dreary mansion. Just before, Romeo
had been unusually joyful and light-hearted. He had
dreamed in the night that he was dead (a strange dream,
that gave a dead man leave to think), and that his lady
came and found him dead, and breathed such life with
kisses on his lips, that he revived, and was an emperor !
And now that a messenger came from Verona, he thought
surely it was to confirm some good news which his dreams
had presaged. But when the contrary to this flattering
vision appeared, and that it was his lady who was dead in
truth, whom he could not revive by any kisses, he ordered
horses to be got ready, for he determined that night to
visit Verona, and to see his lady in her tomb. And as
mischief is swift to enter into the thoughts of desperate
men, he called to mind a poor apothecary, whose shop in
Mantua he had lately passed, and from the beggarly appearance of the man, who seemed famished, and the
wretched show in his shop of empty boxes ranged on dirty
shelves, and other tokens of extreme wretchedness, he
had said at the time (perhaps having some misgivings that
his own disastrous life might haply meet with a conclusion
so desperate), " If a man were to need poison, which by
the law of Mantua it is death to sell, here lives a poor
wretch who would sell it him." These words of his now
came into his mind, and he sought out the apothecary,

who, after some pretended scruples, Romeo offering him gold which his poverty could not resist, sold him a poison, which if he swallowed, he told him, if he had the strength of twenty men, would quickly dispatch him.

With this poison he set out for Verona, to have a sight of his dear lady in her tomb, meaning, when he had satisfied his sight, to swallow the poison and be buried by her side. He reached Verona at midnight, and found the churchyard, in the midst of which was situated the ancient tomb of the Capulets. He had provided a lantern, and a spade, and a wrenching-iron, and was just proceeding to break open the monument, when he was interrupted by a voice, which, by the name of *vile Montague*, bade him desist from his unlawful business. It was the young Count Paris, who had come to the tomb of Juliet at that unseasonable time of night to strew flowers, and to weep over the grave of her that should have been his bride. He knew not what an interest Romeo had in the dead, but knowing him to be a Montague, and (as he supposed) a sworn foe to all the Capulets, he judged that he was come by night to do some villainous shame to the dead bodies, therefore in an angry tone he bade him desist; and, as a criminal, condemned by the laws of Verona to die if he were found within the walls of the city, he would have apprehended him. Romeo urged Paris to leave him, and warned him by the fate of Tybalt, who lay buried there, not to provoke his anger, or draw down another sin upon his head, by forcing him to kill him. But the count in scorn refused his warning, and laid hands on him as a felon, which Romeo resisting, they fought, and Paris fell. When Romeo, by the help of a light, came to see who it was that he had slain, that it was Paris, who (he learned on his way from Mantua) should have married Juliet, he took the dead youth by the hand, as one whom misfortune had made a companion, and said that he would bury him in a triumphal grave, meaning in Juliet's grave, which he

now opened, and there lay his lady, as one whom death
had no power upon to change a feature or complexion in
her matchless beauty, or as if death were amorous, and
the lean abhorred monster kept her there for his delight ;
for she lay yet fresh and blooming, as she had fallen to
sleep when she swallowed that benumbing potion, and near
her lay Tybalt in his bloody shroud, whom Romeo seeing,
begged pardon of his lifeless corse, and for Juliet's sake
called him *cousin*, and said that he was about to do him a
favour by putting his enemy to death.

Here Romeo took his last leave of his lady's lips, kissing
them, and he here shook the burden of his cross stars
from his weary body, swallowing that poison which the
apothecary had sold him, whose operation was fatal and
real, not like that dissembling potion which Juliet had
swallowed, the effect of which was now nearly expiring,
and she about to awake to complain that Romeo had not
kept his time, or that he had come too soon.

For now the hour was arrived at which the friar had
promised that she should awake, and he, having learned
that his letters, which he had sent to Mantua, by some
unlucky detention of the messenger, had never reached
Romeo, came himself, provided with a pickaxe and lantern,
to deliver the lady from her confinement ; but he was
surprised to find a light already burning in the Capulets'
monument, and to see swords and blood near it, and Romeo
and Paris lying breathless by the monument.

Before he could entertain a conjecture, to imagine how
these fatal accidents had fallen out, Juliet awoke out of
her trance, and seeing the friar near her, she remembered
the place where she was, and the occasion of her being
there, and asked for Romeo ; but the friar, hearing a noise,
bade her come out of that place of death and of unnatural
sleep, for a greater Power than they could contradict had
thwarted their intents ; and being frightened by the noise
of people coming, he fled ; but when Juliet saw the cup

closed in her true love's hands, she guessed that poison
had been the cause of his end, and she would have swallowed
the dregs if any had been left, and she kissed his still warm
lips to try if any poison yet did hang upon them, then
hearing a nearer noise of people coming, she quickly un-
sheathed a dagger which she wore, and, stabbing herself,
died by her true Romeo's side.

The watch by this time had come up to the place.
A page belonging to Count Paris, who had witnessed the
fight between his master and Romeo, had given the alarm,
which had spread among the citizens, who went up and
down the streets of Verona confusedly exclaiming, " A
Paris ! a Romeo ! a Juliet ! " as the rumour had imper-
fectly reached them, till the uproar brought Lord Montague
and Lord Capulet out of their beds, with the prince, to
inquire into the causes of the disturbance. The friar had
been apprehended by some of the watch, coming from the
churchyard, trembling, sighing, and weeping in a suspicious
manner. A great multitude being assembled at the Capulets' monument, the friar was demanded by the prince to
deliver what he knew of these strange and disastrous
accidents.

And there, in the presence of the old Lords Montague
and Capulet, he faithfully related the story of their children's
fatal love, the part he took in promoting their marriage,
in the hope in that union to end the long quarrels between
their families. How Romeo, there dead, was husband to
Juliet, and Juliet, there dead, was Romeo's faithful wife ;
how before he could find a fit opportunity to divulge their
marriage, another match was projected for Juliet, who,
to avoid the crime of a second marriage, swallowed the
sleeping draught (as he advised), and all thought her dead.
How, meantime, he wrote to Romeo, to come and take
her thence when the force of the potion should cease, and
by what unfortunate miscarriage of the messenger the
letters never reached Romeo. Further than this the friar

could not follow the story, nor knew more than that, coming himself to deliver Juliet from that place of death, he found the Count Paris and Romeo slain. The remainder of the transactions was supplied by the narration of the page, who had seen Paris and Romeo fight, and by the servant who came with Romeo from Verona, to whom this faithful lover had given letters to be delivered to his father in the event of his death, which made good the friar's words, confessing his marriage with Juliet, imploring the forgiveness of his parents, acknowledging the buying of the poison of the poor apothecary, and his intent in coming to the monument, to die, and lie with Juliet. All these circumstances agreed together to clear the friar from any hand he could be supposed to have had in these complicated slaughters, further than as the unintended consequences of his own well-meant yet too artificial and subtle contrivances.

And the prince, turning to these old lords, Montague and Capulet, rebuked them for their brutal and irrational enmities, and showed them what a scourge Heaven had laid upon such offences, that it had found means even through the love of their children to punish their unnatural hate ; and these old rivals, no longer enemies, agreed to bury their long strife in their children's graves, and Lord Capulet requested Lord Montague to give him his hand, calling him by the name of brother, as if in acknowledgment of the union of their families by the marriage of the young Capulet and Montague, and saying that Lord Montague's hand (in token of reconcilement) was all that he demanded for his daughter's jointure ; but Lord Montague said he would give him more, for he would raise her statue of pure gold, that while Verona kept its name, no figure should be so esteemed for its richness and workmanship as that of the true and faithful Juliet. And Lord Capulet, in return, said that he would raise another statue to Romeo. So did these poor old lords, when it was too late, strive to outgo each other in mutual courtesies ; while, so deadly had been their rage and enmity in past times, that nothing but the fearful overthrow of their children (poor sacrifices to their quarrels and dissensions !) could remove the rooted hates and jealousies of the noble families.

HAMLET,
PRINCE OF DENMARK

GERTRUDE, Queen of Denmark, becoming a widow by the sudden death of King Hamlet, in less than two months after his death married his brother Claudius, which was noted by all people at the time for a strange act of indiscretion, or unfeelingness, or worse ; for this Claudius did no ways resemble her late husband in the qualities of his person or his mind, but was as contemptible in outward appearance as he was base and unworthy in disposition ; and suspicions did not fail to arise in the minds of some that he had privately made away with his brother, the late king, with the view of marrying his widow and ascending the throne of Denmark, to the exclusion of young Hamlet, the son of the buried king, and lawful successor to the throne.

But upon no one did this unadvised action of the queen make such impression as upon this young prince, who loved and venerated the memory of his dead father, almost to idolatry ; and being of a nice sense of honour, and a most exquisite practiser of propriety himself, did sorely take to heart this unworthy conduct of his mother Gertrude, insomuch that, between grief for his father's

death and shame for his mother's marriage, this young
prince was overclouded with a deep melancholy, and lost
all his mirth and all his good looks ; all his customary
pleasure in books forsook him ; his princely exercises
and sports, proper to his youth, were no longer acceptable ; he grew weary of the world, which seemed to him
an unweeded garden, where all the wholesome flowers
were choked up, and nothing but weeds could thrive.
Not that the prospect of exclusion from the throne, his
lawful inheritance, weighed so much upon his spirits—
though that, to a young and high-minded prince, was a
bitter wound and a sore indignity ; but what so galled
him and took away all his cheerful spirits was that his
mother had shown herself so forgetful to his father's
memory ; and such a father !—who had been to her so
loving and so gentle a husband ! And then she always
appeared as loving and obedient a wife to him, and would
hang upon him as if her affection grew to him ; and now,
within two months, or as it seemed to young Hamlet,
less than two months, she had married again—married his
uncle, her dead husband's brother, in itself a highly improper and unlawful marriage, from the nearness of relationship, but made much more so by the indecent haste with
which it was concluded, and the unkingly character of
the man whom she had chosen to be the partner of her
throne and bed. This it was which, more than the loss
of ten kingdoms, dashed the spirits and brought a cloud
over the mind of this honourable young prince.

In vain was all that his mother Gertrude or the king
could do or contrive to divert him ; he still appeared in
court in a suit of deep black, as mourning for the king his
father's death, which mode of dress he had never laid
aside, not even in compliment to his mother upon the day
she was married, nor could he be brought to join in any
of the festivities or rejoicings of that, as appeared to him,
disgraceful day.

What mostly troubled him was an uncertainty about
the manner of his father's death. It was given out by
Claudius that a serpent had stung him, but young Hamlet
had shrewd suspicions that Claudius himself was the
serpent : in plain English, that he had murdered him for
his crown, and that the serpent who stung his father did
now sit on his throne.

How far he was right in this conjecture, and what he
ought to think of his mother—how far she was privy to
this murder, and whether by her consent or knowledge,
or without, it came to pass—were the doubts which continually harassed and distracted him.

A rumour had reached the ear of young Hamlet that
an apparition, exactly resembling the dead king his father,
had been seen by the soldiers upon watch on the platform
before the palace at midnight for two or three nights suc-
cessively. The figure came constantly clad in the same
suit of armour from head to foot which the dead king was
known to have worn, and they who saw it—Hamlet's
bosom friend Horatio was one—agreed in their testimony
as to the time and manner of its appearance : that it came
just as the clock struck twelve ; that it looked pale, with
a face more of sorrow than of anger ; that its beard was
grisly, and the colour a *sable silvered*, as they had seen it
in his lifetime ; that it made no answer when they spoke
to it, yet once they thought it lifted up its head and addressed
itself to motion as if it were about to speak, but in that
moment the morning cock crew, and it shrank in haste
away and vanished out of their sight.

The young prince, strangely amazed at their relation,
which was too consistent and agreeing with itself to disbelieve, concluded that it was his father's ghost which
they had seen, and determined to take his watch with the
soldiers that night that he might have a chance of seeing
it, for he reasoned with himself that such an appearance did not come for nothing, but that the ghost had

something to impart, and though it had been silent hitherto, yet it would speak to him ; and he waited with impatience for the coming of the night.

When night came, he took his stand with Horatio and Marcellus, one of the guard, upon the platform where this apparition was accustomed to walk ; and it being a cold night, and the air unusually raw and nipping, Hamlet and Horatio and their companion fell into some talk about the coldness of the night, which was suddenly broken off by Horatio announcing that the ghost was coming.

At the sight of his father's spirit, Hamlet was struck with a sudden surprise and fear. He at first called upon the angels and heavenly ministers to defend them, for he knew not whether it were a good spirit or bad, whether it came for good or for evil ; but he gradually assumed more courage, and his father—as it seemed to him— looked upon him so piteously, and as it were desiring to have conversation with him, and did in all respects appear so like himself as he was when he lived, that Hamlet could not help addressing him. He called him by his name, " Hamlet, King, Father ! " and conjured him that he would tell the reason why he had left his grave, where they had seen him quietly bestowed, to come again and visit the earth and the moonlight, and besought him that he would let them know if there was anything which they could do to give peace to his spirit. And the ghost beckoned to Hamlet that he should go with him to some more removed place, where they might be alone ; and Horatio and Marcellus would have dissuaded the young prince from following it, for they feared lest it should be some evil spirit, who would tempt him to the neigh- bouring sea or to the top of some dreadful cliff, and there put on some horrible shape which might deprive the prince of his reason. But their counsels and entreaties could not alter Hamlet's determination, who cared too little about

life to fear the losing of it ; and as to his soul, he said,
what could the spirit do to that, being a thing immortal
as itself ? And he felt as hardy as a lion, and bursting
from them, who did all they could to hold him, he followed
whithersoever the spirit led him.

And when they were alone together, the spirit broke
silence and told him that he was the ghost of Hamlet, his
father, who had been cruelly murdered, and he told the
manner of it : that it was done by his own brother Claudius,
Hamlet's uncle, as Hamlet had already but too much
suspected, for the hope of succeeding to his bed and
crown. That as he was sleeping in his garden—his custom
always in the afternoon—this treasonous brother stole
upon him in his sleep, and poured the juice of poisonous
henbane into his ears, which has such an antipathy to the
life of man, that swift as quicksilver it courses through
all the veins of the body, baking up the blood, and spreading a crust-like leprosy all over the skin. Thus, sleeping,
by a brother's hand he was cut off at once from his crown,
his queen, and his life ; and he adjured Hamlet, if he
did ever his dear father love, that he would revenge his
foul murder. And the ghost lamented to his son that
his mother should so fall off from virtue as to prove false
to the wedded love of her first husband and to marry his
murderer ; but he cautioned Hamlet, howsoever he proceeded in his revenge against his wicked uncle, by no means
to act any violence against the person of his mother, but
to leave her to Heaven and to the stings and thorns of
conscience. And Hamlet promised to observe the ghost's
direction in all things, and the ghost vanished.

And when Hamlet was left alone, he took up a solemn
resolution, that all he had in his memory, all that he had
ever learned by books or observation, should be instantly
forgotten by him, and nothing live in his brain but the
memory of what the ghost had told him, and had
enjoined him to do. And Hamlet related the particulars

S

of the conversation which had passed to none but his dear friend Horatio ; and he enjoined both to him and Marcellus the strictest secrecy as to what they had seen that night.

The terror which the sight of the ghost had left upon the senses of Hamlet, he being weak and dispirited before, almost unhinged his mind, and drove him beside his reason. And he fearing that it would continue to have this effect, which might subject him to observation, and set his uncle upon his guard, if he suspected that he was meditating anything against him, or that Hamlet really knew more of his father's death than he professed—took up a strange resolution from that time to counterfeit as if he were really and truly mad ; thinking that he would be less an object of suspicion when his uncle should believe him incapable of any serious project, and that his real perturbation of mind would be best covered and pass concealed under a disguise of pretended lunacy.

From this time Hamlet affected a certain wildness and strangeness in his apparel, his speech, and behaviour, and did so excellently counterfeit the madman that the king and queen were both deceived, and not thinking his grief for his father's death a sufficient cause to produce such a distemper—for they knew not of the appearance of the ghost—they concluded that his malady was love, and they thought they had found out the object.

Before Hamlet fell into the melancholy way which has been related, he had dearly loved a fair maid called Ophelia, the daughter of Polonius, the king's chief counsellor in affairs of state. He had sent her letters and rings, and made many tenders of his affection to her, and importuned her with love in honourable fashion, and she had given belief to his vows and importunities. But the melancholy into which he fell latterly had made him neglect her, and from the time he conceived the project of counterfeiting madness, he affected to treat her with

unkindness and a sort of rudeness ; but she, good lady,
rather than reproach him with being false to her, persuaded herself that it was nothing but the disease in his
mind, and no settled unkindness, which had made him
less observant of her than formerly ; and she compared
the faculties of his once noble mind and excellent understanding, impaired as they were with the deep melancholy
that oppressed him, to sweet bells which in themselves
are capable of most exquisite music, but when jangled out
of tune or rudely handled, produce only a harsh and
unpleasing sound.

Though the rough business which Hamlet had in hand
—the revenging of his father's death upon his murderer—
did not suit with the playful state of courtship, or admit
of the society of so idle a passion as love now seemed to
him, yet it could not hinder but that soft thoughts of
his Ophelia would come between ; and in one of these
moments, when he thought that his treatment of this
gentle lady had been unreasonably harsh, he wrote her a
letter full of wild starts of passion, and in extravagant
terms, such as agreed with his supposed madness, but
mixed with some gentle touches of affection, which could
not but show to this honoured lady that a deep love for
her yet lay at the bottom of his heart. He bade her to
doubt the stars were fire, and to doubt that the sun did
move, to doubt truth to be a liar, but never to doubt that
he loved ; with more of such extravagant phrases. This
letter Ophelia dutifully showed to her father, and the old
man thought himself bound to communicate it to the
king and queen, who from that time supposed that the
true cause of Hamlet's madness was love. And the queen
wished that the good beauties of Ophelia might be the
happy cause of his wildness, for so she hoped that her
virtues might happily restore him to his accustomed way
again, to both their honours.

But Hamlet's malady lay deeper than she supposed,

or than could be so cured. His father's ghost, which he had seen, still haunted his imagination, and the sacred injunction to revenge his murder gave him no rest till it was accomplished. Every hour of delay seemed to him a sin and a violation of his father's commands. Yet how to compass the death of the king, surrounded as he constantly was with his guards, was no easy matter. Or if it had been, the presence of the queen, Hamlet's mother, who was generally with the king, was a restraint upon his purpose, which he could not break through. Besides, the very circumstance that the usurper was his mother's husband filled him with some remorse, and still blunted the edge of his purpose. The mere act of putting a fellow-creature to death was in itself odious and terrible to a disposition naturally so gentle as Hamlet's was. His very melancholy, and the dejection of spirits he had so long been in, produced an irresoluteness and wavering of purpose, which kept him from proceeding to extremities. Moreover, he could not help having some scruples upon his mind whether the spirit which he had seen was indeed his father, or whether it might not be the devil, who, he had heard, has power to take any form he pleases, and who might have assumed his father's shape only to take advantage of his weakness and his melancholy, to drive him to the doing of so desperate an act as murder. And he determined that he would have more certain grounds to go upon than a vision, or apparition, which might be a delusion.

While he was in this irresolute mind, there came to the court certain players in whom Hamlet formerly used to take delight, and particularly to hear one of them speak a tragical speech, describing the death of old Priam, King of Troy, with the grief of Hecuba, his queen. Hamlet welcomed his old friends the players, and remembering how that speech had formerly given him pleasure, requested the player to repeat it, which he did in so lively a manner, setting forth the cruel murder of the feeble old king, with the destruction of his people and city by fire, and the mad grief of the old queen, running barefoot up and down the palace, with a poor clout upon that head where a crown had been, and with nothing but a blanket upon her loins, snatched up in haste, where she had worn a royal robe ; that not only it drew tears from all that stood by, who thought they saw the real scene, so lively was it represented, but even the player himself delivered it with a broken voice and real tears.

This put Hamlet upon thinking, if that player could so work himself up to passion by a mere fictitious speech, to weep for one that he had never seen—for Hecuba, that had been dead so many hundred years—how dull was he, who having a real motive and cue for passion, a real king and a dear father murdered, was yet so little moved, that his revenge all this while had seemed to have slept in dull and muddy forgetfulness ! And while he meditated on actors and acting, and the powerful effects which a good play, represented to the life, has upon the spectator, he remembered the instance of some murderer, who, seeing a murder on the stage, was by the mere force of the scene and resemblance of circumstances so affected, that on the spot he confessed the crime which he had committed. And he determined that these players should play something like the murder of his father before his uncle, and he would watch narrowly what effect it might have upon him, and from his looks he would be able to gather with more certainty if he were the murderer or not. To this effect he ordered a play to be prepared, to the representation of which he invited the king and queen.

The story of the play was of a murder done in Vienna upon a duke. The duke's name was Gonzago, his wife Baptista. The play showed how one Lucianus, a near relation to the duke, poisoned him in his garden for his estate, and how the murderer in a short time after got the love of Gonzago's wife.

At the representation of this play the king, who did not know the trap which was laid for him, was present, with his queen and the whole court, Hamlet sitting attentively near him to observe his looks. The play began with a conversation between Gonzago and his wife, in which the lady made many protestations of love, and of never marrying a second husband if she should outlive Gonzago, wishing she might be accursed if she ever took a second husband, and adding that no woman ever did so but those wicked women who kill their first husbands. Hamlet observed the king, his uncle, change colour at this expression, and that it was as bad as wormwood both to him and to the queen. But when Lucianus, according to the story, came to poison Gonzago sleeping in the garden, the strong resemblance which it bore to his own wicked act upon the late king his brother, whom he had poisoned in his garden, so struck upon the conscience of this usurper, that he was unable to sit out the rest of the play, but on a sudden calling for lights to his chamber, and affecting or partly feeling a sudden sickness, he abruptly left the theatre. The king being departed, the play was given over. Now Hamlet had seen enough to be satisfied that the words of the ghost were true, and no illusion ; and, in a fit of gaiety, like that which comes over a man who suddenly has some great doubt or scruple resolved, he swore to Horatio that he would take the ghost's word for a thousand pounds. But before he could make up his resolution as to what measures of revenge he should take, now he was certainly informed that his uncle was his father's murderer, he was sent for by the queen his mother, to a private conference in her closet.

It was by desire of the king that the queen sent for Hamlet, that she might signify to her son how much his late behaviour had displeased them both ; and the king.

wishing to know all that passed at that conference, and thinking that the too partial report of a mother might let slip some part of Hamlet's words, which it might much import the king to know, Polonius, the old counsellor of state, was ordered to plant himself behind the hangings in the queen's closet, where he might unseen hear all that passed. This artifice was particularly adapted to the disposition of Polonius, who was a man grown old in crooked maxims and policies of state, and delighted to get at the knowledge of matters in an indirect and cunning way.

Hamlet being come to his mother, she began to tax him in the roundest way with his actions and behaviour, and she told him that he had given great offence to *his father*, meaning the king his uncle, whom, because he had married her, she called Hamlet's father. Hamlet, sorely indignant that she should give so dear and honoured a name, as father seemed to him, to a wretch who was indeed no better than the murderer of his true father, with some sharpness replied, " Mother, *you* have much offended *my father*." The queen said that was but an idle answer. " As good as the question deserved," said Hamlet. The queen asked him if he had forgotten who it was he was speaking to. " Alas ! " replied Hamlet, " I wish I could forget. You are the queen, your husband's brother's wife, and you are my mother. I wish you were not what you are." " Nay, then," said the queen, " if you show me so little respect, I will set those to you that can speak," and was going to send the king or Polonius to him.

But Hamlet would not let her go, now he had her alone, till he had tried if his words could not bring her to some sense of her wicked life ; and, taking her by the wrist, he held her fast, and made her sit down. She, affrighted at his earnest manner, and fearful lest in his lunacy he should do her some mischief, cried out, and a

voice was heard from behind the hangings, " Help, help
the queen ! " which Hamlet hearing, and verily thinking
that it was the king himself there concealed, he drew his
sword, and stabbed at the place where the voice came from
as he would have stabbed a rat that ran there, till the
voice ceasing, he concluded the person to be dead. But
when he dragged forth the body, it was not the king, but
Polonius, the old officious counsellor, that had planted
himself as a spy behind the hangings. " O me ! " exclaimed
the queen, " what a rash and bloody deed you have done ! "
" A bloody deed, mother," replied Hamlet, " but not
so bad as yours, who killed a king and married his
brother."

Hamlet had gone too far to leave off here. He was
now in the humour to speak plainly to his mother, and
he pursued it. And though the faults of parents are to
be tenderly treated by their children, yet in the case of
great crimes the son may have leave to speak even to his
own mother with some harshness, so as that harshness
is meant for her good, and to turn her from her wicked
ways, and not done for the purpose of upbraiding. And
now this virtuous prince did in moving terms represent
to the queen the heinousness of her offence, in being so
forgetful of the dead king his father, as in so short a
space of time to marry with his brother and reputed murderer ; such an act as, after the vows which she had sworn
to her first husband, was enough to make all vows of
women suspected, and all virtue to be counted hypocrisy,
wedding contracts to be less than gamesters' oaths, and
religion to be a mockery and a mere form of words. He
said she had done such a deed that the heavens blushed
at it, and the earth was sick of her because of it   And
he showed her two pictures, the one of the late king,
her first husband, and the other of the present king, her
second husband, and he bade her mark the difference :
what a grace was on the brow of his father, how like a

god he looked ! the curls of Apollo, the forehead of Jupiter, the eye of Mars, and a posture like to Mercury newly alighted upon some heaven-kissing hill ! this man, he said, *had been* her husband. And then he showed her whom she had got in his stead : how like a blight or a mildew he looked, for so he had blasted his wholesome brother. And the queen was sore ashamed that he should so turn her eyes inward upon her soul, which she now saw so black and deformed. And he asked her how she could continue to live with this man, and be a wife to him who had murdered her first husband, and got the crown by as false means as a thief—— And just as he spoke the ghost of his father, such as he was in his lifetime, and such as he had lately seen it, entered the room, and Hamlet, in great terror, asked what it would have ; and the ghost said that it came to remind him of the revenge he had promised, which Hamlet seemed to have forgot ; and the ghost bade him speak to his mother, for the grief and terror she was in would else kill her. It then vanished, and was seen by none but Hamlet, neither could he, by pointing to where it stood, or by any description, make his mother perceive it, who was terribly frightened all this while to hear him conversing, as it seemed to her, with nothing, and she imputed it to the disorder of his mind. But Hamlet begged her not to flatter her wicked soul in such a manner as to think it was his madness, and not her own offences, which had brought his father's spirit again on the earth. And he bade her feel his pulse, how temperately it beat, not like a madman's. And he begged of her with tears to confess herself to Heaven for what was past, and for the future to avoid the company of the king, and be no more as a wife to him ; and when she should show herself a mother to him, by respecting his father's memory, he would ask a blessing of her as a son. And she promising to observe his directions, the conference ended.

And now Hamlet was at leisure to consider who it was that in his unfortunate rashness he had killed ; and when he came to see that it was Polonius, the father of the Lady Ophelia, whom he so dearly loved, he drew apart the dead body, and his spirits being now a little quieter, he wept for what he had done.

This unfortunate death of Polonius gave the king a pretext for sending Hamlet out of the kingdom. He would willingly have put him to death, fearing him as dangerous, but he dreaded the people, who loved Hamlet ; and the queen, who, with all her faults, doted on the prince her son. So this subtle king, under pretence of providing for Hamlet's safety, that he might not be called to account for Polonius' death, caused him to be conveyed on board a ship bound for England, under the care of two courtiers, by whom he dispatched letters to the English court, which at that time was in subjection and paid tribute to Denmark, requiring for special reasons there pretended, that Hamlet should be put to death as soon as he landed on English ground. Hamlet, suspecting some treachery, in the night-time secretly got at the letters, and skilfully erasing his own name, he in the stead of it put in the names of those two courtiers who had the charge of him, to be put to death ; then sealing up the letters, he put them into their place again. Soon after the ship was attacked by pirates, and a sea fight commenced, in the course of which Hamlet, desirous to show his valour, with sword in hand singly boarded the enemy's vessel, while his own ship in a cowardly manner bore away ; and leaving him to his fate the two courtiers made the best of their way to England, charged with those letters the sense of which Hamlet had altered to their own deserved destruction.

The pirates, who had the prince in their power, showed themselves gentle enemies, and knowing whom they had got prisoner, in the hope that the prince might do them

To this brook she came one day

1

a good turn at court in recompense for any favour they might show him, they set Hamlet on shore at the nearest port in Denmark. From that place Hamlet wrote to the king, acquainting him with the strange chance which had brought him back to his own country, and saying that on the next day he should present himself before his majesty. When he got home a sad spectacle offered itself the first thing to his eyes.

This was the funeral of the young and beautiful Ophelia, his once dear mistress. The wits of this young lady had begun to turn ever since her poor father's death. That he should die a violent death, and by the hands of the prince whom she loved, so affected this tender young maid, that in a little time she grew perfectly distracted, and would go about giving flowers away to the ladies of the court, and saying that they were for her father's burial, singing songs about love and about death, and sometimes such as had no meaning at all, as if she had no memory of what happened to her. There was a willow which grew slanting over a brook, and reflected its leaves in the stream. To this brook she came one day when she was unwatched, with garlands she had been making, mixed up of daisies and nettles, flowers and weeds together, and clambering up to hang her garland upon the boughs of the willow, a bough broke and precipitated this fair young maid, garland, and all that she had gathered, into the water, where her clothes bore her up for a while, during which she chanted scraps of old tunes, like one insensible to her own distress, or as if she were a creature natural to that element ; but long it was not before her garments, heavy with the wet, pulled her in from her melodious singing to a muddy and miserable death. It was the funeral of this fair maid which her brother Laertes was celebrating, the king and queen and whole court being present, when Hamlet arrived.

He knew not what all this show imported, but stood

on one side, not inclining to interrupt the ceremony. He saw the flowers strewed upon her grave, as the custom was in maiden burials, which the queen herself threw in ; and as she threw them, she said, " Sweets to the sweet ! I thought to have decked thy bridal bed, sweet maid, not to have strewed thy grave. Thou shouldst have been my Hamlet's wife." And he heard her brother wish that violets might spring from her grave ; and he saw him leap into the grave all frantic with grief, and bid the attendants pile mountains of earth upon him, that he might be buried with her. And Hamlet's love for this fair maid came back to him, and he could not bear that a brother should show so much transport of grief, for he thought that he loved Ophelia better than forty thousand brothers. Then discovering himself, he leaped into the grave where Laertes was, all as frantic or more frantic than he, and Laertes knowing him to be Hamlet who had been the cause of his father's and his sister's death, grappled him by the throat as an enemy till the attendants parted them. And Hamlet, after the funeral, excused his hasty act in throwing himself into the grave as if to brave Laertes ; but he said he could not bear that any one should seem to outgo him in grief for the death of the fair Ophelia. And for the time these two noble youths seemed reconciled.

But out of the grief and anger of Laertes for the death of his father and Ophelia, the king, Hamlet's wicked uncle, contrived destruction for Hamlet. He set on Laertes, under cover of peace and reconciliation, to challenge Hamlet to a friendly trial of skill at fencing, which Hamlet accepting, a day was appointed to try the match. At this match all the court was present ; and Laertes, by direction of the king, prepared a poisoned weapon. Upon this match great wagers were laid by the courtiers, as both Hamlet and Laertes were known to excel at this sword-play ; and Hamlet taking up the foils, chose one, not at all suspecting the treachery of Laertes, or being careful to examine Laertes' weapon, who, instead of a foil or blunted sword which the laws of fencing require, made use of one with a point and poisoned. At first Laertes did but play with Hamlet, and suffered him to gain some advantages, which the dissembling king magnified and extolled beyond measure, drinking to Hamlet's success, and wagering rich bets upon the issue ; but after a few passes Laertes, growing warm, made a deadly thrust at Hamlet with his poisoned weapon, and gave him a mortal blow. Hamlet incensed, but not knowing the whole of the treachery, in the scuffle exchanged his own innocent weapon for Laertes' deadly one, and with a thrust of Laertes' own sword repaid Laertes home, who was thus justly caught in his own treachery. In this instant the queen shrieked out that she was poisoned. She had inadvertently drunk out of a bowl which the king had prepared for Hamlet, in case that being warm in fencing he should call for drink : into this the treacherous king had infused a deadly poison to make sure of Hamlet if Laertes had failed. He had forgotten to warn the queen of the bowl which she drank of, and immediately died, exclaiming with her last breath that she was poisoned.

Hamlet, suspecting some treachery, ordered the doors to be shut while he sought it out. Laertes told him to seek no further, for he was the traitor ; and feeling his life go away with the wound which Hamlet had given him, he made confession of the treachery he had used, and how he had fallen a victim to it. And he told Hamlet of the envenomed point, and said that Hamlet had not half an hour to live, for no medicine could cure him ; and begging forgiveness of Hamlet, he died, with his last words accusing the king of being the contriver of the mischief. When Hamlet saw his end draw near, there being yet some venom left upon the sword, he suddenly turned upon his false uncle and thrust the point of it to his heart, fulfilling the promise which he had made to his father's spirit, whose injunction was now accomplished, and his foul murder revenged upon the murderer. Then Hamlet, feeling his breath fail and life departing, turned to his dear friend Horatio, who had been spectator of this fatal tragedy, and with his dying breath requested him that he would live to tell his story to the world—for Horatio had made a motion as if he would slay himself, to accompany the prince in death; and Horatio promised that he would make a true report, as one that was privy to all the circumstances. And thus satisfied, the noble heart of Hamlet cracked; and Horatio and the bystanders with many tears commended the spirit of their sweet prince to the guardianship of angels; for Hamlet was a loving and a gentle prince, and greatly beloved for his many noble and prince-like qualities, and if he had lived would no doubt have proved a most royal and complete king to Denmark.

OTHELLO

BRABANTIO, the rich senator of Venice, had a fair daughter, the gentle Desdemona. She was sought to by divers suitors, both on account of her many virtuous qualities and for her rich expectations. But among the suitors of her own clime and complexion she saw none whom she could affect ; for this noble lady, who regarded the mind more than the features of men, with a singularity rather to be admired than imitated, had chosen for the object of her affections a Moor, a black, whom her father loved and often invited to his house.

Neither is Desdemona to be altogether condemned for the unsuitableness of the person whom she selected for her lover. Bating that Othello was black, the noble Moor wanted nothing which might recommend him to the affections of the greatest lady. He was a soldier, and a brave one, and by his conduct in bloody wars against the Turks had risen to the rank of general in the Venetian service, and was esteemed and trusted by the state.

He had been a traveller, and Desdemona, as is the manner of ladies, loved to hear him tell the story of his adventures, which he would run through from his earliest recollection : the battles, sieges, and encounters which he had passed through ; the perils he had been exposed to by land and by water ; his hair-breadth escapes, when he had entered a breach or marched up to the mouth of a cannon ; and how he had been taken prisoner by the insolent enemy and sold to slavery ; how he demeaned himself in that state, and how he escaped : all these accounts, added to the narration of the strange things he had seen in foreign countries, the vast wildernesses and romantic caverns, the quarries, the rocks, and mountains whose heads are in the clouds ; of the savage nations, the canni-bals who are man-eaters, and a race of people in Africa whose heads do grow beneath their shoulders. These travellers' stories would so enchain the attention of Des-demona that if she were called off at any time by household affairs, she would dispatch with all haste that business, and return and with a greedy ear devour Othello's dis-course. And once he took advantage of a pliant hour, and drew from her a prayer that he would tell her the whole story of his life at large, of which she had heard so much, but only by parts, to which he consented, and beguiled her of many a tear when he spoke of some dis-tressful stroke which his youth suffered.

His story being done, she gave him for his pains a world of sighs. She swore a pretty oath that it was all passing strange and pitiful, wondrous pitiful ; she wished, she said, she had not heard it, yet she wished that Heaven had made her such a man ; and then she thanked him, and told him if he had a friend who loved her, he had only to teach him how to tell his story, and that would woo her. Upon this hint, delivered not with more frankness than modesty, accompanied with a certain bewitching prettiness, and blushes, which Othello could not but understand, he spoke more openly of his love, and in this golden opportunity gained the consent of the generous Lady Desdemona privately to marry him.

He spoke more openly of his love

Neither Othello's colour nor his fortune was such that it could be hoped Brabantio would accept him for a son-in-law. He had left his daughter free, but he did expect that, as the manner of noble Venetian ladies was, she would choose ere long a husband of senatorial rank or expectations. But in this he was deceived ; Desdemona loved the Moor, though he was black, and devoted her heart and fortunes to his valiant parts and qualities. So was her heart subdued to an implicit devotion to the man she had selected for a husband, that his very colour, which to all but this discerning lady would have proved an insurmountable objection, was by her esteemed above all the white skins and clear complexions of the young Venetian nobility, her suitors.

Their marriage—which, though privately carried, could not long be kept a secret—came to the ears of the old man Brabantio, who appeared in a solemn council of the senate as an accuser of the Moor Othello, who by spells and witchcraft, he maintained, had seduced the affections of the fair Desdemona to marry him without the consent of her father, and against the obligations of hospitality.

At this juncture of time it happened that the state of Venice had immediate need of the services of Othello, news having arrived that the Turks, with mighty preparation, had fitted out a fleet, which was bending its course to the island of Cyprus, with intent to regain that strong post from the Venetians, who then held it. In this emergency the state turned its eyes upon Othello, who alone was deemed adequate to conduct the defence of Cyprus against the Turks ; so that Othello, now summoned before the senate, stood in their presence at once as a candidate for a great state employment, and as a culprit charged with offences, which by the laws of Venice were made capital.

The age and senatorial character of old Brabantio

T

commanded a most patient hearing from that grave assembly ; but the incensed father conducted his accusation with so much intemperance, producing likelihoods and allegations for proofs, that when Othello was called upon for his defence he had only to relate a plain tale of the course of his love, which he did with such an artless eloquence, recounting the whole story of his wooing, as we have related it above, and delivered his speech with so noble a plainness—the evidence of truth—that the duke, who sat as chief judge, could not help confessing that a tale so told would have won his daughter too ; and the spells and conjurations which Othello had used in his courtship plainly appeared to have been no more than the honest arts of men in love, and the only witchcraft which he had used, the faculty of telling a soft tale to win a lady's ear.

This statement of Othello was confirmed by the testimony of the Lady Desdemona herself, who appeared in court, and professing a duty to her father for life and education, challenged leave of him to profess a yet higher duty to her lord and husband, even so much as her mother had shown in preferring him (Brabantio) above her father.

The old senator, unable to maintain his plea, called the Moor to him with many expressions of sorrow, and, as an act of necessity, bestowed upon him his daughter, whom, if he had been free to withhold her (he told him), he would with all his heart have kept from him, adding that he was glad at soul that he had no other child, for this behaviour of Desdemona would have taught him to be a tyrant, and hang clogs on them for her desertion.

This difficulty being got over, Othello, to whom custom had rendered the hardships of a military life as natural as food and rest are to other men, readily undertook the management of the wars in Cyprus, and Desdemona, preferring the honour of her lord (though with danger) before the indulgence of those idle delights in which new-married people usually waste their time, cheerfully consented to his going.

No sooner were Othello and his lady landed in Cyprus, than news arrived that a desperate tempest had dispersed the Turkish fleet, and thus the island was secure from any immediate apprehension of an attack. But the war which Othello was to suffer was now beginning, and the enemies which malice stirred up against his innocent lady proved in their nature more deadly than strangers or infidels.

Among all the general's friends, no one possessed the confidence of Othello more entirely than Cassio. Michael Cassio was a young soldier, a Florentine, gay, amorous, and of pleasing address, favourite qualities with women. He was handsome and eloquent, and exactly such a person as might alarm the jealousy of a man advanced in years (as Othello in some measure was), who had married a young and beautiful wife ; but Othello was as free from jealousy as he was noble, and as incapable of suspecting, as of doing, a base action. He had employed this Cassio in his love affair with Desdemona, and Cassio had been a sort of go-between in his suit ; for Othello, fearing that himself had not those soft parts of conversation which please ladies, and finding these qualities in his friend, would often depute Cassio to go (as he phrased it) a-courting for him, such innocent simplicity being rather an honour than a blemish to the character of the valiant Moor ; so that no wonder if, next to Othello himself (but at far distance, as beseems a virtuous wife) the gentle Desdemona loved and trusted Cassio. Nor had the marriage of this couple made any difference in their behaviour to Michael Cassio. He frequented their house, and his free and rattling talk was no unpleasing variety to Othello, who was himself of a more serious temper, for such tempers are observed often to delight in their contraries, as a relief from the oppressive excess of their own; and Desdemona and Cassio would talk and laugh together, as in the days when he went a-courting for his friend.

Othello had lately promoted Cassio to be lieutenant, a place of trust, and nearest to the general's person. This promotion gave great offence to Iago, an older officer, who thought he had a better claim than Cassio, and would often ridicule Cassio, as a fellow fit only for the company of ladies, and one that knew no more of the art of war, or how to set an army in array for battle, than a girl. Iago hated Cassio, and he hated Othello, as well for favouring Cassio, as for an unjust suspicion which he had lightly taken up against Othello, that the Moor was too fond of Iago's wife Emilia. From these imaginary provocations the plotting mind of Iago conceived a horrid scheme of revenge, which should involve both Cassio, the Moor, and Desdemona, in one common ruin.

Iago was artful, and had studied human nature deeply, and he knew that, of all the torments which afflict the mind of man (and far beyond bodily torture), the pains of jealousy were the most intolerable and had the sorest sting. If he could succeed in making Othello jealous of Cassio, he thought it would be an exquisite plot of revenge, and might end in the death of Cassio or Othello, or of both, he cared not.

The arrival of the general and his lady in Cyprus, meeting with the news of the dispersion of the enemy's fleet, made a sort of holiday in the island. Everybody gave themselves up to feasting and making merry. Wine flowed in abundance, and cups went round to the health of the black Othello, and his lady the fair Desdemona.

Cassio had the direction of the guard that night, with a charge from Othello to keep the soldiers from excess in drinking, that no brawl might arise to fright the inhabitants, or disgust them with the new landed forces. That night Iago began his deep-laid plans of mischief. Under colour of loyalty and love to the general, he enticed Cassio to make rather too free with the bottle, a great fault in an officer upon guard. Cassio for a time resisted, but he could not long hold out against the honest freedom which Iago knew how to put on, but kept swallowing glass after glass (as Iago still plied him with drink and encouraging songs), and Cassio's tongue ran over in praise of the Lady Desdemona, whom he again and again toasted, affirming that she was a most exquisite lady, until at last the enemy which he put into his mouth stole away his brains ; and, upon some provocation given him by a fellow whom Iago had set on, swords were drawn, and Montano, a worthy officer, who interfered to appease the dispute, was wounded in the scuffle. The riot now began to be general, and Iago, who had set on foot the mischief, was foremost in spreading the alarm, causing the castle bell to be rung (as if some dangerous mutiny, instead of a mere slight drunken quarrel, had arisen). The alarm-bell ringing, awakened Othello, who, dressing in a hurry, and coming to the scene of action, questioned Cassio of the cause. Cassio was now come to himself, the effect of the wine having a little gone off, but was too much ashamed to reply ; and Iago, pretending a great reluctance to accuse Cassio, but, as it were, forced into it by Othello, who insisted to know the truth, gave an account of the whole matter (leaving out his own share in it, which Cassio was too far gone to remember) in such a manner as, while he seemed to make Cassio's offence less, did indeed make it appear greater than it was. The result was that Othello, who was a strict observer of discipline, was compelled to take away Cassio's place of lieutenant from him.

Thus did Iago's first artifice succeed completely : he

had now undermined his hated rival and thrust him out of his place ; but a further use was hereafter to be made of the adventure of this disastrous night.

Cassio, whom this misfortune had entirely sobered, now lamented to his seeming friend Iago that he should have been such a fool as to transform himself into a beast. He was undone, for how could he ask the general for his place again ? He would tell him he was a drunkard. He despised himself. Iago, affecting to make light of it, said that he or any man living might be drunk upon occasion ; it remained now to make the best of a bad bargain. The general's wife was now the general, and could do anything with Othello ; that he were best to apply to the Lady Desdemona to mediate for him with her lord ; that she was of a frank, obliging disposition, and would readily undertake a good office of this sort, and set Cassio right again in the general's favour, and then this crack in their love would be made stronger than ever. A good advice of Iago, if it had not been given for wicked purposes, which will after appear.

Cassio did as Iago advised him, and made application to the Lady Desdemona, who was easy to be won over in any honest suit, and she promised Cassio that she would be his solicitor with her lord, and rather die than give up his cause. This she immediately set about in so earnest and pretty a manner, that Othello, who was mortally offended with Cassio, could not put her off. When he pleaded delay, and that it was too soon to pardon such an offender, she would not be beat back, but insisted that it should be the next night, or the morning after, or the next morning to that at furthest. Then she showed how penitent and humbled poor Cassio was, and that his offence did not deserve so sharp a check. And when Othello still hung back, " What ! my lord," said she, " that I should have so much to do to plead for Cassio—Michael Cassio, that came a-courting for you,

and oftentimes when I have spoken in dispraise of you
has taken your part! I count this but a little thing to
ask of you. When I mean to try your love indeed, I shall
ask a weighty matter." Othello could deny nothing to
such a pleader, and only requesting that Desdemona would
leave the time to him, promised to receive Michael Cassio
again into favour.

It happened that Othello and Iago had entered into
the room where Desdemona was, just as Cassio, who had
been imploring her intercession, was departing at the
opposite door; and Iago, who was full of art, said in a low
voice as if to himself, " I like not that." Othello took
no great notice of what he said; indeed, the conference
which immediately took place with his lady put it out of
his head; but he remembered it afterwards; for when
Desdemona was gone, Iago, as if for mere satisfaction of
his thought, questioned Othello whether Michael Cassio,
when Othello was courting his lady, knew of his love. To
this the general answered in the affirmative, and adding
that he had gone between them very often during the
courtship. Iago knitted his brow, as if he had got fresh
light of some terrible matter, and cried, " Indeed! " This
brought into Othello's mind the words which Iago had
let fall upon entering the room and seeing Cassio with
Desdemona, and he began to think there was some meaning
in all this; for he deemed Iago to be a just man and full
of love and honesty, and what in a false knave would be
tricks, in him seemed to be the natural workings of an
honest mind, big with something too great for utterance;
and Othello prayed Iago to speak what he knew, and to
give his worst thoughts words.

" And what," said Iago, " if some thoughts very vile
should have intruded into my breast, as where is the palace
into which foul things do not enter? " Then Iago went
on to say, what a pity it were if any trouble should arise
to Othello out of his imperfect observations; that it would

not be for Othello's peace to know his thoughts ; that
people's good names were not to be taken away for slight
suspicions. And when Othello's curiosity was raised
almost to distraction with these hints and scattered words,
Iago, as if in earnest care for Othello's peace of mind,
besought him to beware of jealousy : with such art did this
villain raise suspicions in the unguarded Othello, by the
very caution which he pretended to give him against
suspicion. " I know," said Othello, " that my wife is
fair, loves company and feasting, is free of speech, sings,
plays, and dances well ; but where virtue is, these qualities
are virtuous. I must have proof before I think her dishonest." Then Iago, as if glad that Othello was slow to
believe ill of his lady, frankly declared that he had no
proof, but begged Othello to observe her behaviour well
when Cassio was by ; not to be jealous nor too secure
neither, for that he (Iago) knew the dispositions of the
Italian ladies, his countrywomen, better than Othello
could do ; and that in Venice the wives let Heaven see
many pranks they dared not show their husbands. Then
he artfully insinuated that Desdemona deceived her father
in marrying with Othello, and carried it so closely that
the poor old man thought that witchcraft had been used.
Othello was much moved with this argument, which
brought the matter home to him, for if she had
deceived her father, why might she not deceive her
husband ?

Iago begged pardon for having moved him ; but Othello,
assuming an indifference, while he was really shaken with
inward grief at Iago's words, begged him to go on, which
Iago did with many apologies, as if unwilling to produce
anything against Cassio, whom he called his friend : he
then came strongly to the point, and reminded Othello
how Desdemona had refused many suitable matches of her
own clime and complexion, and had married him, a Moor,
which showed unnatural in her, and proved her to have

a headstrong will ; and when her better judgment returned, how probable it was she would fall upon comparing Othello with the fine forms and clear white complexions of the young Italians, her countrymen. He concluded with advising Othello to put off his reconcilement with Cassio a little longer, and in the meanwhile to note with what earnestness Desdemona should intercede in his behalf, for that much would be seen in that. So mischievously did this artful villain lay his plots to turn the gentle qualities of this innocent lady into her destruction, and make a net for her out of her own goodness to entrap her : first setting Cassio on to entreat her mediation, and then out of that very mediation contriving stratagems for her ruin.

The conference ended with Iago's begging Othello to account his wife innocent until he had more decisive proof, and Othello promised to be patient ; but from that moment the deceived Othello never tasted content of mind. Poppy, nor the juice of mandragora, nor all the sleeping potions in the world, could ever again restore to him that sweet rest which he had enjoyed but yesterday. His occupation sickened upon him. He no longer took delight in arms. His heart, that used to be roused at the sight of troops, and banners, and battle array, and would stir and leap at the sound of a drum, or a trumpet, or a neighing war-horse, seemed to have lost all that pride and ambition which are a soldier's virtue, and his military ardour and all his old joys forsook him. Sometimes he thought his wife honest, and at times he thought her not so ; sometimes he thought Iago just, and at times he thought him not so ; then he would wish that he had never known of it : he was not the worse for her loving Cassio, so long as he knew it not. Torn in pieces with these distracting thoughts, he once laid hold on Iago's throat, and demanded proof of Desdemona's guilt, or threatened instant death for his having belied her Iago, feigning indignation that his honesty should be taken for a vice, asked Othello if he had not sometimes seen a handkerchief spotted with strawberries in his wife's hand. Othello answered that he had given her such a one, and that it was his first gift. " That same handkerchief," said Iago, " did I see Michael Cassio this day wipe his face with." " If it be as you say," said Othello, " I will not rest till a wide revenge swallow them up : and first, for a token of your fidelity, I expect that Cassio shall be put to death within three days ; and for that fair devil " (meaning his lady), " I will withdraw and devise some swift means of death for her."

Trifles light as air are to the jealous proofs as strong as Holy Writ. A handkerchief of his wife's seen in Cassio's hand was motive enough to the deluded Othello to pass sentence of death upon them both, without once inquiring how Cassio came by it. Desdemona had never given such a present to Cassio, nor would this constant lady have wronged her lord with doing so naughty a thing as giving his presents to another man : both Cassio and Desdemona were innocent of any offence against Othello ; but the wicked Iago, whose spirits never slept in contrivance of villainy, had made his wife (a good but a weak woman) steal this handkerchief from Desdemona under the pretence of getting the work copied, but in reality to drop it in Cassio's way, where he might find it, and give a handle to Iago's suggestion that it was Desdemona's present.

Othello, soon after meeting his wife, pretended that he had a headache—as he might indeed with truth—and desired her to lend him her handkerchief to hold to his temples. She did so. " Not this," said Othello, " but that handkerchief I gave you." Desdemona had it not about her, for indeed it was stolen, as we have related. " How ! " said Othello, " this is a fault indeed. That handkerchief an Egyptian woman gave to my mother : the woman was a witch and could read people's thoughts ;

she told my mother while she kept it it would make her amiable, and my father would love her; but if she lost it or gave it away, my father's fancy would turn, and he would loathe her as much as he had loved her. She, dying, gave it me, and bade me if I ever married to give it to my wife. I did so. Take heed of it; make it a darling as precious as your eye." " Is it possible ? " said the affrighted lady. " 'Tis true," continued Othello ; " it is a magical handkerchief. A sibyl, that had lived in the world two hundred years, in a fit of prophetic fury worked it ; the silkworms that furnished the silk were hallowed, and it was dyed in mummy of maidens' hearts conserved." Desdemona, hearing the wondrous virtues of the handkerchief, was ready to die with fear, for she plainly perceived she had lost it, and with it, she feared, the affections of her husband. Then Othello started and looked as if he were going to do some rash thing, and still he demanded the handkerchief, which when she could not produce, she tried to divert her husband from too serious thoughts, and cheerfully told him she saw all his talk about the handkerchief was only to put her off from her suit about Michael Cassio, whom she went on to praise, as Iago had foretold, till Othello in perfect distraction burst out of the room, and then Desdemona, though unwillingly, began to suspect her lord was jealous.

What cause she could have ministered to him she knew not ; and then she accused herself for accusing the noble Othello, and thought to be sure some untoward news from Venice, or some state troubles, had puddled his spirits, and made his temper not so sweet as formerly. And she said, " Men are not gods, and we must not look for that observance from them when they are married which they show us on the bridal day ; " and she beshrewed herself for so unkindly judging of his unkindness.

Again Othello and Desdemona met, and he accused her more plainly of being unfaithful and of loving another man, but he did not name whom. And Othello wept, and Desdemona said, " Alas ! the heavy day ! why do you weep ? " And Othello told her he could have borne all sorts of evils with fortitude—poverty, and disease, and disgrace, but her infidelity had broken his heart ; and he called her a weed, that looked so fair and smelt so sweet that the sense ached at it, and wished she had never been born. And when he had left her, this innocent lady was so stupefied with wonder at her lord's untrue suspicion of her that a weight-like sleep came over her, and she only desired her attendant to make her bed and to lay her wedding sheets upon it, saying that when people teach their babes, they do it by gentle means and easy tasks, and Othello might have chid her so, for in good truth she was but a child when she was chidden. And this was all the complaint which this gentle lady made.

Desdemona being retired to bed, expecting her husband would follow her, soon fell into a slumber, the effect of her troubled spirits, when Othello entered the chamber, full of the black purpose which he had meditated of putting his lady to death. But when he saw her asleep, he thought he would not shed her blood, nor scar that white skin of hers, more white than alabaster. But he was resolved she should die, else, as he said, she would live to betray more men as she had done him. Then he kissed her for the last time, as he said, and that kiss was so sweet he must needs kiss her again ; and he wept, but he said they were cruel tears.

Desdemona was awakened with his kisses, and she looked upon Othello, and she saw him gnaw his under lip and roll his eyes, and she knew he was always fatal when he looked so ; and he bade her prepare for death and to say her prayers, for he would not kill her soul. And this innocent wife, as she lay at his mercy, begged for compassion and to know her fault, and then he named Cassio and the handkerchief which, he said, she had given him ; and as the guiltless lady was proceeding to clear herself, he suddenly would hear no more, but covering her up in the bed-clothes, stifled her till she died !

In this instant of time was brought into the house Cassio, wounded and bleeding, whom Iago had set one of his creatures on to assassinate ; but the fellow not succeeding in his attempt to kill Cassio—whom he wounded, but not mortally—and being himself killed by Iago to prevent discovery, in his pockets were found certain letters, which made the guilt of Iago and the innocence of Cassio clear beyond all doubt ; and Cassio now came to beg pardon of Othello, and to ask wherein he had offended him, that he had employed Iago to murder him.

This discovery was as a thunder-stroke to Othello, who now plainly saw that he was no better than a murderer, and that his wife, poor innocent lady ! had been ever faithful to him ; the extreme anguish of which discovery making life insupportable, he fell upon his sword, and throwing himself upon the body of his dear injured lady, expired.

These rash acts raised much passion of horror and amazement in the bystanders, for Othello had borne a fair reputation, and till he was wrought upon by the arts of a villain, which his own noble nature never gave him leave to suspect, he was a loving and a doting husband. He had loved not wisely, but too well ; and his manly eyes, when he learned his mistake, though not used to weep on every small occasion, dropped tears as fast as Arabian trees their gum. And when he was dead, all his former merits and his valiant acts were remembered. Nothing now remained for his successor but to put the utmost censure of the law in force against Iago, who was executed with strict tortures, and to send word to the state of Venice of the lamentable death of their renowned general.

PERICLES, PRINCE OF TYRE

PERICLES, Prince of Tyre, became a voluntary exile from his dominions to avert the dreadful calamities which Antiochus, the wicked Emperor of Greece, threatened to bring upon his subjects and the city of Tyre, in revenge for a discovery which the prince had made of a shocking deed which the emperor had done in secret: as commonly it proves dangerous to pry into the hidden crimes of great ones. Leaving the government of his people in the hands of his able and honest minister Helicanus, Pericles set sail from Tyre, thinking to absent himself till the wrath of Antiochus, who was mighty, should be appeased.

The first place which the prince directed his course to was Tharsus; and hearing that the city of Tharsus was at that time suffering under a severe famine, he took with him store of provisions for its relief. On his arrival he found the city reduced to the utmost distress; and he coming like a messenger from heaven with this unhoped-for succour, Cleon, the governor of Tharsus, welcomed him with boundless thanks. Pericles had not been here many days before letters came from his faithful minister, warning him that it was not safe for him to stay at

Tharsus, for Antiochus knew of his abode, and by secret
emissaries dispatched for that purpose sought his life.
Upon receipt of these letters Pericles put out to sea again,
amidst the blessings and prayers of a whole people who
had been fed by his bounty.

He had not sailed far when his ship was overtaken by
a dreadful storm, and every man on board perished except
Pericles, who was cast by the sea-waves naked on an unknown shore, where he had not wandered long before he
met with some poor fishermen, who invited him to their
homes, giving him clothes and provisions. The fishermen
told Pericles the name of their country was Pentapolis,
and that their king was Simonides, commonly called the
Good Simonides, because of his peaceable reign and good
government. From them he also learned that King
Simonides had a fair young daughter, and that the following day was her birthday, when a grand tournament was
to be held at court, many princes and knights being come
from all parts to try their skill in arms for the love of Thaisa,
this fair princess. While the prince was listening to this
account, and secretly lamenting the loss of his good
armour, which disabled him from making one among these
valiant knights, another fisherman brought in a complete
suit of armour that he had taken out of the sea with his
fishing-net, which proved to be the very armour he had
lost. When Pericles beheld his own armour, he said,
" Thanks, Fortune ! after all my crosses you give me
somewhat to repair myself. This armour was bequeathed
to me by my dead father, for whose dear sake I have so
loved it, that whithersoever I went I still have kept it by
me ; and the rough sea that parted it from me, having now
become calm, hath given it back again, for which I thank
it, for since I have my father's gift again I think my shipwreck no misfortune."

The next day Pericles, clad in his brave father's
armour, repaired to the royal court of Simonides, where

he performed wonders at the tournament, vanquishing with ease all the brave knights and valiant princes who contended with him in arms for the honour of Thaisa's love. When brave warriors contended at court tournaments for the love of king's daughters, if one proved sole victor over all the rest, it was usual for the great lady for whose sake these deeds of valour were undertaken to bestow all her respect upon the conqueror, and Thaisa did not depart from this custom, for she presently dismissed all the princes and knights whom Pericles had vanquished, and distinguished him by her especial favour and regard, crowning him with the wreath of victory, as king of that day's happiness ; and Pericles became a most passionate lover of this beauteous princess from the first moment he beheld her.

The good Simonides so well approved of the valour and noble qualities of Pericles, who was indeed a most accomplished gentleman, and well learned in all excellent arts, that though he knew not the rank of this royal stranger (for Pericles for fear of Antiochus gave out that he was a private gentleman of Tyre), yet did not Simonides disdain to accept of the valiant unknown for a son-in-law, when he perceived his daughter's affections were firmly fixed upon him.

Pericles had not been many months married to Thaisa before he received intelligence that his enemy Antiochus was dead, and that his subjects of Tyre, impatient of his long absence, threatened to revolt, and talked of placing Helicanus upon his vacant throne. This news came from Helicanus himself, who, being a loyal subject to his royal master, would not accept of the high dignity offered him, but sent to let Pericles know their intentions, that he might return home and resume his lawful right. It was matter of great surprise and joy to Simonides to find that his son-in-law (the obscure knight) was the renowned prince of Tyre ; yet again he regretted that he was not the private

gentleman he supposed him to be, seeing that he must
now part both with his admired son-in-law and his beloved daughter, whom he feared to trust to the perils of
the sea ; and Pericles himself wished his wife to remain
with her father ; but the poor lady so earnestly desired
to go with her husband, that at last they consented,
hoping soon to reach Tyre.

The sea was no friendly element to unhappy Pericles,
for long before they reached Tyre another dreadful tempest
arose, which so terrified Thaisa that she was taken ill,
and in a short space of time her nurse Lychorida came to
Pericles with a little child in her arms, to tell the prince
the sad tidings that his wife had died the moment her
little babe was born. She held the babe towards its father,
saying, " Here is a thing too young for such a place. This
is the child of your dead queen." No tongue can tell
the dreadful sufferings of Pericles when he heard his wife
was dead. As soon as he could speak, he said, " O you
gods, why do you make us love your goodly gifts, and then
snatch those gifts away ? " " Patience, good sir," said
Lychorida : " here is all that is left alive of your dead
queen, a little daughter, and for your child's sake be more
manly. Patience, good sir, even for the sake of this
precious charge." Pericles took the new-born infant in
his arms, and he said to the little babe, " Now may your
life be mild, for a more blusterous birth had never babe !
May your condition be mild and gentle, for you have had
the rudest welcome that ever prince's child did meet with !
May that which follows be happy, for you have had as
chiding a nativity as fire, air, water, earth, and heaven
could make. Even at the first, your loss," meaning in the
death of her mother, " is more than all the joys which you
shall find upon this earth, to which you are come a new
visitor, shall be able to recompense."

The storm still continuing to rage furiously, and the
sailors having a superstition that while a dead body remained

U

in the ship the storm would never cease, they came to Pericles to demand that his queen should be thrown overboard ; and they said, " What courage, sir ? God save you ! " " Courage enough," said the sorrowing prince ; " I do not fear the storm ; it has done to me its worst ; yet for the love of this poor infant, this fresh new seafarer, I wish the storm was over." " Sir," said the sailors, " your queen must overboard. The sea works high, the wind is loud, and the storm will not abate till the ship be cleared of the dead." Though Pericles knew how weak and unfounded this superstition was, yet he patiently submitted, saying, " As you think meet. Then she must overboard, most wretched queen ! " And now this unhappy prince went to take a last view of his dear wife, and as he looked on his Thaisa he said, " A terrible fate hast thou had, my dear : no light, no fire, the unfriendly elements forgot thee utterly ; nor have I time to bring thee hallowed to thy grave, but must cast thee scarcely coffined into the sea, where for a monument upon thy bones the humming waters must overwhelm thy corpse, lying with simple shells. O Lychorida ! bid Nestor bring me spices, ink, and paper, my casket and my jewels, and bid Nicandor bring me the satin coffin. Lay the babe upon the pillow, and go about this suddenly, Lychorida, while I say a priestly farewell to my Thaisa."

They brought Pericles a large chest, in which (wrapped in a satin shroud) he placed his queen, and sweet-smelling spices he strewed over her, and beside her he placed rich jewels, and a written paper, telling who she was, and praying if haply any one should find the chest which contained the body of his wife, they would give her burial ; and then with his own hands he cast the chest into the sea. When the storm was over Pericles ordered the sailors to make for Tharsus. " For," said Pericles, " the babe cannot hold out till we come to Tyre. At Tharsus I will leave it at careful nursing."

After that tempestuous night when Thaisa was thrown
into the sea, and while it was yet early morning, as Cerimon, a worthy gentleman of Ephesus and a most skilful
physician, was standing by the sea-side, his servants
brought to him a chest, which they said the sea waves
had thrown on the land. " I never saw," said one of
them, " so huge a billow as cast it on our shore." Cerimon ordered the chest to be conveyed to his own house,
and when it was opened he beheld with wonder the body
of a young and lovely lady, and the sweet-smelling spices
and rich casket of jewels made him conclude it was some
great person who was thus strangely entombed ; searching further, he discovered a paper, from which he learned
that the corpse which lay as dead before him had been a
queen and wife to Pericles, Prince of Tyre ; and much
admiring at the strangeness of that accident, and more
pitying the husband who had lost this sweet lady, he said,
" If you are living, Pericles, you have a heart that even
cracks with woe." Then observing attentively Thaisa's
face, he saw how fresh and unlike death her looks were,
and he said, " They were too hasty that threw you into
the sea ; " for he did not believe her to be dead. He
ordered a fire to be made, and proper cordials to be
brought, and soft music to be played, which might help
to calm her amazed spirits if she should revive ; and he
said to those who crowded round her, wondering at what
they saw, " I pray you, gentlemen, give her air : this queen
will live ; she has not been entranced above five hours ;
and see, she begins to blow into life again : she is alive ;
behold, her eyelids move ! this fair creature will live to
make us weep to hear her fate." Thaisa had never died,
but after the birth of her little baby had fallen into a deep
swoon, which made all that saw her conclude her to be
dead ; and now by the care of this kind gentleman she
once more revived to light and life, and opening her eyes
she said, " Where am I ? Where is my lord ? What

world is this ? " By gentle degrees Cerimon let her understand what had befallen her, and when he thought she was enough recovered to bear the sight, he showed her the paper written by her husband, and the jewels, and she looked on the paper and said, " It is my lord's writing. That I was shipped at sea I well remember, but whether there my babe was born, by the holy gods I cannot rightly say ; but since my wedded lord I never shall see again, I will put on a vestal livery and never more have joy." " Madam," said Cerimon, " if you purpose as you speak, the temple of Diana is not far distant from hence ; there you may abide as a vestal. Moreover, if you please, a niece of mine shall there attend you." This proposal was accepted with thanks by Thaisa, and when she was perfectly recovered Cerimon placed her in the temple of Diana, where she became a vestal or priestess of that goddess, and passed her days in sorrowing for her husband's supposed loss, and in the most devout exercises of those times.

Pericles carried his young daughter (whom he named Marina, because she was born at sea), to Tharsus, intending to leave her with Cleon, the governor of that city, and his wife Dionyza, thinking, for the good he had done to them at the time of their famine, they would be kind to his little motherless daughter. When Cleon saw Prince Pericles, and heard of the great loss which had befallen him, he said, " Oh, your sweet queen ! that it had pleased Heaven you could have brought her hither to have blessed my eyes with the sight of her ! " Pericles replied, " We must obey the Powers above us. Should I rage and roar as the sea does in which my Thaisa lies, yet the end must be as it is. My gentle babe, Marina here, I must charge your charity with her. I leave her the infant of your care, beseeching you to give her princely training." And then turning to Cleon's wife, Dionyza, he said, " Good madam, make me blessed in your care in bringing up my child " ;

and she answered, " I have a child myself, who shall not
be more dear to my respect than yours, my lord ; " and
Cleon made the like promise, saying, " Your noble services,
Prince Pericles, in feeding my whole people with your
corn (for which in their prayers they daily remember you)
must in your child be thought on. If I should neglect
your child, my whole people that were by you relieved
would force me to my duty ; but if to that I need a spur,
the gods revenge it on me and mine to the end of genera-
tion." Pericles being thus assured that his child would
be carefully attended to, left her to the protection of Cleon
and his wife Dionyza, and with her he left the nurse
Lychorida. When he went away the little Marina knew
not her loss, but Lychorida wept sadly at parting with her
royal master. " Oh ! no tears, Lychorida," said Pericles ;
" no tears ! look to your little mistress, on whose grace
you may depend hereafter."

Pericles arrived in safety at Tyre, and was once more
settled in the quiet possession of his throne, while his
woeful queen, whom he thought dead, remained at Ephesus.
Her little babe Marina, whom this hapless mother had
never seen, was brought up by Cleon in a manner suitable
to her high birth. He gave her the most careful education,
so that by the time Marina attained the age of fourteen
years the most deeply-learned men were not more studied
in the learning of those times than was Marina. She sang
like one immortal, and danced as goddess-like ; and with
her needle she was so skilful that she seemed to compose
Nature's own shapes, in birds, fruits, or flowers, the
natural roses being scarcely more like to each other than
they were to Marina's silken flowers. But when she had
gained from education all these graces, which made her
the general wonder, Dionyza, the wife of Cleon, became
her mortal enemy from jealousy, by reason that her own
daughter, from the slowness of her mind, was not able
to attain to that perfection wherein Marina excelled ; and

finding that all praise was bestowed on Marina, whilst
her daughter, who was of the same age and had been educated with the same care as Marina, though not with the
same success, was in comparison disregarded, she formed
a project to remove Marina out of the way, vainly imagining that her untoward daughter would be more respected
when Marina was no more seen. To compass this she
employed a man to murder Marina, and she well timed
her wicked design, when Lychorida, the faithful nurse,
had just died. Dionyza was discoursing with the man
she had commanded to commit this murder, when the
young Marina was weeping over the dead Lychorida.
Leonine, the man she employed to do this bad deed,
though he was a very wicked man, could hardly be persuaded to undertake it, so had Marina won all hearts to
love her. He said, " She is a goodly creature ! " " The
fitter then the gods should have her," replied her merciless enemy : " here she comes weeping for the death
of her nurse Lychorida. Are you resolved to obey me ? "
Leonine, fearing to disobey her, replied, " I am resolved."
And so in that one short sentence was the matchless
Marina doomed to an untimely death. She now
approached with a basket of flowers in her hand, which,
she said, she would daily strew over the grave of good
Lychorida. The purple violet and the marigold should
as a carpet hang upon her grave while summer days did
last. " Alas for me ! " she said, " poor unhappy maid,
born in a tempest when my mother died ! This world
to me is like a lasting storm, hurrying me from my
friends." " How now, Marina ! " said the dissembling
Dionyza, " do you weep alone ? How does it chance
my daughter is not with you ? Do not sorrow for
Lychorida, you have a nurse in me. Your beauty is quite
changed with this unprofitable woe. Come, give me
your flowers, the sea air will spoil them, and walk with
Leonine ; the air is fine and will enliven you. Come,

Leonine, take her by the arm and walk with her." " No, madam," said Marina, " I pray you let me not deprive you of your servant ; " for Leonine was one of Dionyza's attendants. " Come, come," said this artful woman, who wished for a pretence to leave her alone with Leonine, " I love the prince your father, and I love you. We every day expect your father here, and when he comes and finds you so changed by grief from the paragon of beauty we reported you, he will think we have taken no care of you. Go, I pray you, walk and be cheerful once again. Be careful of that excellent complexion, which stole the hearts of old and young." Marina being thus importuned, said, " Well, I will go, but yet I have no desire to it." As Dionyza walked away she said to Leonine, " *Remember what I have said !* "—shocking words, for their meaning was that he should remember to kill Marina.

Marina looked towards the sea, her birthplace, and said, " Is the wind westerly that blows ? " " South-west," replied Leonine. " When I was born the wind was north," said she ; and then the storm and tempest, and all her father's sorrows and her mother's death, came full into her mind ; and she said, " My father, as Lychorida told me, did never fear, but cried, *Courage, good seamen,* to the sailors, galling his princely hands with the ropes, and, clasping to the mast, he endured a sea that almost split the deck." " When was this ? " said Leonine. " When I was born," replied Marina : " never were waves nor wind more violent." And then she described the storm, the action of the sailors, the boatswain's whistle, and the loud call of the master, " Which," said she, " trebled the confusion of the ship." Lychorida had so often recounted to Marina the story of her hapless birth, that these things seemed ever present to her imagination. But here Leonine interrupted her with desiring her to say her prayers. " What mean you ? " said Marina, who began to fear, she knew not why. " If you require a little space for prayer, I grant it," said Leonine ; " but be not tedious : the gods are quick of ear, and I am sworn to do my work in haste." " Will you kill me ? " said Marina ; " alas ! why ? " " To satisfy my lady," replied Leonine. " Why would she have me killed ? " said Marina ; " now, as I can remember, I never hurt her in all my life. I never spake bad word, nor did any ill turn to any living creature. Believe me now, I never killed a mouse, nor hurt a fly. I trod upon a worm once against my will, but I wept for it. How have I offended ? " The murderer replied, " My commission is not to reason on the deed, but to do it." And he was just going to kill her, when certain pirates happened to land at that very moment, who, seeing Marina, bore her off as a prize to their ship.

The pirate who had made Marina his prize, carried her to Mitylene, and sold her for a slave, where, though in that humble condition, Marina soon became known throughout the whole city of Mitylene for her beauty and her virtues ; and the person to whom she was sold became rich by the money she earned for him. She taught music, dancing, and fine needlework, and the money she got by her scholars she gave to her master and mistress ; and the fame of her learning and her great industry came to the knowledge of Lysimachus, a young nobleman who was the Governor of Mitylene, and Lysimachus went himself to the house where Marina dwelt, to see this paragon of excellence, whom all the city praised so highly. Her conversation delighted Lysimachus beyond measure ; for though he had heard much of this admired maiden, he did not expect to find her so sensible a lady, so virtuous and so good, as he perceived Marina to be ; and he left her, saying he hoped she would persevere in her indus- trious and virtuous course, and that if ever she heard from him again, it should be for her good. Lysimachus thought Marina such a miracle for sense, fine breeding, and ex- cellent qualities, as well as for beauty and all outward graces, that he wished to marry her, and notwithstanding her humble situation, he hoped to find that her birth was noble ; but ever when they asked her parentage, she would sit still and weep.

Meantime at Tharsus, Leonine fearing the anger of Dionyza, told her he had killed Marina ; and that wicked woman gave out that she was dead, and made a pretended funeral for her and erected a stately monument ; and shortly after Pericles, accompanied by his loyal minister Helicanus, made a voyage from Tyre to Tharsus on purpose to see his daughter, intending to take her home with him ; and he never having beheld her since he left her an infant in the care of Cleon and his wife, how did this good prince rejoice at the thoughts of seeing this dear child of his buried queen ! but when they told him Marina was dead, and showed the monument they had erected for her, great was the misery this most wretched father endured, and not being able to bear the sight of that country where his last hope and only memory of his dear Thaisa was entombed, he took ship, and hastily departed from Tharsus. From the day he entered the ship a dull and heavy melancholy seized him. He never spoke, and seemed totally insensible to everything around him.

Sailing from Tharsus to Tyre, the ship in its course passed by Mitylene, where Marina dwelt ; the governor of which place, Lysimachus, observing this royal vessel from the shore, and desirous of knowing who was on board, went in a barge to the side of the ship to satisfy his curiosity. Helicanus received him very courteously, and told him that the ship came from Tyre, and that they were conducting thither Pericles their prince. " A man, sir," said Helicanus, " who has not spoken to any one these three months, nor taken any sustenance, but just to prolong his grief : it would be tedious to repeat the whole ground of his distemper, but the main springs from the loss of a beloved daughter and a wife." Lysimachus begged to see this afflicted prince, and when he beheld Pericles, he saw he had been once a goodly person, and he said to him, " Sir king, all hail, the gods preserve you, hail, royal sir !" But in vain Lysimachus spoke to him ; Pericles made no answer, nor did he appear to perceive any stranger approached. And then Lysimachus bethought him of the peerless maid Marina, that haply with her sweet tongue she might win some answer from the silent prince ; and with the consent of Helicanus he sent for Marina, and when she entered the ship in which her own father sat motionless with grief, they welcomed her on board as if they had known she was their princess ; and they cried, " She is a gallant lady." Lysimachus was well pleased to hear their commendations, and he said, " She is such a one, that were I well assured she came of noble birth, I would wish no better choice, and think me rarely blessed in a wife." And then he addressed her in courtly terms, as if the lowly-seeming maid had been the high-born lady he wished to find her, calling her *Fair and beautiful Marina*, telling her a great prince on board that ship had fallen into a sad and mournful silence ; and, as if Marina had the power of conferring health and felicity, he begged she would undertake to cure the royal stranger of his melancholy. " Sir," said Marina, " I will use my utmost skill in his recovery, provided none but I and my maid be suffered to come near him."

She, who at Mitylene had so carefully concealed her birth, ashamed to tell that one of royal ancestry was now a slave, first began to speak to Pericles of the wayward changes in her own fate, telling him from what a high estate herself had fallen. As if she had known it was her royal father she stood before, all the words she spoke were of her own sorrows ; but her reasons for doing so was that she knew nothing more wins the attention of the unfortunate than the recital of some sad calamity to match their own. The sound of her sweet voice aroused the drooping prince; he lifted up his eyes, which had been so long fixed and motionless, and Marina, who was the perfect image of her mother, presented to his amazed sight the features of his dead queen. The long-silent prince was once more heard to speak. " My dearest wife," said the awakened Pericles, " was like this maid, and such a one might my daughter have been. My queen's square brows, her stature to an inch, as wandlike straight, as silver-voiced, her eyes as jewel-like. Where do you live, young maid ? Report your parentage. I think you said you had been tossed from wrong to injury, and that you thought your griefs would equal mine, if both were opened." " Some such thing I said," replied Marina, " and said no more than what my thoughts did warrant me as likely." " Tell me your story," answered Pericles : " if I find you have known the thousandth part of my endurance, you have borne your sorrows like a man, and I have suffered like a girl ; yet you do look like Patience gazing on king's graves, and smiling Extremity out of act. How lost you your name, my most kind virgin ? Recount your story, I beseech you. Come, sit by me."

How was Pericles surprised when she said her name was *Marina*, for he knew it was no usual name, but had been invented by himself for his own child to signify *sea-born*. " Oh, I am mocked," said he, " and you are sent hither by some incensed god to make the world laugh at me." " Patience, good sir," said Marina, " or I must cease here." " Nay," said Pericles, " I will be patient ; you little know how you do startle me, to call yourself Marina." " The name," she replied, " was given me by one that had some power, my father, and a king." " How, a king's daughter ! " said Pericles, " and called Marina ! But are you flesh and blood ? Are you no fairy ? Speak on : where were you born ? and wherefore called

Marina ? " She replied, " I was called Marina because I was born at sea. My mother was the daughter of a king ; she died the minute I was born, as my good nurse Lychorida has often told me weeping. The king my father left me at Tharsus, till the cruel wife of Cleon sought to murder me. A crew of pirates came and rescued me, and brought me here to Mitylene. But, good sir, why do you weep ? It may be you think me an impostor. But indeed, sir, I am the daughter to King Pericles, if good King Pericles be living." Then Pericles, terrified as it seemed at his own sudden joy, and doubtful if this could be real, loudly called for his attendants, who rejoiced at the sound of their beloved king's voice ; and he said to Helicanus, " O Helicanus, strike me, give me a gash, put me to present pain, lest this great sea of joys rushing upon me overbear the shores of my mortality. Oh, come hither, thou that wast born at sea, buried at Tharsus, and found at sea again. O Helicanus, down on your knees thank the holy gods ! This is Marina. Now blessings on thee, my child ! Give me fresh garments, mine own Helicanus ! She is not dead at Tharsus, as she should have been by the savage Dionyza. She shall tell you all, when you shall kneel to her and call her your very princess. —Who is this ? " (observing Lysimachus for the first time). " Sir," said Helicanus, " it is the governor of Mitylene, who, hearing of your melancholy, came to see you." " I embrace you, sir," said Pericles. " Give me my robes ! I am well with beholding—— O Heaven, bless my girl ! But hark ! what music is that ? " for now, either sent by some kind god, or by his own delighted fancy deceived, he seemed to hear soft music. " My lord, I hear none," replied Helicanus. " None ! " said Pericles ; " why, it is the music of the spheres." As there was no music to be heard, Lysimachus concluded that the sudden joy had unsettled the prince's understanding, and he said, " It is not good to cross him, let him have his way." And then they told him they heard the music; and he now complaining of a drowsy slumber coming over him, Lysimachus persuaded him to rest on a couch, and placing a pillow under his head, he, quite overpowered with excess of joy, sank into a sound sleep, and Marina watched in silence by the couch of her sleeping parent.

While he slept, Pericles dreamed a dream which made him resolve to go to Ephesus. His dream was that Diana, the goddess of the Ephesians, appeared to him and commanded him to go to her temple at Ephesus, and there before her altar to declare the story of his life and misfortunes; and by her silver bow she swore that if he performed her injunction he should meet with some rare felicity. When he awoke, being miraculously refreshed, he told his dream, and that his resolution was to obey the bidding of the goddess.

Then Lysimachus invited Pericles to come on shore and refresh himself with such entertainment as he should find at Mitylene, which courteous offer Pericles accepting, agreed to tarry with him for the space of a day or two; during which time we may well suppose what feastings, what rejoicings, what costly shows and entertainments the governor made in Mitylene to greet the royal father of his dear Marina, whom in her obscure fortunes he had so respected. Nor did Pericles frown upon Lysimachus's suit when he understood how he had honoured his child in the days of her low estate, and that Marina showed herself not averse to his proposals; only he made it a condition, before he gave consent, that they should visit with him the shrine of the Ephesian Diana, to whose temple they shortly after all three undertook a voyage; and the goddess herself filling their sails with prosperous winds, after a few weeks they arrived in safety at Ephesus.

There was standing near the altar of the goddess, when

Pericles with his train entered the temple, the good Cerimon, now grown very aged, who had restored Thaisa, the
wife of Pericles, to life. And Thaisa, now a priestess of
the temple, was standing before the altar ; and though
the many years he had passed in sorrow for her loss had
much altered Pericles, Thaisa thought she knew her husband's features, and when he approached the altar and
began to speak, she remembered his voice and listened
to his words with wonder and a joyful amazement. And
these were the words that Pericles spoke before the altar :
" Hail, Diana ! to perform thy just commands I here confess myself the Prince of Tyre, who, frighted from my
country, at Pentapolis wedded the fair Thaisa : she died
at sea, but left a maid-child called Marina. She at Tharsus
was nursed with Dionyza, who at fourteen years thought
to kill her, but her better stars brought her to Mitylene,
by whose shores as I sailed, her good fortunes brought
this maid on board, where by her most clear remembrance
she made herself known to be my daughter."

Thaisa, unable to bear the transports which his words
had raised in her, cried out, " You are ! you are ! O royal
Pericles "——and fainted. " What means this woman ? "
said Pericles ; " she dies ! gentlemen, help ! " " Sir," said
Cerimon, " if you have told Diana's altar true, this is
your wife." ' Reverend gentleman, no," said Pericles ;
" I threw her overboard with these very arms." Cerimon
then recounted how, early one tempestuous morning,
this lady was thrown upon the Ephesian shore ; how,
opening the coffin, he found therein rich jewels and a
paper ; how, happily, he recovered her and placed her
here in Diana's temple. And now Thaisa, being restored
from her swoon, said, " O my lord, are you not Pericles ?
Like him you speak, like him you are. Did you not name
a tempest, a birth, and death ? " He, astonished, said,
" The voice of dead Thaisa ! " " That Thaisa am I,"
she said, " supposed dead and drowned." " O true

Diana ! " exclaimed Pericles, in a passion of devout astonishment. " And now," said Thaisa, " I know you better : such a ring as I see on your finger did the king my father give you when we with tears parted from him at Pentapolis." " Enough, you gods ! " cried Pericles ; " your present kindness makes my past miseries sport. Oh, come, Thaisa, be buried a second time within these arms."

And Marina said, " My heart leaps to be gone into my mother's bosom." Then did Pericles show his daughter to her mother, saying, " Look who kneels here ! flesh of thy flesh, thy child born at sea, and called Marina because she was yielded there." " Blessed and my own ! " said Thaisa ; and while she hung in rapturous joy over her child, Pericles knelt before the altar, saying, " Pure Diana, bless thee for thy vision ; for this I will offer oblations nightly to thee." And then and there did Pericles, with the consent of Thaisa, solemnly affiance their daughter, the virtuous Marina, to the well-deserving Lysimachus in marriage.

Thus have we seen in Pericles, his queen, and daughter, a famous example of virtue assailed by calamity—through the sufferance of Heaven, to teach patience and constancy to men,—under the same guidance becoming finally successful, and triumphing over chance and change. In Helicanus we have beheld a notable pattern of truth, of faith, and loyalty, who, when he might have succeeded to a throne, chose rather to recall the rightful owner to his possession than to become great by another's wrong. In the worthy Cerimon, who restored Thaisa to life, we are instructed how goodness directed by knowledge, in bestowing benefits upon mankind, approaches to the nature of the gods It only remains to be told that Dionyza, the wicked wife of Cleon, met with an end proportionable to her deserts. For the inhabitants of Tharsus, when her cruel attempt upon Marina was known, rising in a body to revenge the daughter of their benefactor, and setting fire to the palace of Cleon, burnt both him and her and their whole household, the gods seeming well pleased that so foul a murder, though but intentional and never carried into act, should be punished in a way befitting its enormity.

THE END

PRINTED FOR THE PUBLISHERS BY WILLIAM CLOWES AND SONS, LIMITED, LONDON AND BECCLES.